Contents

Prologue ....

Chapter 1 6

Chapter 2 11

Chapter 3 18

Chapter 4 30

Chapter 5 35

Chapter 6 38

Chapter 7 41

Chapter 8 51

Chapter 9 60

Chapter 10 76

Chapter 11 83

Chapter 12 86

Chapter 13 94

Chapter 14 101

Chapter 15 117

Chapter 16 127

Chapter 17 135

Chapter 18 147

Chapter 19 159

Chapter 20 165

Chapter 21 167

Chapter 22 169

Chapter 23 172

Chapter 24 176

Chapter 25 182
Chapter 26 185
Chapter 27 188
Chapter 28 190
Chapter 29 195
Chapter 30 198
Chapter 31 201
Chapter 32 204
Chapter 33 206
Chapter 34 209
Chapter 35 218
Chapter 36 221
Chapter 37 224
Chapter 38 227
Chapter 39 230
Chapter 40 236
Chapter 41 239
Chapter 42 241
Chapter 45 249
Chapter 47 255
Epilogue 261

This is a work of fiction. Names, characters, businesses, places, events, and incidents are either the products of the author's imagination or used in a fictitious manner. Any resemblance to actual persons, living or dead, or actual events is purely coincidental.

Prologue

For Saffi,
Her deep blue eyes, just like her mother
The secrets beneath, she will uncover
Our story told; our hidden truth
Of love endured, beyond our Island of Youth
Love Jack

As Jack looked through the dense trees of the rainforest, and down the moonlit mountainside, he could sense Raoul behind him. He knew he had come to kill Jack, and his thoughts immediately turned to Saffi, his daughter and prayed for her forgiveness for having abandoned her. He heard Raoul's footsteps behind him; his awkward shuffle gave his identity away even in the darkness, a limp that Jack had given him years before in another violent encounter.

'It's over Jack.' Raoul whispered as he edged closer to Jack. 'There's no escape for you this time.'

'Don't tell me Raoul, you've got a gun pointed at my back and you'll shoot me if I run.' Jack could not hide his sarcasm.

'I thought something a little less obvious, maybe a car accident. You know how dangerous these mountain roads are, no barriers for protection as you misjudge a corner and you and the car go over the edge, no-one would ever suspect there had been a bomb in the car.' Raoul spoke cautiously, not wanting to alert Jack to his position and to what was about to happen. Slowly and precisely Raoul lifted the baseball bat and brought it down hard against the back of Jack's head. Jack fell forward and slumped to the ground.

Raoul struggled to haul Jack's limp body to the car he had already hidden in the rainforest. Jack's dead weight was difficult to move, but eventually he strapped the lifeless body into the driving seat and secured it with the seatbelt. Raoul leant in and started the car, engaged the automatic gearshift and released the handbrake. With a forceful push, the car began its final journey down the mountainside.

As the car careered downwards, Jack's consciousness returned and he opened his eyes, he felt a searing pain as he lifted his slumped head from the steering wheel, but it was the seriousness of his situation, that jolted him awake. He didn't know where on the mountain road Raoul had pushed the car over, but he had a good idea. Jack knew the mountain roads of Trinidad intimately, and his only thoughts now were of how to escape before the car reached the bottom and exploded. His years spent training with the Special Forces would pay off now, and instinctively this training took over. He could feel the wheels jarring on the uneven ground as the car plummeted down the slope, through the rainforest, crashing as gravity took control of him and the car, plunging him to the bottom of the mountain. Jack controlled his breathing to stop panic from setting in, but with each crash against the mountainside, Jack's body smashed against the car. As he was thrown forward, he felt his ribs crack against the steering wheel. Dazed and in pain, he grabbed hold of the steering wheel with one hand to stop himself from being thrown around, the other hand he wrapped around his torso, trying to protect his broken ribs. A final crash against a rock sent the car flipping onto its roof, and instinctively moved his hands up to protect his skull, and prepared for an unknown landing on the rocky shoreline at the bottom of the mountainside.

Strapped in and hanging upside down in the car, Jack was confused. He forced the door open, undid the seatbelt, and dropped out of the upturned car. Trying to orientate himself, he staggered to his feet. He could hear the ocean to his left and, as his eyes adjusted to the darkness, he could see the moon reflecting on the sea, and the mountainside above silhouetted against the sky. Jack knew he needed to get into the water before Raoul detonated the bomb. Panic was taking control of his mind and he tried to put his injuries out of his thoughts. Taking only shallow breaths to stop the pain in his ribs, he scrambled over the rocks. With a final burst of energy, he dived into the ocean just as the car exploded behind him, showering wreckage in all directions. As burning debris landed above him, Jack swam deeper, under the waves, but the pain in his head was too great and Jack's world finally went black.

Looking down the mountainside, Raoul watched the car roll out of control, down to the rocks that would become Jack's grave. He sneered as he detonated the bomb with the remote control. If the explosion didn't kill him, the sea would, pounding him against the rocks, an appropriate ending for Jack, Raoul thought as he got into the car that had arrived to collect him. He watched the smoke rise upwards, filling the sky, as his car pulled away. Raoul picked up the car phone and dialled his boss, Luis Leppe; known as 'El Jeffe', meaning 'The Boss', not only by his staff, but also by friends and enemies alike, Luis Leppe was a living legend in the drug world, and Jack's enemy.

'It's done, Jeffe.' Raoul said.

'Did you see Jack die?' Luis spat the words.

'Si, Jeffe, I personally sent him to his grave.'
'There's no way he could have survived?' Luis questioned.
'No-one could survive that explosion.'
'You're certain? There must be no mistake this time.'
'Si, Jeffe.' Raoul said and replaced the phone. A single bead of sweat rolled down his forehead. 'Move', Raoul shouted to the driver. 'Get away before anyone sees us'.

Chapter 1

Saffi sat quietly listening to her father's solicitor, Mr Smith, as he repeated the details of her father's death.

'As The British Embassy told you, your father requested no family or friends to attend his funeral. All I can do is to reiterate what you have already been told, that he died in a car accident in Trinidad, and of course pass on my condolences.'

But Saffi didn't care what Mr Smith had to say about her father; she had stopped caring about her father, Jack Simpson, many years before, after he left her Nana to look after her, when her mother had died.

~~~

Two weeks previously, Saffi had received a telephone call from the British Embassy in Trinidad. The news that her father had died in a terrible car accident had no impact on her.

'Initial investigations showed that he lost control on a notoriously dangerous mountain road, and that the car exploded at the bottom of the mountain.' The Embassy Official told her. Without wanting to distress her unnecessarily, he did not tell her that there had not been much of a body to recover, but Saffi had not been listening to the voice on other end of the telephone; his words fell onto the cold black floor of her subconscious. She neither knew, nor cared who this person was; he was just another man bringing her bad news this week. The first had told her of her impending redundancy at the end of the month.

'Your father checked-in with the Trinidad Customs and Immigration Department within the last two weeks, and that as a UK Citizen, The British Embassy took charge of finding details of his next of kin.' He continued, not waiting for any response from Saffi. Whilst searching his sailboat, they found a letter giving instructions in the event of his death. This letter gave details of you, Saffi, and your father's solicitor. The boat is currently in one of the marinas in Chaguaramas here in Trinidad. You will have to make separate arrangements to have it moved.' The man continued, but none of it made any impression on Saffi, apart from knowing she would need to visit her father's solicitors.

~~~

Mr Smith, Jack's solicitor continued to talk at Saffi. 'Your father was a good man, many thought of him as a hero, so I'm told.' He said, but Saffi continued to stare blankly out of the window. As far as she was concerned, Jack was no more a hero than the stray dog on the marina quay below. Saffi looked out at the boats and became mesmerised by their slow movements, bobbing rhythmically in the breeze.

Mr Smith interrupted her thoughts. 'I realise this must be difficult for you Miss Simpson, after losing your mother when you were so young, but I'll need to see some identification in order to release your father's estate.' He paused, 'May I call you Saffi?'

'No! Only my friends call me Saffi, my name is Saffrina, or Miss Simpson.' She continued looking out the window as memories of her mother's death came flooding back. She was only six years old when she died; too young to understand what had happened, or why Jack had left her in her grandmother's care.

'I'm sorry, Miss Simpson, but did you do as your grandmother asked, and read the documents your father left you?'

~~~

After talking to the British Embassy, Saffi telephoned her Nana to tell her the news, her Nana asked her to come to her house as soon as possible. Arriving at her grandmother's house Saffi saw the net curtains twitch, she knew Nana would already have made a pot of tea. She remembered her Sunday afternoon visits to her Nana's with her parents when she was small. They would arrive at 4 o'clock; Nana had already prepared tea in china cups and barley water for Saffi. Afterwards she and Nana would walk around the garden looking at the flowers; bright pink dahlias with their heads drooping heavy with rain. Nana would tell her stories of her Grandpa who had died before she was born. Sunday tea with Nana had always been the highlight of her week.

Walking up the front path, Saffi saw that Nana had already opened the front door and she could see her sitting at the dining table. Nana called out to her.

'Hello Saffi, do you want some tea?'

Saffi nodded as she came into the dining room and sat down, the china cup rattled against its saucer as Nana poured the tea. She passed the cup to Saffi and then got up, Saffi watched affectionately as Nana walked to the bureau by the garden window. She remembered Nana's garden back in London and thought how dreary this one was looking; she didn't notice Nana return with a large padded envelope, which she handed to Saffi. 'Your father instructed me to give you this in the event of his death.' Nana said, not able to look directly at Saffi.

Saffi took the envelope and opened it. Inside Saffi found a hand written letter addressed to her, along with boat registration documents, copies of her father's sailing and flying licences and numerous keys and a memory stick. Finally, there was an official looking letter addressed to her formally, Miss Saffrina Simpson. Saffi opened the letter and began to read it aloud; it was from her father, giving instructions in the event of his death.

> '. . . I Joseph (Jack) Simpson, being of sound body and mind, hereby request that in the event of my death, full ownership of all my worldly possessions are to pass directly to my daughter Saffrina Simpson. My solicitors, Messrs Smith & Son, of Ipswich have all the relevant paperwork and my daughter is to contact them to arrange completion of said paperwork.
>
> I have left three sealed packages; these must remain sealed until after my death. One copy is with Smith & Son, the second with Mrs Elizabeth Lee, Saffrina Simpson's maternal grandmother, the third with Mr Andreas Romani. Mrs Lee will give the second package to Saffrina Simpson upon my death and instruct her to read the contents. Each package contains the following information; -
>
> A copy of this letter, a personal letter to each recipient, a copy of ownership papers for Sailing Vessel (SV) Linalli, copies of my sailing and flying licences. Andreas Romani will have custody of SV Linalli until Saffrina Simpson contacts him to arrange for the physical transfer to her. Separate instructions regarding my bank accounts are held with my bank, and with Saffrina Simpson.
>
> Messrs Smith & Son are to instruct Saffrina Simpson that she does not have permission to sell, destroy or dispose of any of the items left to her. She can use them in any way she wishes, for as long as she is alive. She can bequeath them to whosoever she wishes upon her own death.
>
> Finally, under no circumstances, is Saffrina Simpson to be told of my whereabouts prior to my death, my employment, or employer.
>
> Signed: Jack Simpson

Saffi looked at her Nana, not knowing what to say, or do. 'I don't want any of his stuff, especially not that old boat of his; I don't even know where it is. Why would he want me to keep it, why can't I just sell it?' She asked Nana.

'I don't know Saffi, I'm sure there's a very good reason, you're just angry right now, which is understandable. Why don't you go home and read the other letters and things later? Perhaps he explains more about what he has done in the other letters.' Nana said. The loss of her son-in-law was not unexpected to Nana and there was no love lost between them. However, Saffi needed to deal with this in her own way, and in her own space.

Saffi began to question her Nana about the package but she refused to say anything further and Saffi knew there was no point pressing her; Nana never said anything for the sake of it. Saffi finished her tea and kissed Nana good-bye as she began to leave, but as she did, she sensed something in Nana, something she had not felt before; a sadness, not of Jack's death, but of something she couldn't place. As Saffi drove away, a chill came over her and a tear finally dropped onto her cheek, she brushed it away, quickly dismissing any feelings towards her father. How dare he make me feel like this after all these years she thought as she drove away.

~~~

Meanwhile, on the other side of the world, Luis Leppe sat overlooking the beautiful tropical gardens of his Columbian mansion. He was very satisfied with the job Raoul had carried out in Trinidad.

'We need to get the news of Jack's death out fast', he said looking at his men sitting on the veranda with him. 'And we need to find Andreas. Jack no doubt left him instructions as to where he has hidden MY money.'

He looked directly to one of his men, a huge man dressed in a badly fitting black suit, sweating profusely in the oppressive heat. His jacket hung open, revealing his handgun. Tariq was Luis' number two, after Raoul, and had worked for him for over five years, but his ambition was not just to take Raoul's place, but to take Luis Leppe's.

'Tariq, what was Andreas' last known location?' Luis asked.

'St Kitts.' Tariq replied and pre-empted the next question. 'We have someone on the island we can use, Carina, my cousin. She'll get any information from him.'

'Get to it immediately, and get Raoul back here quickly, I want him working on this as soon as possible.' Luis stood up. He needed to clear his head, he indicated to a stable boy to prepare his Palomino horse for riding. Turning to his men he said, 'This is a good day, Jack Simpson finally dead. But there is still more information we need to know.'

Luis Leppe picked up the telephone and dialled his secretary. 'Did you get the number of Jack Simpson's solicitor? Good and you confirmed the information about the affair he is having with his secretary.' He paused while his secretary confirmed the information. 'And we have proof that she is the wife of one of the board of directors of the firm. Good then get him on the phone.'

Moments later his secretary put him through to Mr Smith, who was unaware of who Luis Leppe was, or what danger he was about to get into.

'Mr Smith, my name is Luis Leppe and I was wondering if I might employ your services for something which is say, a little delicate, involving a client of yours who has recently deceased Mr Jack Simpson.'

~~~

The call from Luis Leppe had come out of the blue, and Mr Smith had no idea how this stranger had found out about his affair with Mrs Somerset. However, Mr Leppe had made it very clear on the phone what would happen if he didn't find out the information from Saffrina Simpson, but also how much he would pay him if he did. He would have to work very carefully to get the answers he needed when Saffi came in for her appointment the following week.

Chapter 2

When Saffi arrived back at her father's solicitors, she wondered why she had bothered. She had not read or even looked at the remainder of the package her father had left her; somehow, she didn't feel she was ready to hear what he had to say. He'd had nothing good to say to her for the past few years, so why should she be bothered now. When she entered Mr Smith's office, Saffi noticed an identical package on his desk. Mr Smith indicated for her to sit down, as she did she looked directly into his expressionless eyes.

'Like I said the last time we met, I will need some proof of identity to release your father's estate. Have you brought any with you?' he asked.

'Of course' she replied and handed him her passport. Using the intercom, he called his secretary.

'Mrs Somerset, would you come and take a copy of Miss Simpson's passport and place it in her father's file.'

Mrs Somerset entered the office and looked straight through Saffi. She walked behind Mr Smith's desk and leant him over to retrieve Saffi's passport. Saffi found it embarrassing and difficult to ignore the sexual tension between Mrs Somerset and Mr Smith.

She sat awkwardly, waiting for Mr Smith's secretary to return. All she wanted was to get this unpleasant business over with and finally have Jack out of her life. She didn't care what Jack's letter said, she would find a way to sell everything he owned and take Nana on holiday. Yes, she thought sea air and walks along the coast.

At that moment, Mr Smith snapped her out of her daydream. 'Have you read the contents of the package?' He stared at her coldly, with an air of expectancy.

'Obviously I've read the letter of instruction from him, or I wouldn't be sitting here, but I haven't read anything else before meeting you.'

Mr Smith could feel his aggression rising in the pit of his stomach; he needed to know what was in Saffi's personal letter from Jack, Mr Leppe had made that very clear. He took a deep breath before he responded. 'It is what your father requested in his instructions.

Saffi did not understand what all the fuss was about.

'So you've not read the letter from your father or checked the contents? Shall I give you some time now, you can read it here?'

'No, I think I want to read the remainder of the package at home.' Saffi replied, still not understanding why Mr Smith was making such a big thing about her letter.

'I understand, but perhaps it would be a good idea if you kept a copy of the letters here in our safe, along with your father's other papers?'

Mr Smith had become very intimidating and was making her feel uncomfortable. 'No thank you, I'll take it home. I understand you have some papers for me to sign, that's why I'm here, isn't it?' She asked, standing up from the table and picking up her package.

'If you insist, but my advice would be to keep copies of important documents with a solicitor. Who better to use than your fathers'?'

'Thank you Mr Smith for your concern, but I'd like to get on my way.' Saffi replied.

'As you insist, but if you change your mind...' he tailed off mid-sentence.

'Yes, I know where you are.'

'In which case, you just need to sign the release documents.' Mr Smith said handing her the paperwork.

Saffi read the documents, signed them and left with her belongings. As she walked away from the office she thought that it was strange how aggressive Mr Smith had become, but she dismissed the thought and walked down to the waterfront to clear her mind.

~~~

Finding an empty bench Saffi sat down, took out the hand-written letter addressed to her, and immediately recognised the handwriting from the birthday cards she used to receive from her father, until her Nana took over the job of sending them on his behalf, when he had given up caring about her.

> *'Darling Saffi, if you are reading this letter then the inevitable has happened to me, and you are now an orphan, for which I am deeply sorry. I only hope that you are old enough to forgive me for letting you down as a father. Explanations are not good enough for failing you. I wish my life had been different and I am truly sorry that I was not able to watch you grow into the beautiful, intelligent woman I know you are. You will never know how much pain and regret I have felt for not being able to be there for you. Although I have sometimes watched you from afar, it was never enough to stop the pain in my heart.*

Saffi stared at the letter. There were no words to describe how she was feeling as her father spoke to her from beyond his grave; she could not remember a time that he had ever shown her any emotion or remorse before. She continued reading.

> *'I know that the items left in this package may seem strange, especially as you don't know what I have been doing, but all will become clear if you follow my instructions. The Gstaad branch of Credit Suisse will complete the transfer of my bank accounts to you. There is an account ready for you to use. You will need to go to Gstaad and meet with Benedict Constantine the Manager. I have known him for a very long time and he has instructions to enable you to carry out the transfer. Take Nana with you, for a holiday, it will be my way of saying thank you to her for looking after you for all these years. As a special treat indulge yourselves and take a suite at the Palace Hotel, the view of the mountains is breathtaking.*

Saffi could not take in what she was reading in his letter. Gstaad, Swiss bank accounts and suites at the Palace Hotel. She emptied the contents of the package onto her lap. There were his pilot and sailing licences, some keys and a memory stick. She was hesitant about reading any further, but curiosity forced her to continue.

> *'I have left my home, the sailing boat Linalli, with Andreas, he has been my closest friend for many years. He will make contact with you soon. Talk with him to sort out the arrangements for Linalli and where you might want to moor her, he can help you with this.*
>
> *Finally, Saffi, you were and always will be my angel, and in my sadness of writing this, I will always watch over you. Take every chance to explore the world, its people and its places, for out there are things that are truly yours.*
>
> *Jack x'*

Saffi stared at the letter, not really comprehending what she had read. She looked at her father's photograph in his pilot's licence, but she didn't recognise the face that looked back at her. She knew her father even less than before now, and who was Andreas Romani?

She had never heard his name mentioned. She decided it was time to go back to Nana's to see if she knew about any of this. She put the keys, memory stick and letter in her bag, and licences back in the envelope and headed towards the car park.

~~~

Saffi didn't see Mr Smith staring at her from his office window, but she did recognise Mrs Somerset in the car park. Quickening her pace, Mrs Somerset caught up with Saffi.

'Miss Simpson,' she said, catching her breath. 'I just wanted to pass on my condolences to you, about your father.'

Saffi stopped in her tracks, 'Oh, thank you. Did you know him well?' Saffi asked suspiciously.

'I met him twice, everyone liked him, he was a real gentleman, but you already know that.' Mrs Somerset replied.

'Actually I didn't know him very well at all.' Saffi stopped mid-sentence, she didn't need to explain anything to this woman about her relationship with Jack. 'I'm sorry, if you would excuse me, I'm in a bit of a hurry.' Saffi said.

'Oh I'm sorry, I didn't mean to hold you up, I just wanted to say, well, you know. Here let me help you with your bag.' Without waiting for an answer, Mrs Somerset grabbed Saffi's bag and intentionally dropped it on the floor. The entire contents went everywhere, scattering keys, lipstick and pens under Saffi's car, both women instantly bent down to pick up the contents. Without Saffi seeing, Mrs Somerset grabbed Jack's letter and slipped it into her own bag. When Saffi stood up, she handed the padded envelope and a lipstick back to her.

'I'm so sorry Miss Simpson, I'm so clumsy sometimes, I best get out of your way before I do any more damage.' Mrs Somerset said and backed away from the car. Saffi grabbed the envelope from her, visibly annoyed she found her keys and opened the car. Incensed Saffi sat in her car for a few moments trying to calm down and gather her thoughts. She started to think about what she was going to do. Swiss bank accounts and strangers who will contact her, it was all nonsense.

As Saffi drove to Nana's house, her head was full of questions. Did Nana know about Jack's Swiss bank accounts? Did she know who Andreas Romani was? She became angry. He'd done it again. All these years she'd been fine, not thinking of him or knowing anything about him, and now, in his death, he'd complicated her life once more. All I want to do is get on with my life and he's messed things up again, she thought. Why couldn't he just leave me alone?

Switzerland, what's he talking about, take a trip to Gstaad, I don't even know how to pronounce Gstaad, let alone know where it is!

Nevertheless, driving back to Nana's she began to calm down and thought more about Jack's letter, slowly she began to change her mind. Why not go to Switzerland, give Nana that holiday she deserved, and there were his bank accounts to sort out, she thought, it's not as if I've a job to worry about any more and I could do with the money.

~~~

Back at Nana's house, the kettle was on, as expected.

'How did it go?' Nana's voice was soft.

'OK. I've had everything signed over to me.' Saffi called as she hung up her coat. 'Jack's left details of his bank accounts I need to transfer into my name,' she paused, 'in Switzerland.' She waited for a reaction from Nana. 'He left me details in another letter, and he says I have to go there in person, suggested we make a holiday of it, a sort of thank you to you.'

'Switzerland, what's Jack doing with Swiss bank accounts?' Nana asked.

'I've no idea, there were no other details in his letter, but I need to meet the manager to transfer the accounts. I think it's quite a nice idea, we could go for a long weekend, what do you think?' Saffi sat down opposite Nana. 'Let's look up Gstaad on the internet.'

Saffi opened her laptop, entered Gstaad as a search and from one of the tourist information sites she read to Nana.

'In terms of size, Gstaad is just your average Swiss village, but its reputation as a fashionable Mecca for the jet-set is global.'

'That's us Nana, the jet-set.' Saffi laughed. 'I'll look up the hotel Jack suggested.'

She found the hotel's website and read the opening words.

> *'The Gstaad Palace has earned an unrivalled reputation for discrete, refined hospitality over the years, and has always welcomed the most discerning international clientele'.*

'I'm not sure we're very discerning, let alone international, 'Saffi said and continued.

> *'There are over a hundred rooms and a luxurious three-bedroom Penthouse Suite, five restaurants, and a nightclub,* so we can go clubbing and won't have to worry about getting home,' Saffi joked.

'Oh, I'm not sure you'd get me 'clubbing' at my age, 'Nana smiled at Saffi.

'It looks amazing,' Saffi said, showing Nana the website. 'I wonder if Jack ever stayed there. He said in his letter to take a suite, I wonder what a normal room costs.' Saffi clicked on the rates page, and took a sharp intake of breath. 'That's about a week's wages. I don't think we'll be staying there.' Saffi looked at Nana who looked over the top of her glasses at Saffi.

'I always knew Jack had expensive taste.'

'I think I'll check if there are any cheaper hotels in the town,' Saffi said.

Nana was sipping her tea, looking quietly on, amazed as always with the wonders of computers. She looked at Saffi.

'Well if Jack said to go there, let's blow the expense and go, book two single rooms.' She was intrigued, why would Jack want them to go to Switzerland and suggest this particular hotel?

Saffi looked at Nana. 'I can't afford that.'

'I know, but I can. I'll pay for it Saffi.'

'But it's ridiculously expensive Nana,' Saffi said. 'Don't be daft.'

'If I want to pay for this I will, and in any case, Jack has been sending me money for your upkeep over the years, and I've been saving it for just such an occasion. Now how do we book the rooms?' Nana was insistent.

Saffi stared at her, she knew nothing about any money Jack had been sending, but she would pay Nana back when she could. As it was, she didn't know how much Jack had left her in the bank accounts.

Finally, she agreed with Nana and booked low cost flights into Geneva and they would get a train to Gstaad, they would leave on the 17th October, the following week. Saffi hoped she wasn't making financial commitments she wouldn't be able to repay. Just then, her phone rang.

~~~

Back in Mr Smith's office, he was pleased with Mrs Somerset for being able to obtain the letter from Saffi, he would thank her properly later that night, but first he had to call Luis Leppe.

'Mr Smith for you.' Luis Leppe's secretary announced as she transferred Mr Smith's call.

'Good afternoon Mr Leppe. I have discovered that Jack has instructed Saffi to go to Switzerland to sort out Jack's finances in Gstaad,' Mr Smith said, hoping the information would be sufficient for Luis Leppe to now leave him alone and remove his threat. 'Do you want me to find out when they are going?' Mr Smith continued.

'No, I have contacts in Switzerland. They will inform me of the details and carry out any necessary jobs. However, you have done well Mr Smith.' Luis Leppe replied, 'I will make arrangements for your payment as agreed, and you will not hear from me again. Thank you again for the information.' Luis Leppe said as he ended the telephone call.

As he replaced the telephone, he turned to another of his men, 'Please deal with Mr Smith and his secretary in the usual way, leave no trace of me or our organisation, and then go to Gstaad and find the girl.'

~~~

Pleased with Leppe's reply, now he would be able to give Mrs Somerset a proper treat tonight and book into her favourite restaurant and a four-star hotel, but first he needed to return Saffi's letter to her before she became suspicious. He dialled her number.

'Miss Simpson, Mr Smith here. I understand you bumped into my secretary, after you left my offices.'

'Yes,' Saffi replied, remembering how annoyed she had become.

'It's just that as you drove away, Miss Somerset noticed that a letter had fallen out of your bag, the letter from your father. Would you like me send it onto you?'

'Yes, if you wouldn't mind,' she replied abruptly, annoyed by the whole incident.

Mr Smith had already taken a copy of Jack's letter, and he would e-mail it to Luis Leppe in the morning; he was more in a hurry to meet up with Mrs Somerset and repay her for her good work. What he didn't know was that he and Mrs Somerset wouldn't be alive by the morning.

Chapter 3

After an early start, and a short flight, Nana and Saffi arrived in Geneva. The airport was busy and Nana found it quite exhausting watching all the people rushing everywhere with their suitcases on wheels. Saffi found her a seat.

'We've got about half an hour wait before the train leaves. Will you be all right on your own here? Saffi asked Nana as she looked around for the ticket office.

'Yes, I'll be fine, but have you noticed that very smart dressed gentleman over there, holding a placard with your name on it? Are you expecting someone to meet us?'

'No,' Saffi replied, looking quizzically at the man holding the card.

He was dressed in a smart uniform, and as she got closer, she could see the words 'The Palace Hotel' discretely embroidered above his top pocket. She walked towards him.

'Mademoiselle Simpson?'

'Yes,' Saffi replied.

'The Hotel has sent a car for you and your grandmother, how many bags do you have?'

'Two,' She replied, almost stammering. 'I didn't request a car to be sent, I'm not sure I can afford. What I mean is my Nana wanted to go through the mountains on a train.'

'That's perfectly understandable Mademoiselle, but the car will take you along the same route as the train and it is much more comfortable. And Mademoiselle, do not worry, the transport is all part of the hotel service,' he smiled, but Saffi knew that the driver wasn't telling the truth, she had seen on the website, the "exclusive airport transfer" was expensive. However, she handed the bags to the driver and she and Nana followed him out to the car.

'Aren't we going on the train after all?' Nana asked.

'Apparently the hotel has sent a car for us. At least we can sit in comfort for the last part of the journey. The driver's told me that you can see just as much of the mountains from the road as you can from the train.'

Sitting in the car Nana smiled at Saffi, she knew Saffi was hiding something but she wasn't going to pry. The hotel hadn't arranged a car she thought. This was more of Jack's doing, there was more to this trip than Saffi was letting on, or knew; Jack hadn't sent them to Switzerland just for a holiday, but she had no idea why he had.

Leaving the airport, the car followed the road along the edge of Lake Geneva; the driver pointed out the Jura Mountains on their left. The bright green hills rising gently above the villages and the undulating mountaintops picked out by lines of pine trees. The road twisted and turned, up and down through the hills, then back along the edge of the lake, which glistened in the sunshine. On the far side of the lake, the Alps rose up out of the dark blue water, high into the clear blue sky, topped off with virgin white snow.

The journey took them through towns and villages, all set on a backdrop of a 'chocolate box' picture. Before long, the car reached the outskirts of Gstaad, and the driver explained that 'the 'Centre de Ville' is a car free zone, so shopping is quite safe and very pleasant'.

Arriving at the hotel the magnificence of it overwhelmed them. Neither of them said a word as the porter opened the car door and they stepped out of the air-conditioned car and into the warmth of the summer air. The porter led them into the reception, which, like the exterior, was also grand and imposing. Saffi felt inadequate and uneasy; she had never been anywhere so luxurious. She walked to the Reception Desk and before she had time to speak, a tall, thin man spoke to her.

'Welcome Mademoiselle Simpson, my name is Gerald Lintz and I am the Hotel Manager. Firstly, on behalf of the staff and myself may I give you our condolences? Your father was a frequent visitor here at 'The Palace'. All the staff will miss him dearly. We have kept his suite for you, just as he instructed. Is there anything we can do for you after your long journey? Tea perhaps, taken on the balcony?'

Saffi stared at Mr Lintz not knowing what to say. Nana stepped in and took control.

'Thank you Mr Lintz for your kind words, I'm sure Jack enjoyed his time here.' Nana paused, 'Yes I think tea on the balcony would be most acceptable. We would also like some sandwiches, if that is possible. And um', Nana stumbled, 'can you confirm which suite will be ours?'

Saffi stared even harder at Nana, how did she know what to say, surely she had never been anywhere like this before. Nana turned to her and whispered.

'It's all those romantic novels I've read over the years, that's the sort of thing they say, now let's get up to the room and have some tea. I want to see what the suite is like.'

However, Saffi was in no rush, she knew nothing about a suite; she turned back to the hotel manager.

'Excuse me Mr Lintz that's very kind of you, but I booked two single rooms one in my name, the other for Mrs Lee.'

'Yes Mademoiselle, that is correct, however we have received instructions from Monsieur Constantine at the Credit Suisse Banque to change your rooms to The Penthouse, as instructed by your father. Do you have a problem with the Penthouse Suite?' he said raising an eyebrow in a kindly fashion.

'No, well yes, I mean no, it's just that, well it's rather expensive, isn't it, the Penthouse Suite and...', Saffi lowered her voice so that Nana couldn't hear, 'It's just that my Nana has paid for the rooms on her credit card and I don't think she will be able to...'

Mr Lintz leaned over the reception desk and interrupted her quietly. 'My dear Mademoiselle Simpson, the Penthouse and all other expenses have been paid for in full by Monsieur Constantine on the instructions that your father left him. You and your grandmother need not worry yourselves with anything as', he coughed, 'as vulgar as money whilst you are staying at the Palace. Your wish, as they say, is my command. So please, let me arrange for some tea, my staff have taken your bags to the Penthouse and Walter, the butler, is hanging your garments as we speak. There is a private elevator for you to use at your convenience.'

Smiling at Saffi, Mr Lintz gave her directions to the private elevator and waved his arm in a gesture to send them up to the Penthouse. As she and Nana stepped into the elevator Lintz smiled, 'What a charming young lady, so much like her father, it will be a pleasure having her stay with us', he thought.

Bemused by all that had just happened, Saffi and Nana took the private elevator to the Penthouse. Walter, the butler, met them and showed them around a spectacularly huge apartment. It had three lavishly decorated bedrooms all with en-suite bathrooms, the grandest of dining rooms and a sumptuously cosy lounge with a log fireplace, all with breathtaking views of the Alps and Gstaad, each room revealing more luxury. There was the biggest flat screen TV Saffi had ever seen, along with every conceivable piece of audio equipment available. Outside on the balcony they discovered a Jacuzzi, a sauna, and a steam room ready for their use. Everything had been thought of, nothing more could be added to enhance the suite. Neither of them said a word.

Walter showed them to their rooms and explained how everything worked, and asked if there was anything further he could assist with.

They sat in silence on balcony, while they took tea and digested all they had seen. Neither had ever experienced anything like this before. A few minutes later, and without saying a word, Nana got up and went into the lounge. When she returned, she said 'I just thought that we should celebrate, or commiserate, or do something special, so I've ordered some champagne. It just seemed the right thing to do. We should at least toast your father. After all we wouldn't be sitting here if it wasn't for him.'

A few minutes later Walter arrived with the champagne and poured two glasses. Nana raised her glass. 'To Jack'.

'Yes, to Jack Simpson, whoever he was.'

'What do you mean by that Saffi?'

'Oh nothing much, it's just that I never really got to know Jack, but over the last week he's started to reveal himself to me and it's not what I was expecting.'

Nana looked at Saffi carefully, as she had thought, there is more to this trip than Jack was letting on, but she wouldn't interfere, just yet. Although she felt Jack had let her and Saffi down over the years, he was still Staff's father and she had always loved him like a son.

It had been a long day, so they had dinner in their suite and went to bed early. Saffi lay on her bed pondering on what had happened in the past week. She felt like she was looking in on someone else's life, and tomorrow she would be opening a Swiss bank account. She wasn't expecting that a week ago.

The next day they took breakfast on the balcony in the cool morning air. The previous afternoon Saffi had asked Mr Lintz to make an appointment for her with Mr Constantine at Credit Suisse for 3pm the following day. After breakfast, they walked into Gstaad to go shopping and have lunch. Walking the short distance into the village the breeze was warm and the air fresh, they could hear the sound of the river flowing down the mountains and into the stream below. They stopped at the entrance to Hauptstrasse, the main shopping street of Gstaad, with its pretty buildings, most of which resembled gingerbread houses, their roofs picked out with carved wooden edges, some with beautiful window boxes still in full bloom.

They walked up the street and looked in the shop windows, staring at all the beautiful things, most of which they neither could afford nor needed. They came to a Chocolatier and stared at the wonderful array of chocolates.

'Shall we treat ourselves Nana, just a few each?'

Opening the door, the bittersweet smell of chocolate hung in the air and they breathed in the powerful aroma. Looking at the trays of chocolate, they were unable to decide which to choose, and asked the 'confectioner' to give them a selection. She wrapped them delicately in cellophane and then put them into a pale blue box with a ribbon. Like children with Easter Eggs, they left the shop quickly, and found a bench to sit on. Nana carefully untied the ribbon and opened the box. They each chose a different one, and carefully bit into the thick chocolate layer and murmured ooh's and aah's as the liquid centres revealed their inner flavours.

'Mmmm, I've never tasted anything like this before,' Nana said, ensuring that she didn't miss a drop of the sweet liquid centre.

'Let's have another,' Saffi said, her fingers already choosing the next. Before long, they devoured the entire box.

They continued along the Hauptstrasse, past Credit Suisse Banque, and Saffi took note of where it was. They had lunch in one of the cafés and sat outside watching the people of Gstaad going about their daily business. At two o'clock Saffi took Nana back to the hotel and got ready for her appointment.

Inside the Bank, she informed the cashier that she had an appointment with Mr Constantine, the cashier indicated to a seat, and Saffi sat down. A few minutes later a broad man, wearing a dark pinstripe suit opened the office door. He was in his early sixties and had a welcoming face. He greeted Saffi with a big smile and firm handshake. He recognised her instantly, although she had blonde hair, her features definitely reminded him of Jack. However, just like the photographs of Lillian he had seen, it was her piercing blue eyes, that struck him most, so blue that you felt like you were looking into a beautiful ocean.

'Mademoiselle Simpson? I am Benedict Constantine, the Manager. Do come into my office.'

Saffi followed Mr Constantine through the door and upstairs into a small office, decorated in a modern style, with just a touch of tradition about it. He offered her a chair at a large oak table by the window, looking down onto the street.

'My condolences Mademoiselle Simpson, I have known your father for many years. He will be sadly missed by many people.' Benedict paused in a gesture of remembrance and out of politeness for Saffi. He spoke gently to her, almost in a fatherly manner. 'If there is anything I can do for you, at any time, day or night, you have only to ask. Here is my card. It has my office and my mobile telephone numbers, and I have put my home number on the back.' He passed Saffi the card. 'And so to the matter of business, I need for you to sign some papers and then I can take you to your Safe Deposit Box and arrange for your account to be activated. Do you have your passport with you? I am sure you know it is just a formality.'

'Yes' said Saffi, bewildered by all that was happening.

She watched Benedict open a filing cabinet. People here liked Jack, just as they did at the hotel, she thought. Benedict returned to the table with various papers, he had marked a cross on each of them, indicating where she was to sign. He explained what each form was for and gave her time to read through before she signed. Transfer of Funds. Activation of Account. Release and Transfer of Safe Deposit Box. Saffi read each one carefully and signed in the relevant boxes. He in turn checked each one, removed the Customer Copy and returned these to Saffi.

As Benedict rose from his chair, he looked at Saffi with sympathetic eyes and a heavy heart. He had known Jack well and knew how much he was worth, but he also knew that money did not necessarily bring you happiness and in Saffrina Simpson's case, he wasn't sure that money was what she needed. She needed someone to watch over her.

'And now, I shall take you to your Safe Deposit Box while I will get the accounts transferred to your name.' He opened the door for Saffi and showed her down two flights of stairs to the basement, through two heavily bolted doors and finally into the vault room. He gave Saffi two keys marked A and B, which unlocked a box numbered 1279.

'There is a telephone on the desk. You can call me when you are finished or if you need anything, extension twenty-seven.'

Saffi stared at the rows of Safe Deposit Boxes, not really knowing what to do, she turned to ask Mr Constantine a question but he had already left the room. She looked at the keys; they looked insignificant in her hand. Moving toward the row of boxes, she looked for 1279. Finding it, she stood there, looking. Snapping out of her gaze she thought to herself, 'Come on Saffi, pull yourself together, it's only a box'. She moved towards the box and slid the key marked 'A' into the keyhole. The key made a loud clunk as she turned it in the lock. The lock opened and she slid the box out of its housing. It was not as heavy as she expected, holding it tightly she moved over to the desk and put it down. The box also had a lock and she opened it with the key marked 'B'. She lifted the lid warily, it was stiff and difficult to open, but eventually the lid fell back. Not knowing what to expect inside the box she tilted it toward her and the sound of items sliding down the metal box startled her. She dropped the box on the table. The sound made her jump and she stood up and looked around her.

She sat down again and took a deep breath. In the box were two envelopes, one contained various foreign currencies she had not seen before, Bahamian dollars, Eastern Caribbean dollars and Cuban Pesos. She closed the envelope and put it to one side. She picked up the second envelope, her name in Jack's familiar handwriting on the front. It was laying on top of a velvet pouch tied with a turquoise cord; when she picked it up it felt heavy. She untied the cord and poured the contents onto her hand. Out slid a simple pendant hanging from a piece of well-worn black leather cord. The pendant was quite large, about 3 centimetres in diameter and half a centimetre thick, and was made of a green, opaque stone that looked like marble. Its shape was mainly circular but not uniform or symmetrical. Along the bottom, it looked like a piece had been broken off. Small blue stones, linked together on a silver chain, led up to the leather cord. There were turquoise stones along the right edge, and along the inside of the pendant where, it looked broken. Set within the marble was one large gold coloured stone. The pendant was set in silver and on the back was a strange, almost jigsaw pattern, with small letters inscribed in italics which were difficult to decipher. It was pretty, in an unusual way, but not the sort of thing Saffi would chose to wear. She slid the pendant back into the velvet pouch and then opened the letter addressed to her; again, she read her father's handwriting.

> *Dearest Saffi,*
> *If you are reading this, then you have taken my advice and are in the care of Benedict and he has sorted everything out with the Palace Hotel. He's a good man, I've known him for a very long time and you can trust him.*
> *What I am about to tell you will not make sense to you, and it is no excuse for leaving you alone all these years.*
> *My work, such that it was, took me all over the world and I met many wonderful people. Unfortunately, for reasons I*

cannot say, I cannot tell you exactly where I have been or what my work entailed. The work was not exactly 'secret', but it relied on anonymity on everyone's part.

During my time away from you, I discovered many wonderful things. These things and much more I have left for you to discover, but because of the reasons stated above, I have had to conceal the whereabouts of your inheritance. However, it will all become clear if you follow my instructions, and meet with Andreas.

You've probably looked in the pouch and seen the pendant. It was your mothers. She had it made to remind her of a special place, our special place, our Island of Youth. Keep it with you at all times. I can't tell you why, but you'll know when you'll need it, it will be obvious.

Stay in Gstaad for a week, enjoy the hospitality of Mr Lintz and Walter, and then return home. Andreas will then contact you, if he hasn't heard back from you within a week, he will send one further message. If you still choose not to get in touch with him, he will never contact you again. He will assume, sadly, that you are not going to try to find what I have left for you, what is rightfully yours.

I urge you to go and meet him, and when you do, you must take the things I left in the previous package, the keys and contact lists. You will need Andreas' help to find all the answers you are looking for. Please go and meet him, as it will be worth it in the end.

I have left a small quantity of currencies that you will need when you meet with Andreas, he will let you know if you need anything else. I have left instructions with Benedict for you to use the Account Credit Card for travelling expenses, do so, and he will settle the account each month automatically.

When, and I hope, not if, you start to look for what is yours, use your senses; look for what is not there, and what you can't hear. Remember the things we did together when you were small. The places we went, the things we saw and the times we spent together. These things need to be in your memory always.

Saffi, please, please go, find what is yours, and I promise you will find the answers to all your questions and in doing so, I hope you will finally get to know me, who I was, and why I left.

Love forever Jack

Saffi took the pendant out of the pouch again and held it in her hand. It felt warm and cold at the same time, sort of like porcelain but not as delicate. She clutched it in her hand and she felt a warm flush run through her body. The sensation made her drop the pendant on the table. She picked it up again and placed the leather cord over her head, the pendant seemed to lie perfectly around her neck. She took a compact mirror from her bag and looked at herself, it looked as though she had always worn it and for some reason, it made her smile.

She adjusted the leather cord so that the pendant was out of sight, under her blouse. She collected the two envelopes and put them in her bag along with the pouch. She locked the lid and returned the box to its place in the housing. She sat back down and reached for the pendant once more. Perhaps I will meet with Andreas Romani, what harm could it do, she thought to herself. She picked up the receiver on the phone and told Mr Constantine that she was ready to leave the vault.

Benedict showed Saffi into his office once more. 'Please sit down Saffi. We have completed the activation of the accounts and there is nothing further for you to do. However, can I ask you to return in a couple of days when you can collect your credit card? Of course, if you need an advance until that time, you need only ask.'

'Thank you very much, but that won't be necessary, and thank you for organising everything at the hotel, 'Saffi replied.

'It is what your father wished and I would be most delighted if you and your grandmother would join me for lunch on Friday.'

Walking back to the hotel, she felt compelled to reach for the pendant, stroking it gently, thinking about Jack's letter, not really knowing what to do next. She went up to the Penthouse and Walter greeted her.

'Was everything satisfactory with Mr Constantine, Mademoiselle?'

'Yes, thank you Walter, in fact he's invited us to lunch on Friday.'

'Lunch.' Nana called from the balcony, 'Who with?'

'Mr Constantine, the Bank Manager, he has invited us to lunch with him. He is a very nice man and he was very helpful today. I have to collect my credit card for the account at mid-day on Friday.'

'Oh, OK. Anything else happen?'

'Yes, he took me down to a vault, to a safe deposit box. There was another letter from Jack and this pendant he's left me.'

Saffi pulled the pendant from under her blouse. Nana scrutinised it carefully on both sides.

'It doesn't look very expensive to be hauled up in a safe deposit box.'

'It's not about the value Nana, it was mum's, and he left it for me, but it rather reminds me of him in a funny way.'

'What's it made off, it feels like china or porcelain? What are those markings? Are the stones real?'

'So many questions Nana, I don't know. I just got it out of a velvet pouch along with a letter from Jack as I said, he doesn't say what it's made of or anything, just that it was mums, she had it made to remind her of a special place, an island, or something.'

Saffi stopped, realising that she was saying too much, and that if she continued she would have to explain about everything else she had received from Jack. However, she didn't like to keep things from Nana. At least if she knew what was in the letters she would be able to advise Saffi what to do. Nana already knew about the sailboat Jack had left her, he'd had that for ages, so she may as well tell her about the letters.

'Nana' Saffi said. 'Did you know what was in the package Jack left for me?'

'Not the personal letter to you dear and it's not for me to pry.'

Saffi got out the letter from the package and handed it to Nana.

'Are you sure Saffi, this is personal between you and your father.'

'Go ahead Nana, I want you to know what's going on, and anyway I think I'm going to need some help from you.'

Nana began to read Jack's letter, half way through she sat down, and by the end of the letter she began to look pale and her face had glazed over, Saffi came over to her to make sure she was OK.

'Is this true Saffi?'

'As far as I know, so far everything he's said has been the truth, Gstaad, the hotel, Mr Constantine, I've no idea who Andreas Romani is, have you ever heard of him?'

'No, it's not a name I've ever come across. Was there anything else?' Nana asked.

Saffi gave her the letters from the Safe Deposit box to read. Nana looked up at Saffi, took the pendant in her hands again, and rubbed her fingers across it.

'What does it mean Saffi, what are you going to do?'

'Well, we'll stay here for the rest of the week, meet Mr Constantine on Friday and see if he can tell us anything else. Otherwise, wait until we get back home and start trying to find out who this Andreas is.'

'It all sounds a bit strange to me, you need to be careful. You don't want to get yourself involved in things you don't know about.'

'Oh stop it Nana, I think this is Jack's way of making me get out of my boring life and go and see the world. He has come up with some wacko idea with a friend of his to make it sound exciting. Well, I'm all up for that, it's not as if I've a job to go back to, and what harm can it do to meet one of Jack's oldest friends, perhaps I will find out something about him I didn't know.

Friday arrived and they both seemed a bit more relaxed and looking forward to lunch with Mr Constantine. Neither of them were sure why. They had a leisurely morning before going to the village to meet him. Promptly, at noon, Benedict came out of his office and greeted Saffi with his now familiar smile and she introduced him to Nana.

'Enchantè Madam Lee, it is my pleasure to meet with you, I have booked a table at my favourite restaurant; it is only a few minutes to walk.'

'Oh please call me Elizabeth, Mr Constantine.'

'Very well, then we must all be on first name terms, you must both call me Benedict. Shall we go?'

For the first time in many years, Nana Lee blushed. Benedict was a handsome man with whom she immediately felt at ease. She was going to enjoy lunch, she thought. The three of them walked out of the bank and up Hauptstrasse until they reached the restaurant. Benedict was the perfect gentleman; he had reserved a table on the terrace looking out onto the mountains and ordered champagne whilst Saffi and Nana looked through the menu.

'Please, be my guests. Do not be embarrassed, as I know the English can be. I have waited a long time to meet Jack's daughter, and I am very pleased also to meet the woman who has cared for her in his absence all these years. You have indeed done a wonderful job and I raise a glass to you Elizabeth.'

'Thank you Benedict, you are too kind, but what else could one do when your only grand-daughter was left as she was. It's funny, after the death of my daughter, over the years, Jack and I grew apart. I never really knew him after that. He never told me what he was doing. Can you shed any light, Benedict? Did you know Jack well?'

Saffi looked at Nana, she was not expecting her to turn the conversation to Jack so soon, but she was glad that she had taken the initiative and raised the subject of Jack. In fact, Nana and Benedict had been getting on rather well she thought, considering they only met an hour ago.

Benedict lifted Nana's left hand, drew it to his mouth, and kissed it in an old-fashioned way.

'My dear Elizabeth, I wish I could be of more assistance. Although I have known Jack for many years, not just as a customer, but also as a dear friend, he never divulged anything more than daily comings and goings, so to speak. He kept himself very much to himself and mainly spoke of Saffrina and your charming self. If I can be of help to assist you in any other way, please let me know.'

Nana let the subject drop, knowing that Benedict was too much of a professional businessman to let anything slip that he shouldn't about Jack, or any of his clients.

Saffi, Nana and Benedict enjoyed a wonderful lunch, and as they chatted of everyday things and the time flew by. Finally, at 3pm Benedict suggested that they should return to the bank to collect Saffi's credit cards.

Back at the bank Benedict handed Saffi a dark blue leather wallet, explaining that everything she needed for her accounts was in there and of course, as always, if there was anything further she was only to call. He turned to Nana. 'Elizabeth, if ever you are in Gstaad again it would be my utmost pleasure to escort you to dinner.'

Blushing again, Nana replied that she would be delighted, but doubted very much that she would be returning in the near future. 'But thank you for being such a perfect host and for all your help while we have been here.' She said as she and Saffi left the bank. Little did she know how soon she would be seeing Benedict Constantine again?

Chapter 4

THE journey back to the UK seemed longer and left Saffi and Nana feeling exhausted. The next morning, they began looking through Nana's post to see if Andreas had sent her something. They assumed the only way he could contact them would be by some sort of letter.

'What are we looking for Saffi?'

'I don't really know.'

They went through each item, putting them into piles, bills, junk mail, local papers, but could find nothing of significance. Nana put the post on the table and sat down to watch television. Joining her, Saffi picked up the local paper to see what was going on in the area. She came across the 'Entertainment' section, the usual 'What's On' at the cinema and car boot sales and then the puzzle page.

'Are you any good at crosswords, Nana?'

'I've been known to do the odd one or two. Every now and then I attempt the Times, but it takes me an ago.'

'This shouldn't be too difficult then,' Saffi said as she began to read the clues aloud.

'One across: Boston's afternoon Party, three letters. Well that's simple, TEA.' She entered the letters into the puzzle.

'Two across: Doctors and nurses do this for patients. Begins with T, five letters.'

'Treat.' Nana replied.

'OK. Three across: 'Rearrange the plug, to stop the noise of fear'.' She repeated the clue, slowly, 'rearrange the plug, to stop the noise of fear?' Saffi said. 'I'm not sure what that's all about?'

'Gulp,' Nana replied.

'Gulp?' Saffi repeated.

Yes, gulp. Rearrange the PLUG, P-L-U-G becomes GULP, G-U-L-P, it's an anagram don't you see, you gulp when you are frightened. That's quite an easy one. The clue gives you an instruction and you have to decide what word it is that you have to change. Like this one, 'rearrange', it's not an action, it's an instruction for you to rearrange the letters,' Nana explained.

'I suppose that makes sense,' Saffi said. 'Did you finish going through the post?'

'Oh I've gone through the bills, but nothing else. Here, why don't you look through the junk mail?' Nana said, handing Saffi the pile.

Saffi sifted through quickly and then something caught her eye. It looked like a mail shot for a holiday company, or hotel, designed as a postcard.

'Did you see this Nana?' Saffi said as she held up the card. She turned it over in her hands. On the front was a picture of a hotel, set on a white sand beach and crystal blue water. At the top in italic writing was the marketing message, 'Welcome to the Breezes Hotel, Nassau, Bahamas'. On the reverse, in very neat writing was the following:

Hi S,
I hope you enjoyed your trip to Switzerland and are ready for another holiday.
I've been staying here, it's lovely and it would be wonderful if you could join me. J has told me so much about you that I can't wait to meet you personally.
Give me a call on the number below and let me know what your plans are. I can book a room at the hotel for you, once I know what flight you're going to take.
If you decide to come, we can fly kites on the beach and take every chance to explore the world, its people and its places.
A

Saffi read the card aloud to Nana, and looked for a phone number below the writing, but all she could see was the name of the hotel.

'This has to be from Andreas. He's addressed it to 'S', which I assume is for Saffi, referred to J, which I guess will be Jack, and signed it A, which can only mean Andreas. Right at the end, he talks about when Jack and I used to fly kites on the beach. He's uses the same sentence as Jack, explore the world. Strange, though, he's mentioned a number and then not put one anywhere.' Saffi said.

'Let me look,' Nana said, taking the card from Saffi. 'I see what you mean, what about this number at the bottom, could it be his, rather than the hotel's?'

'I'll look up the hotel details on the internet, see what number they give.' Saffi did so and saw that the number was completely different, even the dialling code. 'I suppose there's only one way to find out if it is his number.' Saffi said, as she picked up the phone and dialled the number. It rang. She paused, and then cut off the call.

'What if it is him, what am I going to say? Hello, I am the daughter of your dead best friend. You've sent me a postcard, what do you want me to do now? It might not be him, 'Saffi said, looking at Nana.

'Why don't you wait for him to answer and see what he says?'

'What if he doesn't say anything, what do I do then?'

'You need to ask him a question that only you and he would know the answer to, maybe ask him if he knows the name of Jack's boat, Linalli?' Nana suggested.

Then, for the first time, Saffi thought about the name of Jack's boat, and said. 'Oh, it's an anagram of Lillian. He named the boat after mum, Linalli.'

'Well then, what are you waiting for?' Nana said.

Saffi's hand was shaking as she picked up the phone. She redialled the number, and waited for someone to answer.

'There's no reply,' she said, looking at Nana, and then a voice answered.

'Hello, how may I help you?' The accent was odd, sort of Spanish, with an American drawl.

'Hello, I'm not sure if I have the right number and this might sound a bit strange, but can you tell me the name of Jack's boat?' Saffi asked.

'Who wants to know?' The voice replied.

'A friend,' she said.

'And how do I know you're a friend?'

Saffi paused, and then saw the postcard. 'Ah, yes. I'm enquiring about a holiday at the Breezes Hotel, in the Bahamas, and was wondering when would be the best time to visit.'

'Oh, in that case, in answer to your first question, the answer would be Linalli. Does that satisfy your enquiry?' The voice replied.

Saffi thought for a moment, wanting further confirmation. 'Possibly, but what's so special about the Breezes Hotel?' She questioned, unexpectedly enjoying the tension of the conversation.

'Ah that's easy. At the Breezes Hotel you can fly kites on the beach and explore the world, its people and its places,' the voice replied without hesitation.

'And why is that so special?' She asked.

'When I was writing this particular postcard I was reminded that this was something a good friend of mine would say to his little girl when they were flying kites on the beach. Does this satisfy you Saffi?'

She wasn't expecting his reply. 'Err, yes it does.' She fell silent, not knowing what to say next.

'Did you enjoy your time with Benedict?' Andreas asked, sensing her nervousness. 'Did you get everything sorted out?

'Yes I met with him very recently.' Her response was sharp.

'Good, good, so you have everything you need? Have you decided to come to meet me?'

'Meet you? Well I'm not sure. I'll need time to think about it,' Saffi said, having not really thought about the prospect of actually meeting Andreas.

But Andreas interrupted her, not really listening to her excuses. He knew they needed to move quickly; he knew what was at stake. 'Can you get here in a week? I can book a room, ready for when you arrive. I've checked the flights, BA operates five flights a week, direct to Nassau, so you shouldn't have a problem getting a flight,' Andreas said, but Saffi took none of the information in, it was all becoming too much.

'Stop, please. I need time to think, I wasn't expecting to have to meet you so far away. Jack never mentioned anything about the Bahamas. I'm not sure. I'll need to call you back when I've decided,' Saffi said, as she put the phone down without saying goodbye. She needed time to think this trip through before committing to anything.

Andreas was not surprised by Saffi's response, she had, after all, led a very ordinary life compared to Jack and him. He would give her time. As it was, it had taken him a few days to adjust to the news about Jack.

Andreas put his phone away. He was surprised Saffrina had phoned him so quickly, and then he thought about her parents. He wondered who she was most like, Lillian or Jack. Both were resilient, headstrong and resourceful. Lillian's attention to detail sometimes drove Jack to distraction, but her kindness and compassion made up for any fickle ways she had. Jack had the same fastidious mind, but his strength was in his pedantic planning, meticulously checking any project before he even started. They had been a great team, but Lillian's death had devastated Jack; and afterwards he could have gone either way. Drink or work. Drink was an easy road, one that Jack had trodden before, but finally, Jack threw himself into his job alongside Andreas. He would never have been able to bring up Saffi, and they both knew that, not in their line of work.

A week before, Andreas had been sitting in his favourite bar on St Kitts, when the 'Agency' telephoned to tell him the news that Jack had died. They informed him that they were sending him a package, which would arrive in a few days.

He sat at the bar drinking a cold beer, the first of what would be many that day. He sat alone, quiet in his thoughts, not believing the news he had received. Jack dead! He never believed it would happen, not to Jack. Jack was so careful; something must have gone wrong. He knew Jack too well; he wouldn't have made any mistakes, not now.

He had another sip of his beer, and took out a photograph of a teenage girl from his wallet. It was unmistakeable who she was, so much like her mother, those same blue eyes, same pale complexion and slender features. 'Saffi', he said quietly to himself, looking at the photograph, 'I'm not sure you should come and find me, I won't know what to tell you. It's all become so complicated.'

The waitress started to open another beer for him.

'No thanks Carina, I need something stronger, whisky, make it a large one.'

Carina had known Andreas long enough to know that he only drank whisky when there was trouble in store. Handing him the glass she looked down at the photo of Saffi.

'She's very pretty, a relation?' she asked.

'Not related to me, but someone very special to me.'

'Is she visiting the island?'

'No, but I'm hoping to meet up with her soon. Will you excuse me Carina?'

Picking up his drink, Andreas walked out to the veranda. He stared out to the Caribbean Sea and beyond. Carina left him to his thoughts knowing not to pry any further, but she thought how sad he looked. However, her loyalties lay with Luis Leppe. Dialling his number out of sight of Andreas, she would let him know what she had discovered.

Chapter 5

Saffi had a disturbed night's sleep, mulling the thoughts repeatedly in her head. She was first to rise and made some breakfast, Nana was not too far behind her.

Before Saffi even said good morning, Nana asked whether she would be going to the Bahamas. 'I don't know Nana, it's seems so far-fetched, but Jack's letters were so, so. . .' she couldn't think of the words. '. . . convincing? I just feel as though I ought to go, but...'

'You're scared?' Nana said, realising how well she knew her granddaughter.

'I've never been anywhere remotely exotic. The closest I've been to the Caribbean is the Jamaican food shop in Cambridge. I mean really, The Bahamas?' Saffi was wringing a tea towel nervously as she spoke. 'And even if I were to go, how would I pay for everything.'

'The Credit Card, the one Benedict arranged for you. You said Jack had left it for you to use for travel expenses. Don't you think he may have done that on purpose, so you wouldn't have to worry about the cost?' Nana said. 'But this is a decision is for you to make. My only word of advice would be, whatever decision you come to, make sure that you won't regret it later in life, 'she said as she began to make breakfast.

Now she was even more confused, such a poignant thing to say, Saffi thought. Should she go to the Bahamas and meet a complete stranger? Jack had been so specific in his letters. It's not as if she'd just met him on the internet. He knew all about her childhood, the kites and the beach. He knew about Jack's boat. Her head was full of questions and no answers. She still needed time to think.

'I'm going out Nana; I need some fresh air to clear my mind. I won't be long.'

Saffi walked down the lane and out behind Nana's house, she knew a short cut through to the meadow beyond, over to a stream. With the questions still overwhelming her, she found a spot near the stream, sat down on the grass and closed her eyes. For some reason she felt for the pendant around neck. She rubbed her fingers across it, and lay back on the grass and looked up at the clear sky above. She remembered that one of Jack's letters was in her coat pocket. She got it out and read it again. It was the letter about the pendant, as she read it, she could hear his voice in her head, urging her to go and find Andreas. To go and discover 'a world she never knew existed'. She folded the letter away and thought of Nana's words of advice. What do I have to lose if I go? More to the point, what will I regret if I don't go?

As she got up, she felt very calm. She reached for the pendant, and thought of her mother wearing it. She felt as though her mother was standing by her, touching her hand, and as outrageous as it seemed she decided this was a sign that she should go.

When she got back to Nana's house, she told her of her decision. 'I need to call Andreas, let him know I'm coming. I think they're a few hours behind us, so I'll call him this afternoon. I don't want to wake him in the middle of the night.'

But Andreas was awake in the middle of the night.

~~~

A few days after he received the news of Jack's death, his package arrived. It contained the same as the other packages and, like the others, included a personal letter to Andreas. The words cascaded over him and landed in a hollow place in his heart as he read them.

> *Well my friend, this is it, the day we hoped would never come, the demise of one of us. As we had said on many occasions 'we were surprised it had not come sooner, all things considered!' But hey, it appears that I beat you to it, but let's not dwell on the past for too long, we knew the risks and we were paid in full.*
>
> *And so to business, as we discussed many times, I leave the safety of Saffi's future in your hands. She has her mother's spirit and I believe that it won't take long for her to take up the challenge and come to find you. The clues have been set and you have all the information you need to solve them. They are as we agreed they would be, so think like the team that we have been for all these years and you will find the prize. The memory stick is in Saffi's possession; make sure it stays that way. I have arranged everything with Benedict so you needn't worry financially, not that you ever did. However, Saffi will. She is after all an accountant; you may need to change that in her. You will know the password when the time comes.*

> *Be aware my friend, I believe there may be 'enemies in the camp', someone close. Not everything may be as comfortable as we would have hoped.*
>
> *My final words to you, my friend, are to enjoy the challenge. Until our spirits meet once more!*
>
> *Your friend Jack*

Andreas smiled. Only Jack could write a departing letter with a warning within. He can't have written this long ago, he thought. He looked through the remainder of the package. He and Jack had spoken many times of his wish for Andreas to show Saffi his world, if he died before he could show it to her. He knew many people would be after Jack's 'legacy' and this was the only certain way of ensuring that Saffi got what was rightfully hers. He gathered his thoughts; he was just about to go out when his phone rang. He looked at the screen and recognised the four-digit code he had entered to recognise Saffi's number.

'Have you come to a decision?' He asked.

'Yes, I think I have, I'll be arriving on the 12th November. Can you book the hotel please? Saffi said, saying it quickly, before she changed her mind.

'Yes of course, but are you sure you're OK with all this Saffi. Say so now before it's too late.' He didn't want to scare her, but needed to make sure she was certain.

'Yes, I'm positive, besides, I've got more to lose by not coming than if I don't, so let's grab the bull by the horns, as they say', she said.

'Very philosophical,' he said, 'just like your mother. Send me the flight details and I'll meet you at the airport,' Andreas replied.

'Like my mother, did you say? Did you know her well?' Saffi asked.

But Andreas had again hung up.

'What did he say?' Nana looked at her impatiently, waiting for Saffi to tell her everything.

'He asked if I was sure, said he'd arrange the hotel and then he said something about my mother, but he hung up before I could ask him about her. He must have known her. Did you know of him Nana, before all this?'

'Like I said before, the first I knew of him was in Jack's letter,' Nana replied. 'What did he say about Lillian?'

'He said I was very philosophical, just like my mother. What was she like Nana?'

Chapter 6

Looking at Saffi, Nana sighed. She knew she would finally have to tell Saffi all the things about Lillian she had never told her before. Things she had always wanted to tell her, but it had been too painful a memory.

'Sit down Saffi.' Nana started slowly. 'Lillian, your mother, was a beautiful child, full of life and adventure. She was a good girl, did well at school. It was hard for her when her father died. She never understood why he went away when she was so young. She was the same age as you were when Lillian…' Nana stopped, took a deep breath and continued, 'When she was 20 she met Jack. She was studying to be a nurse. It was back in the early 70's when all that flower power stuff was still going on. He was a nice lad and your grandfather would have liked him. Bright, but not very mature at that time, if you know what I mean. He had been away at sea on a merchant trade ship or something for a few years and was home visiting his family. They met at some sort of demonstration rally, you know the sort of thing, I'm sure you've seen it on the telly. Well, it wasn't very long before Jack had proposed and they wanted to get married. It was like a railway train running down a track, one minute they'd met, the next they were getting married. I was so excited. I got a new dress and hat, the whole works. It was a lovely day and she looked beautiful. She wore one of those 'Maid Marion' dresses, with long swooping sleeves, and just some flowers in her hair.'

Nana stopped and went over to a drawer in the cabinet. She took out Jack and Lillian's wedding album and started showing Saffi the photos. Saffi had seen them many times before, but looking at them this time her parents seemed different. Lillian looked more beautiful than she had remembered, and somehow Jack did not seem as bad as she recalled. She started to look at him in a different light. The way he looked at mum and held her hand, how they both looked overjoyed. Nana continued.

'It was a few days after the wedding when they told me they were going travelling rather than have a normal honeymoon. Something about wanting to help those less fortunate than them, you know all that hippy stuff that went on in those days, well I suppose you don't, but anyway. They were going to go and see the world they said, go and see a world they never imagined could exist.' Staring at the photos, tears came to Nana's eyes; she stroked Lillian's face in the photo.

'She was too young to die.'

Saffi passed Nana a handkerchief. 'Nana don't go on, it's too painful for you.'

'No, no, there are things you need to know. They left in 1975. They were going to visit all sorts of places they said, India, Africa, and South America. They ended up in the Caribbean. Lillian would write to me all the time, great long letters describing everything they had seen and done. It sounded wonderful, maybe a little scary, all those strange places and people. Funny smells and food, not for me at all, but they seemed to be enjoying themselves.

'It was while they were in the Caribbean they found a sailboat for sale. Said it would be cheaper than hotels, and they'd be able to see lots more places. Eventually they got to Venezuela. I know my geography is not that good, but I knew that Venezuela is not far from Colombia and Colombia in the 70s was not a good place to be, all that business with drugs. They kept insisting that it was fine and they were meeting lots of nice people.'

Saffi listened with keen interest and intrigue and let her Nana continue.

'It was Christmas of 1976 when they told me they sailed into Colombia, I wasn't very happy about this, but what could I do all these miles away? Anyway, Lillian got involved with an orphanage or a hospital or something to do with sick children. Apparently, she felt she needed to help in some way and so they stayed in Colombia for a long while. I did miss her terribly, but she wrote and called as often as she could.

'It was the winter of '79 that I got the phone call.' Nana stopped and wiped another tear from her eye, she looked at the photos of Lillian with such affection. She composed herself and continued.

'Where was I, yes November 1979, it was Jack on the phone, there had been an accident, he wasn't clear, the phone line wasn't very good. He was trying to say that there had been a shooting or something in the city. I never did find out the truth of what happened, but somehow, in all the commotion, Lillian found herself in the middle of the crossfire and that's all he told me. He said they were operating on her in a hospital in Colombia and he didn't know what to do. I couldn't believe what he was telling me, but he said he would phone when he had more news. He phoned a few hours later, telling me she was OK, and that I was going to be a grandmother.'

Tears were flowing down Nana's cheeks now, and Saffi stroked her hand. Finally, the emotion was too much and for the first time Nana broke down in front of Saffi. She cradled her grandmother like a child, rocking her to a fro. Saffi had never seen Nana like this, but Nana had never told her this story of her mother before.

Eventually, Nana composed herself and looked at Saffi. I'm sorry Saffi. I should never have told you any of this.'

'Yes you should, I can't believe you dealt with this pain alone all these years. You should have told me; we could have helped each other. I understand why you didn't, but I think I have a right to know what happened to my parents, so I'm glad you have told me. Now it makes so many other things much clearer to me. I never understood this feeling between you and Jack and now I do, you blame him for your daughter's death. If she hadn't gone with him, she would still be here, but then I might not have been here?' Saffi said.

Nana looked at her granddaughter and saw now that she was no longer the child she raised, but was now a young woman. She started to see a mature Saffi, and perhaps this Saffi should go and find out what her father had left her?

Saffi got Nana a glass of sherry and they continued to look at the photographs. 'Is there anything else I should know, before I set off and meet Andreas?' Saffi asked.

Chapter 7

The morning of her flight Saffi said goodbye to Nana. I'll call from the hotel, when I get there.'

'Won't it be cheaper from your mobile? It'll cost a fortune phoning from the hotel,' Nana said.

'No, I'm not taking my phone. It doesn't work outside of Europe.' Saffi wasn't really into the latest mobile phones; she only ever used hers to call Nana, and in her naivety, she didn't know she could have changed her phone easily. She checked and double-checked she had her tickets and passport and waited for the taxi to arrive to take her to the airport. Saffi was not a well-travelled person and had never been on a trans-Atlantic flight. She tried hard to stop the butterflies in her stomach, but to no avail. She had managed to get a window seat and sat with a young couple on honeymoon, after a brief chat, she settled down to watch a film and then tried to get some sleep.

The plane landed in Nassau, just after 1pm local time. Tired and feeling a bit dishevelled, Saffi looked around the airport for any sign of Andreas, not that she knew what he looked like. However, she spotted a young lady, holding a sign with her name on it and went over to her.

'Hello, I'm Saffrina Simpson.'

'Ah, yes. I have a message for you,' and she handed Saffi a sealed envelope, then walked off.

Saffi opened the letter and read the contents.

> *Saffi, I am so sorry that I cannot be at the airport to meet you – something came up that I can't get out of doing. Take a taxi to the Breezes and I'll meet you there when I can. Once again, I'm sorry not to have been here for you.*
> *X A*

Disappointed that he had not met her, she did as Andreas said, and took a taxi to the hotel. On arrival, the receptionist gave her the room key and a letter.

She found her room, and with a huge sigh, put her suitcase down and slumped onto the enormous bed. The room was big and airy, and had a patio with a small garden set with a table, chairs and a sun-lounger. The patio looked out onto a white beach with the bluest sea beyond she had ever seen. Sitting on the bed, she sighed again as she lay down. Assuming the letter would be from Andreas she opened it.

> *Dear Saffrina*
>
> *I apologise again for not meeting you at the airport. I hope your flight was not too exhausting, and that you have arrived safely in the hotel. Unfortunately, I cannot meet you until tomorrow, but take your time to enjoy the hotel facilities. The restaurant here is excellent, try the chef's specials, they are always superb.*
>
> *If it's OK with you, I shall meet you tomorrow for lunch at Raymond's Beach Bar. I'll be there at 12.30; I have a photo of you, so should be able to recognise you from that. Tomorrow we will acquaint ourselves properly and decide what to do next.*
>
> *Until tomorrow*
> *A*

Saffi was beginning to feel let down by the so-called 'friend of Jack'. Twice he had failed to meet her. However, she placed the letter back in the envelope and put it in her bag. She lay down and within a few minutes was in a deep sleep.

When she woke again, it was 5pm, and although confused as to where she was, she soon adjusted to her surroundings. She checked the time and decided to shower and go for dinner.

Saffi had never stayed in a hotel on her own before, and she felt very self-conscious walking into the hotel restaurant, but remembered to bring a book with her to read, hoping it would make her look inconspicuous. Entering the restaurant, a waiter directed her to a table on the veranda and told her of the day's specials. She ordered a drink and, on Andreas' advice, ordered the Chef's Special.

After dinner, back on her patio she stared up at the stars. She had never seen so many before. The waves gently lapped the shore, glistening with the reflection of the moon. It had been a long day, and she thought about all that had happened in the last couple of weeks, not really comprehending it all, before going to bed and falling into a deep, comfortable sleep.

Saffi woke the next day just after sunrise feeling surprisingly refreshed. She spent the morning exploring the hotel gardens, pools and shops. It was only 10.30, so decided to spend an hour on the beach. Sitting in the shade of a beach umbrella, she felt herself drawn to the colours of the sea; her eyes did not move from the spot they had settled on. Her book lay unopened by her side as she continued to stare out into the ocean. Feeling very relaxed her eyes began to droop and she was soon dozing. Thinking she could hear her mother talking calmly to her, she tried to listen, but the voice disappeared, and she realised it was just the sound of the ocean lapping the shore. An hour had gone by without her realising; she just had time to change before she was due to meet Andreas.

Back in her room, she was finding it difficult to decide what to wear; she had packed as Nana had suggested, 'something for every occasion', but she had never been on an occasion like this. She decided on 'smart casual', white linen trousers and a pale blue top. She checked her reflection in the mirror and realised that she was feeling nervous. I wonder what he will be like, she thought. What shall I say to him? Will I like him? Will he like me? Why am I worried about whether he will like me or not? I'm only meeting him to decide what to do with Jack's boat, and find out whatever my inheritance is. He's only here as a chaperone.

She looked in the mirror again, and then changed her hair for the third time, and left her room. She felt nervous as she walked along the corridor, and tried to calm down as she headed for the beach bar.

Raymond's Bar was a typical 'tropical beach paradise', a round bar, topped with a palm fringed roof and high stools set around the circumference, so that everyone could see everyone else. The barman, Raymond, created his cocktails in a central area that allowed him to see all of his customers. He was a native Bahamian, about 40 years old, wearing a bright, Hawaiian shirt and black trousers, and had the warmest smile of anyone in the hotel. Seeing Saffi arrive, and take a seat at the bar, he noticed how nervous she looked.

'Good afternoon Miss. What can I get you?' his voice deep, but friendly.

'I don't know' she said, 'nothing too strong, what do you recommend?'

'A Raymond Special on the 'Soft Side' is what I would suggest.' Raymond moved around his bar putting all manner of rums into a blender and adding various fruit juices, a whole banana and lots of ice. After whizzing the blender thoroughly, he poured the creamy mixture into a tall glass and topped it with a cherry and a straw, setting it down in front of her he asked Saffi her name.

'Saffrina' she replied. 'I'm waiting for a friend.'

She looked around the bar trying to see if she could spot Andreas. Directly opposite she could see a young couple, probably on honeymoon, never taking their eyes off each other. Next to them was a very large, and very loud, American in his early 60s, wearing an oversized checked shirt, smoking a huge cigar and perspiring from the whole of his upper body. To Saffi's right was a middle-aged woman, with immaculate make-up. She was very well dressed and wearing a large amount of what seemed to Saffi to be very big diamonds. Although quite slim and tanned, she was also very wrinkly, Saffi thought. Far too much sun and too much jewellery, she concluded. There was no one else at the bar, but it was only 12:15. Saffi took a sip of the Raymond Special, turned on her stool, and stared out to sea.

Meanwhile, in the hotel bar, Andreas sat looking out to the beach bar. It was obvious which one was Saffi and for some reason he had lost all his normal bravado. The photo he had of Saffi was of when she was a teenage girl with braces on her teeth. Instead, in front of him was a beautiful young woman, whose good looks aroused something in him. This is Jack's daughter, he thought. I am supposed to be protecting her, not fall for her. Picking up his beer, he finished it in one gulp, as if to prepare himself to meet with her. He looked at Joe, and said 'well, here goes nothing' and strolled out to the beach bar.

Walking to the bar Andreas was still not sure how he should introduce himself. Hi, I'm Andreas, friend of Jack and protector of Saffi. No far too macho, he thought. Hi, Andreas here, been waiting for you to arrive, watching you from afar, as it were. No, no, that will frighten her. Hi Saffi, I'm Andreas, pleased to meet you. No. Way too formal.

By the time he reached the bar, he had no idea what to say. He felt like a teenager on a first date, his palms were sweating and his heart was pounding. The closer he came to the bar the faster his pulse raced. He walked around to the opposite side of the bar, as if hiding behind the central pillar. He was still planning what to say when Raymond interrupted his thoughts.

'Andreas, my man. How you doing? The usual?' He winked as he spoke. 'Any news about this babe you're meeting?'

Andreas turned bright red and looked over to Saffi. Had she heard? Did she realise that Raymond was talking about her? He could only hope that the pillar in the middle of the bar had hidden him from view. He slid onto one of the bar stools, and beckoned Raymond closer to him.

'I'd be really grateful if you could keep the vocals down, I think the young lady you're referring to is on the other side of the bar, and yes, the usual please.'

Raymond opened a bottle of Kalik beer, placed a slice of lime into the top, passed it to Andreas, and apologised. He held his hand up as if to say 'give me five minutes and I'll check things out.' Raymond went over to Saffi and asked if she needed anything more.

'No, this is quite delicious but I think you may have added a little too much rum for this time of the day. Do you have a glass of water?'

'No problem, Saffrina.' and he went to get a bottle of water from the fridge. When he returned, he also topped her cocktail glass up with some pineapple juice.

'This will help it go down a bit smoother.' He paused. 'This friend, what time are you expecting her, or him?'

'Oh, his name's Andreas, he's due at 12.30 and I'm a little early. Please, my friends call me Saffi.'

Andreas, listening to her response, was relieved to hear that she had not heard Raymond's unhelpful comments. He stood up from his bar stool and walked around the bar. Trying very hard to look as casual as you can when walking on hot sand, he headed towards Saffi. When he reached her and before he had time to speak, Saffi looked at him, thinking it must be him, she tried to get off the tall bar stool to greet him. As she did, she caught her foot on the bar rail, tripped and threw her 'Raymond Special on the Soft Side' all over Andreas.

'Oh, I'm so sorry, here let me get you a cloth.' Raymond passed her a clean bar towel. Taking it, she proceeded to wipe banana daiquiri all over Andreas' shirt. Not knowing what else to do, and without thinking, she grabbed her glass of water and threw that over him to in order to 'take out the stain'. Andreas stood in front of her dripping wet, covered in banana and smelling like a rum distillery, he asked her very politely to 'stop and not to worry.'

Saffrina could not have been more embarrassed, even more so, when Andreas started to take off his shirt and revealed his suntanned torso. Andreas handed his to shirt to Raymond, who immediately called reception to send someone to come and take the shirt to the laundry; he passed Andreas a dry towel. Meanwhile Andreas held out his hand and introduced himself.

'Hi, I'm Andreas, and you must be Saffrina.'

'I am so sorry, I can't believe I've been so clumsy, it's just that the stools are very high and I thought it was you and so I tried to get up to say hi and well, then I got caught up in the rail and. What can I say? I'll pay for the dry cleaning and please let me get you a drink.' She gabbled on, wanting the floor to open up and swallow her. She had never felt so embarrassed or stupid.

'Don't worry, it's not a problem, it's only an old t-shirt and it will wash out.' He turned to Raymond, 'can you have a 'uniform shirt' sent down for me to wear, and we'll have another two more Raymond Specials please.'

'Oh, I'm not sure I could drink another one. I won't' be able to walk back to the room.'

'Well it's not like you finished the first is it, and after all, you're supposed to be on a bit of a vacation, aren't you?' Andreas smiled at her, she wasn't sure if she felt that it was a sincere smile or whether he was just appeasing her.

'Well OK, if you insist,' Saffi said.

'Shall we take a seat over here?'

He pointed to one of the tables away from the main bar area and headed towards it. He pulled a seat out for Saffi and Raymond brought the drinks over, a clean, dry shirt and some snacks in an upturned coconut shell. Raymond smiled at Saffi, as if letting her know that everything was OK. She liked Raymond; he somehow made her feel special!

Andreas stared at Saffi, and she stared back at him. Neither knew what to say. They both started speaking at the same time and eventually Saffi let Andreas start the conversation.

'Would you like something to eat, lunch here is very good?'

'If you like, do they have a menu? Or just a salad, that would be nice.' Her voice was nervous and she knew she was gabbling.

Andreas signalled to Raymond who brought them menus and he told them of the day's specials. They ordered and sat once again in an awkward silence. Finally, Saffi spoke.

'Did you know Jack, my father, very well?'

'Jack! Did I know Jack well?' His voice rose as he spoke. Andreas stumbled, he was not sure how much Saffi knew about Jack and what he should, or should not say.

Saffi spoke again. 'Yes, did you know him very well? You must have been quite close for him to entrust me, as it were, to you. It's just that…' She stopped, not knowing how much to reveal to a complete stranger on a first meeting. They looked at each other again, then down at the table and then at their drinks. Luckily, Raymond arrived with lunch to break the silence.

'Crab salad for the lady and the usual 'cheeseburger in paradise' for the gent. Enjoy. Are you both OK for drinks?' They told Raymond they were fine and started eating in silence.

Finally, Andreas looked at Saffi, 'Look Saffi, shall we leave all this Jack stuff until tomorrow, can we try to get to know each other today, it's just that I think it's probably as awkward for me as it is for you.'

'I think you're right, it's a bit difficult. Why don't you tell me a bit about yourself instead?'

Andreas looked at her, how much should he tell her, how much did she know about him already? If he told her everything now, would it be the end of this relationship before it even began. Nervously he started to talks', I'm 43, but hopefully don't look it. I'm originally from Columbia, but I've been in the Caribbean so long, it feels like I've always been here. I'm single and have no family that I know of. In my spare time, I like to go sailing and fly aeroplanes. How's that for starters?'

'Not bad, but what do you do for a living?' She asked him wondering if he did the same as Jack and hoped this might spread some light on this elusive subject.

'What I do for a living? I, um…' He hesitated as he started to speak, what should he tell her. 'What I do for a living is, well, I sort of help those who need my help, as it were.'

'What exactly does that mean?' She asked.

'Well, it's a bit difficult to explain, I, when people, um, if there is someone who, well…'

He stopped again, should he just tell her everything and get it out of the way or should he try to skirt around the subject. He changed the subject.

'How much do you know about your father, Jack?'

Realising that he was avoiding the question, she let the subject change. 'Not very much really, he left, well in my opinion, abandoned me when mum…' She stopped and looked at Andreas to see if there was a reaction on the mention of Lillian. She watched his eyes divert to the floor uncomfortably. Saffi continued.'…After mum died', finally she had said the words, 'After mum died, Jack made it clear that it would be better if I stayed with Nana rather than him, and over the years his visits became less frequent, for what they were worth anyway.' Her voice was bitter as she recalled the memory of his visits.

Andreas interrupted her, he knew why Jack had left her, and that he had not abandoned her. He tried to defend his friend.

'It wasn't like that Saffi, he couldn't, it wouldn't have worked out, he was always travelling, it wouldn't have been safe for you…' He stopped and he looked at her face, had he said too much already. 'Look, shall we start again? Tell me something about you.'

'Yes, you're right, I'm sorry. OK, I'm nearly 27 and I did work as a trainee accountant and am, well was, taking my final exams, but then they made me redundant, which was why I was able to come out here at such short notice. Other than that, my life is a little boring really. I wanted to be a vet but I wasn't bright enough at school, but that's probably the story of my life.' She looked at her hands, twisting the napkin around like a child, not able to look him in the eyes. Why was she embarrassed about her past? She was doing fine in life, all things considering. She continued.

'I suppose life for you is one big adventure, I'm not sure I'm going to be cut out for this lifestyle.' She tried to laugh as she spoke, she was way out of her depth and didn't know how to control the conversation, but she was not sure if she wanted to.

'No, no, my life can be very tedious if there's no work, I just have to hang around until I'm needed, which is why I like to sail and fly. Oh, I nearly forgot to tell you, I've brought Jack's boat, Linalli, here for you. I'm not sure what you will want to do with her. She's in lovely condition for her age and glides through the water like a dream. Have you ever sailed?' Andreas asked.

'No, never. I wouldn't know what to do with a sailing boat. In fact, I'm not sure what I AM going to do with a sail boat.' The emphasis on 'what I AM going to do with a sail boat' was very clear to Andreas.

'Why don't I take you sailing tomorrow, just around the coast to see how you like it, come on, what d' you say.' He knew if he could get Saffi out on the water, she would love it. 'Look, we seemed to have got off on the wrong foot. Why don't we start all over again?' He looked directly at her. 'In fact, would you do me the honour of having dinner with me this evening, nothing fancy, a little restaurant I know just down the way, I'll pick you up at 6:30, how does that sound?'

Saffi looked at him, she did not know what to make of Andreas, he seemed OK, friendly enough, quite attractive, he was supposed to be helping her, and she didn't exactly have any plans for this evening.

'OK, 6:30, I'll wait in reception for you.'

They finished their lunch chatting about nothing much, mainly the people on the beach until Andreas walked her back to reception. He left the hotel feeling that the day had gone well, so far, and hoping that dinner would be better.

Saffi on the other hand waited until he had left the hotel and returned to Raymond's Bar, she thought she would get the 'lo down' about Andreas from Raymond.

Raymond saw her walking towards the bar, he was already waiting for the questions; so many women had asked the same thing about Andreas. However, Andreas seemed to act differently with Saffi. Not like a date, more like a brother-figure, and he wasn't used to Andreas acting in such a way.

'Hi Raymond, could I have a fruit punch please?'

'Of course Saffi, how was lunch?'

'Very good, thanks, best crab salad in these parts they say.' She was trying to keep the conversation as low key as she could. 'So, how long have you known Andreas, Raymond?'

'Andreas? Oh many years, he's always coming and going around these parts. 'Raymond knew not to give too much away about any of his customers.

'OK, but what's he really like, will I be safe with him at dinner, for instance?' Again, Saffi tried to inject some humour into her voice but she knew it sounded like a feeble attempt to pry about Andreas, and she knew by the look on Raymond's face, that he knew what she was trying to find out.

'Look Saffi.' Raymond leaned over his bar and spoke softly, but sincerely to her. 'I've known Andreas for a long time and he's a real good friend, but if you were my daughter, I wouldn't let you near him. Tells me he has women all over the place, but I'm not your papa. However, I watched Andreas today with you, and he was not acting like the Andreas I know, he was…he was somehow different, more like your brother. Does that make any sense to you?'

Saffi looked at him; she thought she knew what he meant. He certainly looked like the type of man that would 'have a woman in every port'. Sort of swarthy Mediterranean type, wine and dine you and only want one more thing from you. She knew she was naïve when it came to men and relationships, but somehow Andreas didn't act the way he looked. Under normal circumstances, she would have tried her best to avoid the likes of Andreas, but this was different. Jack had sent her to meet him. How did Jack and Andreas ever become such good friends? Again her mind was beginning to fill with questions, none of which she had the answers for. She looked back at Raymond.

'Well, I'm here to meet him on behalf of someone else so I don't see this becoming a romantic affair, more of a business proposition, so I can't see that I'm in too much danger of being 'whisked off my feet' by the infamous Andreas. But I'm glad you told me the truth, at least I can be prepared.' She smiled at Raymond and finished her drink.

'My advice to you Saffi is to just go ahead and enjoy your time while you're here, you're only on this planet for a short while and, as they say, life's not a practice.'

Saffi walked back to her room, happy that she had at least found something out about Andreas. She liked Raymond and felt that she could trust him, 'the art of a good barman'. She thought. 'Life's not a practice.' Raymond's words ran through her mind like a rhyme, she had never thought about life like that.

Chapter 8

Andreas drove back to Nassau, where he had left Linalli in a marina, just off from the 'Dockside' Restaurant; he had already booked a table for this evening. He knew this would be the best place for Saffi to see the boat for the first time.

It had just gone 4 o'clock when he got back on board Linalli. Sitting in the cockpit, he reflected on his first meeting with Saffi. Maybe a little strained, but what else did you expect from a 27-year-old who lost her mother when she was young, then abandoned by her father, only to find out he's not who she thinks he is. He mulled the thought over in his mind, what exactly was he going to tell her, and what wasn't he. He and Jack had never discussed that. They had just agreed that Andreas would do this one last favour for him if it came to it.

He wondered how much she knew about Jack, or himself for that matter. Does she know anything about Colombia? Luis Leppe? Does she know about the shooting? And if she doesn't, is it up to me to tell her? His mind reeled with questions.

He looked around at Linalli with affection. She had been his home for the last six months, he moved on board when Jack had gone back to Venezuela to 'tidy things up'. At the time, he thought it was odd how Jack had insisted that he move onto her permanently. Had Jack known something was wrong before he left? He still had that mystery to clear up, as well as the mystery he had left for Saffi. He poured himself a glass of Pussers Rum, and stared at the other boats in the marina, losing his thoughts in the tangle of masts that stretched above him. He sighed as he drank the last drops before heading to the shower. It had been a long day and it wasn't over yet he thought to himself.

Saffi spent the remainder of the afternoon trying not to think about how badly lunch had gone and tried to relax by the pool, but it had not worked. Questions continued to fill her mind. 'How much does he know about Jack, how much will he tell me tonight, and do I really want to know?' She returned to her room to get ready for dinner. Again, she found herself worrying about what she was going to wear, and not knowing why. Having changed twice she finally put on a simple black chiffon dress, printed with tropical flowers. She picked up her purse and shawl and went to reception.

She was early and as there were no free seats in reception, she decided to wait for Andreas at the bar. Walking through, she could see a man sitting at the bar, with his back to the door, and she didn't realise it was Andreas. The barman smiled at Saffi as she walked in and Andreas turn to see who it was. As she walked across the room, her dress floated elegantly around her, and as she reached the bar, she still had not recognised Andreas. He was dressed in navy trousers, a white linen shirt, clean-shaven, and his hair was slicked back, allowing his dark curls to drop down over his shoulders; he looked nothing like the Andreas she had met that afternoon in shorts and a baggy t-shirt. Embarrassed that she had not recognised him sooner, she started gabbling again.

'I didn't see you there, you surprised me, I'm sorry. I can't have been looking properly, how long have you been here, am I late…' Eventually she took a breath and Andreas took the opportunity to speak.

'Saffi, it's not a problem. I came early to see Joe,' Andreas said, gesturing to the barman. 'You look stunning?' Saffi blushed and avoided any eye contact with Andreas. 'Shall we go outside to watch the sunset?' He said as he picked up their drinks and went outside.

Saffi followed Andreas out to the veranda and they watched the sky turn from pale yellow, through amber, and to violet. She watched the first stars begin to twinkle as if they were winking their approval at her. They finished their drinks and Andreas led Saffi to the car park. She tried to guess which car was his. Looking around the car park, she knew he would have a sports car. It could be nothing else. She imagined him with the roof down, one of his many 'girls' in the passenger seat, the wind blowing through their hair as he sped around the island. So it came as quite a shock when he led her to a battered old Jeep, covered in dents and scratches, and he obviously had not washed it in months.

'You expect me to get in that, in this dress?' She protested.

'Trust me, it's spotless on the inside, I had it cleaned this afternoon.' He opened the door and helped her in. 'It's not what you expected was it?' He said, smiling knowingly. 'There's no point having a decent car out here, it will either get stolen, scratched or go rusty before you can say wax and polish. No one is interested in this old thing, but it can take me anywhere on the island without a single complaint.'

She smiled to herself. She was doing exactly what Nana told her never to do. 'Don't judge a book by its cover, not least until you've read the contents page!'

Although the sun had set, in the distance there was still a thin line of brilliant orange lighting up the edges of the remaining clouds, as Andreas drove along the coast road. Saffi looked out at the changing colour of the sky, just making out the islands in the distance, until the lights of Nassau Harbour took over the skyline. He took the back road to the restaurant. He did not want Saffi to see Linalli before they reached the restaurant. Parking the car, he turned to Saffi.

'I know this must be difficult for you Saffi and probably very confusing, as it is for me. Shall we make a pact?' He paused and looked down. 'No embarrassing questions tonight, what d' you say.'

'I'd say that's probably the best suggestion you've made today. But, how do we know what is and isn't an embarrassing question?'

'What about, if there's something we don't want to talk about, we just say 'taking the fifth', and then change the subject, no questions asked?'

'OK.' Saffi agreed.

'Good, shall we go in?'

Andreas jumped out, ran around to the passenger door, and opened it for Saffi, if nothing else Andreas was a gentleman. He offered his arm for her to take and they walked into the 'Dockside' Restaurant. As Saffi expected, he knew the owner by name and he greeted them personally. Showing them to their table overlooking the quay, Andreas asked the waiter to bring the champagne. 'I took the liberty of having a bottle of champers put on ice, I hope you like pink champagne?'

'Are you sure, we should be ordering…'

He interrupted her. 'Absolutely, if I can't order champagne for the daughter of my oldest friend, who can I order it for?'

The waiter poured two glasses and placed the bottle in an ice bucket. She looked over to Andreas who had already taken hold of his glass and was raising it to make a toast.

'To you and all that lies ahead.' He said as he chinked his glass with Saffi's and took a sip, as did Saffi. She giggled, as she always did whenever she took the first taste of champagne, but this time she tried not to laugh. She raised her glass to Andreas.

'To Jack and all he has laid ahead for us.' She chinked her glass against his, took another sip and this time the bubbles got the better of her and an unladylike giggle came out of her mouth.

'Oh I am so sorry, this happens every time I have champagne, the bubbles…'

He interrupted, 'The bubbles go up your nose and make you giggle. I know it does it to most people. I find it a great ice-breaker.'

As he was saying this, she took another sip and giggled again. She looked at him and they laughed aloud. They opened the menus and Andreas offered his recommendations. After they had ordered, Andreas noticed Saffi staring out to the marina.

'It's huge here, so many hotels, I'm finding it a bit overwhelming. I think I prefer the simpler things in life,' she said.

'And how do you know that, have you tried all the luxuries of life?' He was teasing her, for his ideals were the same.

'Well not all of them, but I recently had the pleasure of staying somewhere very luxurious thank you.'

'Oh you did, and where was that may I ask?'

'The Palace Hotel in Gstaad.' She said with a satisfying grin; as if she had stayed somewhere he obviously had never heard of.

'And I suppose you stayed in the Penthouse did you?' Andreas replied, knowing that was where Jack would stay when he was in Switzerland, and he had stayed there himself a few times. 'How is Walter these days? Is his arthritis any better?'

Saffi glared at him, her blue eyes cutting right through him.

'So you've been there yourself have you, at Jack's expense I shouldn't wonder.'

Her voice was bitter, now Andreas was the enemy and she was defending Jack. Andreas was not ready for this turn of the conversation.

'Actually I've been there on more than one occasion, with and without Jack.'

He needed to rescue the conversation but he wasn't sure that he could manage that. Saffi looked at him through her champagne glass and realised she had perhaps made assumptions that maybe weren't correct.

'I'm sorry, it's just that I'd never stayed anywhere quite like that before and I sort of wanted to keep it for myself. Childish I know; will you forgive me?'

Andreas looked up, her blue piercing eyes had softened and calmed, and she looked like the girl in the photo again. She's so like Lillian he thought. He picked up her hand and gently kissed it.

'Apology accepted and just so you know, I agree with you, I think the simpler things in life are best.'

Over dinner they spoke of nothing in particular, favourite films, music and books, trying to learn about each other without venturing onto dangerous ground. After dessert, they ordered coffee and sat looking out to the marina. Saffi had not seen Linalli moored in the marina, as the boat's name was only painted on the stern. Andreas waited until Saffi had finished her coffee and suggested taking a walk along the quay. He was eager for her to see Linalli, she was a beautiful boat and after all, she did belong to Saffi.

'I have something to show you while we're here,' he said.

He paid the bill and put her shawl around her shoulders. As they walked down the steps of the restaurant Andreas guided her off the quay and onto the pontoon, walking past the first two boats on either side. He waited to see if there was any reaction, these were beautiful boats, both a reasonable size, quite modern in their design. Saffi looked on without any comment, it was not until they started to walk further along the pontoon that she saw the beginning letters of the next boat, first the Li. Andreas let her walk slightly ahead of him. As she went further, the rest of the letters came into view on the stern of Linalli. Her hull was dark blue and her decks were teak. Her lines were sleek and smart, giving her the appearance of speed and beauty all at the same time. Saffi stood still, her mouth dropped open, her eyes were drawn up to the top of the mast before they ran down to her decks again and then onto her stern where the name was painted in gold letters.

'It's Linalli.' She looked back at Andreas; her eyes were bright and excited. 'She's beautiful.' That is all she could say, her eyes were darting all over her hull and decks and back up the mast again. Andreas had done a fine job of bringing her into top condition, he had oiled the decks, the stainless steel was glistening in the lights of the marina, and he had carefully left the warm glow of the cockpit light on so that she could see inside. Taking her hand, he guided her into the cockpit.

'Welcome on board, Captain Saffi.' He smiled, waiting for her to send him an indignant look, but she just smiled back, a huge broad grin. She looked at Andres' is this really her, Linalli?'

'Yes Saffi. And she's all yours. Do you want a tour below decks?'

'Downstairs? Oh, no not yet, I want to stand here and look at her, she's not what I imagined at all, she is beautiful.'

'Why don't you take a seat and I'll get us a drink, coffee or something stronger?'

'Oh anything.' She replied.

Her eyes were tracing Linalli's lines along the deck past the mast up to the bows and back down the other side. She dared not move. Having never been on any sort of sailboat before, there were so many ropes and unknown objects; she didn't know where to step, so she sat very still, exactly where she was.

'I think rum is in order, drink of all skippers.' Andreas passed her the glass and she took it without question, still staring all around her, her mouth open, ready to ask questions, but not knowing what to ask. Andreas watched her with interest. I think she's hooked; he thought and smiled. After a few moments, when she had finally taken in as much as she could, she looked at Andreas, and asked, 'Do you know how to sail her?'

'Do I know how to sail her? That Saffi is such an understatement, if you don't mind me saying. I've been living on her for the past six months, I sailed her up from Venezuela after Jack asked me to bring her back here.' He stopped, had he said too much again, he waited for the reaction from Saffi.

'Venezuela.' She said, 'how far away is that?'

'About a thousand miles.'

'A thousand miles, how long did that take?'

'I didn't sail it all at once, I stopped at various islands and places on the way. Knowing Jack, we'll probably be visiting some of them very soon.' Andreas' mind whirled, he had mentioned Jack twice now; he looked at Saffi.

'Do you think so? Do you think I'll get to see some of the places you've been to while I'm here?'

Her voice was gentle, not in the way she had reacted before, when he'd made the mistake of mentioning Jack. Had he broken through, he wondered. 'I'm not sure Saffi, I've no idea what he has in store for you, or me for that matter.'

'Tell me about him, tell me about the Jack you knew.' Her voice was calm and her face relaxed.

'Jack!' Andreas paused. 'Jack was my best friend.' He decided to keep this on a personal level and leave the professional elements to another time. 'Jack treated me like a son, like the father I never had, I learned about the sea and the air from him. He had a way about him, a natural way. Behind the wheel of any vessel, that's where he was most at home. He loved nature. He loved to watch the world in its truest form. He would do anything for you, and would put himself out for you, whatever the cost. I don't imagine you see him in that way.' Andreas stopped; he just described the perfect father, not the one that Saffi knew at all. He was hoping he hadn't gone too far.

'Oh.' Saffi's eyes dropped to the floor, 'that's not what I was expecting you to say, it's not exactly the way I remember him, not that I really remember him.' She continued to recall the memories of Jack.

'He used to come and visit me a couple of times a year, he would take me to the beach; we'd fly kites and play in the dunes.' She stopped and looked at Andreas, remembering the postcard he had sent, and then continued. 'We used to go there when my mother was alive, when I was little.' Her voice was soft and peaceful when she spoke of Lillian. 'Then, after she died, I used to look forward to his visits, but then they became less and less frequent. My Nana used to make out he'd sent presents, but I soon realised that it was her doing, bless her, what else could she tell me. She tried so hard to protect me from the truth.' She took a large drink of rum and handed the glass to Andreas.

'Another?' He asked, she was finally letting him in, he didn't want her to stop and thought perhaps the rum had 'loosened her grip' on her memories.

'No I'm fine thank you.'

'Carry on; you were talking about your Nana.'

'It must have been hard for her, all those years, not knowing where he was, not knowing what to tell me. I can't imagine what it must have been like for her when my mother died.' She looked at Andreas again. 'You said on the phone that you knew my mother, what was she like?'

Andreas got up, his heart sank, what could he tell her that would not cause her any more pain. 'Are you sure I can't fill your glass again, I'm having another.' He picked up her glass without waiting for an answer and went below to fill the glasses. When he returned Saffi was standing, staring up into the sky.

'I don't think I've ever seen so many stars.' She turned to him and took the glass without question.

'You should see the stars when you're not in port, there's a lot of light pollution here, from all the hotels. When you anchor in a bay, with nothing around you but the night sky, all you can see for miles are stars, millions of stars.'

Saffi looked back at Andreas; he too was now staring into the night sky.

'Look there, you see those three stars in a row, up to the left'. He pointed to a constellation. 'That's Orion's Belt, you can normally always find Orion.' He looked around the sky again. 'There, you see up there, that's the Big Dipper, can you see it looks a bit like a cooking pan.' Andreas pointed to the Big Dipper, and tried to show Saffi the stars that made up this constellation. Acknowledging that she could see it, he continued. 'If you find the Big Dipper, you can then find the North Star, if you take the two stars from the edge of the 'pan' and following them, past the 'handle of the pan' you will come to the North Star. There, that's your first bit of celestial navigation, if you learn enough about the stars you can navigate the seas.' He looked back at her as he sat down. She looked so alone standing there, looking at the stars. What was he going to tell her about Jack and Lillian, he was dreading her bringing the subject up again?

Saffi sat opposite him, putting the full glass on the table. 'I think I've had enough for one day; can you take me back to the hotel please.' Suddenly her face looked drained.

'We'll take a cab, I've had too much to drink tonight, you sit here and I'll organise one.' He got up to leave the boat, when she spoke again.

'Thank you.' She said very quietly.

'What for, the cab, it's no bother, they're just outside.' She interrupted him.

'No for being here, for helping me, I'm not really sure what I'm meant to be doing, it all seems like a dream at the moment.' She said.

He sat beside her and took her hand in his. 'There is nothing to thank me for, you are Jack's daughter; what else could I do but help?' He smiled as he let her hand go and went to get a taxi. Saffi pulled her shawl around her shoulders and picked up her bag. Her eyes moved along the decks of Linalli, a small smile appeared on her lips as she ran her hands along the sides of the cockpit. 'I own a sail boat' she thought to herself, 'how unbelievable is that?' She walked through the cockpit and down the plank onto the dock and waited for Andreas to return.

They sat in silence on the way back to the hotel, Saffi staring into the night sky. As they arrived at the hotel Andreas got out and opened the door for her.

'I'll walk you to your room.' He turned to the cab driver, 'wait here, I won't be long.'

Saffi collected her key from reception and they walked down the corridor to her room. Reaching the door, she turned to Andreas, 'Thank you for a wonderful evening and thank you for listening.'

'That's perfectly OK, in fact, my pleasure. What do you want to do tomorrow?'

'Tomorrow, I hadn't really thought about tomorrow. I suppose you know about the memory stick. I'm not sure what's on it, or what it's about, but perhaps we ought to look at it sooner rather than later.' She said.

'Or we could go sailing, if you want?' Andreas looked at her, he was not ready to become the mystery solver yet, he wanted to show her Linalli at her best. 'We could just go out for an hour or so. We could take a picnic and be back before two, and then look at what's on the memory stick, what d' you say?'

She looked at him; she had not thought about sailing Linalli, she became quite fearful of the thought.

'Sailing, oh I'm not sure I'm ready for that, it's all a bit too much in one go.' Her eyes fell to the floor, she thought she might be letting him down, he had after all told her what a wonderful boat she was.

'OK' he said 'what if I meet you here, and then we go to Linalli and I show you around her, in the marina, we have lunch on board and look at the memory stick after lunch. How does that sound as a plan?' He was hoping to get her used to being on board whilst still in the safety of the marina.

'OK, that sounds like a plan, how about you meet me at 10:30, I think I want a bit of a lay in tomorrow after all the excitement I've had these last couple of days.'

'Great, that's agreed, 10:30 in reception, I'll be waiting. Do you like fish?'

'Well, yes, I suppose so.' She said.

'Good, I'll arrange lunch and pick you up at 10:30.' He was like an excited schoolboy inviting his girlfriend to meet his parents for the first time. He stopped and looked at her, wanting to kiss her goodnight, he held back, instead he took her hand and kissed it gently. 'Good night Saffi, sleep well, I'll see you tomorrow.' He turned and almost skipped back along the corridor. Saffi watched him leave, she was still not sure what she thought of him, in the back of her mind she found him attractive, but she also thought he was a bit like an older brother. She opened the door and flopped onto the bed exhausted.

Chapter 9

Saffi woke early, and lay in bed watching the sunlight spill through the gap in the curtains. She thought of the previous evening and what lay ahead today. After breakfast, she decided to give Nana a call.

'Hello Nana, its Saffi, how are you? Is everything OK?'

'Oh hello dear. Everything's fine here. How are things there? How was your flight? What's Andreas like? What's the hotel like, what have you done so far, has he told you anything?' Nana finally stopped.

'Nana, so many questions.' Saffi paused, deciding where to start. 'I didn't get off to the best start with Andreas; in fact, I threw a drink over him. I didn't mean to; it was an accident. It's all a bit odd really; we don't really know what to say to each other. We went for dinner last night and that cleared the air a bit, and then he showed me Jack's boat, Linalli.' She paused again reflecting on how the boat had made her feel. 'She's a beautiful boat Nana. Today we're having lunch on board.'

'It all sounds like a far too much excitement for me, but are you having a nice time?' Nana asked. Given all the circumstances, Saffi thought it was an odd question, but typical of Nana.

'Yes, yes, I suppose so. Andreas is acting quite the gentleman, he's tall and dark,'

Nana interrupted her 'and handsome?'

'Yes, I suppose he is, if you want to look at it that way, yes I think he's quite handsome.'

Nana interrupted again. 'Benedict called yesterday to check that you were OK, I said I'd call him and let him know when I'd heard from you.'

'How did he know I was away?' Saffi asked.

'Oh I asked that, but of course you're paying with the credit card, aren't you dear, so he will have seen charges coming through. Anyway he just wanted to make sure everything was fine.'

'I think he just wanted to talk to you Nana. He's a very handsome man, don't you think, for his age?'

'Oh stop it Saffi, don't be daft. Romance, at my age?'

'Why not, you can enjoy yourself at your age, why don't you give him a call and let him know I'm fine.' Saffi had watched the way Benedict had looked at Nana, nothing wrong in a romance at their age.

Nana changed the subject. 'What did you say you were doing today?'

'We're having lunch on board and then looking at some information Jack left. Why don't I give you a call in a couple of days and let you know how it's going?'

'OK dear, you do that, and perhaps I'll give Benedict a call too. Take care dear, speak to you soon.'

~~~

At 10:30 Saffi went to reception to meet Andreas as arranged. This time she had not spent hours pondering what to wear before meeting him, she felt much more relaxed today. Walking into reception Andreas was waiting and his smiled said everything to her.

'You look like you had a good night's sleep.' He said as he greeted her, this time he moved forward and gave her a kiss on the cheek.

'Yes' she replied 'I feel ready for anything today, I've spoken to Nana this morning and that's put my mind at ease. So I'm raring to go, as they say.' They walked out to the car park and towards the Jeep, Saffi smiled. 'You've washed the jeep. It looks much better, thank you.'

They got in and Andreas headed in the direction of the marina. He looked over to Saffi and asked, 'Have you got the memory stick with you?'

'Yes, apparently you've got the password; do you know what it is?'

'Nope, I'm completely in the dark about that one.' He replied. Andreas thought she seemed different today, no sarcasm in her voice, almost jovial.

They parked the jeep and walked over to Linalli, the boat looked different in the daylight, Saffi thought.

As they boarded her, Andreas said, 'So do you want to see below decks now?'

'Yes, I suppose I do, lead the way. You know I don't know a thing about boats, I think you'd better tell me what everything's called, as we go through.'

'OK, we're currently standing in the 'cockpit' and going to go down the 'companionway' into the 'saloon'.' He gesticulated with his hands as they went down the steps of the companionway.

'Right, got that.' Saffi said, nodding her head and watching her step.

She followed Andreas down the companionway stairs into what she would describe as 'lounge' come 'dining room' come 'kitchen' type room. The interior was wood throughout, a dark cherry colour. There was a table on the right with a built-in sofa around it. On the left, there was a small cooker, a sink and small work surfaces. Behind her on the right was a desk with maps and compasses strewn over it and a built in seat. There were all manner of dials and electronic devices on the wall, what looked like a microphone and a walkie-talkie radio. She stood in the middle of the room not knowing which way to turn.

'Does it have a bathroom and bedrooms?' She asked shyly.

'Yes of course, but we call the bathroom the 'heads' and the bedrooms are 'cabins', over there is one of the heads and beyond that door is one of the cabins, there are two, go ahead, take a look, I'll put the kettle on, coffee OK, I don't have any tea I'm afraid.'

'Coffee is fine.' She said as she walked around opening doors and drawers.

There were cupboards everywhere, each containing something she was not expecting. Crockery, glasses, tins and packets of food, bottles of water; there was even a drinks cabinet. She moved to the rear of the boat and through into the master cabin. There were books on every shelf; she assumed they were her fathers. As she turned the corner, she found herself in a very small bathroom. A toilet, a basin and a shower room all in one. She looked around her and then sat on the bed, without thinking she started to stroke the cover, was this really Jack's bed? She looked along the row of books and found one marked 'Saffi'. It looked like a scrapbook. Tentatively she removed it from the shelf and opened the cover, on the first page was a photo of her and Jack on the beach, when she was about three. Mum must have taken this, she thought to herself. She ran her fingers over the photo. He looked so young. She turned the pages; each one contained just one photo of her, taken at either a birthday or Christmas, sometimes a school photo. Underneath was Jack's handwriting, giving the date and place the photo was taken, sometimes a comment. The edges of the photographs were very worn; she assumed he had rubbed the edges with his fingers. She turned each page cautiously and watched herself growing up through the photographs. Nana must have sent them, she thought; she started to feel sorry for him, alone all this time. She closed the book and put it back carefully on the shelf, as she did so she saw Andreas in the doorway looking on.

'You OK.' He said, although her face said a thousand words.

'Yes. It just seems a bit…a bit odd watching yourself grow up page after page. I never knew he had them.'

'I think there's a lot you don't know about Jack.' He turned and walked away. 'Coffee's ready.'

She followed him out of the cabin and noticed another album on the shelf, this one labelled 'Lillian: My Blue Eyes'. She placed her fingers tenderly around the spine but stopped, she was not ready for that book yet and she knew it. She went up to the saloon where Andreas had taken the coffee. Rather than sitting opposite him she sat down beside him, she wanted to cry but didn't know how.

'Tell me some nice things about him, please.'

He looked at her, sensing her pain 'If you're sure.'

'Yes, I think I need to know some good things about him, I've only ever thought bad things.'

He decided not to start at the beginning as that would involve talking about Lillian and he knew she wasn't ready for that. 'Jack…Jack was a lover of all things good and despised all things bad, not so much a case of black or white, more of right and wrong. You could be bad, but right, that didn't make you good, it just made the person not wrong.' He stopped. 'I'm not making a very good job of this am I?'

'No, it's OK, I understand, I think a bit like that, I think it's a problem sometimes as I'm always trying to find the good in people, no matter what.'

'That's what I meant to say, that's what Jack was like, always trying to find the good in everything. He believed there was good in everything and everyone, even if you didn't know it yourself. It's like when I first met Jack, he found the good in me that not many other people had seen.' She interrupted him

'When did you meet Jack?' She looked up at him with her deep blue eyes, wanting to know everything. He stopped; he didn't want to go down this road yet.

'A long time ago, but let's not talk about that yet.'

'Why not?' She asked.

He coughed 'I'm taking the fifth' he said with an uncomfortable laugh. He looked at her and his imploring eyes said it all. She hadn't really thought whether this would be painful for him, talking about Jack, after all he had lost his best friend.

'I'm sorry,' she said 'let's leave it for a while.'

'Do you have the memory stick; shall we take a look at what's on it?' He asked.

'Yes, it's here in my bag. Do you have any idea what this is about?' She said as she opened her bag and took the memory stick out. 'Oh, and do you have a computer; I didn't think to bring my laptop?'

'All I know is that some of the people Jack encountered in the last few years believe he owes them money. Jack thinks they will try everything in their power to get it, even if that includes taking it from you. He often told me that he would hide your inheritance, but I never knew what he meant, until now.' He paused while he brought over his laptop. 'I think this might be a way of keeping them off our backs, perhaps.'

'Oh, it's not going to be dangerous, is it?' Saffi said as she looked at the laptop. 'How do you keep the laptop charged if you're not on the land?' She asked.

'Firstly, no, I do not believe Jack would get you to do anything dangerous.' He said, knowing that he may not be telling her the full truth. 'However, you ask a very sensible question regarding power sources.' He continued, changing the subject as quickly as possible. 'While we're in a marina, we connect to the mains shore power but I have, or rather you have, a wind generator and solar panels, which provide all the power Linalli needs. The energy is stored in the batteries, and we convert into power we can use via an inverter. That allows us to use electrical things on board when we are away from land.'

'Oh!' She said, not quite understanding anything he had said.

He opened the laptop and it whirred into life, he inserted the memory stick, the option to read the file popped onto the screen.

'Shall we?'

'Yes, yes.' she was getting impatient.

There was only one file on the memory stick, an excel spreadsheet called 'Test.xls'. Andreas clicked on the file to open it. A message appeared, or rather a question.

'What was Lillian protecting?'

They looked at each other, clueless. Andreas repeated the question and Saffi looked at him and asked, 'Well, what was Lillian protecting?'

'That's the thing, I don't know what he's talking about.'

'Why would he ask a question that you don't know the answer to?'

'Why is it me that knows the answer, it could be you.'

'No, he was very specific in his letters, I have the memory stick, and you have the password. Didn't you get the same information as me?'

'I assume so, let me get the package'.

He got up and went to a cupboard that contained folders and files. He took a file marked 'For your eyes only' and brought it back to the table.

'For your eyes only? What's all that about?' Saffi asked, smirking at him.

'It's my filing system. I mark all my files with film names that mean something to me. Jack reminded me of a sort of James Bond character. Silly, I know, but I'm not very good at filing.'

Saffi just stared at him and smiled mockingly.

He opened the file and reread the original letter. She was correct, she had the memory stick, he has the password, but he did not have a clue to what Jack was referring.

'I didn't think Lillian was protecting anything, not that I knew of anyway.'

'It must be something you're not thinking of, something cryptic.'

'What do you mean?' He looked at her with staring green eyes, he felt useless.

'Is he using the word figuratively or actually? Was she physically protecting something or mentally protecting him from something that you knew about?'

'Nothing I know about.'

'She wasn't ill or anything?'

'No, but...' he stopped, and remembered that day, the day Lillian was shot. Jack didn't know she was pregnant, but Lillian might have known. She was pregnant with Saffi, but Andreas was not sure how to tell her this. She looked at him.

'No secrets' she said, 'we have to be completely open with each other.'

'I'm not sure how to say this to you Saffi.'

'Just say it.'

'I think she was protecting you, Jack didn't know she was pregnant when she...' He stopped again, did she know about the shooting? Saffi knew what he was about to say, Nana had told her what she knew about the accident and perhaps Andreas would shed more light.

'When she was shot?' Saffi said.

He looked shocked 'You know about that?'

'I know there was an accident and mum was caught in a shooting or something, Nana told me about it a few days before I came out here, I knew nothing about it before then. Why don't we try my name as the password?'

Andreas typed in the letters S A F F R I N A. Beep, nothing

'Try Saffi, that's what I've always been known as.'

Again Beep, nothing.

'I think that's the wrong tree we're barking up.' Andreas looked downhearted as he said it.

'Nana said they didn't find out mum was pregnant until she was in hospital, there must be something else, think Andreas, think.'

'I AM thinking. It was a long time ago.'

She looked at him and stared, her voice softened, 'where were you when the shooting happened?'

He wasn't sure if this was a question about the clue or about his past, but she had said 'no secrets'.'I was at the farmhouse, the orphanage that is, when Father Caleb found me. He said the children were fine but that Lillian had been shot.'

Startled, she replied 'The children? Farmhouse? What are you talking about?'

He sighed, now he knew she didn't know about any of this. 'Jack and Lillian had bought a farmhouse, they used it to help some of the street kids who needed looking after, they'd come for food and shelter, a bit like an orphanage.'

'Orphanage, street kids, where, when?' Her voice raised now, she knew nothing about this.

'Back in the 70s, when they were in Columbia, they lived on a boat and then they bought this old farmhouse in the hills, Lillian wanted to help as many kids as she could.'

'But how do you know all about this, this is the first I've heard about it. I knew they travelled and Nana said mum was working in a hospital or something. Tell me Andreas, please tell me.'

He looked deep into her eyes; this was going to be a long day. 'Saffi, I think we should take this very slowly, one bit at a time, there's a lot to tell you. Do you trust me that I will tell you everything eventually, but just one bit at a time for now?'

'Why can't you tell me everything now, surely I need to know everything?'

'Yes, and you will, but it is a very long story and we have other things to work on as well. Please trust me, I will tell you everything.' His eyes pleaded with her.

'OK, I trust you, Jack did, so why shouldn't I, but please tell me about the farmhouse.'

Andreas continued to tell her his story. 'I grew up on the streets of Cartagena, after my parents abandoned me, when they could no longer afford to feed me.'

'Oh my God that's awful, why didn't you go to the police or something.'

'Saffi, try not to interrupt, I will explain everything.' He got up, went downstairs and grabbed a couple of beers. 'I think I am going to need a drink to tell you all this.'

He cracked the bottles open and passed one to her. He continued. 'Kids being left on the streets by their parents in Columbia in the 60s and 70s, even today, wasn't and isn't unusual. There's not enough money, work or food. It's just the way it is, it's not right, it just is.' He took a gulp of beer and set the bottle on the table. Saffi did the same and watched him intensely.

'By the time I was 10 I was involved in the drug world, it's a much easier way of life, when there are guys who ask you to take a message to someone and they give you a couple of bucks for doing so, now you can buy food, but now they've bought you...it's a vicious circle. It was fine while I was still a kid, but as I got older, they wanted me to do more and more. I was using the money to help the other little kids, to get them food and stuff, a few of us lived in a derelict barn on the edge of town for shelter. Well, by the time I was 13 the drug gang were demanding more of me. They wanted me to sell drugs. Selling to businessmen and prostitutes is one thing, but forcing little kids into drugs was not what I wanted to do. They wanted to get them 'hooked' see. I'd seen what it did to people, I'd never touched any of the stuff and never wanted to, I didn't want these little kids touching the stuff either.'

He took another drink, her eyes fixed on him, she had never heard anything so awful, she wanted to ask so many questions, where were the police, why didn't they get involved, but he had asked her to stay quiet.

'Well, when I continued to say no to their demands they found I wasn't 'useful' any more so they beat me up and left me to die on the streets. Luckily, I knew how to play their game and acted as if they had knocked me unconscious so they would give up. I lay in the street for 2 hours to make sure they didn't return. It was really hard lying there with rats running over me and trying not to move.'

Saffi gasped at the thought of rats. . .

'Finally, as it became dark, I got up and dragged myself to the local hospital. I say hospital, it didn't have much of anything, including medicines but I didn't know where else to go. I walked through the door and collapsed on the floor. It was Lillian who found me and she picked me up like a wet rag and took me into a small room.'

'Lillian, my mother was there, how, why?' Andreas looked at her; tears were already filling his eyes.

'Please Saffi, let me finish. By the time I 'came to' properly I was lying in a bed, washed up and in new clothes lying in Jack's boat, Lillian was sitting on the bed looking at me, she'd been there two days. That's how I met your parents.'

A tear finally ran down his cheek as he looked at the floor. Saffi moved closer to him, put her arm around his shoulders and sat quietly holding him. After a short while, he pulled himself away from her and took another drink from his beer. He looked at her with sorrowful eyes. 'I'm sorry you had to hear about my life, it wasn't a great childhood, but I can say that Jack and Lillian did make the rest of it much more bearable.'

'Tell me about the farmhouse, what was that all about?' Saffi asked.

'When I was well enough to speak I told Lillian all about life on the street and the other kids that were out there, she was appalled, she kept asking questions and saying to Jack 'we've got to do something to help these kids'. Of course, Jack agreed but they had no idea what or how to help them. It's fine giving them some food, but it doesn't help in the long run, and Lillian wanted to help, she wanted to make a big difference. They went and spoke with Father Caleb at the local church, to see what could be done.'

'What did he say, how could they help.' This was the most Saffi had learnt about her mother, and father for that matter, from anyone, and it was fascinating.

'Well, as I say, there's not a lot you can really do, but he said these kids need somewhere safe to stay, a roof over their heads, away from the streets. When Lillian understood this, she was determined to get something sorted out, which is why they bought the farmhouse. As soon as it was safe enough and I was well enough they moved me there, I suppose I was their first 'street kid'.'

'How many were there'

'At first, not many at all, they were too scared of strangers. The other kids thought it wasn't safe, so in the end it was up to me to convince them to come and stay in the farmhouse, just overnight to start, to get them used to the idea. I remember bringing Maria and Stephano to the house as soon as possible. I'd been helping Maria on the streets; she was left like me by her parents, only she had a little brother to feed as well.'

'Oh my god, that's awful, how can parents do such a thing to their own children.' Saffi was outraged.

'Because it's the only way Saffi, in a country like that, you hope that someone will be good enough to help your kids when you can't.'

'How old were Maria and Stephano?'

'When they were first on the streets Maria was 6 and Stephano 3, I took them to the farmhouse as soon as I could, in fact that's who you're named after, it's sort of a combination of the two names. They were always with Lillian and Jack; in fact, they were with Lillian when the shooting happened.'

He grabbed his beer again, feeling drained by recalling the memories.

'What did you say then?' She looked at him, intrigued.

'Your name, Saffrina, is a sort of combination of Maria and Stephano.'

'No, you said they were with them when the shooting happened. Do you think that's what she was protecting, Maria and Stephano?'

'What do you mean?'

'Well, if there was a shooting going on and she had these children with them, don't you think the first thing she would do is try to protect them?'

'Oh, I see what you mean, I suppose so.'

'Well, which name shall we try first? I'm not sure how many times we can try to get this password.'

'Maria, she was always hanging around Lillian.'

'Yes, but was Lillian protecting HER when the shooting happened?' Saffi asked.

'I don't know, but come to think of it, Stephano was always in her arms, he was the smallest little boy. I wonder if she had him in her arms when the shooting started.'

'I think we should try 'Stephano', agreed?'

'Agreed.' said Andreas.

They both looked back at the screen, scared to enter the letters. Andreas typed them in S T E P H A N O. He clicked on the enter key, there was no beep, just the screen coming to life. It opened to a spreadsheet that had two work tabs. The first looked much like a blank crossword, and the other was entitled 'clues'.

'No clue in guessing what we've got here then.' Andreas said with a smirk, it was almost too easy he thought.

'Well I suggest we look at the clues before we decide how easy this is going to be, don't you?'

Saffi and Andreas opened the workbook entitled 'Clues', staring at the screen Saffi knew she would be about as useful as a chocolate teapot. On the screen was a list of clues, crosswords, as she knew, were not her strongpoint. There was a grid with two types of questions, one called 'Island Clue, and directly beneath it another called 'Answer Clue'. To the right of the clues were two columns, one headed 'Answer', the other 'Contact'. Looking at each other and then back to the screen, they read through the clues quickly. After a few moments, they realised that this would be a long and arduous task. On the screen, there was a set of instructions. Saffi read them aloud.

> 'To my darling Saffi, if you are reading this then you are with Andreas and are probably very confused, don't be, it will all make sense in the end. I'm sure Andreas will have told you about the need to hide your inheritance; I didn't work hard all these years for someone to come and take away what rightly belongs to you. So, I came up with this idea, and I hope you will enjoy yourself while you are searching. Indulge me! Think of it as a treasure hunt and enjoy the places I send you to visit.
>
> The first set of clues, are the 'Island Clues'. These will identify an island that you will need to visit. The second step is to solve the 'Answer Clue'. Once you have resolved this clue, put your answer in the adjacent box and, if it is correct, a contact name will appear. Refer back to the list you already have and make contact with this person and ask if you can meet with them. They in turn, will give you the across or down co-ordinate for where you should place this 'Answer Clue' in the crossword, which is shown on the next workbook. Good luck Saffi, love Jack.'

Island Clue
This chain in the Bahamas says it has a Cay for every day of the year
Answer Clue
When Her Majesty needs protecting, she chooses this hosiery to stand in front of this Great land
~~~
**Island Clue**
This island mixes up A Unit Garage to become one of this group's largest islands
**Answer Clue**
Although mainly flat, head to the smallest of the high points.
~~~
Island Clue
Find an island split in two and look for the Doctor
Answer Clue
Find an Old French Cape in the North and stare at the point, which, in 1641, it was the end for the Beginning.
~~~
**Island Clue**
A predominantly Spanish island with predominantly American features. An island that 'listens' for 'ET'.
**Answer Clue**
Find the town on the south coast that has something belonging to the World's Fair, and then look for the twin bell towers to find Our Lady of Guadalupe.
~~~
Island Clue
Originally named after a 4th C princess who was raped and murdered, along with 11,000 maidens.
Answer Clue
Running between a Spanish turtledove and a fat virgin, this piece of water was named after an English Privateer.
~~~
**Island Clue**
In confusion, I sat at, in a place known by a much shorter name
**Answer Clue**
Would you write about this extinct volcano or rather take a 'hike'?
~~~

Island Clue
Carib name of Karukera, 'island of lovely waters'
Answer Clue
Between two islands with mistaken lands, lies a salty pass between
~~~
**Island Clue**
When Columbus had a 'day of rest', he stumbled on this island
**Answer Clue**
The 18th Century left this town with a mixed identity
~~~
Island Clue
This French Island was birthplace to one of Frances' moot famous Empresses
Answer Clue
Then find the 19th hole of her birthplace
~~~
Island Clue
This floating island has a place of memories, on which 'I'll nail' my own.
Answer Clue
A secret life, hidden beneath my blue eyes.

    Andreas continued to look at the clues, his eyes running up and down the list, searching for anything recognisable, or easily solvable. They looked at each other, both knowing what the other was thinking. Saffi clicked the mouse onto the next work sheet to reveal a blank crossword, only the numbers indicating where the across or down answers should fit it.

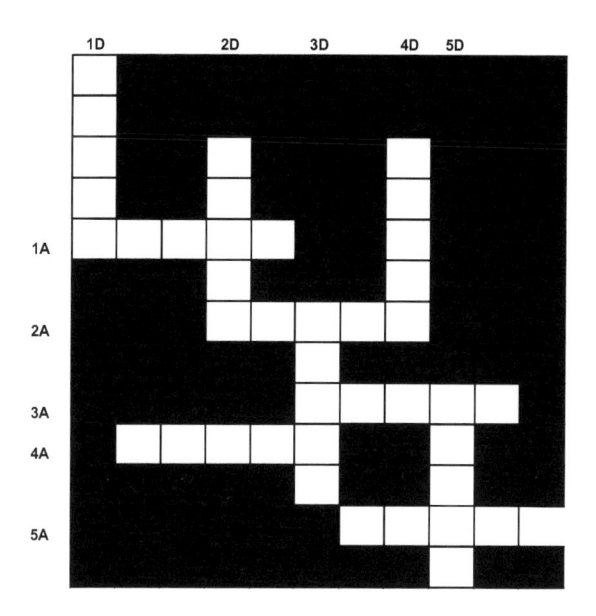

'So the clues don't have numbers, so we don't know where the answer will fit.' Saffi commented as she moved the mouse around the screen, 'and they all have five letters. What did Jack's instructions say again?' She read aloud again.

'The second step is to solve the 'Answer Clue'. Once you have solved this clue, put your answer in the adjacent box in the grid, if it is correct a contact name will appear. Refer back to the list you already have and contact this person. They will give you the across or down co-ordinate for where you should place this answer in the crossword shown on the next workbook'.

She looked at Andreas, who looked as confused as she felt. 'So once we've solved the second clue that will give us a name of a person, who we then need to find, in order that they can give us the crossword position. It's nothing if not convoluted.' She said.

'I think this is a wild goose chase and it's going to take some time to meet ten people. How long can you be away from home?' Andreas asked, the tone of his voice sharing his lack of physical enthusiasm.

Saffi didn't answer his question, she hadn't thought about how long she would be away from home, she would think about that later. 'What about the other information he left me, he left me a list of contacts with numbers and things. I'll need to go back to the hotel to get it.'

'Not so fast. Jack also left me a list of names and stuff.' He replied as he pulled out an identical package to Saffi's one. 'Perhaps we need to start at the beginning and see where it gets us, Clue one.' He read the clue aloud.

''*This chain in the Bahamas has a Cay for every day of the year.* 'Well that is an easy start, we are already in the Bahamas and not all the islands are part of a chain. I reckon he's describing the Exumas. There are many cays in the Exumas and all beautiful.' His voice sounded more enthusiastic when he mentioned the Exumas.

'How do you know that?'

'Because, Saffi, I have spent a lot of time flying up and down the Exumas. What's the next part of the clue?'

Saffi read from the screen ''*When Her Majesty needs protecting, she chooses this hosiery to stand in front of this Great land.* 'Any ideas?' She looked at Andreas.

'Hosiery, that's sort of underwear and stuff, yeah?'

'Actually, it's mainly socks and tights.' She replied.

'And stockings' he said with a cheeky grin.

'Yes and I suppose stockings.' She smirked.

'I'm being serious, there is an island called Stocking Island in the Exumas, let's check the Bahamas guide.'

He returned to the cockpit with an armful of books, guides, dictionaries and maps. 'I think we're going to need these. You look in the 'Lonely Planet Guide' and I'll check the Bahamas guide.'

Andreas didn't really need to look in any book, he knew exactly where Jack was sending them and who to see, but he wanted to see if Saffi could figure it out for herself. Saffi picked up the Lonely Planet Caribbean Islands guide and checked the index. 'Bahamas, pages 58-100.' She turned to page 58 and read from the first page.

'*The Bahamian islands may have tourism's footprints in their sands and millionaires hiding in their cays but fishing is still the main livelihood…*'

'Look up the Exumas, Saffi, that's where I think we're going.'

She turned the page and saw a map of the Bahamas islands, moving her finger slowly across the page she found Nassau so she could get her bearings, it was not hard to find as it was in large letters in the centre of the page. She moved her finger down again and saw the 'Exuma Cays'. Again, as she moved down the page she found Great Exuma and Stocking Island marked on the map. 'OK, I've found Stocking Island on the map but I'm not sure what that has to do with the Queen?'

'That's why I think you need to look up the Exumas pages, go ahead see what it says.'``

Again, she started to flick through the pages, she found a large map of Nassau and found the marina where Linalli was, and she turned some more pages and eventually found a page headed 'Exumas'. She began to read aloud. *'The Exumas are a 100-mile-long necklace of 365 cays'.'* She stopped, 'did you hear that Andreas, 365 cays, one for every day, like in the clue. I think you're on the right track.'

Andreas smiled, he knew exactly where this was leading, he thought to himself, he knew Jack better than he'd realised. 'Carry on, what else does it say?'

She skimmed down the page to the next paragraph. *'the main settlement on Great Exuma stands on the west shore of Elizabeth Harbour sheltered from the Atlantic by Stocking Island'.* Saffi looked back at the screen and re-read the clue *'When Her Majesty needs protecting, she chooses this hosiery to stand in front of this Great land'.* 'Hosiery is stockings, Stocking Island protects Elizabeth Harbour, Elizabeth is the Queen and great land is Great Exuma, do you really think it's that easy Andreas?' She turned to him and saw a huge smile staring back at her. 'What, what's that big smile for?'

'I think I even know who we are going to meet.' Andreas said grinning.

'Oh come on, he won't have made it that easy, surely?'

'Well, what shall we do if I'm right?' he asked.

'I don't know, who do you think it is?'

'I think we're off to see old Gus Ambrose, he runs the ferry to and from Stocking Island. If I'm right I get to fly you down there tomorrow and if I'm wrong, you get to chose what we do next, deal?' He said, grinning. He looked at Saffi, he knew he was right and flying her down to the Exumas would be one of life's pleasures and he wondered whether Jack was doing this on purpose.

Saffi was excited now, but not sure why. 'OK, you're on. Let me type in the word.' She turned to the keyboard and typed in 'EXUMA' in the column and clicked the enter button. She was not sure if she was happy or not to see the name Gus Ambrose appear in the contact box. She looked at Andreas with scared eyes. 'How big is the plane?'

Chapter 10

The next morning Saffi waited patiently for Andreas to meet her, and was extremely apprehensive when he arrived just after breakfast.

'I've never been in a small plane.' She announced, hoping he'd changed his mind.

'A deal is a deal, and don't worry, you are going to have a wonderful time. You do have an overnight bag, haven't you? As I said, Gus won't let us get away without staying the night.'

Andreas had made the relevant calls the night before, after he had taken Saffi back to the hotel. He'd organised a Cessna 172, a modern 4-seat plane, out of Nassau Airport. The flight would only take about an hour and a half, but he knew that it would take about two hours to get everything sorted and 'off the ground'. He took hold of Saffi's bag and then, looking at the expression on her face, he took hold of her hand.

'There's nothing to worry about.'

'How long have you been flying?' She asked, trying to hide her nerves.

'Me, flying, most of my adult life, Jack introduced me to it, I have been flying around these waters for a long, long time. I know them like the back of my hand.'

That's fine for him to say, she thought, what if the plane stops working, what then. She sat nervously in the Jeep, thoughts rushing through her head constantly worrying about the upcoming flight. They reached Nassau International Airport and Andreas drove to the 'General Aviation' area. They parked and he told her to wait while he checked that everything was OK.

After about ten minutes, he returned, 'Come on then, we have a green light, let's get this show on the road' he said as he grabbed both their bags and told Saffi to follow him. She looked all around her trying to take everything in. There were small planes everywhere, squeezed in amongst huge private jets. They walked around parts of an airport she didn't know existed. Andreas came to a halt, dropped the bags to the ground and held his arm towards the small plane.

'You want me to get in that? That tiny little plane and fly over the sea. You are kidding me.' She looked at him aghast. The Cessna was no bigger than a 4-door saloon car with wings.

'Stop panicking, these planes are great for this type of trip, it's only ninety minutes and you get a great view, come on, just get in and sit in it, you'll see what I mean.'

Saffi looked at Andreas. She really wasn't sure but moved slowly toward the plane. Andreas opened the door, 'put your foot here, and hold on there,' he said showing her the best way to get in. Inside the plane was very lavish, tan leather seats, front and back, headsets already in place, what looked like a computer screen and all sorts of dials.

Once she was seated, Andreas leaned in the plane. 'See, it's much bigger than you thought, go-on tell the truth.'

'Well, I suppose it is, the seats are comfy and windows are much bigger than I imagined.'

Andreas ran around the other side of the plane and got in. 'Shall I explain some of these things to you? That might make it easier for you.'

'Well, if you think so, but don't expect me to remember anything.'

'That's fine. You'll need to put on a life jacket as we're flying over water, and if I raise my hand it means I'm about to speak to Air Traffic Control, so don't speak. Once we're out of the control you can talk as freely as you like, but I explain more on the way. Shall we get going?'

'If you sure it's going to be safe.' She looked across at him with apologetic eyes, he was clearly excited and wanted to get going, and she was very nervous.

'You will have one of the best 90 minutes of your life, and I can promise you sights like you have never seen before. Do you trust me?'

'Yes, I suppose so.' She said, but deep in the pit of her stomach, all she could feel was fear churning inside her.

'Then I will get everything ready and we can go.'

He helped her on with her life jacket. He put the bags in the luggage hold, walked around the plane, and did his final pre-flight checks. He got back in and helped her with the seat belt and head set. Then he started to switch things on, and the interior of the plane came to life, the computer screen lit up and dials began moving around. Andreas started the engine and the propeller spun into life. He looked across at Saffi, he read 'fear' in her eyes, but he knew she would be all right.

'I'm just going to call Air Traffic Control, so no talking for a minute please.' He waited for Saffi to acknowledge him. 'Nassau

Ground, this is November Five Five Six Sierra Papa requesting taxi clearance for VFR departure to George Town.'

Saffi heard his words in her headset, she was about to say something, Andreas raised his hand as if to say 'not yet'.

'November Five Five Six Sierra Papa, this is Nassau Ground, taxi via runway Two Three to holding point Bravo for departure Runway Zero Nine and contact Nassau Tower on One One Nine decimal five when ready for departure.'

Andreas repeated the message back to Nassau Ground Control. He made one final visual check around the surrounding area, increased the power and released the brakes, the plane started to roll forward. Saffi sat with her feet wedged against the floor. 'Oh my god, tho plano'o moving' she thought to herself, 'this is it, take deep breaths'. Andreas manoeuvred the plane skilfully along the taxiway and around to 'holding point Bravo' where he turned the plan into the wind and completed his pre-flight checks.

'Nassau Tower, this is November Five Five Six Sierra Papa, at Bravo, ready for departure.' Andreas said into his microphone.

'Six Sierra Papa, after departure, right turn on track Norman's Cay as filed. Climb Two thousand feet and contact Nassau Departure on One Two One Decimal Zero. Cleared to line up, depart, Runway Zero Nine.'

Again, Andreas repeated the message back as confirmation. He taxied the plane to the end of the runway and lined up for takeoff. He increased the power, but kept the brakes on when he reached the correct rpm, he checked the engine temperature and pressures, released the brakes and increased to full power. The plane started to roll down Runway Zero Nine. Saffi held on for dear life. As the plane left the ground, she let out a scream, 'What's happening?'

'We're flying. Open your eyes and look out the window.'

Saffi finally removed her hands that were gripping the edge of the seat, opened her eyes and looked out of the window, she watched as the ground disappeared beneath her. She grabbed the edge of the seat again and shouted to Andreas. 'Is it really safe, we're not going to crash?'

'Not if I have anything to do with it.' He smiled as he looked at her and he started to turn the plane to the southeast. Once the plane was stabilised in the climb he called Nassau Departure on the radio.

'Nassau Departure this is November Five Five Six Sierra Papa, passing One Thousand for Two Thousand feet, on track Norman's Cay.'

'Six Sierra Papa, continue as cleared, report Norman's Cay in sight.'

'Continue as cleared, report Norman's Cay in sight, Six Sierra Papa.' Andreas confirmed with Nassau Departure. He looked at Saffi and said, 'You can talk all you want now, we don't have to talk to Air Traffic until we see Norman's Cay.' He watched as she looked around. They were flying at 2,000ft, a good vantage point to see the whole of the Exuma islands when they came into view.

'What was all the talking about, I'm not sure I understood any of it, they talk so fast.' Saffi asked.

'Oh, you'll get used to it, I ask to do something, they give me permission, I have to repeat back what they say, they tell me I can do something else, and so it goes on until we get out of their airspace and they leave us alone, so now we can talk freely. You only have one job to do, well maybe two.'

'What are they? I thought this was a pleasure trip, no work involved?'

'Well firstly you have to enjoy the trip, that's job number one, but job number two is a bit more important, you have to help keep a look out for other traffic, you know other planes that might be around.'

'Why? Don't Control, or whatever they're called, tell you who's around?' Saffi was quite shocked that she would have to do this.

'In this part of the world sometimes they do, but sometimes they don't so it's always best to keep a good look out, see over there, in your ten o'clock position, about two miles away, there's another plane. However, he's going the same way as us and he's faster than us, so we just need to keep an eye on him.'

Saffi looked in what she thought was her 'Ten o'clock position' but could see nothing. What she could see was a vast amount of blue water and not a lot else in sight.

'How do you know where we're going?' She looked at all the dials; she had forgotten everything he'd told her earlier.

'Before we did anything, in fact after I dropped you back at the hotel last night, I plotted a course on this chart here.' He handed her a paper chart with a line drawn from Nassau to Norman's Cay and then down to Great Exuma.

'Is that our course?' She asked as she studied the map.

'Yes, that's what we have put on the flight plan that we've filed with Nassau. That lets them know where we are intending to go and where we will go if we have to divert. So if anything were to happen, which it won't, there is someone on the ground who knows roughly where we will be.' As he said it, he knew he shouldn't have.

'Oh well that's good news then, there I was thinking we were just flying around aimlessly. What do all these dials do again?'

'These are the mechanical versions of what we have on the GPS here. Look, can you see the moving map? We can put our course into the GPS and it gives us information on which direction to fly, it gives us course, speed, height, distance and time to our destination so at any time you can see where we are and how long we have to go. And, if all this breaks down, which it won't, then we can use the manual dials, which also show us speed, direction, height. Do you want to have a go at flying?'

Saffi looked horrified at him, was he serious, her, fly the plane. 'Oh I don't think so! I don't know what to do.'

'Well I'll tell you what to do, it's perfectly safe. Take a hold of the yoke, that's the steering wheel to you, while I still have control of it, and just see if you can 'feel' the plane.'

Saffi moved her hands to the yoke and held on gently; other than some vibrations, she couldn't feel anything, apart from sweaty palms and sheer panic.

'Now, if we just push the yoke forward, away from us, very gently, watch what the horizon in front of us does.' Andreas pushed gently on the yoke and allowed the plane to descend very slightly, just enough for her to see the horizon rise slowly. 'Now, if we pull the yoke back again, very gently, the horizon will drop down back to its original place. If we do that again, watch what the altimeter does.'

Andreas carried out the same actions, pointing out to Saffi that the altimeter decreases and increases as the plane descends and rises. He did the same with a turn, banking the plane slowly to the right and then to the left, pointing out when they were back on track. He asked her to watch the 'artificial horizon' and to tell him when they were straight and level again.

'Are you sure you don't want to take control, it's a very liberating feeling, and I promise that we won't crash, I'll keep my hands right by the yoke.'

Saffi nodded, but she could feel the sweat on her top lip as she moved her hands around the yoke again. She squeezed it so tightly that her knuckles turned white.

'Not so hard, you don't have to hold on so tightly.' He said.

She released her grip slowly and began to relax, Andreas still had hold of the yoke, or so she thought. The Exuma islands had just come into view and he told her to find a fixed point in front of her, on the horizon and to fly towards it and see if she could fly straight and level. She was doing fine until Andreas finally released his hold on the yoke. The plane began to rise slowly.

'Watch your horizon, don't grip too hard and don't pull back, gently come back down, you've gone up 100 feet.'

'What, aren't you holding on anymore?' She panicked and let go of the yoke completely.

'OK, I have control, let's try again, gently take the yoke, and watch the point on the horizon and try to keep the plane level.'

Saffi put her hands back on the yoke, she looked out of the window and found a point on the horizon; concentrating, she was determined to keep the plane level this time', I'm ready now.'

'Actually, you've been flying for the last few minutes I moved my hands off a little while back, you're doing fine. Just keep going.'

She started to panic again and the plane moved upwards, she took a deep breath and moved the yoke forward slowly and the point on the horizon come back into view. She steadied herself and felt a strange sensation; she was in control of an aeroplane.

'Do you want to try a turn?' He asked.

'Do you think I can, just a little one.'

'OK, keeping your eye on the horizon, find a spot just a little bit to the left of your original spot, as you start to turn, the plane will try to drop, so you have to pull back a little bit on the yoke as you turn, not too much, when you're happy straighten back up. Off you go.'

Saffi looked at her original point and looked to the left. She found another point to aim for. As she started to turn the yoke she could feel the plane start to descend, she did as Andreas had said and pulled back on the yoke to maintain her horizon. She lined up with her new point and levelled the plane back up.

'That was perfect, now do the same the other way and come back onto our original heading, your original point on the horizon.' He said.

Saffi did the same again, although it felt easy it was taking all of her concentration, she liked the feeling of being in control of a plane. She looked back at Andreas; she had no idea how big her grin was. He loved this reaction when he took people flying for the first times', I have control again, I need to talk to Nassau Radio and you need to look out the window as we come over the Exumas.' Andreas called Nassau and they gave him permission to continue onto Great Exuma, and to call Exuma Tower when he was passing the northern end of Great Exuma.

The Exuma cays were just becoming visible. This was his favourite place to fly. From above, the waters of the Exumas were unbelievable. You could see every single shade of blue and turquoise in the rainbow, all swirling around the banks, reefs and islands. Deep blue strips of water with boats anchored against shallows, only inches deep. Tiny cays, some inhabited, some just a scrap of land, some with runways, and some with nothing but a dirt track running through the middle. Everything these islands needed came from either the sea or the air. It could be a harsh and barren existence, but also one of the most beautiful. He couldn't wait for Saffi to see it, just as Jack had wanted her to, from the air.

Chapter 11

As the Cessna flew closer to the edge of the Exuma islands, Andreas could see the first of the islands coming into view. He looked over at Saffi and pointed the island out for her to see.

'That's Norman's Cay over there. Back in the 1980s, an infamous drug lord took it over. They came in one night, threatened people with guns and made them leave their homes and possessions. If you look closely, look down there, you can see the remains of one of their planes that crashed after takeoff. You can snorkel around it now. Can you see it?' Andreas said as he pointed out the window.

'God that's awful, what happened to the islanders?' Saffi asked, looking out of the window, trying hard to see the plane in the water below. She looked down at the island; it seemed so small and insignificant. Finally, as they passed over the end of the runway she could see the wreck of the plane in the water.

'The DEA finally caught up with them all and banged them away for a long time. The islanders got their homes and their island back, eventually. It's a great island. The restaurant by the runway, makes the best cheese-burger I know of, perhaps we'll stop here on the way back.' Andreas said.

Saffi didn't know what to say, she'd never seen anything like this before. As Andreas took the plane lower, he flew over the sunken plane he had pointed out. She could see it clearly now, it's cockpit half sitting out of the water.

Saffi peered over at Andreas, a question was looming but she wasn't sure if she should ask it. Andreas looked at her, 'No secrets' he said, 'they were your words not mine, ask me anything?'

'Did you know them, the drug people who took over that island?' She dared not wait for the answer. Here she was, sitting in a plane with someone who had been involved in drugs, OK a long time ago, but he still could be, couldn't he?

'No, I was clear of all that stuff by the time these guys came along, but I'm sure they knew some of my old associates, it's not something I like to think about these days.'

'Oh' Saffi wasn't sure what to say to that.

'If we have no secrets, I have a question for you.' He said.

'OK, I suppose, go ahead.'

He looked her straight in the eye. 'Do you know what it is we're looking for, what your inheritance is, what Jack is trying to get us to find?'

She had assumed, incorrectly, that he knew more than her, his question surprised her. 'No, I thought you would know, all I know is what Jack told me in the letters which was there is an inheritance for me to find and you will help me find it? I don't even know why he's hidden it in all these clues; why not just give it to me, if it's mine?'

'I have some ideas about what it might be. Like I said, some of Jack's 'associates' believe he owes them. Did he say anything else in his letters, anything at all about other people wanting your inheritance?

'No, he didn't. Surely whatever it is, it's mine I have the letters to prove it. Who are these 'associates anyway?' She looked at Andreas, 'is there something more I've not been told. Did Jack have a secret family or something? Don't tell me, I have half brothers and sisters all looking for the same inheritance. You know, whoever finds it first, gets it?' She was angry now. What sort of man was Jack, and what sort of 'wild goose chase' had he sent her on?

'No, nothing like that, there was only ever Lillian and you, and he lost both of you, in one way or another. However, I have some ideas who 'the others' might be, but they're just guesses.' He stopped, not knowing where this conversation would end. 'Jack and I upset quite a few people in the last few years.'

'Oh! You did, like whom?' She said, unable to hide the fury in her voice.

'Just people.' He stopped, trying to calm the situation. 'Let's not have this conversation now, you'll miss the show outside, and we can talk about it over dinner?'

She'd noticed that every time Andreas said something interesting about his past with Jack, he put off talking about it, 'he knows much more than he's letting on' she thought. 'OK, we'll talk over dinner.' She would not let this conversation slip, no matter how hard he tried.

However, Andreas knew there would be no time to talk at dinner; Gus would make sure of that, he'd want to spend as much time with Saffi as he could, and he would put off talking about his and Jack's past for as long as he could.

Andreas continued to fly the plane down the Exuma Cays, pointing out each island as they passed, explaining to Saffi about the more interesting ones, but it was the colour of the water that kept her eyes fixed on the scene below. She could see boats at anchor at most of the islands and wondered what it would be like to bring Linalli here, not that she had any idea how to sail. She wondered what it would be like sailing around, living on a boat. Her mind was wandering as she continued to take in the shapes and colours of the tiny islands.

Andreas called Exuma Tower and asked permission to land at Great Exuma, Saffi looked out but could see no sign of a runway. 'Land, where?'

'Down there, we've still a few miles to go yet, you'll see as it gets nearer. Don't worry it's a proper runway, not just a dirt track if that's what you're thinking.'

'Me! Worry! Why on earth would I do that?' Saffi looked out of the window again; this was all too much to take in, in one day.

Gradually the runway came into sight as Andreas began his decent. In fact, the runway was coming into view very quickly, but she decided to stay quiet; Andreas needed all his concentration for landing she thought.

He brought the Cessna to the ground with perfect precision and the plane began to slow as it continued down the runway. At the end, he slowed down, turned the plane around and backtracked down to the first exit. He found a place to park on the hard standing and applied the brakes. He let the engine run for a few minutes while he completed some paperwork and before shutting everything down. He looked over at Saffi. You OK? You look petrified.'

'I'm not sure what I am. I think I'm in shock, that's what I think. I'm not sure how many people get to have their first experience in a small plane over such an amazing place. I can't believe what I was just looking at, the islands, and the water, the water is so' she stopped, she couldn't think of enough words to describe the sea she had just seen.

'Blue?' Andreas interrupted, not meaning to sound sarcastic but he knew exactly how she felt, the waters around the Exumas were beyond compare.

'Well, yes, blue.' Saffi said.

'You wait until you see the beaches and meet the locals. They really will blow you away.'

Chapter 12

Andreas helped Saffi from the plane and got the bags from the hold. He could see she was bewildered and didn't know what to do next.

'This way.' He pointed. 'We just need to let the 'authorities' know we're here, it'll only take a couple of minutes and then we can get a taxi to Gus's place.'

They walked across an open concreted area, of what Saffi could only describe as a 'plane car park' or rather a 'plane park'. They walked up a ramp and into the 'arrivals lounge'. Behind a desk was a big Bahamian Customs Officer, who looked quite fearsome, she thought, but as soon as the Customs Officer recognised Andreas, his eyes lit up and his sullen mouth turned into an enormous grin.

'Andreas, my man, where you been these past months, you not been around these parts for a long time now.'

Saffi listened hard, although he spoke English, his strong Caribbean accent was difficult to understand at times.

'Jeremiah, what can I say, business always keeps me away from this wonderful place for too long, but I'm back now.' Andreas said, slapping the Customs Officer friendly on the back.

'You here on business, or pleasure?' He asked, smiling as he looked at Saffi.

'Oh pure pleasure.' Andreas looked at Saffi and gestured to her come closer. 'May I introduce Saffrina Simpson, Jack's daughter?'

'Saffrina, it is a real pleasure to finally meet you.' Jeremiah said, taking both Saffi's hands and gently cupping them in his enormous grasp. 'For many years, I have heard only wonderful things about you from Jack. I, we, on the island, was so sad to hear of his early passing. He was always good to us here. I hope you enjoy your stay as much as Jack enjoyed his time with us. Where you off to now?'

Saffi stuttered. She wasn't expecting this reception. 'Oh, thank you, um, we're off to see Mr Ambrose, I think.'

'You off to see Gus, I think Gus is already here to find you. Let me see your passports and I'll get you through to 'Old' Gus' as quick as possible.'

Jeremiah checked their paperwork and after giving them both a hug, they went through to the main airport area. As they walked through, Andreas heard the deep voice of Gus calling over.

'Oh heavens above, what a great surprise, I can't believe you back to see us Andreas. And this, this must be Saffrina, oh how many years have I wanted to meet you my dear child.' Gus said taking her in his arms and hugging her as though he had known her all her life, which in a way he had. Jack had spent many hours talking about Saffi to Gus and his family, and about his sadness of not be able to see her grow up, and even more of his disappointment of not seeing her as often as he wanted.

Gus was a gentle looking man, of medium build, a few inches under six feet tall. He had a warm smile and a face that looked 'lived in'. Saffi liked him immediately.

Saffi didn't really know what to say to Gus. 'I'm very pleased to meet you Mr Ambrose, it would be nice to be able to say that I've heard a lot about you too, but I only heard of you yesterday. I'm sorry, but I think I will enjoy getting to know you, I'm sure.'

Gus looked over to Andreas, 'my my, she is a polite one, you sure she belongs to Jack.'

'Oh I'm sure.' Andreas replied 'Luckily for Saffi her Grandmother raised her, so she had a proper upbringing.'

'Ah yes, Nana Lee, I've heard many good stories of Nana Lee, how is she, missing you I've no doubt.' Gus enquired.

'Thank you for asking, she's fine, I spoke to her a few days ago.' Saffi stopped, not knowing how to ask the next question. 'Excuse me for being rude Gus, but how did you know we were coming.'

'Nothing stays quiet in the Bahamas for long, child. You'll get to know this.' He looked at Andreas. 'You rent the plane from Wesley, right?'

Andreas nodded, but he knew how the islands worked, the coconut telegraph, and how the news had made it there before them.

Gus looked back at Saffi; he took her by the hand and led her out to his truck. 'Wesley's brother-in-law, called his sister Tara, who called Mary at the store, who told her son Rupert to come tell me and 'Ma' that you were on your way.' Gus took a deep breath.

Saffi had given up trying to keep up with the links that got the news to Gus that they were on their way, but it appeared to work.

'Now 'Ma' has made up the spare room for you, Saffi, Andreas you be sleeping on the porch, the mosquito nets are fixed tight so there's no need to worry. Now let's take you off to meet 'Ma' and the others.' Gus said has he showed Saffi to the truck parked outside the airport.

Andreas helped Saffi into the front of the truck and he and the bags went in the rear, but he was used to this. Gus drove out of the town, and down a long, and well-maintained road. Although the day was hot and dry, Saffi was enjoying this 'guided tour'. She watched in amusement, as goats and chickens ran wild along the side of the road. She was surprised how green and clean everything was. Eventually they turned off the main road and into a small settlement, with just a few houses. Gus turned off another street and onto a dusty drive, at the end of which was a reasonably sized, wooden house, with a white painted picket fence. Sitting in a rocking chair on the porch was, Saffi assumed, 'Ma'.

Gus stopped the truck and they all got out, and 'Ma' came down to greet them all. As she came closer, Saffi thought that 'Ma' reminded her of 'Grandma' from the Walton's, only a Caribbean version. Wearing a flower print dress with an apron tied around her waist, her face was gentle and her eyes sparkled as she approached. Then all of a sudden about a dozen small children were running around them, all shouting at Andreas and clambering for his attention. 'Ma' came over to Saffi and with the gentlest of voices greeted her.

'My, my you are a picture to behold child. It has been many a year I've been wanting to meet with you, and now, it's with such sadness in my heart.' She took hold of Saffi and wrapped her arms around her and Saffi felt as if Nana Lee were there. When she let go she put her arm through Saffi's and they walked together up to the porch. 'I've made lemonade and cookies, I hope you like lemonade and cookies.'

'Yes I do, thank you, err, 'Ma'?' Saffi replied, not knowing what to say.

'That's right child, everyone calls me 'Ma'. Now tell me everything that's happened to you since the dreadful news about your father.' 'Ma' pointed to the chair next to the rocker as she poured the lemonade.

Saffi was feeling bemused and wasn't sure how she'd ended up here. Within two weeks she'd been in Switzerland, back home to England, in a hotel in Nassau, and now she was drinking lemonade with 'Grandma from the Walton's' who seemed to know more about her and her father than she did.

She sat down. It didn't matter, somehow it felt 'OK' being here, and she started to tell 'Ma' all that had happened. 'Ma' made her feel easy and relaxed, it was like talking to Nana Lee and she felt at home. Finally, Andreas and Gus came up to the porch and 'Ma' took hold of Andreas hugged him, until he had no breath left inside, as though he was one of her own children. 'Now, you listen to me,

Andreas.' She said as she let him go. 'You make sure you look after this dear child, while she's in your care'. Andreas looked embarrassed but promised 'Ma' that nothing bad would happen to Saffi.

They sat on the porch reminiscing for a couple of hours, about the times Jack and Andreas had been to the house, and of all the good things, 'these boys had done for the town and its folk'. Gus recalled fondly the times that Jack had joined him on his ferry, skippering it between Great Exuma and Stocking Island. 'Sadly, we only got to meet Lillian the one time, when they were travelling through the islands.' 'Ma' said as she got up and invited everyone indoors for supper. She went to the kitchen and brought out a huge pot of chicken casserole, as Gus showed them to the table.

'This is delicious,' Saffi said, having never tasted anything quite like it before.

'It's all in the seasoning, and home grown vegetables, and chickens that run around free, and then let it cook real slow.' Ma explained.

After dinner, they moved back out to the porch where Gus opened beers for everyone, including 'Ma', and they continued to talk well into the night. It wasn't long however before 'Ma' could see Saffi's eyes start to droop and announced it was 'time for bed'. She showed Saffi to her room while Gus and Andreas made up the hammock in the porch.

Saffi sat on the bed and looked around her; the room was immaculately clean with white and lilac bed linen and wicker furniture. She thought of her room back home and Nana Lee. 'What am I doing here' she thought, 'this is just a wild goose chase. I've no idea how long this is going take'. Nerves and doubts were getting to her. She started to empty her bag and put her things on the dresser. As she did, she found the pendant; she had put it away for safekeeping. She felt the smooth feel of the pendant as she ran her fingers across the surface. 'And what is it about this pendant?' She thought as she carefully re-placed it in the pouch, and put it back in her bag before getting ready for bed. Once in bed, she fell into a deep sleep.

The next morning, Saffi woke to the noise of 'Ma' knocking gently on her door. 'Breakfast is ready when you are, Saffi.' 'Ma' said.

When Saffi went into the kitchen, everyone was already eating a huge breakfast. 'Ma' poured her a glass of orange juice, handed her a plate and told her to 'help herself'.

After breakfast Andreas and Gus went outside to the yard, apparently the truck needed 'fixing'. Saffi helped 'Ma' with washing the dishes, and unexpectedly, 'Ma' turned to Saffi saying, 'Do you think you're ready for this trip Saffi?'

'What do you mean? What do you think I need to be ready for?'

'Oh nothing really, just round here, in these parts, it's not the same as back in your home, people have different attitudes and ways.' 'Ma' paused. 'Jack and Andreas knew some shady characters if you ask me.'

Saffi looked at 'Ma'.'What do you mean, what sort of shady characters', Saffi paused, 'Ma, do you know what Jack did for a living? I've not been able to find anything out about what it was he did.'

Ma looked directly at Saffi, her huge brown eyes staring deep into her. 'Jack did a lot of good things in this part of the world, but sometimes it meant he had to be involved with, as I say, shady characters. I was never too sure what it was he and Andreas got up to, but I know there are a few bad cookies out there, some of them are not as sad as we are that your father has passed away.'

'But how can I find out what he did, and why I'm here?'

'You say Jack has left you a puzzle to solve?'

'Yes, it's like a crossword with a difference. Each clue puts me in contact with people, like you and Gus. And then somehow, you have some more information for me about the puzzle.' Saffi still thought it all sounded farfetched.

'I'm sorry Saffi. I don't know anything about a puzzle. What I do know is that your father will not have sent you to do this for no reason. He wants you to meet these people for a purpose, so I suggest you keep going and find out what that purpose is.' 'Ma' said, thinking it was sound advice.

'But what about the puzzle 'Ma', don't you have anything for me? Maybe a letter or something?'

Ma started to think, and as she did, she moved away from the sink and the dishes. 'Come with me child, there is something I want to show you.'

They moved through the house and into 'Ma's' bedroom. She crossed over to the dresser and opened a beautiful box covered in shells. She pulled something from the box that Saffi couldn't quite see. 'Come, sit next to me Saffi.' 'Ma' indicated for Saffi to sit beside her on the bed. 'Many years ago, maybe 10 years after your mother died. Jack gave me this, he told me to keep it safe for all time. He didn't say there was a purpose for it, just to keep it safe.' Slowly

'Ma's' hand unfolded and in her palm was a pendant, almost identical to Saffi's. Saffi gasped. 'What is it child, what's the matter?'

Saffi got up and beckoned 'Ma' to follow her to her room, she reached into her overnight bag and pulled out the pendant and showed it to 'Ma'.'Jack left this for me in a safe-deposit box in Switzerland, along with a letter telling me to keep this with me at all times and that it will become clear why.'

They sat on the bed and looked at the pendants, although similar, they were not exactly the same. Ma's pendant hung on the same leather cord as hers. It was the same shape and made of the same green marble stone, with a large gold stone. However, this stone was different in shape. As Saffi started to speak, Ma interrupted. 'Look here, this gold stone comes out and underneath there is some writing. Can you make out what it is, Saffi?' 'Ma' asked as Saffi scrutinised the pendant.

'There are some words and I think it's a number, it looks like 'X Jack 1A,".' Saffi said, peering at the stone.

'X Jack is probably obvious, but what does 1A mean. Do you know Saffi?' Ma asked.

'Oh how clever,' Saffi said, 'I think it might be a grid reference for the puzzle, let me get my laptop and we can check.'

Saffi started up her laptop and opened the file with the crossword, and typed E X U M A into the spaces headed 1A, but nothing else happened.

'How do you know if it's right?' 'Ma' asked.

'I don't, I guess we have to wait until we have all the answers and see what happens then.'

Saffi sat with her pendant on her lap and the gold stone from 'Ma's in her hand. Remembering that there were markings on the reverse of her own pendant she picked it up and looked closely. 'Ma', look at this, on the back of my pendant there are some markings and a jigsaw pattern, your stone fits exactly into the shape marked 1A. This must be what Jack left with you, for me.'

Saffi went out to the porch and called to Andreas. He shut the bonnet of the truck and he and Gus came over. Saffi explained about 'Ma's' pendant and the markings on the back, she showed him the crossword. 'Do you think when we eventually get all the answers it will tell us where to go?' Saffi said, looking at everyone.

'Well without looking at the clues, we won't get anywhere,' Andreas said. 'What's the next clue?'

Saffi opened the page with the clues and read it aloud. 'The island clue reads, *"This Island mixes up A Unit Garage to become one of this group's largest islands".'* Saffi paused. 'Can anyone make any sense of that? The second part reads, *"Although mainly flat, head to the smallest of the high points".* Does anyone have any ideas?' Saffi said, pleading.

Gus got up and went to the back room, he returned with a map for everyone to look at. There were hundreds of islands all with different sorts of names.

Saffi continued to look at the clue and remembered the crossword she'd completed with Nana. It's an anagram, 'A Unit Garage'; we just need to work it out.' Saffi looked at everyone; they all looked back at her blankly, as she explained. 'The beginning, *"This island mixes up",* is telling us to mix up the next set of words or letters, *A Unit Garage*. OK,' she said, grabbing some paper and a pen from her bag. 'We need to get working on this. If we do this the way Nana showed me, it shouldn't take very long.'

Saffi began to write the letters down, backwards. E G A R A G T I N U A then tried to pronounce this word. 'Backwards it reads Egaragtinua, does that help anyone?' Again, blank looks from everyone. Saffi set to work while the others looked on carefully.

'What words can we make from Egaragtinua? Tina? Nit, Tin, Rag, Rat, Ear, Earring, perhaps it's something to do with pirates?' She continued. 'Tan, Gear, Art, Great. Any islands begin with Great?'

'Great Cay, Great Isaac, Great Stirrup Cay, Great Harbour' Gus called from the table. 'I'm searching through the index.'

'Matt Fennis.' Andreas said, lifting his head and smiling.

'Matt Fennis, how do you get Matt Fennis from Egaragtinua?' Saffi enquired.

'Of course, Matt Fennis.' Gus joined in. 'I've not seen him in a good few years.

'Would someone like to tell me who Matt Fennis is, and what he has to do with Egaragtinua?' Saffi looked around the room.

'Ma' came and sat with Saffi, her warm smile making Saffi feel more comfortable than she realised.

'Matt Fennis is a US Coast Guard and Volunteer Park Ranger on Great Inagua, which is an anagram of A Garage Unit, if I'm not mistaken. Lovely man, be good to see him. He can tell you some stories about your father, I'm sure.' 'Ma' said.

'Great Inagua is just about 200 miles away, two hours by plane. If Gus and 'Ma' could let us stay another night, we could make an early start and be there before lunchtime? Andreas looked over to 'Ma', already knowing her answer.

'Of course you can stay another night, if this means getting another clue solved, and spending some more time with you both.'

Chapter 13

The next morning Saffi sat in the departure building reading up on Great Inagua while Andreas completed the relevant paperwork for the flight. They walked to the plane and got themselves set for the two-hour flight. Saffi felt just as apprehensive as she had the previous time. However, as soon as they were airborne, and she could see the beautiful colour of the sea below, she relaxed and tried to enjoy the flight.

They headed southeast towards Great Inagua and Andreas pointed out the island in the distance. The sea between the islands was of the deepest blue, and became more transparent as they got closer to the island. Andreas manoeuvred the plane into position for landing and, as he approached the runway, Saffi was a little more prepared. Only this time the landing was not as smooth as the previous one. The plane hit the runway hard, and it immediately bounced up again and then hit the tarmac even harder the next time, Andreas did whatever was necessary to keep the plane on the runway, as they hit the ground for a third bounce. Andreas finally brought the plane to a standstill. He looked at Saffi, 'Not every landing can be a 'greaser' as they say, sorry about that.'

As they reached the parking area Saffi's face said it all. She was very glad to be back on solid ground and out of the plane; she chose not to comment on his landing ability. They walked to what looked like a small terminal building. When they entered, no one was around but as always, Andreas had telephoned ahead to say they were coming. Soon two Customs Officers arrived, after official formalities, Andreas introduced Saffi as Jack's daughter.

'Is Matt Ferris about?' Andreas asked.

'Matt's up on James Hill, some guys wanted a tour around the island,' One of the Officer's replied.

'What's on James Hill?' asked.

'James Hill, nothing much, view's good I suppose.'

'Is it high?' Saffi looked at Andreas, 'wasn't that part of the clue, something about going to the smallest of the high points?'

'You want me to drive you there now, you might still catch Matt?' replied one of the Officers.

'If it's not out of your way, it may save us some time later.' Andreas suggested.

Donald, the bigger and older of the Customers Officers showed them to the truck and headed towards James Hill. 'Why you looking for Matt? Don't tell me Jack's in trouble again?'

'Haven't you heard?' Andreas looked at Saffi. 'I'm afraid Jack's dead.'

Donald screeched the truck to a halt. 'Dead! What happened?'

'An accident in Trinidad,' Andreas said.

'Oh, I'm so sorry Saffi; I just assumed you were here to visit Jack.' Donald said, not really knowing where to look.

'We were told it was a road accident but it's all a bit of a mystery.' Andreas answered. 'Saffi's here to look up some of Jack's old friends, sort of a posthumous gathering. Saffi didn't really know Jack that well, she lives in England.' Andreas explained, not really knowing why.

'Well in that case we need to get you to Matt up on James Hill.'

Donald headed to a small hill on the north of the island where they found Matt's truck. Andreas took Donald's mobile number and he agreed to collect them if they needed him. Standing at Matt's truck Saffi got out her laptop and opened the clues and crossword files. She typed in 'JAMES' to see what would happen on the clue sheet, and as Andreas had guessed the name Matt Fennis appeared next to the clue.

'OK, so you were right, it is Matt we are looking for and JAMES is the answer to clue two. What next?' She asked.

'We can either wait here for Matt to return, or we could take a stroll up the hill and see if we can find him, the view's nice from up there, it's not very high and you may as well see some of the island while you're here. Come on.'

Andreas grabbed Saffi's hand and they started up the hill, about half way up they could see three men coming towards them. Andreas called Matt's name. In a few moments they had reached each other and, what was becoming a regular practice, Andreas hugged Matt and they continued with the distinctive Caribbean handshake, interlocking fingers and clenched fists touching each other. Saffi had not yet learned the technique, or what it meant, but apparently, everyone did it as a welcome. After brief introductions Matt suggested he meet them in an hour when he had finished the tour he was conducting. Andreas called Donald to pick them up and take them into town.

~~~

Saffi had already type-cast Matt Fennis as a stereo-typical American and when they met later in a local bar he was dressed in the obligatory checked shirt and shorts that she imagined every American wore, topped and tailed by a worn-out baseball cap and 'sneakers', finished off with a deep Texan drawl. However, as Matt passed on his condolences to Saffi, she noted how articulate he was. Matt already knew about Jack's death and when they met in the bar he hugged Saffi a little too long for her liking, but as the evening wore on, she grew to like Matt more and more. As 'Ma' had said, 'Matt will have some stories to tell about Jack,' and she was right.

    Throughout dinner and into the early hours of the morning, Matt relayed story after story about Jack and himself getting into "small scrapes with slightly unsavoury characters, in one or two of the more unsavoury places in the Caribbean."

    'Nothing ever illegal mind, just one too many rum punches followed by one too many fist punches. Mind you, we weren't just giving the punches. We got to receive them as well.' Matt recalled, rubbing his hand over his check as if soothing an imaginary pain. 'It seemed that whenever I went out with Jack, I would be worse for wear in the morning, with a pain in my head from either a hangover or a fight. And it was always over something stupid like a ball game or cards, I wouldn't have minded if it was over a woman, but not Jack, never another woman for Jack, not after Lillian.' Matt stopped. 'Oh I am sorry Saffi. That was insensitive of me, talking bout your Momma like that. I recall the time I rescued them, that's when we met…'

    'Rescued them?' Saffi said, 'What happened?'

    '…it was back in the mid 70s, 'bout '75 or '76, I had just joined up, the Coast Guard that is, we were on exercises out of Puerto Rico, monitoring 'traffic' if you get my drift. One night we get a PAN PAN call on the radio',

    Saffi interrupted, 'what's a PAN PAN?'

    Matt explained, 'Well Saffi, a PAN PAN is an emergency call but not quite a MAY DAY,' he continued, 'So we radio the boat back and ask what the situation was and where they were. Turns out to be Jack and Lillian, they'd just bought this old boat from a local on St Martin and were heading to St Kitts and started taking on water, nothing too serious, but enough to put out a call. Luckily, we were heading that way and got to them within an hour, by which time your Momma was up to her ankles in water, bucket in hand and bailing as fast as she could while Jack was trying to get them into shallow water around St Kitts, which is difficult at the best of times. If only they'd headed over to Anguilla, they could have beached the boat no problem. Well we towed them to safety, helped them patch the boat up and drank a bottle of rum well into the early hours of the morning. We've been meeting every few years ever since.'

Saffi didn't quite know what to make of the story, it all sounded plausible and Andreas was nodding his head in agreement throughout. She liked Matt. He made her laugh, and told her stories that made her father seem real. What did make her sad was the thought that she was beginning to like Jack and now she would never get to be with this Jack. This Jack seemed to have friends everywhere; people liked him and said good things about him, why had she never met this Jack.

As they walked back to the guesthouse, Matt asked Andreas if he could have a private word with Saffi. Andreas continued on, and sat on the porch waiting, keeping an eye out for Saffi, and Matt for that matter – Jack may not have played around with any women, but Andreas had been out socially with Matt a few times. He knew exactly what he was like. Saffi stood and listened to Matt.

'Saffi, this may all sound a little odd and emotional, and maybe you'll think it's the drink talking. However, the last time I was with Jack he gave me a present, told me not to open it, but to give it to a girl 'with Lillian's eyes'. Well, you're the first woman I've ever met who has eyes the same blue eyes as your mother, so whatever Jack was on or whatever Jack wanted me to do with this present I think it was meant for you.'

He opened his jacket, reached inside the pocket and brought out a package wrapped in brown paper, tied with string. He handed her the package, kissed her on the cheek and headed off into the darkness. Saffi stood quite still and watched him walk away. She sensed sadness in him that she had not felt all evening. For no reason she reached for the pendant, which she had put on that morning, and hidden beneath her t-shirt. She looked over to Andreas, walked towards him, and she sat down next to him when she reached the porch.

'Matt gave me this.' She passed him the package.

'What is it?' Andreas said, moving the package around his fingers.

'Jack gave it to him the last time they met, saying he was to give it to the first woman he met who had Lillian's eyes, and apparently that's me.'

Andreas passed the package back to her. 'Are you going to open it?' He looked on, edging himself closer so that he could see.

Saffi began to untie the string, and unrolled the package, which was cylindrical in shape. Finally, a wooden salt grinder rolled out from the brown paper onto her lap. She picked it up and looked at it with confusion. 'Any suggestions?' She was tired and in no mood for trying to work out any more mysteries today.

'It's a salt shaker.' Andreas replied.

'Very good, I can see that, but why has Jack sent me a salt shaker?'

'They produce salt on this island and he knows you like salt?' He could sense her exhaustion as she glared at him.

'Well, let's suppose it has nothing to do with my culinary taste and see if it's something to do with the clue.' Exasperated she began grinding the salt pot, and, as expected, freshly ground salt dropped from the bottom.

'So we now know it has salt in it, any other suggestions?'

'Let's open the top and see if there's anything else in it.' Andreas took the saltshaker and began unscrewing the top, just as the top released and before Andreas could turn it over Saffi took it back and poured the contents into her lap, onto her skirt.

'Let's make sure we don't drop anything on the floor and lose it, shall we.'

They looked at the pile of salt sitting in her skirt and a small green stone within it. Carefully Saffi picked out the green stone and poured the salt back into the pot.

'What's that?' Andreas tried to peer closely at the green stone, but Saffi already knew what it was and what to do with it. She took the pendant from around her neck, laid it on her lap and turned it over. Looking closely at the shape of the stone she then matched it up with one of the marks on the back of the pendant.

'Two down.' She said, very pleased with herself.

'Two down.' Andreas replied very confused with her.

'Two down. That's where we have to put the clue 'JAMES' in the crossword, two down.'

'Are you sure, how do you know?'

'See here, on the back of this pendant there are numbers and letters within the shapes. It just came to me, all the letters are crossword references, one through five across and down, see 1a, 2a, 3a, and 1d, 2d, 3d, can you see?' Saffi showed Andreas the back of the pendant so that he could make out the numbers and letters.

'When 'Ma' showed me her pendant, the stone in the middle came out and fitted into the place marked 1a. I think it's a formula.' Her mood had lightened and she felt excited by the progress she thought she had made.

'If you say so, how do you know for certain?' Andreas asked, not convinced by her explanation.

'I don't, but we don't have any other suggestions either, so I propose we go with this one until we have a better idea. Come on, let's get the laptop open and see if we can work out the next clue.'

Saffi opened the relevant files, typed the letters J A M E S into 'two down' and read out the next clue aloud. *"Island Clue three; Find an island split in two and look for the Doctor."* And the next part reads –*"Find an Old French Cape in the North and stare at the point which, in 1641, it was the end for the Beginning."* Saffi looked at Andreas.

'An island split in two, that could be Hispaniola or St Martin, St Martin is half French and half Dutch. Hispaniola is made up of Haiti and Dominican Republic, which is a beautiful place. I remember once, a long time ago, Jack and I were going to the D R and we were running low on fuel...' Andreas' voice trailed off as Saffi interrupted.

'Did you say the D R?'

'Yes, you know the D R, Dominican Republic, why?'

'Don't you see, D R is short for Doctor, like M R is short for Mister, the island is split in two and one side is known as the D R.' Saffi looked at Andreas for confirmation of her assumption.

'Yes, I suppose you could be right, what's the second part again?' he asked.

'Find an Old French Cape in the North and stare at the point which, in 1641; it was the end for the Beginning. Old French Cape start with capitals, which leads me to think it's a place and a beginning also, starts with a capital B, which leads me to think, well, think nothing. Any ideas Andreas?'

'An Old French Cape, an Old French Cape, 1641, 1641, end for the Beginning.' Andreas repeated the words of the clue, running it over and over, something was lurking in his sub-conscious but nothing came to mind. He turned to Saffi. Getting to Dominican Republic isn't going to be easy in Linalli, not just the two of us; that will take a good week, and only if the conditions are right.'

'What do you suggest,' she asked, 'surely we need to get there as soon as possible?

'There are two options, we can continue to fly the plane to the DR and I can arrange for some crew to bring Linalli to meet us in there, or wherever we end up, or we can fly back to Nassau and sail her down to the DR. The choice really is yours; do you have enough clothes and things with you to carry on from here? It would be the better option.'

'Clothes are not a problem, but I think time is of the essence so, if you can get someone to bring the boat to us we could meet them on the way, either in the DR or wherever the next stop is. I don't really want to be sailing around in a boat for a week with nothing to do. I know I haven't got a job to get back to, but I still don't exactly have all the time in the world.' She said.

'OK, I'll make some calls in the morning and we can fly into Puerto Plata on the north of the DR, from here, it's only a few hours away. Let's get some shut eye now and we can head off first thing tomorrow.'

They agreed on this plan and went to bed with their minds full of the latest clue, but something was niggling at Andreas, he knew Jack was getting at something, but he could not bring it to mind.

~~~

The next day, after Andreas had made necessary phone calls including one to Carina back on St Kitts. He asked if she would keep an eye on his place, as he would be away longer than expected. She managed to get him to tell her where he was heading, which she immediately reported to Luis Leppe.

'Is the girl with him Carina?' Luis had enquired.

'He hasn't said and he didn't say how long he'd be gone. Normally he gives me some indication, but he did mention something about getting crew to bring a boat to him from Nassau, nothing specific, but I thought I should mention it to you. I told him I had a cousin who could do it for him, and he asked me to look into it. He's going to call me in a day or so.'

'You have done very well Carina, you will be rewarded accordingly, and remember, anything he tells you, no matter how insignificant, inform me immediately.'

'Thank you "El Jeffe"' Carina replied, but the phone was already dead.

Chapter 14

The trip to Dominican Republic was uneventful and on arrival, they checked into a small hotel in Sosua town. While Saffi was using the internet to see if she could unravel the next part of the clue, Andreas was looking over maps and guidebooks, checking every inch of the North coast of Dominican Republic.

'So, we're looking to *"Find an Old French Cape in the North, and stare at the point which, in 1641, it was the end for the Beginning."* Any new ideas?' Saffi asked.

'Old French Cape, perhaps we are looking at this the wrong way, I'm thinking cape, as in something to wear, but a cape can be geographical, and the DR's coast is full of Cabos, which is Spanish for Cape. See what you get if you Google 'Old French Cape Dominican Republic?'

Saffi entered the words, but the search engine returned too many results to be of any use. Then she added 'in Spanish' to the search to see what result she would get.

'Look at this Andreas, 'Cabo Frances Viejo' is Spanish for Old French Cape. So I entered the Spanish 'Cabo Frances Viejo Dominican Republic' and look at the second entry.'

Andreas read aloud. *"Cabo Francés Viejo is located on a headland with views over the area's cliffs and beaches. Offshore lies the wreck of the 'Concepción', which sank in 1641… ".* 'Of course, The Concepcion - which is Spanish for conception.' But Saffi didn't get the connection. Andreas explained further.

'Don't you see? An Old French Cape, or this case Cabo Francés Viejo, is a place on the north coast of the DR. From there you can 'stare at a point', in this case the Silver Shoals, which are named because when a Spanish Galleon, 'The Concepcion' sank, it scattered its "pieces of eight" over the reef that it crashed on. That's when The Concepcion, or in the clue *"the Beginning"*, sank, or in other words its 'end'. Oh he's clever your Dad, even if I say so myself. OK, now all we need to do is put the answer into the puzzle.'

Saffi opened the file, looking at all the words from their solution, only one had five letters, and so she entered 'VIEJO' and when she hit the Enter key, the name Julio Ferdandido appeared next to the answer. 'Julio Ferdandido, do you know him?' Saffi asked Andreas.

'Yes, Julio is a diver. He runs courses on all things to do with water sports. Jack and he used to go scouring around wrecks to see what they could find. I'm not sure they ever found anything. Do we have any phone numbers? We can give him a call and see if we can meet up, he's a good two-hour drive away.'

Saffi checked the information and found a number for Julio. Andreas called him and, after explaining what was happening, he agreed to meet them the following day. He said he wasn't sure if he would be able to help in any way, but he had a few things that belonged to Jack that he had left the last time they went out on a dive.

That evening, over dinner, Saffi decided she would try to find out some more about Jack and her mother, and may be delve a little more into Andreas' background.

'After my mother was shot in Columbia, what happened?' Saffi decided on the direct approach.

Andreas felt guilty about telling Saffi the next part of the story; he had always felt that somehow he was indirectly responsible. He took a deep breath and began to recall the story.

'A couple of months before the shooting, I'd left the farm house, I'd been made 'an offer' I couldn't refuse.' His head dropped at the shame he felt. 'I needed money, Jack and Lillian needed money, and the orphanage they were trying to set up really needed money. I thought I could help out, you know, 'on the side'. I said nothing to Jack or Lillian, I just packed my bags, left and got myself a job as a Falcon for the 'opposition', mind you, they are all 'opposition' in my opinion.' Andreas sensed her confusion and explained. 'A falcon is the lowest of the low in a drug gang, you watch the police and rival gangs, and pass info back to your boss.'

Saffi could see how difficult this was for Andreas. She leant over the table and took his hand. 'Go on.' She said, trying to comfort him.

'I also took messages between 'organisations' although I never knew what was in them. Anyway, after a few weeks, I decided I needed to let Jack and Lillian know I was OK, and give them some of the money I had earned. Well, as I passed the edge of town I could hear shooting in the Market Square. I decided that it was best to stay out of it and so I didn't investigate. Instead, I ran towards the farm. When I got there, it was empty, I could see Lillian's shopping bags were gone and assumed they'd gone into town for provisions. I decided to hang around and wait until they got back. But they didn't come back.' He sighed as he said the words.

'It was Father Caleb who came to the farmhouse, to get some things for Jack. When he saw me there, he told me what had happened. I ran as fast as I could to the hospital. When I got there,

Jack was pacing up and down, not knowing what to do. I felt so ashamed at what I had done I collapsed in tears in front of him.'

'Why, what had you done, you weren't involved with the shooting?' She said.

'Not directly, but I had played my part by taking the messages to set it up. I felt disgusted with myself. I couldn't believe I had put them in so much danger.'

'But you weren't to know, surely, Jack must have known that,' Saffi said.

'He did, he made me take Maria and Stephano back to the farmhouse and look after them until he knew that Lillian would be OK. Jack stayed at the hospital for days and I looked after the children, as best I could. I was, after all, still only a kid myself. They wouldn't release Lillian from the hospital for fear of repercussions from the drug gangs, not that Jack, or Lillian, had anything to do with them, it's just they were witnesses and might have caused a problem.'

'What happened then, what did Jack do?'

'That's when he decided he needed to get Lillian back to England. It wasn't fair on her mother, or Lillian, to be stuck in a Columbian hospital, not knowing what the outcome would be. So, with the help of the British Embassy flights were arranged to take them back to the UK.'

'What about you and the children, what was going to happen to you?'

'Jack made me promise to look after the farmhouse and any children who wanted to go there, he left enough money with Father Caleb, and then kept sending money back from England so that we could run the farmhouse. Back in England he got a job back on the ships, and sent nearly everything he earned to us, you were born six months later, and well, the rest you know.'

'I'm not sure I do know the rest. I only really knew him while mum was alive and after that, it seems that you saw more of him than me. What happened after mum died? Did he come back to the farmhouse?' Saffi asked expectantly.

'It was Father Caleb who told us that Lillian had died. Everyone here was devastated and we never thought we'd see Jack again. But just about a year later, he arrived, out of nowhere, just like that. He was in a real state, I think he'd drunk his way through the Caribbean, he was living on a boat, what is now Linalli, but at the time, it was a wreck. I'm not sure how it made it all the way down from Dominica. Before he bought it, it had been caught up in a hurricane; the insurance company just wanted rid of her so he'd picked her up really cheaply.'

Andreas slouched back into his chair, took a sip from his beer and closed his eyes. 'That was all a very long time ago and a lot has happened since then.' He looked at Saffi with appealing eyes. 'I think I've had enough for one night; can the rest wait for another day?'

Saffi stood up, finished her drink and nodded in agreement. There was another piece of the puzzle to find tomorrow.

~~~

Julio put the phone down, pulled open the drawer beneath his desk and took out the bottle of Pusser's rum, he didn't bother with a glass he just swigged the golden liquid straight from the bottle.

'Shit!' He shouted and looked around for something to throw, luckily, the nearest thing he could find were his car keys and he hurled them at the filing cabinet.

Jacqui, his long-standing dive partner, girlfriend and confidante, came running into the office to see what has caused this outburst. 'What is it, you look like you seen a ghost.' She said.

'What did I say to you last time Jack was here, I said something was wrong.' He took another long gulp from the bottle of Pusser's.

'Yes, I remember saying you were talking nonsense, as always.'

'He's dead.' Julio said.

'Who is?'

'Jack is.'

'What Jack Simpson? How do you know?' Jacqui asked as she sat down opposite Julio.

'That was Andreas on the phone. He's just explained everything to me.'

'What, what did he explain, for god's sake Julio, what happened, was it an accident or something?' She took the bottle from the table and poured herself a large glass.

'Supposedly a car accident, but no-one has told Andreas the full story. It all smells bad to me. Andreas and Jack's daughter, Saffi, are coming here tomorrow.'

'Here? Why?' She asked.

'From what I can gather Jack's daughter wants to meet up with 'some of his old friends', but Andreas wouldn't say any more than that. They didn't even get to go to his funeral. Christ I can't believe Jack's swallowed a bullet, not this late in the game. Someone must have known something, someone on the inside.' He reached for the bottle again as a tear ran down his cheek. Jacqui tried to console him but knew better, and let him stare at the photo of him and Jack with their 'prize find' as they finished the bottle of rum.

~~~

Saffi and Andreas hired a Jeep and set off early to meet Julio. Saffi stared out of the window as the ever-changing scenery went by, and her mind wandered. Her life had become a dreamlike world of ever changing places and people. Was she sure she wanted to continue with this search, she was thousands of miles away from home, chasing after an unknown man's life with someone she'd known less than a month.

'Why are we doing this Andreas?' She asked, breaking the silence.

'Because this is the way to Julio's house.' He looked over and saw Saffi's expression; a mixture of confusion and doubt in her eyes.

'No, not going to Julio's, this.' She pointed to the list of clues. 'This is supposed to be a treasure hunt. I mean we don't even know what it is we're looking for. I've known you less than a month and so far, you've taken me to all manner of islands and places and shown me a boat that I've no idea what I'm going to do with. What am I doing here, really?'

Andreas didn't know how to answer. He would do anything for Jack, as he knew Jack would have for him. But Saffi, why should she bother, he left her without a true father and now he wants her to drop everything and search for an unknown inheritance. He didn't know what to say to her. He pulled the car off the road and stopped.

'I can't answer that Saffi, I knew a different Jack to you, my Jack would do anything for you, and that's why I am doing this. For him, because it's something he asked me to do a long time ago, and I promised I would. But if you don't want to carry on, you need to let me know now, before we head further down the islands. It's not a decision I can make for you.' He said, in all sincerity.

'It's just that I've become caught up in something that's bigger than me. Everyone I meet loved him, and they all have great stories to tell about their time with him. I've led such a...' she paused, '. . . such an uninteresting life, and suddenly I've been thrust into a world way beyond anything I could imagine, and I think I'm confused by it all. I just wish I knew more about what we're searching for, that's all, whether it's really worth it.' She said, as she continued to stare out of the window.

'Perhaps that's the point, if you knew what you were searching for then maybe you wouldn't search for it. Perhaps this is just another of Jack's challenges, or maybe there's a reason we don't know what we're looking for.' He looked for some change in her expression, but she just stared out of the window. 'Why don't we go and see what Julio has to say and make a decision after that. I've arranged for Linalli to be sailed down to The Virgin Islands, we can fly over there from here if you change your mind and, if you really want to, you can fly back home, to England, but let's see what Julio has to say.'

'OK.' She said, looking back at him, her deep blue eyes hiding her true feelings. She'd never done anything so impulsive in her life before and she wasn't sure if the feelings she was experiencing were of excitement or fear.

As they continued, the scenery held her attention more than she'd realised, the north coast of the DR, famed for its dramatic and rugged coastline, high cliffs and stunning beaches backed by lush rainforest. Within an hour they arrived at Julio's Dive Centre, above which was his house. Jacqui greeted them as they got out of the Jeep; she hugged Andreas tightly, but was unsure how to greet Saffi in such unusual circumstances.

'Julio's down on the beach, do you want a beer, I'll bring them down to you. Go through Andreas, you know the way?'

Once again, Andreas had not let on how well he knew these people, and Saffi followed sheepishly behind, as he led the way out to the beach. Jacqui followed minutes later with a beer for each of them. Julio spotted Andreas, and he called out to him as they approached where he was sitting.

'Andreas, my man, good to see you, although I wish it were in better circumstances. This must be Saffi?' Julio's Caribbean vocabulary mixed with his strong Spanish accent took Saffi by surprise as he moved to greet her. She put out her hand for him to shake, but he embraced her tightly, as if he'd known her for years.

She was caught off guard and began to gabble, 'Oh! Nice to meet you, how do you do.'

Andreas cut it in. 'Julio, what gives, long time, no speak, how's business?'

Julio released his grip on Saffi and gestured for them to sit on the large bean bags arranged on the beach, beneath signs advertising diving and windsurfing lessons. Jacqui joined them and handed out the beers. Saffi sat down awkwardly not knowing what to say; fortunately, Andreas and Julio had known each other long enough to start the conversation.

'Andreas, what the hell happened to Jack, give me all the info you have, I can't believe it. Do you know what went down?' Julio asked.

Andreas moved closer to Saffi, he was beginning to realise that she felt uncomfortable every time they met another of Jack's friends. Someone else who was going to tell her something more about him, something else she didn't know.

'The details are all a bit hazy at the moment. All we know is that it was some sort of accident.' Andreas intended to keep the details vague and close to his chest for the time being.

Saffi interrupted, 'I met with my father's lawyer and he couldn't, or maybe wouldn't, tell me anything about how he died. I got a letter, like Andreas telling, or rather, asking me to visit some of his friends. Do you know why he wanted me to meet you?'

Julio lent forward and looked Saffi directly in the eyes, 'do you know anything about me and Jack. Has he ever mentioned anything about our past?'

'I'd never heard of you before yesterday, but I'd never heard of any of Jack's friends before he died. We weren't what you'd call close.'

'So he never mentioned diving or salvage or anything like that?' Julio asked.

'No', she replied, 'the first I knew of you was in the last clue we solved.'

'Clue, what clue?' He leaned further in towards them, his eyes inquisitive.

'The clue about The Concepcion, that's how we knew to come and talk to you.' Saffi said.

'What are you talking about? Andreas is she making any sense to you?' Julio said, sitting back.

'It's all a bit long-winded, but if you must know, Jack is keeping the identity of everyone he wants Saffi to meet a mystery. He set up an elaborate series of cryptic clues, each of which tells us how to find the person we're looking for. I'm sure there's a very good reason for it.' Andreas said, trying not to show his annoyance to Saffi.

'Damn right there's good reason, I don't want all of Jack's enemies crawling around here, never know what they'll find, or what they'll be after.'

'Enemies, did Jack have enemies?' The word startled Saffi.

Andreas cut in quickly, 'it's just a phrase Saffi, you know, most people have someone who doesn't like them.'

'I don't,' she snapped.

Julio interrupted. 'No, I'm sure you don't Saffi, but you've not been pissing off the wrong guys in the Caribbean for the last 10 years have you, taking what they believe to be rightly theirs?'

Andreas needed to get this conversation away from where Julio was heading. The last thing he needed was Julio scaring Saffi. He looked directly at Julio, hoping he would understand his meaning when he interrupted, 'let's not exaggerate, eh Julio, and let's not let Saffi think her father was some kind of trouble maker.'

'Well what was he?' Saffi asked, 'that's the one thing no-one seems able to, or want to, tell me about my father, what exactly was it that he did do?'

Julio looked at Andreas and Andreas looked at Julio, both stumped for words.

'Your father,' Jacqui had decided to sort the mess out that the men had caused. 'Your father, apart from being one of the nicest guys I've ever met, used to go diving in search of treasure, it was Julio who taught him to dive, isn't that right Julio?' She frowned at him, hoping he'd understand and that he should just agree with her.

'Yeah, that's right, I taught Jack to dive, must've been at least 15 years ago, if not more.'

Jacqui continued, 'It was during some of those dives, that Jack found a few things, that some other people think belong to them. Julio, why don't you tell Saffi about the big find? I'll get the photos.' Jacqui went into the house and returned a few moments later with a scrapbook, which she handed to Saffi. The first page was a newspaper cutting from 4th April 1993, the headline read, 'The Drinks are on you!' Saffi continued to read the cutting,

> 'Local salvage expert Julio Ferdandido and his dive partner Jack Simpson couldn't believe their luck when they found what they believed to be a relic from the sunken wreck of The Concepcion, which sank off Cabo Frances Viejo in 1641. The area has been the searching ground for many divers hoping to find the elusive 'pieces of eight', which history tell us were scattered over the reef, giving it the name the 'Silver Shoal.'
>
> 'The last known finding was in 1978 when the bulk of her treasure was discovered in her strong room, but many believe there is still much more to be found.
>
> For Julio and Jack, the waiting must continue as the sealed bottle of rum, which they found hidden within the reef,

has yet to be identified, date tested and authenticated as coming from The Concepcion. If confirmed, then this may be the 'beginning of the end' of the search for the remainder of The Concepcion's long-lost treasure. Or to put it another way, the end of the beginning [The Concepcion], it may yet bear riches for those willing to take up the challenge and explore the world for its hidden treasures discovering the legacies which are kept as well guarded secrets.'

Saffi could not believe what she was reading. So many similarities to what was written in Jack's letters, the exact words in the clue 'the end of the beginning', take up the challenge and explore the world, discovering legacies', was this what Jack was trying to tell her, that he'd found the treasure of The Concepcion? She needed to speak with Andreas alone and explain what she thought, but she also needed to know more from Julio. She handed the scrapbook to Andreas, 'Have you seen this before Andreas? Did Jack ever tell you any more about it?'

'Yes, there's a copy on Linalli, Jack was always getting his scrapbook out and showing me stuff, he never did tell me if the bottle was from The Concepcion though. Was it Julio?'

'You must have been so excited; did you have to wait long to find out?' Saffi asked.

'No and yes, sorry that sounds confusing. No, we didn't have to wait long and yes it was confirmed that it was a bottle of rum, but not from The Concepcion, but it was about a hundred years old and we sold it to some collector in the States, got a few thousand dollars, back when a few thousand dollars was a lot of money.'

'Did you ever find anything else?' Saffi asked. She was sure that Jack was telling her something through the newspaper cutting.

'Yeah, the odd piece of broken china and a few bits and bobs, nothing of any real monetary value, but the museum in Santo Domingo was happy to buy them and display them there.'

'Did Jack dive here a lot with you? Saffi asked.

'Off and on, we saw each other at least once a year, when he was on his travels.'

'He didn't leave anything here, didn't mention anything he wanted you to give to someone?' She asked, she needed to know the co-ordinates for the answer to the clue, where was it to go in the crossword.

'Nope, he used to turn up, bag in one hand, boat or plane parked somewhere on the island and came to dive and drink. Oh! And eat Jacqui's mofongo.'

'Mo...fong...? What's that? Some kind of Chinese dish?' Saffi asked

'It's a local speciality, bananas fried, mashed and mixed with pork rind, you want to try some? I can have some ready in no time.' Jacqui answered.

Without a thought for anyone else Andreas nodded eagerly, 'you've never tried anything like this in your life, especially Jacqui's version, it's amazing.'

'Do you guys want to stay the night, there's room in the guest house if you don't mind sharing a room?' Julio asked.

Andreas looked at Saffi, 'up to you, it's a two-hour drive back and we could start to work on the next clue while we're here, plus the beer's cold here.'

Saffi smiled, agreed and took another beer from Jacqui. A pattern was emerging, solve a clue, meet old friends, reminisce, drink beer and solve another clue. But no closer to any kind of answer. She sighed, accepting that this adventure would go on for a little while longer.

Saffi flicked through the pages of the scrapbook, it contained more photos of Jack and Julio, mainly them standing with huge fish hanging from a hook, but nothing more on the Concepcion, or any evidence as to where the answer should go. She sat and listened to stories of shipwrecks, dives and fishing, late into the night. After a while, the beer stopped and the rum came out.

'You know this was your father's favourite drink, not just any old rum, but Pusser's Rum, that's why he was so excited about the bottle we found on the reef. Jacqui go get the leaflet that explains about Pusser's please, I'm not sure I can stand up!' Julio said.

Jacqui wobbled on her feet as she went back to the house and returned with an unopened bottle of Pusser's Rum, which had a label hanging around its neck. She read aloud. *'For 330 years from about 1640',*

Julio interrupted, 'That's the important bit you need to remember, 1640, that's the year before The Concepcion sank, sorry, continue my dear.' Julio waved his hand around gesturing her to continue,

'For 330 years from about 1640 until 31st July 1970, Great Britain's Royal Navy issued a daily rum ration to its sailors. This

daily allotment was known as the 'tot' and its issue, and the ritual that went with it, was one of the longest running traditions in maritime history. The rum issued was a unique rum called Navy or Admiralty Rum or sometimes PUSSER's, a corruption of the word purser, after the officer in charge of the daily issue.',

Jacqui took a long breath, 'There's a whole lot more, but I think you get the point, Jack loved the stuff. Shall we raise a glass to Jack?'

'To Jack.' Everyone said and lifted their glasses to the sky.

Saffi sat silently watching everyone remember their good friend and she felt lonely again. 'I think I'm ready for bed, can someone show me the way please?'

'I think it's about time we all turned in.' Jacqui acknowledged, 'Andreas, you know the way, and there are clean towels and sheets already laid out for you. Come on Julio time for you also.' But Julio was already asleep on the beanbag. 'He'll find his own way back to bed when he finally wakes up.' Jacqui said.

In the guest room, Saffi sat on the bed looking at the scrapbook, the article and photographs. 'Did you pick up on the words in the article, end of the beginning and the other bits? Andreas shook his head, 'Well listen to this,' Saffi read aloud the article and explained what she thought she was reading into the article. 'Do you think he was trying to tell us something?'

'What like? It might just be a coincidence that the same words are used.' He said.

'It seems too similar to be a coincidence, we have no idea where to put the answer in the crossword, perhaps there's something in the article we're missing.'

She read and re-read the article until she finally fell asleep. Andreas watched and waited for her to close her eyes, removed the scrapbook from her hand and covered her with a blanket, and then he quietly slipped out of the room and back down to the beach, where he knew Julio would still be. Julio was snoring loudly, but with a quick kick to the ankle, Andreas bought him round.

'What gives, what time is it, where are the girls?' Julio's eyes were bloodshot from too much rum over the past two days.

'They went to bed hours ago; I need to make sure you're telling me everything you know Julio. The last time you saw Jack did he say anything, you know, out of the ordinary or worrying like?'

'Funny you should say that, last time Jack was here I said to Jacqui that things weren't right, nothing in particular, just his mood, things he said.' Julio answered.

'What like, what did he refer to, it's important Julio and you, more than most, know that.' Andrea's voice sounded soberer than he actually was.

'No, nothing specific, he was just odd. What's all this with these clues and why has he dragged Saffi out here?'

'That's my concern, I always knew he wanted me to show her the Caribbean, but never in these circumstances, something isn't right. I can't put my finger on it, but my gut feel is that someone somewhere knows more than they are telling. Someone I don't think we can trust.'

'That's what I said to Jacqui. What makes you think that Andreas?'

'Firstly, Jack alluded to it in his letter to me, but I've just got a bad feeling and I don't like it when I have a bad feeling. I may need to call you on again, sooner than you think. Can I rely on you Julio, drop of a hat?' Andreas asked.

'Man, you know that you can, anything, anything at all, you just call.'

With that, they hugged and finally both went to bed and slept through until Jacqui called them for breakfast.

~~~

Saffi and Jacqui had been up for an hour, and had had coffee on the beach, getting to know each other. Finally, Saffi had another woman to talk to about how she felt. Jacqui had told Saffi her life story, that she was ten years younger than Julio was and, like Jack, she'd met Julio because she wanted to learn to dive. That was fifteen years ago when she was 30, it was a birthday present from her family.

'At that time, the US army had a big presence in Puerto Rico, and because my father was in the army, he had the whole family moved over there the previous year. As a surprise, he had arranged a family holiday in the Dominican Republic. That's when I met Julio. We fell for each other immediately and within a year I'd moved to the DR and in with him, and that's when I met Jack.' Jacqui said, and continued.

'I'm really sorry about your father, I thought Jack was wonderful. Handsome, witty, and adventurous, not unlike Julio in that respect, obviously the sort of man I like. He would always let us know when he'd been home to the UK to visit, but he never said anything to anyone, he kept his past very close to his chest, as he did with most things. He may have been all those things I've mentioned, but above all he was a very private man, Andreas was probably the closest person to him.'

'Thank you for telling me about him Jacqui, so far I've only heard adventure or drinking stories about him, it seems that everyone liked, even loved him, but no-one has told me about the person he was, did you meet him often?' Saffi asked.

'Only a few times, sadly. When he was passing through, he'd always stop by. He was a great storyteller; he would grab everyone's attention as he told of scrapes he'd been in and out of with Andreas. Luckily, they got out of most of them unhurt it would appear. However, when he talked about Lillian, that's when you saw the true Jack, the passionate, gentle, loving Jack, and the sad Jack. You could see through his eyes, straight into his broken heart. I never met Lillian, before my time, but he's shown me photos of her, you look so similar, he would be very proud of you for taking this trip, I hope it leads you to what you want.'

'What do you mean by that? I don't even know what it is I'm searching for?' Saffi said.

'Perhaps that's the point, perhaps Jack's helping you to discover what it is you're searching for, treasure isn't always tangible, or even something we think we're looking for. Sometimes we have to look beyond what is written, and look deeper. In fact, sometimes treasure can be just a state of mind.' With that, Jacqui got up and called the guys for breakfast.

Saffi sat and pondered what Jacqui had said, maybe she was reading too much into the article and not looking beyond what she had found here, she followed Jacqui back into the house.

'Morning sleepy heads, you've finally risen from your pits then?' Jacqui said to Julio and Andreas as she handed them a mug of strong, black coffee, 'you'll probably need this.'

'What do they put in that rum? Every time I drink that stuff with you I feel like someone has kicked me in the head in the morning.' Andreas thanked Jacqui for the coffee and sat next to Saffi.

'I think you'll find it's not the quality of what you drink, more likely the quantity, we did get through, two bottles last night, plus all the beer. Eggs Ranchos for everyone?' Jacqui said as she opened the fridge and took out the eggs.

'No further forward on finding where the answer goes then, Saffi?' Andreas asked, 'it didn't come to you in a dream last night?'

'No and no, but unlike you I don't have a stinking hangover and am going to look at the next clue to see where we're meant to be heading,'.' Saffi said, smugly.

'Please don't shout; my head is pounding.' Julio asked as he sidled slowly up to the table. 'Every time you come here Andreas I get a hangover, I think I'm going to ban you.'

'Let's see what we have next,' Saffi said as she opened the list of clues. 'Island clue first; *A predominantly Spanish island with predominantly American features. An island that 'listens' for 'ET'.*'

Jacqui looked over from the stove, 'that's easy, Puerto Rico.'

'How and why do you know that for certain?' enquired Andreas.

'Oh come on Andreas, you know better than that, Puerto Rico, America's 51st state, where I spent time before moving here.'

'What's it got to do with ET and Spain?' Saffi asked.

'OK everyone, listen up. School girl Puerto Rican history in a nutshell. Juan Ponce de Leon found the island in the fifteen hundred's when he returned with his old chum Chris Columbus. Then the Spanish Conquistadores enslaved, raped, murdered and starved the natives, the others died of smallpox or whooping cough, not dissimilar to the rest of the Caribbean islands. Typical, along comes some European, thinks he knows it all and manages to kill everyone off and strips the island of its treasures. Then the good Old Dutch and French traders turn up, and they use the island to drop off slaves from West Africa, until eventually half the population were West African slaves. This all carried on until the Spanish-American War of 1898 when Puerto Rico finally pried itself away from Spain and became a commonwealth of the US.'

'How do you know all this?' Saffi asked.

'I went to school there, just a typical history lesson. Anyway, the USA, via 'Operation Bootstrap' poured money into the island, building roads, post offices, supermarkets and military posts; that's why my dad was stationed there. So you can see from Jack's clue, a predominantly Spanish island, with predominantly US features, is why I think it's Puerto Rico.'

'OK, I get that, but what about the ET bit?' Andreas asked.

Jacqui continued, 'in the north of Puerto Rico there is the Arecibo Observatory, the world's largest radio telescope which runs SETI, the Search for Extra Terrestrial Intelligence, you know ET.'

'Oh.' Julio, Saffi and Andreas replied.

'Come on then, read the next bit, it can't be that difficult, I know most places on the island.' Jacqui said.

Saffi read aloud again, '*Find the town on the south coast that has something belonging to the World's Fair. Then find the Our Lady of Guadalupe.*'

Everyone looked at Jacqui and Jacqui looked at everyone, 'well that's stumped me, I didn't know that something from the World's Fair lived on Puerto Rico, Julio get a map out and look at the towns along the south coast while I finish breakfast.'

'Can't we just look on the internet, I'm sure we must be able to find something.' Saffi asked.

'Well you would under normal circumstances, but as luck would have it, we haven't got any connection at the moment, we don't have much of one at the best of times, but currently the service is 'not being provided'.' Julio explained.

'You mean you haven't paid the bill again.' Jacqui said.

'No, I haven't paid the bill, because they don't provide me with the service they say I'm getting, so no service, and no payment.' Julio replied.

'OK, so it's back to the old fashioned way of research through books.' Andreas interjected, sensing an argument brewing between Julio and Jacqui. 'Do you have any guide books around?' He asked.

'I've a guide for the Caribbean Islands that might help.'

Andreas opened the guide at the section on Puerto Rico, 'OK, towns along the south coast, Saffi write these down as I read them out, La Parguera, Guanica, Yauco, Guayanilla, Ponce, Santa Isabel, Salinas.'

'Stop, take a look at Ponce, that's a main historical centre, loads of pretty buildings and stuff like that, it has a main square, oh what's it called?' Jacqui called from the stove.

Andreas flicked through the pages until he found Ponce and read aloud for them all to hear, '*The historical centre of this otherwise modern city is full of great charm and quaint architecture,* nothing about the World Fair yet, 'he ran his eyes over the section, '*Plaza Las Delicias is a quintessential Spanish-colonial plaza, translates into 'Plaza of Delights'.*'

'Yes, that's the place I'm thinking of, what does it say about that?' Jacqui called out.

Andreas read the paragraph, muttering under his breath, children playing, men sitting under shady trees, pretty cafes, still nothing about the World's Fair. Best at night when pink lights dance in the waters of the Fuente de Leones, oh, here we go, *Fuente de Leones, the Fountain of Lions, a monument rescued from the 1939 World's Fair*. Oh, and here further down it says about the blue and white bell tower of the Catedral Nuestra Senora de Guadalupe, wasn't that the last bit of the clue, something about Guadalupe?'

Saffi read the clue again, '...*something belonging to the World's Fair, then find the Our Lady of Guadalupe.*'

'There you go,' Julio said, 'Catedral Nuestra Senora de Guadalupe, Our Lady of Guadalupe. Job done, clue solved.'

'Well not quite. We need to find out what word goes in the puzzle, so we can find out who we are meant to be finding on Puerto Rico, I'll get my laptop.'

'What's she talking about Andreas, haven't we just solved the clue?' Julio asked.

'Well yes and no. First we have to work out what island we're meant to be going to, and then we find the place on the island, and then, if we managed to put the correct, five letter word that we've found, into the puzzle, it then tells us, by some piece of computer wizardry, who we need to go and visit. I can't believe Jack set this by himself, he was never that much of a computer geek, but it seems to work.' Andreas took a deep breath.

'Oh.' Julio said as he took a plate of eggs Ranchos from Jacqui.

Saffi returned with the laptop already booted up and put it on the table, 'there are only two words of five letters, either Lions or Ponce.' She tried 'LIONS' first, with no luck, but having entered 'PONCE' it returned a name, 'Father Tomas Melia' Saffi said aloud.

'No surprises there then, eh Andreas? I'd like to be a fly on the wall for that conversation and no mistake.' Julio said raising his eyebrows at Andreas him.

'I wondered when he'd turn up on the list.' Andreas replied.

'Why, is it good or bad?' Saffi asked.

'Well, in a way, very good, but don't think that just because he's a priest that he and Jack always got along.' Andreas said.

'Why, what happened, how did he know Jack?'

'It was Father Tomas who saved your father from the dreaded drink when he first got back to Columbia after your mother died, and let's just say that they didn't quite see eye to eye on the whole 'not drinking' scenario.' Julio replied before Andreas began to tell her the whole story.

Andreas stood up, 'Shall we take our coffee outside before I begin this bit of Jack's history, it may take some time...' he trailed off as he walked outside to the beanbags. Saffi followed, looking to Jacqui for some sort of indication, Jacqui just shrugged her shoulders.

Chapter 15

Saffi sat next to Andreas, ready to hear another happy instalment of her father's life, but somehow Andreas' demeanour told another story. He looked at her with his dark brown eyes, hiding so many secrets within.

'It wasn't a good time for your father when he returned to the farm, he'd been drinking hard.' He sat back and sighed as he began to tell her the story.

'After Lillian died and he decided the best thing for you, was to leave you with your Nana, Jack needed to get away, from everything. Although returning to the Caribbean would bring back memories of their time together, he also knew the Caribbean is a place where you can lose yourself, in any way you care to choose, especially in those days.

'As I've told you he arrived back at the farm in a real state. He'd bought Linalli, at the time she was called "Soul Searching" or "Island Chasing" or some name that people call their boats when they leave their "normal life and go and explore the world". They think sailing the Caribbean is seeing the world, one hurricane and they get the first flight back home. That's what Linalli was, a casualty of Hurricane David, a big hurricane that hit Dominica in '79, where she'd lay ever since. With the help of some local lads, he managed to get her sea worthy. Sea worthy for him, maybe not for anyone else; but to him she became home. He renamed her Linalli and for the next eighteen months, she protected him from everything he and nature could throw at him, depression, anger, storms and drink. That's the other problem with the Caribbean, rum is cheap, and with a splash of lime and an ice cube in it, and you can drink the roughest, rawest stuff without flinching.

'He somehow managed to negotiate and navigate his way back down the island chain. Stopping at some islands, avoiding others, until one day, in a drunken hue, he arrived back at the farm. He told me some of the stories of his return trip, not all; he probably couldn't remember them all. I'm sure he had pissed off a few people along the way, but it was Father Tomas he had the biggest problem with.' Andreas finished his coffee and looked out to sea then back to Saffi, 'Jack wasn't pleasant to know then, so much anger pent up in a drunken sailor, who had nothing left to live for.'

'He had me. He could have spent his time looking after me, rather than feeling sorry for himself, and deserting me and leaving Nana with the hardship. Sounds like an excuse for not taking your responsibilities seriously.' Saffi was angry now, 'everyone always feeling sorry for Jack, what about me, left with no parents, no idea what had happened and no-one ever telling me.' The words spat from her mouth.

'You're right Saffi, perhaps he should have stayed and taken care of you, but to be honest, I think watching you grow up, looking so much like Lillian would have killed him, on the inside. It may have been a coward's way out, but it was the only way Jack could see, doesn't make it right, but it's what happened.'

'Well what happened at the farm, Father Tomas, what did he have to do with anything?'

'When Jack arrived at the farm Father Caleb had had to leave town for a while, his own mother was sick, and Father Tomas had arrived to stand in as the local priest. He took over keeping an eye on the farm, and the kids who stayed or visited, and like Father Caleb, he was very good with the children. Always telling them stories, from the bible you know, but making them sound fun or adventurous, but he was a strict man, wouldn't stand for any nonsense.

'So, when Jack arrived, making demands around the place, after all it was Jack's place, Father Tomas was having none of it. *'It may be your place in name, but these children are my responsibility, and you are in no fit state to start making demands around here, until you clean yourself up. And I don't just mean with good clean soap and water, because if no one's told you Jack, you stink. I mean clean yourself up from the demon drink and get your soul cleaned up too. When was the last time you even entered a house of God?* He said.

'I can remember the words as if it were yesterday, and Jack's face, that was a picture. Within minutes Jack was seeing red, and was not about to take any crap from some priest who'd just arrived, and was giving out orders willy-nilly. Without a thought for the kids who were looking on, Jack took an almighty swipe at Father Tomas, aiming straight for his jaw. However, unbeknown to Jack, Father Tomas was a schoolboy-boxing champion, who was already ahead of Jack's game. As Jack's left hook came toward him, he grabbed his fist with his left hand and punched Jack square in the stomach with his right. Jack fell to the floor, coughing and gasping for breath. He wobbled to his feet and lunged again at Father Tomas, who, quick as a flash, jumped out of his way, and Jack went head first into wall, he fell to his knees once more. But that wasn't stopping Jack. He got up again and charged at Father Tomas, grabbing him around the waist, with his clenched fists locked around his back, they both fell backwards and onto the floor. Within a split second, Father Tomas was kneeling over Jack, pinning his shoulders to the ground. Finally, Jack surrendered and Father Tomas allowed him to sit up before shooing the children away.'

'Where were you when this was going on?' Saffi asked.

'Watching from the porch, it was a great show.'

'Typical, you didn't try to stop them?'

'Why would I, Father Tomas had everything in control, who was I to butt in?' Andreas said, smiling as he remembered the day well.

'Well what happened after that?'

'Immediately after that Father Tomas grabbed a bucket of water and threw it over Jack and told him to get inside and clean himself up properly. Father Tomas knew all about Jack and Lillian, and you, and he was well versed in dealing with sad old drunks who needed some direction in their lives. However, it wasn't going to be easy, or pleasant. Nevertheless, if it wasn't for Father Tomas, I'm not sure Jack would have made it. He cleaned him up and set him on a path of determination and a reason to live. Some say that path may have led to revenge on Jack's part, others used the word avenge. Either way, you can thank Father Tomas that Jack found his way out of his drunken stupor. I'm sure he'll tell you more when we meet him. I suppose we ought to find out if he's going to be around. Come on Saffi, let's get back inside and get ourselves sorted out.' With that, Andreas stood up and walked back to the house.

'But, what do you mean revenge, avenge, who did he take revenge out on, what did he do?' She ran after him, but he had already locked himself in the bathroom, taking a shower, he knew she'd have a million questions for him now, and he'd yet to contact Father Tomas, another phone call he wasn't looking forward to making.

~~~

After breakfast, they said their goodbyes to Julio and Jacqui and returned to the plane. The flight to Puerto Rico took them down the spectacular north coast of the DR, above Julio and Jacqui's house, and over what Andreas described as one of the most awful sailing passages in the Caribbean, the Mona Passage, before reaching the north-west coast of Puerto Rico.

'Down there,' he said pointing, 'is exactly why I didn't what you to sail Linalli here.'

Saffi looked out of the window; she could see white beaches lapped by blue water, which sparkled in the sun. 'Looks wonderful from here, what's wrong with it?'

'It's a notorious passage for sailing, everything against you, wind, waves, current, even migrating whales, you name it, it throws everything at you. I've done it a few times; only once did I enjoy it.'

'Who's sailing Linalli down?'

'A good friend of mine, Carina, she has a cousin who's a sailing instructor, sailed all his life. He and a couple of friends are sailing her down, they're going to meet us in Puerto Rico, on the east coast, hopefully in the next couple of days. From there the sailing's pretty easy; the two of us can do it, no really long passages.'

'Oh.' Saffi said, not really understanding what he was saying.

Andreas looked at her, 'What's wrong?'

'I've got quite used to flying now, funny it scared me at first, and now I'll have to get used to a boat. Will it be safe?' She looked worried. Anything new scared Saffi.

'Of course it's safe, and I promise not to make you do anything you don't want to. By the way, I took the liberty of calling your hotel and having your things packed and delivered to the boat, I hope you don't mind?'

However, Saffi's mind was now wandering and worrying about boats and sailing. Andreas left her to her thoughts; he had his own problems to worry about when they got to San Juan. He hadn't seen Father Tomas in a long, long time and he wasn't looking forward to meeting him.

~~~

They landed at San Juan Airport a few hours later and cleared through Customs, Andreas had booked them into a hotel and he hailed a taxi.

'Casa de Playa, por favour.' he said in fluent Spanish.

'Si Señor.'

'This is a great place Saffi, you'll love it, set right in hoards of palm trees, great bar too.'

'Oh', she said, not really knowing where they were going.

'Only problem is the noise from the airport, but we'll only be here tonight, we can get a car sorted tomorrow, after I've checked with Father Tomas, then we can go down to Ponce.

'You mean he doesn't know we're coming yet?' Saffi was surprised to learn that Andreas had not contacted Father Tomas yet.

'Well, no, I didn't get around to calling him before we left, and what with all the 'good-byes' with Julio and Jacqui, it sort of slipped my mind.' He blushed.

'You mean we've flown over here and we don't even know if he's on the island, what do we do if he's not here?' She sounded angry.

'He will be,' Andreas paused, 'but if he's not we'll find out where he is and go and find him.' He looked out the taxi window to avoid eye contact with her.

'What is it Andreas, why don't you want to talk to Father Tomas?'

'What, nothing, there's no problem, I just haven't got around to it yet, don't worry, chill out, look we've arrived at the hotel. Come on Saffi, get your bag.'

As Saffi got out, Andreas paid the taxi driver and almost ran into the hotel. Saffi followed slowly, taking in her surroundings. At least they were near the beach, she thought, she could have some time to herself, to think a few things through. She walked into reception and found Andreas standing with keys to a villa in one hand and a beer in the other, chatting to Bonita, the receptionist. Clearly, Andreas knew Bonita from previous visits, probably on a more personal level than he was letting on, especially the way Bonita's smile dropped when she saw Saffi.

'Thanks Bonita, I knew you'd sort things out, I owe you, as usual.' He winked at her as he walked toward Saffi, 'there you are. Come on, I'll show you around.'

'Know her well, do you?' Saffi's tone was accusing.

'Yes, as a matter of fact I do, this is one of my favourite haunts and Bonita always looks after me.'

'With a bit more material, she'd have made a nice dress out of what she's wearing.' Saffi had taken an instant dislike to Bonita and didn't know why.

'Well if you've got a great body like that, you may as well flaunt it.'

'Not exactly what I'd call suitable attire for a receptionist.' Saffi said looking back over her shoulder to Bonita.

'Oh I don't know, it's always so damn hot here, and anyhow, she's married to the manager, so no-one's going to take advantage of her.'

'Oh', Saffi replied, feeling a little embarrassed by her preconceived ideas. 'I just thought you two seemed to know each other very well.'

'You got all that from a two-minute conversation; you're reading way too much into things. It's the way of the Caribbean, everyone loves everyone and you'll see a lot more of that, I've no doubt. Come on, let's get you a drink and show you the villa.'

'Villa, don't you mean rooms?'

'Ah, well, there we have a problem, well not a big problem but they didn't have any rooms and only had one villa left, which only has one bedroom, but I'm happy with the sofa, honest.'

'Well I hope it's comfortable.' I'm sure we could have found a hotel with two rooms available she thought as she followed him outside.

They stopped at the bar, and of course, Andreas knew the barman, Moses. Why was she even surprised, but she was surprised at how she was feeling, it wasn't anger, or resentment or anything she could put her finger on, but since they had landed Andreas was just annoying her. She sat quietly and listened to Andreas and Moses for a while, and then she went and sat on a beach chair to gather her thoughts.

What's wrong with me, she thought. Everything he says today bugs me, he's always so damn cheerful, and knows everyone in the whole world it seems. He's able to do anything he puts his mind to, some sort of superman, flying, sailing, diving, next thing I know he'll be telling me that he loves sky diving too. She took a gulp from the bottle of beer she had. And what's with me drinking beer, I've never drunk beer in my life, let alone out of a bottle, but she took another sip despite herself. But why am I so angry, she felt for the pendant and realised she didn't have it on, in fact she hadn't had it on for a while now. She began to think back to when she last wore it, it was back in the Bahamas, Great Inagua, when she showed Andreas the numbers on the back, then she'd put it away. It was after that that she had started to feel agitated, firstly with Julio, for no reason, now with Andreas, and then with Bonita and Moses. She stood up, went to the villa, and found her bags. Knowing exactly where the pendant was she found it and placed it around her neck again. She sat on the bed and took a deep breath, sighing as she did. She had no idea why, but she felt calm. Maybe it just reminds me of my mother, she thought. Whatever it was, she was in a better mood now.

After a few minutes, she changed into a cooler dress and returned to the bar. Andreas and Moses were still catching up on gossip. She moved her bar stool closer to Andreas.

'Ah, there you are, wondered where you'd got to.' Andreas said with a smile.

'I just popped back to the villa to change, I was too hot.' She moved her hand up to the pendant and smiled.

'Moses has just told me that Father Tomas is on the island, still down in Ponce, he's going to get Bonita to give him a call and arrange for us to visit tomorrow, and they've got a car we can borrow. If we set off after breakfast, we could be there by lunchtime.' He indicated to Moses for another beer. 'You seem happier than you did a while ago, is everything OK?' Andreas was still not used to Saffi's mood swings, she ran hot and cold, he never knew if he was saying the right thing.

'I'm fine, in fact I feel much happier than I have been for a few days now. Moses can I have another beer too; I'm rather enjoying this.' Her mind flickered, only five minutes ago she was thinking that she didn't like beer, and now she was enjoying it. In fact, she enjoyed the next four, more than she realised, until they got up to go back to the villa. Saffi got off the bar stool and wobbled, just in time for Andreas to catch her and stop her from falling.

'I'm OK.' She said, as she grabbed Andreas' arm.

'I know you are. I thought you were holding me up.' He lied.

'Ah, yes, well that's more likely the case, because I don't get drunk, you're the one who drinks too much, and we've not had anything to eat this evening, that's why you're feeling as drunk as you are'. She slurred.

He held onto her as tightly as he could without her knowing that he was guiding her back to the villa. He sat her down on the veranda and brought out a glass of water.

'Oh let's have another beer.' She said, waving her arms around.

'I'm not so sure that's a good idea, we've a long day tomorrow, and besides, you don't like beer, you keep telling me so.' Andreas replied.

'Well, I appear to have gained a taste for it, so I am going to have another one.'

With that, Saffi stood up and wobbled her way inside and to the fridge where she took another beer out and opened it. Andreas watched on with a careful eye as she zigzagged her way back through the villa. Seeing that she was about to trip over a bag, he ran in and thought he'd caught her just in time, but, as if in slow motion, she lost balance again and they fell backward onto the sofa, Andreas on his back and Saffi lying on top of him.

'Look, I didn't spill a drop.' She giggled.

'Well done,' he said taking the bottle and placing it on the table, 'I think you've had enough for one day.'

'Haven't you got brown eyes, they're like, really really brown.' The words slurred from her mouth like a teenager drunk for the first time, 'and your hair, I really like your hair, it's really, really black, and sleek, in fact you look a little bit like that actor, you know, played the cat in that cartoon film about a big green ogre thingy, oh what's his name?' She looked up to the ceiling trying to think of the name, 'Antonio Bandage, him, you look like him.'

'I think you mean Antonio Banderas, and I don't look anything like him.'

'Yes you do, he has black hair and tanned skin, I think he's quite cute, oh that must mean I think you're quite cute…' she stopped mid-sentence with the realisation of what she had said and thought suddenly dawning on her. Unexpectedly she kissed him. Without a second thought, Andreas responded accordingly and placed his arms around her as he kissed her back. She stopped and looked him straight in the eyes, suddenly sober; her eyes told him everything he needed to know.

He stood up slowly, turned and picked Saffi up in his arms and carried her through to the bedroom, as he laid her on the bed he whispered, 'are you sure?' to his delight she nodded.

Andreas lifted her up to a sitting position and gently ran his fingertips down her neck and slid the straps of her dress down over her shoulders, and undid the buttons to her waist; he waited for a reaction from her. She smiled at him and moved to kneel across him, as she moved closer to him she lifted his shirt over his head, as she did her dress fell open and her breasts caressed his face and he breathed in her scent, he undid the remainder of the buttons and her dress slid to the floor. He wrapped his arms around her, as close as he dared, and lay her back down on the bed, 'don't move,' he whispered as he kissed her softly along the length of her body. He stood up and closed the curtains to the outside world; this moment was for the two of them only. When he returned, he was naked, he lowered himself down onto Saffi; she moaned gently has he skilfully worked his tongue around her body and along the inside of her thigh. She moved in time with his breathing, and she arched her back as he reached her navel and worked his way back down her body. She began to relax more and more as he worked his magic, she allowed him to move in between her legs and she sighed softly in pleasure, his tongue now playing with her nipples, as he slowly slid inside her. She gasped in pleasure as she allowed him in. Slowly they moved in rhythm with one another, the noise of the fan murmured overhead unheard, but gently cooling their bodies, as they discovered each other. Finally, they reached the heightened moment together, slowing down to make the sensation last as long as possible, before finally laying side by side, in a knowing silence. Knowing that from this moment, their lives would now be unquestionably joined together. Leaning up on one arm Andreas looked at Saffi, he stroked her face and then kissed her passionately. They talked through most of the night, until they finally drifted into a deep sleep, in each other's arms.

Andreas woke before Saffi, he made breakfast and set it out on the veranda, Saffi stirred a while later, having lain in bed catching, her breath as she remembered the night before. Andreas saw she had woken and went over to the bed.
'Good morning sleepy head,' He kissed her gently on the top of her head, 'breakfast is ready when you are.' He walked away allowing her to get up in her own time, he called from the kitchen, 'I've spoken with Father Tomas this morning, he can see us this afternoon, around three, so no rush.' He smiled, perhaps he should just go back to bed and repeat the previous night, but Saffi had walked into the kitchen. She looked sheepish. He'd seen this look before in women. That embarrassed morning after look, not knowing what to say and how to act.
'There's orange juice and coffee out on the veranda, I'm just doing some eggs and toast, and it's a beautiful morning. We could go for a swim if you like before we set off.' He tried to relax her, and still she said nothing. He walked to the veranda and saw her sipping some orange juice, 'are you OK?' he asked.
She looked up at him, her cheeks blushed, 'yes, yes, I'm fine.' He knelt beside her and took her hand; he kissed it lovingly and looked straight into her eyes, 'You are beautiful; you know that, don't you?'
She blushed again and her eyes fell to the floor.
'I thought you were beautiful the first time I saw you, but never imagined for a moment this would happen, I never set out for this to happen, and I know what you think I'm like, some sort of womaniser…'
She interrupted him 'thought. I thought you were a womaniser.'
'And what do you think now?'
'I don't know; nothing like this, like you, has ever happened to me before, I…' she looked at him, deep into his brown eyes,

'everything is happening so quickly, I can't take it all in, I feel like running back to England and wishing none of this had ever happened.' She looked at Andreas, hoping he could make sense of it all for her.

'I'm glad it's happened. I'm glad you came.' He knelt between her legs and took her face in his hands, his kissed her tenderly, and then wrapped his arms around her and she felt her worries melt away. 'Let's go and see Father Tomas this afternoon, see what he has to say, I've a feeling you and he are going to get on just fine. Now let's have a smile from you and some breakfast.'

Chapter 16

The call came as no surprise to Father Tomas, having already heard the sad news of Jack's death. He knew it would only be a matter of time before Andreas visited, with his tail between his legs. He knew Andreas would be feeling guilty. Guilty of forsaking his duties to those who depended on him, and needed him most. The orphanage needed more than money to sustain it now that Jack was gone. The children needed a new leader, someone to look to in times of need, when the church could not be there.

However, having received the call from Bonita, he was surprised to hear that Andreas was travelling with a companion, Jack's daughter, Saffrina. His heart cried out for her, another orphan reaching into his fold. Admittedly, she was not a young child in need of rescue, but why had she made her way here, to Andreas, and to his church? Surely, Jack would not have led her into danger. He knew very well that wherever Jack and Andreas had walked, they had truly encountered danger. This thought reminded him of Psalm 23, though they walked through the valley of death, they would fear no evil; he had prayed for them constantly.

Father Tomas moved to the altar, and knelt beneath and prayed, 'Lord, help me as you send this lost child into my protection, help me to find the way forward. I am unsure what is required of me, or what to do next, and so I ask you to give me wisdom and guidance. Help me to trust in you to give me strength and patience. Amen'. He touched the four points of the cross on his chest and walked out of the church, into the blazing sun. He needed to rest and to contemplate before Andreas and Saffi arrived later that day; they would take tea in the Rectory garden, he thought.

Back in the Rectory, Father Tomas went into his office and sat at his desk. He opened the drawer and removed the Bible that Jack had given him as a peace offering many years before, after their first encounter. It had taken a long time for the healing process to begin. Father Tomas had used his bible reading classes to try to win Jack over, telling him that everyone, 'and I mean everyone' at the orphanage must attend at least one bible reading class a week. As the weeks and months went by, and Jack sobered up, Father Tomas could finally see an opening in Jack's heart that he could reach into; an opening that became a large, cavernous space that needed to be filled. At first, Jack filled it with anger and hate, which he took out on Father Tomas; it took all of Father Tomas' knowledge and skill to teach Jack that he should turn his hate and anger into something positive. 'Do not avenge Lillian's death, but continue the orphanage in her name.' He had said at the time. 'Think of what Lillian would have wanted.' He would remind him that it wasn't just Jack, who had lost Lillian, but Elizabeth had lost a daughter, Saffrina had lost a mother, and the children at the orphanage would lose all hope if he deserted them once more. He would often read Psalm 3 to Jack, the psalm of David when he fled from his son.

Father Tomas opened the bible, turned to Psalm 3 and saw the familiar finger markings alongside the passage, worn by the numerous readings; he read the verses aloud and thought of Jack with affection.

> O' Lord, how many are my foes!
> How many rise up against me!
> Many are saying of me
> 'God will not deliver him.'
> But you are a shield around me, O Lord;
> You bestow glory on me and lift up my head
> To the Lord I cry aloud,
> And he answers me from his holy hill
> I lie down and sleep;
> I wake again, because the Lord sustains me
> I will not fear the tens of thousands
> Drawn up against me on every side
> Arise, O Lord! Deliver me, O my God!
> Strike all my enemies on the jaw;
> Break the teeth of the wicked
> From the Lord comes deliverance

Now the words were clearer than ever before, Jack's foes would always surround him, they would continue to rise up against him, and his family, even after his death. So why had Saffi come? Why would Andreas put her in dangers' way? He closed his eyes and prayed quietly to himself.

~~~

The journey from San Juan to Ponce took a little over two hours and was through some of the most beautiful scenery Saffi had ever seen. The rapid changes in the landscapes astonished her. How quickly the old town of San Juan, with its incredibly narrow, dusty streets had morphed into dense rain forest with steep, winding roads. The southern coast road was dotted with tiny holiday villages, and arriving in Ponce, the town had surprised her once more;

brimming with colourful buildings of all shapes and sizes. They found the Fuente de Leones easily, as described in Jack's clue, a large fountain bordered by statues of lions, and trees providing shade and respite against the heat of the sun. In stark contrast, the bold red and black building, Parque de Bombas, which was once the fire station, but now a museum, overshadowed the tranquillity of the fountain. Within a few minutes' walk, the pale blue building of the Catedral Nuestra Senora de Guadalupe came into view. They were early and spent ten minutes walking around the fountain, trying to take in the enormity of the past twenty-four hours.

Andreas took Saffi's hand and squeezed it. 'Are you OK?'

'Yes, are you? You seemed very quiet on the way here. What's the problem between you and Father Tomas?'

They sat down on a bench near the fountain, Andreas sighed. 'Did you go to Sunday School when you were little?'

'Yes, regularly with Nana, I used to help out with the little ones when the main service was on. Why?'

'Well, I don't know about you, but priests make me nervous, especially Father Tomas.'

'Why?' She asked.

'Don't get me wrong, he is a good man, a very good man, but shall we say he expects, or rather, demands a certain level of respect and commitment.'

'OK, I get that, but you're a grown man who, from what I have seen so far, spends your time flitting from one place to another, so you can't exactly commit to being at Sunday Mass every week.' She said.

'No, it's not that, it's just, now that Jack is gone, I think he's going to expect more of me, to,' he searched for the right words, 'to take Jack's place.'

'What do you mean, what exactly was Jack's place?'

'I'm not sure I can explain what I mean. Jack carried on with the orphanage as you know, but well, he also… we started to take a few things into our own hands.'

'What do you mean, what are you talking about Andreas?' Saffi asked.

'Saffi, this is very long and complicated and will take more than ten minutes to explain, let's go and see Father Tomas and on the way back we can see if Linalli has been delivered and I promise to explain everything then. It will be easier on board; there are things that can only be spoken about in private.'

'What do you mean, was Jack in trouble? Are you in trouble?' Saffi began to feel nervous, even scared, what had Jack been up to?

Andreas stood up and took Saffi by the hand and, before she had a chance to question him any further, they were standing at the door of the church where Father Tomas' housekeeper was waiting to greet them.

The Housekeeper led them through to the garden where Father Tomas was waiting; tea was set out on a table on the lawn under a sprawling sunshade to protect them from the sun. Father Tomas stood and greeted them. Saffi thought how athletic he looked for a man who must be at least seventy, but she recalled the story of the fight between him and Jack, and assumed Father Tomas must keep up some sort of fitness regime. Father Tomas gave his condolences to Saffi and hugged Andreas like a lost son. They sat quietly while the housekeeper poured tea before leaving them in private. An awkward silence fell over the garden.

Finally, Saffi could stand the silence no more. 'Father Tomas, you are probably wondering why we are here?'

Father Tomas placed his teacup back on the table and refilled it. 'Once I heard the news of Jack, I was expecting to see Andreas, maybe not so soon, but certainly not with a companion such as yourself. Why are you here my child?'

Andreas remained silent and felt awkward as Saffi replied.

'As you probably know, you, more than anyone I would imagine, I did not see much of my father after my mother's death; in fact, in the last few years not at all. So it came as a quite a shock to find that he had left specific instructions in his Will for me to seek out and meet some of his friends and acquaintances. I won't go into the finer details, but he has left, for want of a better explanation, encrypted clues as to how to find these acquaintances, and you happen to be on the list. I am not sure to what end this search will take me, and I'm not really sure why I have decided to follow Jack's request to find these people, but here I am.' She was surprised at how succinct she had explained the situation.

'And have you found many of these 'acquaintances' your father wished for you to meet with?' Father Tomas' voice was soft and comforting.

'You're the fourth specific person on the list, but I have met others on our journey.' Saffi found herself talking in the same calming tones as Father Tomas.

'Am I at liberty to know who you have met so far?' Father Tomas enquired.

Saffi thought this was an odd request and looked to Andreas for guidance. He smiled and leant forward to answer. 'Father, you are one of the few people who truly knew the nature of Jack's business, and motivation, and for this reason it is probably better that you do not know any more than is necessary. You have more to protect than most.'

'Andreas, as you would have learnt, had you attended more of the Bible reading classes, the Bible teaches us that God is the only one who can protect us fully, but I will respect your wishes,' Andreas flinched at Father Tomas' reprimand. 'However, I do not believe that Jack would have sent either of you to me in order for us to take afternoon tea on the lawn. What is it that you are searching for?'

His forthright approach shocked Saffi, but she was glad of it, he obviously knew Jack much better than she had realised.

'We are in search of a reference of sorts.' Saffi replied.

'What type of reference, a character reference?' Father Tomas was confused.

'No, we're looking for a sort of grid reference. Did Jack leave anything with you, anything obscure or ambiguous?'

'No, Jack left nothing with me, nothing that could be deemed to be a reference,' Father Tomas poured them some more tea and thought about Jack. 'The only thing I have here, that has anything to do with Jack, is a Bible he gave me many years ago, a peace offering one might say. I was reading it just before you arrived.'

'Could we look at it, if it's not too private?' Saffi asked.

'Of course my dear, let us go inside to my office and I can show it to you.'

Father Tomas led the way back to his office and offered Saffi and Andreas a seat opposite his desk. The simply furnished office had a large desk adorned with papers and books, a simple crucifix upon the wall and a view back over the gardens. Father Tomas took the Bible from the drawer and passed it to Saffi.

Saffi opened the cover and saw Jack's writing.

> *'To Father Tomas, my teacher, without whom I would have been lost, but now not only am I found, I am saved and have a purpose. I will forever be in your debt and always grateful.*
>
> *Your thankful servant, Jack.'*

The words tore deep into Saffi's heart, Father Tomas had obviously been Jack's saving grace in his most desperate hour of need, again she felt ashamed that she had never thought of how devastated Jack had been, how lost he was. She had just assumed he had left her because it was easier. She closed the cover and ran her hands across the Bible; it was a well-used book. There was a bookmark inserted and she opened the Bible at the page, Psalm 3. Father Tomas watched her carefully.

'Jack's favourite passage in the whole Bible, I read it again this morning in his memory, I fear its meaning may be a little closer to home than any of us could have realised.' Father Tomas read the Psalm aloud, verbatim as Saffi followed the words on the page.

> O' Lord, how many are my foes!
> How many rise up against me!
> Many are saying of me
> 'God will not deliver him.'
> But you are a shield around me, O Lord;
> You bestow glory on me and lift up my head
> To the Lord I cry aloud,
> And he answers me from his holy hill
> I lie down and sleep;
> I wake again, because the Lord sustains me
> I will not fear the tens of thousands
> Drawn up against me on every side
> Arise, O Lord! Delivery me, O my God!
> Strike all my enemies on the jaw;
> Break the teeth of the wicked
> From the Lord comes deliverance

Andreas closed his eyes as he listened to the Psalm, how many of their foes had risen up against them, how many times had they been delivered and shielded, Andreas truly believed that they had been protected by God on more than one occasion.

'Psalm 3,' Father Tomas said quietly, 'it's the Psalm of David when he leaves his son, Absalom,' he paused, maybe this was what Jack was sending to Saffi, an explanation of sorts as to why he had left her. 'However, other than this Bible, there is nothing here that belonged to Jack, and I cannot think of any sort of reference, I'm sorry.'

Saffi closed the Bible and repeated, 'Psalm 3, the Psalm of David, the words are very stirring, the message is quite forceful.'

'Yes my child, the Bible has many powerful statements, some with hidden meanings and messages.'

Saffi passed the Bible back to Father Tomas, 'No Saffi, I believe that you should take this now, and try to learn whatever message your father has left for you, if nothing it may bring you closer to him, to understand him more.'

'Thank you Father, I will cherish this memento of yours.'

There was nothing more to say as silence fell across the room. They all knew that their time together was at an end. Andreas stood up, 'we have a long journey, and I think we should be heading on our way Saffi. Thank you Father, for everything.'

Father Tomas knew that Andreas meant more by this than just a farewell, he knew now that Andreas would honour Jack's memory in any way he could. He wished them a safe journey and blessed them before they left.

~~~

For most of the journey back, both Saffi and Andreas were quiet, even contemplative. Saffi continue to read Psalm 3, running the words repeatedly over in her head. 'There has to be something in this, the words are too, too...'

'Meaningful?' Andreas interrupted.

'Yes, that's it. The verses, the fact that it is about David leaving his son, it's as if Jack is trying to tell us something.'

'I particularly like the verse where we get to strike our enemies on the jaw; I've done that a few times,' Saffi scowled at him, 'what, what's the problem, there have been more than a few who deserved it.' He answered.

'I'm sure, but that's not helping now, is it?'

They fell silent again. Saffi quietly repeated the words over and over, Psalm 3, Psalm of David. Psalm of David, Psalm 3. Suddenly, without warning Andreas slammed on the breaks, the car stopped abruptly and he turned and looked at Saffi.

'Three down.' He said.

'Three down?' She questioned.

'Psalm three, 3, Psalm of David, D for David, 3D, three down.'

'It couldn't be that simple, could it?' She said.

Saffi reached into the back of the car and grabbed her laptop. She opened the crossword and typed P O N C E into three down. They knew they would not know if this was the right place until the whole crossword was finished, or so they assumed, but they had nothing else to go on.

'At least we have three entries out of four answers, but we've still no idea where Julio's clue fits in.'

'No, but I've a feeling there is something in that newspaper article that we're not seeing. Come on, let's head to the marina and see if Linalli has arrived.' Andreas said as Saffi continued to look at the crossword and drove directly toward Puerto Del Rey Marina.

Chapter 17

Carina's cousin Tariq, and his two crewmates, Ollie and Conrad, arrived in Puerto Rico, having taken five days to sail the seven-hundred miles. They encountered no problems with either the passage, or Linalli. Although they were exhausted, Tariq had his instructions to call Luis Leppe as soon as they arrived. He left Ollie and Conrad on watch while he called Luis Leppe.

'Buenos noches, El Jeffe.'

Luis could hear the fear in Tariq's voice. 'Where are you?' he asked.

'Puerto Rico, we have just tied up in the marina at Puerto Del Rey.'

'Has Andreas arrived yet?' Luis asked.

'No, we have seen no-one yet; I have left my men on the boat to keep watch.'

'You must call me as soon as you meet with them.' Luis emphasised.

'Can you confirm that the girl is with him?' Tariq asked, fearful of asking a question of his boss.

'Yes, sources have seen them in both the DR, and now in Puerto Rico, you have arrived in good time. You have done well Tariq. I will wait for your call.' Luis hung up and called for Raoul, who was waiting in the next room.

'Have they arrived?' Raoul enquired.

'Yes, the boat is in Puerto Del Rey Marina, but no sign of Andreas yet. We need to find out where they are going next and I need to find a way of keeping Tariq and his boys on the boat with them. Find me a solution and make it fast.'

'Of course.' Raoul replied.

~~~

As Andreas and Saffi continued along the coast road toward Puerto Del Rey Marina Andreas' phone rang, he answered it.

'That's great news Tariq. You made good time then, no problems?' Andreas pulled the car to a stop on the side of the road and mouthed to Saffi that Linalli and the crew had arrived.

'No Andreas, no problems at all, she sails great, we were hitting seven knots along the way and with three of us on board we could go non-stop.' Tariq replied.

'OK, we're just on our way from Ponce, we should be there in about an hour, and the beers are on me when we get there. See you soon.' Andreas replied.

~~~

Tariq telephoned Luis immediately, 'Andreas is on his way back to the boat, with the girl. They'll be here in an hour. What do you want me to do?'

'Can I count on you to continue some, shall we say, "other work" for me? It will take at least two of you, possibly three; can you trust your men?'

'Yes, they can be trusted, and need any 'work' they can get.' Tariq knew the type of 'other' jobs Luis called on people to carry out. It would not be a problem.

'Good.' Luis said, already knowing that Tariq would take on the work. 'I will call you soon when I have a solution; I need to find a plausible way for you to stay on the boat.' Luis was about to hang up when Tariq interrupted.

'That won't be a problem, El Jeffe. I can "create" a technical fault that will need my attention, leave it with me. I will report back when I have set everything up.'

Back on board, Tariq, Ollie and Conrad set about causing some intermittent faults with the autopilot on Linalli. Without an autopilot the boat would need to be hand-steered, for which Andreas would need extra crew if they were continuing down the islands.

~~~

Andreas drove away and updated Saffi on what Tariq had told him.

'It's at least an hour till we get to the marina. Do you want to read the next clue to me?'

'Good idea, it will take my mind off some of the things Father Tomas said.'

Andreas did not enquire as to what she was referring, he would try to avoid all invasive questions from Saffi; he just concentrated on the road ahead.

Saffi opened the file containing the clues. 'OK, Island Clue number five, *"this island was originally named after a 4th Century princess who was raped and murdered along with 11,000 maidens."* that's not very pleasant, any ideas?' Saffi looked at Andreas, and assumed the concentration on his face was from the driving.

'What, sorry, no, no ideas yet, what's the second part of the clue?' he replied.

Saffi continued, *''Running near a Spanish turtledove and a fat virgin, this piece of water was named after an English Privateer'.* So we've got a fourth century princess raped and murdered along with thousands of maidens and now a fat virgin, a turtledove and a crook.'

'Privateers weren't crooks, they were legalised pirates, and in fact England's very own Sir Francis Drake was a privateer. He spent a lot of time attacking Spanish shipping in these waters. Did you know he was so famous in these parts they named a stretch of water after him, Sir Francis Drake Channel in the BVI.' Andreas explained.

'The BVI, where, or what, is the BVI?' Saffi asked.

'The British Virgin Islands, don't they teach you about your own islands at school.'

'I've never heard of the British Virgin Islands, but don't you think it's quite a coincidence that both of the clues have references to virgins, and you're talking about Virgin Islands?'

'Of course,' Andreas hit his palm against his forehead, 'I'm not thinking straight, Sir Francis Drake.'

Saffi interrupted, 'what about Sir Francis Drake, you just said he spent a lot of time here.'

'Yes, yes, but the Sir Francis Drake Channel runs along Tortola.'

'OK, what does that have to do with anything?' Saffi was confused.

'Tortola is the main island in the British Virgin Islands and Tortola in Spanish is Turtledove, like in the clue. And The Sir Francis Drake Channel also runs up to Virgin Gorda, which if you want a literal translation is a fat virgin.' Andreas smiled.

'So I assume we're off to the Virgin Islands next, where are they?' Saffi asked.

'Saffi are you going to love the Virgin Islands, they are a couple of days away, but the sailing is amazing around there, and I think I know who we'll be meeting, but you'd better put the answer in the sheet to make sure.'

'Oh yes, the answer,' Saffi had become distracted, 'we have two five letter words, GORDA and DRAKE, I'll give DRAKE a go first.' Saffi entered the letters and a name appeared, 'so come on Andreas, who do you think it is we're meeting?' She asked.

'My guess would be Cap'n Skip,' Andreas could not contain his smile, 'Am I right? Is that what it says?'

'You seem very excited about 'Cap'n Skip. Who is he?'

'Am I right, come on Saffi, tell me.'

'Yes, you're right. We need to find Cap'n Skip. Now who is he, and what do I need to know before we get there?'

Andreas breathed a sigh of relief, again the conversation would be steered away from him, Jack and their business; it would take him at least thirty minutes to talk about Cap'n Skip, and that would just be scratching the surface of this character. Andreas began.

'Cap'n Skip, short for Captain Skipper, no one was ever very sure if he wanted to be called Captain, or Skipper, so the words morphed and became Cap'n Skip. If you are on really good terms with him you can call him Skip, or Cap'n, depending on how he's feeling that day.'

'I think I'm confused already.' Saffi replied.

'I would imagine he'll let you call him what you want, to say he was close to Jack and Lillian would be a real understatement.'

'He knew my mother?'

'Yes, he was one of the first people they met in the islands once they'd bought their boat. Now I need to get my dates right, but I would imagine it was sometime after Matt, you remember Matt, the coastguard?'

'Yes, of course, it wasn't that long ago.' Saffi replied.

'Yes, sorry, well after Matt got Jack and Lillian sorted out, they carried on down the islands. Now clearly your dad didn't know much about sailing or the Caribbean at that time, cos one of the things you don't do is go from St Kitts, where Matt had left them, directly over the Antigua.'

'Why not, what's wrong with going to Antigua?' She asked.

'It's not Antigua that's the problem; it's the route they took, directly east to Antigua from St Kitts.'

Saffi interrupted, 'I'm sorry Andreas I don't think I'm following you, what's wrong with going east to Antigua, if that's the way Antigua is?'

'It means you're sailing directly into the prevailing wind, otherwise known as the Trade Winds, and directly into the sea and waves. It makes it really uncomfortable; the boat smashing through huge waves and it takes forever.' He replied.

'Oh!' Saffi replied, still as confused as before.

'So, as I was saying, you father put your mother through probably one of the most uncomfortable sails they encountered along their journey, and when they finally got to Antigua they ended up in English Harbour where they met Cap'n Skip.'

'So why aren't we going to Antigua?' Saffi asked.

'Because Cap'n Skip lives in the Virgins now.'

'You just said they met him in Antigua.'

'Yes, but that was back in the seventies, this is now, he's moved since then.'

'Oh, I see. I think!'

'Let me give you a bit more history on Cap'n Skip. Firstly, he's English, like you, from good Old Blighty.'

'How did he end up in the Virgins?' Saffi asked.

'You mean how did he end up in Antigua? His father was a vicar posted to one of the churches on Antigua when Cap'n Skip was a small boy. He didn't move to the Virgins until the late eighties. Now by that time Antigua had became a bit of a political hotbed, after it had achieved independence in the early eighties. In fact, there was a real big hoo-hah when the son of the prime minister was involved in smuggling weapons to a cartel in Columbia from Israel, and to make things worse another of his sons was locked up for smuggling cocaine.'

'You hear a lot of talk about drugs in the Caribbean, it's not something you or Jack have been involved with, is it? Saffi asked, cautiously.

'Jack and me, involved with drugs, what makes you say that?' Andreas was desperately searching for a way out of that question.

'That's not exactly a yes or a no answer, it was a simple question, have you ever been involved in drugs?' Saffi was becoming suspicious.

'I've never taken them, if that's what you mean, well not if you don't include booze, which of course is a drug, and there have been a few times when Jack and I were completely 'out of it' after a few bottles of rum, some of these Caribbean rums really hit the spot,'

Saffi interrupted, 'you're waffling Andreas, which means you're hiding something, I'll ask you again, were you or my father ever involved with drugs, yes or no?'

'It's not quite that simple Saffi.'

'Yes, it is, yes or no?' now she was getting angry.

'Look Saffi, I said that I had a lot to explain to you and that it would be better if we did it in private, on board, and I promised to tell you everything, so can we just drop this question for now, we're nearly at the marina?' His eyes searched her face imploringly and then stared straight ahead. Saffi did not reply.

They arrived at the marina having continued the journey in silence. Andreas parked the car, got out and began looking for Linalli. Saffi had other ideas. She needed some space.

'I think I need some fresh air, I'll come and find you later.' Saffi's tone told Andreas all he needed to know, and so he headed in the direction of the moored boats. Linalli was easy to spot and he could see Tariq waiting on the deck with his two crewmates. As Andreas boarded he could sense something was wrong, Tariq was avoiding eye contact.

'What's wrong?' Andreas asked.

'I'm sorry Andreas, but there's something not right with the autopilot, I didn't want to tell you on the phone, I thought I'd be able fix it before you got here, but it's stumped me.'

'What sort of problem, how long has it been like it?'

'It started about half way down here, it's a good job there were three of us, we've had to hand steer most of the way. I didn't want to get an engineer to look at it until I'd told you.' Tariq voice was apologetic.

'What have you looked at?' Andreas asked.

'I've checked for blown fuses, checked the power, I've checked the wiring from the auto pilot control unit and the wiring from the flux gate compass.'

'What about the power to the rudder actuator unit?' Andreas asked.

'Ollie and Conrad are just doing that.' Tariq called to them to ask how they were getting on.

'Everything's fine down here.' The reply came from Ollie.

'Do you want me to find an engineer to take a look?' Tariq asked.

'No, thanks, I'll just check everything myself first, just in case there's something you've missed, no offence, but I know this boat a lot better than you.' Andreas replied as he headed down the companionway.

'None taken, anything you want me to do, or is it best we all stay out of your way for a while?'

'Thanks for the offer, but probably best I check this out, and besides when Saffi arrives, you probably don't want to be around to hear that conversation, I'm not exactly in her good books at the moment.'

'Saffi? Is that the broad you told me about, where is she?' Tariq asked as he indicated to the others to get off the boat.

'Yes, but for god's sake don't call her a broad within earshot of her. Let's just say she's gone to get some fresh air, and to get me out of her sight. The problem is we need to get moving down to the BVI and without an autopilot that's going to be tricky with a non-sailor on board; this will really piss her off.'

'The BVIs, that's not too far, couple of day hops and you'll be there.'

'Yeah I know, but I don't know where we're going after that.'

'Why's that, the lady can't make her mind up, typical woman.' Tariq didn't want to sound too obvious in his questioning, but he knew this would be good info for El Jeffe.

'If only it was that simple. Look guys, thanks for your help and bringing the boat down here but I need to look at this autopilot before Saffi gets here.' Andreas said as he disappeared below.

Tariq knew when to push further and when to walk away, they would return in an hour and offer their services as crew, 'come on guys, let's go get a beer,' he said to Ollie and Conrad as he walked towards the bar, 'we'll come back shortly.' As they walked along the quay, a young woman came barging through them. She didn't stop to apologise. She just carried on walking. Tariq turned and watched her get on Linalli, 'that must be the infamous Saffi, perhaps we'll come back sooner than planned, eh boys?' Tariq smirked as he said it.

Saffi was still angry with Andreas, but knew that she would solve nothing by not talking to him. She found Linalli and got on board, calling for Andreas as she did.

'Down here, I'm just investigating a little problem we have.' He replied.

'Problem, what sort of problem?'

'It appears that the autopilot has given up the ghost, Tariq has checked the obvious things, but I just want to go over a couple things before I call an engineer.'

'Is that a big problem, no autopilot, does it mean we can't sail?' Saffi asked, her anger diminishing.

'We can still sail, but we will have to hand-steer the whole way and as we don't know how far we're going, that could be a bit of a hindrance.' Andreas said as he came out from behind a panel that was crammed full of wires. He was going to continue with a sarcastic comment about her now talking to him, but he thought better of it.

'Is there anything I can do?' She asked.

Andreas wiped the sweat from his face, 'nope, if I can't fix it, then I'm not sure an engineer can, but I'll just pop over to the marina office to see if there is anyone around. You may as well look at the next clue after the BVI, at least that way we know where we're meant to be heading after that.' He grabbed a clean T-shirt and left Saffi on her own.

She opened the laptop and looked at the next clue. She read aloud to herself, 'Island Clue –"*In confusion, I sat at, in a place known by a much shorter name*", well that makes no sense,' she continued aloud, "*would you write about this extinct volcano or rather take a 'hike?'*" Saffi picked up the Caribbean Island guidebook and looked through the index for extinct volcanoes, but there were only references to active ones. She knew this was pointless, not knowing the islands in detail. She looked at the map at the front of the guide to see if any of the islands near to the BVI would shed any light, they didn't. She was however shocked to see how far they had travelled from the Bahamas, and wondered how much further they would be travelling to unravel the mystery Jack had left them.

She sat down feeling dejected and lonely and looked at the crossword and the entries they'd solved already, EXUMA, JAMES, PONCE, and remembered they had not found a crossword reference for Julio's answer. Andreas had said there was a copy of the newspaper cutting on the boat that Julio had shown them. She went into the main cabin where she had seen her photo album a week or so ago. She saw the album and the other marked Lillian, but again decided it was still too soon to look at that one. She looked further along the shelf and found what looked like a scrapbook. Taking it off the shelf, she sat down on the bed and began to flick through the pages. She realised there would be time to look at everything else on the boat, sometime in the future, for now she was trying to find the newspaper article.

After a few more pages she came across the newspaper cutting, she removed it carefully, and re-read the article, remembering the story of the bottle of rum they'd found. The words still seemed to mean more to her than she understood, but still nothing stood out regarding the crossword. She turned the page over, nothing obvious on that side either, but she was convinced the crossword reference was hidden in the cutting somewhere. She read the article repeatedly and was about to give up. She opened the scrapbook to return the cutting, but as she replaced it, she could see that Jack had written the date above the cutting, 4th April 1993. He had underlined the date, but when she looked carefully he had only underlined the '4' and the 'A' from April, she looked at the newspaper cutting and he had done the same on the date of the newspaper, he had underlined the '4' and 'A'. She smiled as she realised what he had done, 4A, 4 across, the reference had been there all along, just not highlighted on Julio's copy. She went back to the table and entered the clue in the crossword. Four completed, six to go, she thought to herself; let's hope it's all worth it in the end.

Just at that moment Andreas also returned, 'Any luck with the clue?' he asked.

'No, not with the next one, but I have worked out the crossword referenced for Julio's clue,' and explained what she had found, 'any luck with an engineer?' she asked.

'Well at least that's a bit of good news; I had no luck with an engineer, well not one that was available to look at an auto pilot with any great confidence. I'm not sure what to do about this Saffi.' He said, his voice not hiding his concerns. He grabbed a beer from the fridge and went up to the cockpit. Saffi followed and sat next to him.

'Well, what are our options?' she asked.

'Far and few between I'm afraid, especially if we want to keep moving.' He sighed and took another gulp of beer. As he placed the bottle on the table, he saw Tariq walking along the quay.

'Permission to come aboard?' He asked jovially.

'Of course Tariq, this is Saffi. I told you about her, Saffi, this is Tariq and presumably his two crewmates.' Andreas replied. Saffi smiled and moved to sit next to Andreas while the others sat down.

'Yes, this is Ollie and Conrad, without them it would have been a nightmare with no autopilot. Have you fixed it yet?' Ollie and Conrad said hi to everyone and then sat quietly, clearly knowing their places when Tariq was talking.

'No luck I'm afraid, nothing obvious and no engineer available, we are as they say, up a creek without a paddle.' Andreas told them.

'Well can you wait for an engineer?' Tariq enquired.

'No, we really have to keep moving, we need to get to the BVI.'

'And after that, where are you heading?'

'That we don't know yet; it's a bit of a mystery our tour of the Caribbean.' Andreas replied trying to be as evasive as possible.

'Well we would know if we could solve the next clue.' Saffi interjected. Andreas could have kicked her, instead he gave her a look that said, don't say another word.

'Clue, what are you on some sort of treasure hunt or something?' Tariq asked, hoping he would get enough to tell El Jeffe.

'Nothing so exciting I'm afraid, just trying to show Saffi some of the Caribbean, that's all,' Andreas hoped he'd diverted the questions, 'Saffi, why don't you get these guys a beer, there's a love.' She began to protest but realised he wanted her out of the way and she did as he asked. When she was out of earshot Andreas continued, 'I don't want to worry her unnecessarily, she's never sailed before, it won't be a problem just the two of us, but I'm trying to keep the whole thing a bit low key.'

Tariq saw his entry into the solution, 'what about if you had some crew with you, would that make life easier for you and Saffi?'

'It would, but I've no idea how long we are going to be away, who do you have in mind? Andreas already knew.

'We'd be delighted to help you out, for a small fee obviously, but we've nothing to get back for, nothing that won't keep, and hey, there are still a few islands I've not seen in the Caribbean, it will be an adventure for all of us.' Tariq said, Ollie and Conrad nodding in agreement.

'I'll have to run it by Saffi; I'm not sure how she'll react.'

'React to what?' Saffi said reappearing with the beers.

'Oh nothing much, I'll tell you later.' Andreas replied, but Tariq was not working to Andreas agenda.

'I just suggested to Andreas that if you can't get the autopilot fixed me, and the boys here would love to help you out, for a small fee. . . We could help you sail to wherever you want to go, what do you say Saffi?' Tariq gave her the most genuine smile he could muster.

'I don't know, what do you think Andreas?' Saffi knew from her previous mistake not to just agree to anything.

'Look,' Tariq said, 'why don't we leave you two alone to have a think about it, we'll come back in an hour, if you want to go along with the idea great, if you don't it's no skin off our noses.' Tariq, Ollie and Conrad grabbed their beers and left Andreas and Saffi to discuss their suggestion.

~~~

Tariq left Ollie and Conrad in a bar while he made his call to Luis.

'El Jeffe, Tariq here, I have good news for you.'

'Good, go ahead.' Luis needed some good news about catching up with Andreas.

'Andreas has arrived on the boat, with the girl. As you asked, we created a few little 'problems' on the boat, and I think I have convinced them to take us with them. They are just discussing the option and we're going back in an hour to find out their answer.'

'Good, good Tariq, do you know where they are heading next?'

'They are definitely going to the BVI next, but after that we don't know. The girl, Saffi, hinted at some kind of clue they need to solve, but Andreas cut her short, clearly not wanting us to know more.'

'Yes, that would be the sort of thing Jack would do, hide everything from sight. Do you think you can manipulate the girl?' Luis enquired.

'Yes, if I can get Andreas out of the way, it shouldn't be too difficult, she doesn't appear to be, how can I say, very worldly wise, probably trusts everyone without thinking of any consequences. I'll call you when we have their decision.'

'Good work Tariq; I will await your call.' Luis hung up.

~~~

Andreas and Saffi looked at each other, both knowing it would be a good solution having crew on board to help, but neither wished to admit it. Finally, Saffi spoke.

'If they came along, it would leave us both free to work on the clues without having to actually sail the boat.'

'Yes, and I could spend some time teaching you about sailing and navigation.' Andreas replied.

'So what's the problem?' Saffi asked.

'I don't know, I can't put my finger on it, but I'm just not happy with the situation, but I don't see another way out.

'What if we get them to come as far as the BVI with us, and if we're not happy after that we don't take them any further.' Saffi offered as a solution.

'That's not a bad idea actually, and in that way we could go directly from here to the BVI without having to stop at the Spanish and US Virgin Islands, it would save us a few days. If you're happy with that, we'll suggest it to them.'

'And if we still need someone else then perhaps Cap'n Skip can put us onto someone.' Saffi suggested.

When Tariq and the boys returned, Andreas told them of their plan, that they could help them go directly to the BVI, leaving the following day. Tariq agreed this was a good solution, he said they would be back the following morning before 8am to get an early start. El Jeffe would be pleased Tariq thought, and telephoned him as soon as he was out of sight of Linalli.

~~~

'It's arranged, we will sail with them to the BVI at a minimum, we leave tomorrow morning, what do you want me to do El Jeffe?' Tariq asked.

'Just get as close as you can to the girl. Find out everything you can about these clues. They must be leading them to what Jack wants them to find, what is rightfully mine,' Luis' voice became angry. 'I will send Raoul to meet you; we need to get them away from the BVI, it's too public, find out what islands they are visiting, and where they have been already, and if you can, find out who they have met. Send me a text with any information you find out, I may need to take further action. You have done well Tariq, but whatever you do, don't lose them, find a way to stay with them as long as you can.' Luis hung up and called for Raoul. He was already waiting.

'Tariq has done well, he is sailing with Andreas and the girl to the BVI tomorrow morning from Puerto Rico, it will only take a day to get there, I want you to get up there and stay in the shadows. I have told Tariq you are on your way, but I want Tariq to stay as close to them as possible. Andreas doesn't suspect Tariq, yet, but if he sees you, he will know there is something wrong. I need you to be the eyes and ears of what Tariq does not see, and to be available for whatever may need to occur.'

Raoul acknowledged Luis' instructions and arranged for one of the planes to be prepared for his departure, he would leave immediately in order to be in the BVI before Andreas and Saffi arrived. He was glad of the opportunity to get back to the BVI, he had some unfinished business with Cap'n Skip, he was sure that's who Jack would send them to, but if he got their first and dealt with Cap'n, that may slow their progress.

Chapter 18

As agreed, Tariq, Ollie and Conrad came back to Linalli the following morning. They were clean-shaven and smartly dressed which came as a bit of a shock to Saffi and Andreas.

'You scrub up well, what's the occasion, birthday or wedding?' Andreas joked.

'Very funny, Andreas, but we take pride in our work; a good reference is worth much more than a bad one.' Tariq replied. Luis had told him to "get some uniforms, throw Andreas off the scent". They had been shopping and bought matching polo shirts and shorts the night before.

Saffi came up on deck. 'You look smart boys, nice effort, thanks.'

'See, Andreas, it doesn't take much to give a compliment. Thanks Saffi.' Tariq said.

'Sorry guys, it's just that this is not the impression Carina gave me when she pointed me in your direction for crewing on Linalli.' Andreas replied.

'Well that's probably because I haven't seen my cousin for a good few years and she probably doesn't realise that I'm trying to move up in the world. That's a point, do you know if we'll be heading for St Kitts, it would be good to see her.' He knew Andreas trusted Carina, but that's because Andreas had no idea that she'd been working under cover for Luis on St Kitts for too long to remember.

'As I said guys, let's just get to the BVI before we start making our way down the island chain. See how we all get on first. If everyone is ready we need to check out with Customs, I want to be on our way as early as possible.' Andreas replied.

~~~

Andreas and Tariq both knew that the route from Puerto Del Rey to Tortola would take them in between the small islands of the Spanish, US and British Virgin Islands, a tricky route in the best of conditions. Andreas had kept his concerns hidden from Saffi and he was glad to have some experienced sailors on board. When he was happy that they were clear of the initial dangers of the coast of Puerto Rico, he went below to see Saffi.

'Come on then, let's hear the next clue, you said you'd looked at it, but couldn't make any sense of it. If we can get the clues solved en route we may be able to plan ahead and take the quickest route.'

'You don't think Jack has put them in any particular order for a reason. It occurred to me that some of the people we've met so far were able to help with the next clue. Remember, Jacqui helped us with the Puerto Rico clues.' Saffi joined him on the sofa with her laptop and opened it at the required place.

'You can never tell with Jack. It does seem like we're following the islands, but that would make sense from the Bahamas to Puerto Rico, but from here on who knows where he's sending us. Fire away then, clue number six if I'm not mistaken.'

Saffi read aloud as usual. '" *Island Clue - In confusion, I sat at, in a place known by a much shorter name",* and the answer clue reads, "*would you write about this extinct volcano or rather take a hike"?'* I've looked in the guide books for extinct volcanoes but they don't list them, probably too many, and I'm a bit confused by the way he's written the island clue, the commas are in the wrong place.' Saffi said.

'Read it to me as he has written it, word for word, comma for comma.' Andreas asked.

" *In confusion,"* Saffi paused, *"I sat at,"* she paused again, *"in a place known by a much shorter name".* She looked at Andreas, who looked back at her, also confused.

'OK, the way I see it is we are looking for an island that maybe has a nick name, a bit like we call the British Virgin Islands the BVI or the Virgins, but I don't get the bit about being *"confused while I sat at."*The grammar's all wrong. I assume we are looking for an extinct volcano that we can hike up, but I'm not sure about the reference to writing about it, hand me the Caribbean guide.'

He flicked through the pages at random, she interrupted him. 'Why don't we go to the section immediately after the BVI and see where it is, we know we've already been to the islands before there.'

'It's worth a try, I suppose,' and moved to the end of the section, 'here we go, next is Anguilla. There are definitely no extinct volcanoes there, its way too flat. Then it's St Martin, half Dutch, and half French. I've spent a lot of time there and again I don't believe there are any extinct volcanoes there as I know there won't be on St Barth's.' He paused and continued to look through the pages, 'Saba, now there is a mountainous island with lots of hikes, but I'm not aware of it being called by anything other than Saba, not a name you can shorten really.' Then it came to him, he scanned through the pages and put the guide down in front of Saffi and pointed at the page for St Eustatius.

'And from this I am to deduce what?' She asked.

'Nothing, that's the next island, read the first line of the intro.' Andreas pointed it out for her; it read *"St Eustatius – commonly known as Statia."*

'Oh I get it, *"In confusion, I sat at "*is an anagram of Statia, but what about the extinct volcano.' She asked. Again, Andreas pointed to the next page and Saffi read aloud, *"The Quill: Hike to the island's highest point and admire the scenery around this dormant volcano."* Saffi looked back at the clue, 'Quill. Very good. *"Would you write about this extinct volcano or rather take a 'hike'?"*So how far is Statia from the BVI Andreas?

'It's about a hundred and twenty miles; if we only make four or five knots it will take over thirty hours, if not more. If we can't get the auto pilot fixed in Tortola I think 'Tom, Dick and Harry' upstairs will be staying on board for a bit longer.'

'Well why don't we try and solve all the clues now and see exactly where we've got to go, then we can make a better judgement call in the BVI.' Saffi said.

'Not so fast, we need to put the answer from clue six into the puzzle to see who we're meeting.' Andreas said.

Saffi typed in the word QUILL into the puzzle and the name Abigail Jones appeared, 'Do you know her?' she asked.

'I met her once a few years back, but Statia isn't that big an island so she shouldn't be too difficult to find. We can call her from the BVI. No point dithering on that clue, what's next?'

'The island clue reads, *"The Carib name of Karukera, 'island of lovely waters'* and the place clue is *"Between two islands with mistaken lands, lies a salty pass between"*. Saffi read.

'That means nothing; all the islands have lovely waters. Also, does he mean that the main island has two other islands, because loads of the Caribbean islands have little islands lying off them? You look in the book; I'll get the sailing chart over, that will give us an overall view of the Caribbean and all its islands.'

Saffi looked in the guide, moving through each section in turn, looking at the map of the island and reading its history. Andreas laid the chart on the table and waited for her to read from the guide.

'St Kitts and Nevis, isn't that where you live?'

'It's where I have a place to stay; where I live, is wherever I am at the time.' Andreas replied. Saffi tutted, just the sort of thing she expected a wanderer to say. She skimmed through the history section.

'Well it's not there, St Kitts was known as Liamuiga, Fertile Island,' she continued reading, 'wait a minute it says here that the

Caribs knew it as Oualie, Land of Beautiful Waters, isn't that the same thing?'

'No, we're looking for the island of lovely waters, St Kitts is the island of beautiful waters, something entirely different,' He said with a smile, 'please continue with the next island.'

'Yes, but there are two islands, St Kitts and Nevis and the clue said 'between two islands with mistaken lands, and the guide makes a discernible difference between them.' She said.

'OK, tell me the name of the passage between the two islands.' Andreas asked, already knowing the answer. Saffi turned the page and looked at the detailed map.

'The Narrows.' She said.

'Exactly, nothing to do with salt, we are looking for a salty pass.'

'OK, OK, mister know-it-all, you look through the guide. 'But Andreas was too interested in the sailing chart on the table.

'Hey look at this,' he pointed to a big island on the map that resembled a butterfly, 'look up Guadeloupe in the guide, and see what the Caribs used to call it.' He asked.

'Why, that's only one island, we're looking for two?'

'Just look it up please. It may look like one island, it may only have one name, but there are two different names for the landmasses. If you look closely here on the chart, you will see that the River Salee runs through the middle and, if I'm not mistaken, Salee means salt. Yes, look here in the dictionary, the verb "to salt", is saler, or the adjective is salé(e), Salt River.' He smiled smugly at Saffi.

'OK, but what's that got to do with the mistaken lands?' she asked as she found the chapter on Guadeloupe in the guide. 'You were right about the Caribs; they called it Karuker.' She showed Andreas the page in the book; he took it and started to read about its history. As he turned the page, he saw a map of the island and showed Saffi the river.

'Look,' he said, 'the two land masses have different names, Grande-Terre and Basse-Terre.'

'Yes, but more interesting than that is this section here,' she pointed and read the section headed *"What's in a name"*, 'see what it says here, *"the names given to the twin islands are perplexing. The eastern island, which is smaller and flatter is named Grande-Terre, which means 'big land', while the larger, more mountainous western island is named Basse-Terre, meaning 'flat land', just like in the clue 'mistaken lands"*. So we go to Guadeloupe after St Kitts.'

'Yes, but who are we going to see in Guadeloupe, put SALEE in the puzzle.' Andreas said.

She entered the letters and a name appeared, Pablo François. 'Do you know him? Saffi asked.

Andreas shook his head, 'another one of Jacks acquaintances I've yet to meet.'

Just as Saffi had put the word into the puzzle, Tariq sent Ollie down to make some tea. Tariq told him to listen to anything they were saying. 'Tea guys or would you like something cold to drink?' Ollie asked.

'Oh tea would be nice.' Saffi said.

Andreas closed the laptop lid down as she said it, 'yeah, great, thanks. Everything OK 'up top'?' He asked.

'Yeah, fine, calmer than expected for the time of year,' he looked at Saffi, 'you any good with those things?' Ollie pointed to the laptop as he filled the kettle.

'Yes,' Saffi replied, 'I used to use them all day at work, but they can be a real pain when they go wrong. Why?'

'Oh I just get a bit confused with them, it's all a bit beyond me, bit like the chart plotter on the boat and the GPS, I tend to leave that to Tariq and Conrad. I'm more of your hands-on type of guy; I leave the clever stuff to them.' Ollie said. He got the mugs from the cupboard, 'how do you take your tea?'

'Milk, no sugar.' Saffi and Andreas said together.

'I'd love to know how to use them a bit more, but we never seem to have enough time, always on the go or fixing something.' Ollie replied.

'I'm sure you're not that bad at it, but if you'd like some help, I'm sure I could show you a few short cuts.' Saffi offered.

Ollie handed them their tea, 'that would be great if you could. I don't always want to be reliant on Tariq for all my work, thanks Saffi.' Ollie said as he went back up to the cockpit.

'Be careful what you offer, Saffi,' Andreas said, 'I don't know everything about these guys, I only know Tariq because of his cousin on St Kitts.'

'Oh you're so melodramatic sometimes, not everyone's a villain, if I can offer a little bit of help I will, after all where would we be without them. Come on let's look at the next clue.

~~~

Ollie handed Tariq his tea, 'Did you hear anything of interest?' Tariq asked.

'Yes, I hung around a bit before going down; they will be visiting Guadeloupe, some guy called Pablo Francois, or something like that. Andreas doesn't know him. Also I've asked Saffi to give me some help on the computer.' Ollie said with a smile.

'But you know how to use a computer, what's the point of that?' Tariq said accusingly.

'I know I can use a computer, it's a ploy, so that I can get access to their computer and find out the rest of the clues.' Ollie answered, he was fed up with being treated like the imbecile of the group, he had more 'know-how' than Tariq and Conrad put together. He planned to let Luis know that he was the brains behind this job he had sent them on.

'How are you going to do that, it's got passwords and protection, she won't just hand you the computer and say "here you go, here's what we're up to."' Tariq's belittling tone annoyed Ollie, but he held his tongue, he would show him. He would let Tariq think he was still in charge, for the time being.

~~~

Saffi read the next clue to Andreas, *"Island Clue - When Columbus had a 'day of rest' he stumbled on this island."* The answer clue is, *"the 18th Century left this town with a mixed identity."*

'So we're looking for another of Columbus' finds, could be any of the islands.'

'Day of rest is normally what people refer to as Sunday, you know the Lord's Day of rest, there aren't any islands called or sound like Sunday, are there?' Saffi asked.

'Not that I can think of, but then Columbus wouldn't call it Sunday as he was Italian so he would say Dom-én-ica.' Andreas said with an emphasised bad Italian accent.

'OK, so are there any islands that sound like Dom-én-ica.' Saffi replied with a similarly bad Italian accent.

'Well there's Dominica.' He replied without the accent.

'Then I would imagine that's what where were going, what about the second part of the clue, *"the 18th Century left this town with a mixed identity"*.' Saffi repeated.

Andreas looked at the chart on the table and Saffi looked at the map in the guide, Saffi began reading the names of the towns on Dominica, starting at the top and working clockwise around the island. 'Portsmouth, Anse Du Mé, Calibishie, Marigot, Bataka, Salybia, Sinekum, Castle Bruce, La Plaine, Delices, Petite Savanne,

Scotts Head, Soufriere, Roseau, Trafalgar, Massacre, Layou, Mero, Salisbury, Dublanc and back to Portsmouth.' she said.

'Yep, I agree with all those names, and they seem a mixed up bunch if you ask me. I mean there are French, English, Carib and who knows what in that lot, where do we start?' Andreas replied as he sat down back next to Saffi.

'I think we should discount the English names and write a list of the others, get some paper, I'll read the names,' Andreas did as he was asked and wrote the names Saffi read out. Now all we have to do is find out what happened in the 18th Century. Let's see what the guide says,' Saffi read the guide, 'here we are. *"For the remainder of the 18th Century Dominica was caught up in the French and British skirmishes that marked the era, with the island changing hands between the two powers several times"*, that will be why there are so many French and English names, but what does he mean by mixed identity, what's Jack getting at?'

They looked through the list over and over again, but neither of them could decipher the clue's meaning.

'Let's think about this logically, we are looking for a name of a town that is mixed up, but the emphasis is on the 18th Century when the island was fought between the French and the English, so what we are looking for is a name that is...' Andreas interrupted Saffi, '...that is half French and half English.' He said.

'Exactly, so what's on the list that could be half French and half English,' she read the names aloud and slowly breaking them down by syllables, 'Anse-Du-Mé, Cal-i-bi-shie, Bat-aka, Sal-y-bia, Sin-e-kum, La-Plaine, Del-i-ces, Petite-Sav-ann-e, Sou-fri-ere, Rose-au, Lay-ou, Me-ro, Du-blanc, none of them sound half French and English.' She said.

'Perhaps we're going about this the wrong way. Perhaps we need to look at them written down, not how they sound. Let me have a go,' Andreas looked at the list and began rewriting them and read aloud as he wrote, 'An se Du Mé, Cal ib is hie, Bat a ka, Salybia, Sine kum, La Plaine, Deli ces, Petite Savanne, Soufriere, Ro seau, La you, Mero, Dub lanc.'

'Go back, what was that you just said, it began with La.' Saffi was excited.

'La You, Layou?' he replied.

'Yes, that's it, La, French for 'the, and 'you', English for 'you', when I pronounced it I said Lay Ou, not La You, and its five letters, Layou.'

Saffi enter the word into the puzzle and as she expected a name appeared. 'Pico,' she said, 'is that his full name?' She looked at Andreas.

'Yes, that will be his full name, Pico, one of the Indian River's Boat Boys, you'll like him.' Andreas replied.

'I'm sorry, the Indian River's Boat Boys, what in the world is a boat boy.'

'Boat boys are local guides. They are there to help the likes of me and you find our way around Dominica and its sights, in particular the Indian River. Motorised boats aren't allowed up the Indian River. The Boat Boys will row you up there, give you a guided tour and drop you at the rainforest bar at the end of the river for a refreshing, overpriced beer, before brining you back down the river.' He said.

'Is that all they do, must get very boring.'

'No, that's not all they do. They are there to help you with things like mooring your boat, security in the anchorages, getting fresh fruit and bread for you on your boat.'

'Why can't I moor my boat and get fruit and bread on shore, why do I need a boat boy, why do they need to provide security?' Saffi asked.

'Because not all anchorages are paradise. Some of them are not that nice at all, and some of them have quite a lot of crime. You, on your nice expensive boat, clearly have more than most people on the islands, and are classed as a prime target. There is quite a lot of theft, among other things, especially on the more remote, less commercialised islands. So the Boat Boy Schemes were set up to help those on boats to know who to trust and who not to, for a cost, of course.'

'So is it safe to go there, do we need to pay for protection?' Saffi sounded scared now.

'No, because Jack knew almost everyone on the island and has lots of friends there, we'll be fine. You never know, we may still have Tariq and the boys on board when we get there. But let's not worry about that yet,' he could sense Saffi's uneasiness, 'what's the next clue, we must be nearly at the end of them now.'

'Yes, yes you're right, um, let me see, "*Island Clue - This French Island was birthplace to one of Frances' most famous Empresses*" and answer clue, "*Then find the 19th hole of her birthplace*".' Saffi read aloud.

'There are only four French islands in the Caribbean, we're already going to Guadeloupe in the other clue, we've passed St

Bart's and St Martin is only half French. Navigationally, if we're heading south, I think it must be Martinique, which if my school history holds true, is the birthplace of the Empress Josephine.' Andreas said.

'As is 'Josephine and Napoleon'?' Saffi asked.

'Yes, check the guide, but I'm sure she was born somewhere on Martinique, I think there's a museum or something.'

Saffi looked in the guide, 'you're right, there's a whole section about Josephine, I never realised she came from the Caribbean. What about the second part of the clue it says then find the 19th hole of her birthplace.

'OK, the 19th hole is an obvious reference to a golf course, does the guide tell us where she was born and is there a golf course nearby?' Andreas asked.

'It says here she was born in Trois-Îlets in 1763,' she turned to the page for Trois-Îlets and read to Andreas, 'small working town, blah blah, central square, quaint church where Josephine was baptized, blah blah, ah, here we are, *a few miles west of the town the island's golf course and a botanical park.* So do we need to use the word TROIS or ILETS?' Saffi said, as she entered the letters, TROIS and a name appeared.

'Go on then, who is it this time?' Andreas asked.

'Someone called Salvador Hareau, ever heard of him?'

'No, another new friend to meet,' Andreas sighed, 'I think I've had enough mystery solving for one day, at least we know where we heading, come on Saffi, let's go up and help the guys sailing, you can have a go at steering if you like.

~~~

Up on deck Conrad was at the helm, Tariq and Ollie were sitting in the cockpit chatting.

'I hear you're going to give Ollie some computer lessons Saffi, thanks for that, it will be a real help to him.' Tariq smiled at Saffi, she smiled back. She didn't get the same bad feeling about Tariq and his crew that Andreas did, but knew now that she had to be careful.

'Yes, I'm not sure how much help I can be, I just know the basics really, but if I can help I will.' Saffi looked around, the sea was dotted with little islands in every direction, 'is it long to go, we've been going a few hours now?' She asked.

'Considering we going into the wind and sea we're making good time; should be there by mid afternoon.' Tariq turned to Ollie, 'why don't you go down below and get some lunch for everyone?' He gave him a knowing look that Ollie understood immediately, 'Saffi, why don't you have a go at the helm, Conrad can show you how?'

Andreas interrupted, 'Good idea, I'll show you how Saffi, come on.'

Andreas took the helm from Conrad who then offered to help Ollie with lunch; Tariq stayed in the cockpit with Saffi and Andreas and 'helped' him show Saffi the helm, this way he knew he could keep them occupied while Conrad and Ollie would not be disturbed down below.

~~~

Ollie stayed in the galley shouting questions through the companionway, asking where things were, while Conrad started to scout around the boat looking for anything that may be of use to them. He saw Saffi's laptop on the table and next to it was a list of names, he read them to himself and knew immediately that these were all names from Dominica, and whispered to Ollie what he had found.

'Now we know they need to go to St Kitts, Guadeloupe and Dominica. We need to find out how many clues there are and whether they have solved them all.' Conrad said.

'We need to get Tariq here to see what he wants to do, go upstairs and make up an excuse to get him down here,' Ollie said, 'but make sure the others stay up there.

Conrad went up to the cockpit and saw Andreas explaining to Saffi how to steer the boat. He called out as he reached the cockpit.

'It's good to learn a new skill, I'm not very good at helming, do you mind if I listen in, I always find listening to someone different gives you another view, Tariq can you help Ollie down below while I watch Andreas.' Tariq was about to protest when he saw the look on Conrad's face and knew he was needed below.

'No that's fine Conrad, you go sit and listen to Andreas and I will help with lunch. You're doing a fine job Saffi, you're a natural.' He smiled at her as he left the cockpit.

As he went down the companionway, he could see Ollie waiting for him, beckoning him out of sight of the others.

'What is it, this better be important.' Tariq snapped.

'We've discovered that they are heading for Dominica at some point, we already know they're going to St Kitts and Guadeloupe, we wanted to know how you want to proceed. From what we've heard they need to visit these islands to find more out information to do with the clue, and I have a plan.' Ollie said.

'Oh you have a plan do you, well best you fill me in.' Tariq knew Ollie was ambitious and watched his every move, he knew he was someone else he could not trust within Luis' organisation, along with all of his bosses' employees, there was 'no loyalty among thieves' he knew that.

'We need to lose Andreas. He knows El Jeffe will be following their every move, so we need to get Saffi away on her own. I suggest we take her hostage by force, at knifepoint and throw Andreas overboard. There is very little traffic in these waters so it could be days before anyone finds him, if at all. In this way, we have Saffi, the clues and most of the answers. We can force her to do whatever it is Jack has told her, and lead us to the fortune.' Ollie said

'Mmmm, I like you're thinking Ollie, but we will need to get Saffi on her own, down here without Andreas,' Tariq ran his hand through his hair while he was thinking, 'and if we leave it for another hour or two we will be far enough past Culebra and Vieques where there will be fewer boats. That's a good idea, but how do we get her down here?'

'After lunch I will persuade her to give me that computer lesson like she offered, we will have to do that on the table down here. You and Conrad will need to keep Andreas busy. After a while, when she is comfortable with me, I will make an excuse to call you down, you sit the other side of her and grab her at knifepoint. I will act surprised; we need her to still trust me so that she can show me things on the computer; she needs to be able to trust one of us.' Ollie said, pleased with his plan.

'Yes, I like your thinking, good plan. We need to brief Conrad so that he knows what will happen, but I can do that during lunch.' Tariq's mind was full of how this plan would work, but more so, of the praise he knew he would receive from El Jeffe.

Back in the cockpit Andreas was standing behind Saffi at the helm, describing how to steer the boat. 'It's like in the plane, find a spot on the horizon in the direction we want to go and aim at it, the waves and wind will try to push you off your course so you have to turn the helm to counteract their action, like this.' Andreas put his hands over Saffi's and moved the helm to keep the boat steering in the direction they needed. 'You see the compass here in front, we need to head east, or zero nine zero degrees on the compass, so you need to keep an eye on that too.'

Saffi smiled, she was enjoying herself, learning something new, but mainly enjoying the safe feeling of Andreas wrapped around her, since that night in Puerto Rico she had hardly thought of anything else, except solving the clues, and there was only one left. She was looking all around her, taking in the sounds and colours of the sea; little islands dotted all along the horizon, she breathed in the fresh sea air and sighed. She was beginning to enjoy this life.

Chapter 19

After lunch, Saffi whispered to Andreas, 'shall we go and solve the last clue?' She really wanted to be alone with Andreas, just for a short while. They made their excuses and went below.

'OK, here goes nothing, the last clue. Island clue: "*This floating island has a place for memories, on which 'I'll nail' my own*", she paused, 'you notice how *"I'll nail"* is in speech marks?'

'Yes, I saw that, what does the next part say?' Andreas said.

"A secret life, hidden beneath my blue eyes." I've seen a photo album in his cabin called that. I've not looked at it yet; I think its photos of mum.'

Sensing her feelings, Andreas said, 'let's be logical and do as we've done before and solve the island clue first, what was that bit again, I'll nail my own memories, or something?'

Saffi repeated the clue, 'What does he mean by a floating island? Islands don't float; they are just the land poking through the sea.'

'Not unless it's man-made, like a pontoon in a marina or something.' Andreas said.

'Well do you know of any marinas with floating pontoon in the islands?'

'Martinique has a marina with floating pontoons, but we've already got a clue to go there. The bit about nailing memories to it, it's not one of his anagrams again, is it? Write down the letters, see what we get.' Andreas suggested.

Saffi did so, writing the letters forwards, alphabetically and then backwards.

ILLNAIL -AIILLLN-LIANLLI

Now, seeing the letters written down it was obvious that it was an anagram of LINALLI.

'Of course,' Saffi said, 'the boat is a floating island, and I think he must want us to look at that album.'

Inside the cabin, Saffi quickly found the album. She lingered over opening the cover, scared of what it would reveal; her mother's life in photographs that she had never seen before. Andreas understood immediately and sat down beside her. He took the album from her and opened the cover. Saffi's breath caught in her throat and tears began to well in her eyes. The first photo was of the three of them, again when she was about three years old, they were on a beach, she was between Jack and Lillian, they were all smiling, and in her hand, she held a kite. Beneath the picture, Jack had written 'memories of my perfect life, my perfect blue eyes'. Saffi did not hold back her emotions now, she let the tears fall in abundance and Andreas took her in his arms to comfort her. She now understood how Nana felt a few weeks ago when she had finally let her feelings out when they had looked at the wedding album.

As Saffi composed herself Andreas turned the pages, her parents' life unfolding before her, pictures of their travels in the Caribbean, the orphanage, Andreas as a small boy, then back in England, after the accident, after Saffi was born.

Saffi looked at Andreas and smiled, 'I'm OK now, thanks. We need to find the answer to the clue, a secret life, hidden beneath my blue eyes, I've a feeling he's hidden something under a photograph, let's look at the first one.' Taking the album, she turned to the first page and carefully tried lifting the corners of the photograph, it was stuck fast to the page, but she could feel there was something beneath. 'I need something thin, a knife or something.' Andreas reached into his pocket and took out his Swiss Army knife and opened up a small pair of tweezers, 'will this do?' he said as he handed it to her.

'Perfect', she said as she gently slid the tweezers beneath the photograph, she managed to grab hold of what she could feel and pulled out a folded piece of paper. She opened it carefully, and read the words aloud. It was a poem.

> *Her deep blue eyes, just like her mother*
> *The secrets beneath, she will uncover*
> *Our story finally told, our hidden truth*
> *Our love endured, beyond our Island of Youth*

'That's beautiful.' Saffi said as she read it aloud again.

'Yes, it is, but I hate to be the bearer of bad news, but what does it have to do with our puzzle? Andreas asked.

Just as he said it, they could hear Ollie calling from the galley, 'Saffi are you down here?'

'Yes.' She replied, 'quick, put the note back under the picture, we don't want anyone finding it. Just coming, Ollie.' She walked to the galley to see Ollie standing at the stove, putting the kettle on.

'Do you want some tea?' he asked.

'That would be nice, thanks.'

'I wondered if you'd have time to give me a computer lesson this afternoon; I'm not really needed up at the helm.' He gave her a boyish grin.

'Oh yes, um, yes that won't be a problem, I'm just finishing something with Andreas, why don't you make some tea and I'll be right with you.'

She told Andreas what she was doing and, not feeling very happy about it, he went back up to the cockpit to see how Conrad and Tariq where coping.

~~~

Saffi and Ollie sat at the table and stared at the computer, 'so what is it you want to know how to do?' she asked.

'Well I've seen people do stuff with numbers and calculations, I think it's called Excel, or something, that might be useful as I'm not very good at maths.' Ollie said.

'OK, I'll show you a few basic things and how to use the help option, that way you can look up things yourself in the future.'

Saffi started by showing Ollie different examples of simple calculations, she then showed him how to do it and then got him to do the same thing. After about thirty minutes Ollie was becoming confident in what he was doing, 'do you mind if I show Tariq what I've learnt, I'm sure he'll be impressed?' Ollie asked, and he called up the companionway for Tariq to come downstairs. Ollie sat on the far side of Saffi, Tariq came down the stairs and sat on the other side of her and asked what Ollie had learnt.

'Saffi's been great, she's shown me loads of things with numbers, stuff we can use in the business, and it's been really helpful. Here let me show you.' Ollie leant forward toward the computer moving closer to Saffi so that she couldn't move. Tariq did the same on the other side, so that she was stuck between the two of them. Ollie began to show Tariq what he had learnt and as Saffi watched on with pride, she didn't notice Tariq's hand reach behind his back and bring out a large knife. In one swift move, he had pushed her right hand up behind her back and put the knife to her throat.

'Now, don't make a sound, this knife is very very sharp. Ollie, tie her hands behind her back.'

She started to scream, but Tariq pressed the knife harder into her throat.

'What are you doing?' Ollie protested; all part of the act.

'Just do it.' Tariq snarled at Ollie, 'now Saffi, I'd like you to stand up very slowly and move around the table.'

She did as instructed, her breathing was rapid and her heart was pounding.

'Now, walk slowly up the stairs, I'll make sure you don't fall, we don't want any nasty accidents with this knife, now do we?' Tariq said as he pushed her up the companionway. At the top of the stairs, she tried to scream at Andreas, but Tariq pushed the knife harder into her throat.

Up on deck Conrad had suggested that Andreas check the area for other boats through the binoculars, at the sound of Saffi's muffled scream Andreas turned to see her being pushed through the companionway with Tariq's knife at her throat.

'What the hell are you doing, let her go.' He shouted as he rushed towards her, but Conrad was ready with his gun and pointed it straight at Andreas, 'Oh no you don't. You stop right there and do exactly as we say. That way no-one will get hurt.' Conrad pushed the gun into Andreas shoulder and forced him to turn around to face the back of the boat.

'What we want you to do is very simple', Tariq said, 'just take a few steps off the back of the boat and everyone will be very happy and Saffi won't get hurt, do you think you can do that Andreas?'

Andreas' mind was working in overtime, calculating how long they had been travelling, how far they were from the nearest island and whether he could reach over and grab the hand-held VHF radio stowed at the helm before he jumped. He nodded his head in agreement and slowly turned towards Tariq, 'What guarantee do I have that you won't hurt Saffi?' he asked as Conrad grabbed his arm before he could turn a full 180 degrees, it was enough for Andreas to see the radio and it was just within his reach.

'We won't be hurting her as long as you both co-operate, you need to get off the boat and she needs to tell us all about the clues Jack left. Now, I won't ask you again, I have taken command of this boat and you must now get off it.' Tariq said, his voice calm and in control.

'OK, OK, I get the message, but one more question...' As he said this, he reached over and grabbed the hand-held radio, ran and dived off the side of the boat, so as to avoid the engine propeller which had been running for the last fifteen minutes, as he went over the side he shouted to Saffi, 'do as they say, I'll come back for you, don't worry.'

However, they had already taken Saffi below, tears streaming down her face, tears of fear and of sadness, not knowing what was happening. She really was scared now.

~~~

Andreas swam as deep as he could with one breath, and he could see bullets skimming past him; Conrad was shooting at him from the boat. He swam back toward the boat; they would not expect him to do that. Andreas knew there was a swim ladder at the stern, with a line attached to it; Andreas used this when he was cleaning the undersides of the boat. His only option was to see if he could grab hold of the line, and try to stay out of sight for long enough, for them to think one of the bullets had hit him.

Luckily, the current was with him and the boat was not at full power. He knew it would be dangerous and he would have to keep clear of the propeller. Within a few minutes, he had managed to get hold of the line. He pulled himself underneath the swim platform, and out of sight, he took two deep breaths before going under the water again; he made sure the VHF radio strap was securely around his wrist.

After what felt like an age, he could no longer hear them shouting from the deck, and Conrad had stopped shooting into the water. He could feel the vibrations of the engine begin to intensify and he knew they were increasing the power; the added wake would help to cover him as he let go of the line. He took a final deep breath and swam beneath the water one more time, directly out behind Linalli. He stayed under the water for as long as he could, eventually he raised his head above the waves to see if they had seen him, but only Ollie was on deck, looking forward. He swam beneath the waves again, farther away from the boat, back in the direction of Puerto Rico. When the boat was as far away as he felt safe, he began to make emergency calls on all frequencies other than channel 16, he knew they would be listening to that channel.

~~~

Back on board, Tariq shouted to Ollie. Lock her in the main cabin. We don't want her causing any trouble.'

Saffi kicked and screamed as Ollie forced her through the boat and into the cabin.

'Look Saffi, if you calm down this will be a lot easier for you, I have to do what Tariq tells me, otherwise', his eyes said everything as he looked at Saffi, 'you know, he can become very violent, so please, be quiet and do what he says.'

Saffi stopped kicking and looked at Ollie, 'I thought you were my friend, I helped you with the computer, why are you doing this to me? I don't know what you want from me.'

'We want to know what Jack has done with our boss's money, he wants it back.'

'What money, I don't know anything about any money, I never even knew my father; he left me years ago.'

'So why are you here? What are all the clues about? How did you find Andreas? Don't lie to me Saffi, we know you are looking for something, we know where you've been and who you've met, so it would be better for you if you just told us everything you know.'

They reached the cabin, Ollie opened the door and pushed Saffi in; she went in and turned to face him.

'Ollie, if I am to be held captive in my own boat, won't you at least untie my hands, it's not like I can go anywhere.'

'I don't know about that; I think it's safer if I just leave you tied up in here.'

'Look Ollie, you will have me locked in a cabin, on a boat I don't know how to sail, in a place I've never been to and I can't navigate, what exactly do you think I am going to do? Please untie my hands so that I can at least sit comfortably.' She stared directly into Ollie's eyes, imploring him to untie her hands. Ollie thought for a moment and then agreed. He sat her on the bed, untied her hands and locked the door behind him as he left. As she said, where could she go, what could she do? They needed her to co-operate, a bit of give and take on both sides he thought.

As she sat on the bed, she noticed that the photo album was still out and Andreas' army knife was lying beneath it, but he'd managed to put the poem back underneath the photo. She was scared and didn't know what to do, but she knew she had to do something. She took the poem from beneath the photo, in order to memorise the final part of the clue, and then replaced it. She also knew she needed to hide this album from their sight. She removed the label from the spine, looking around she found a pen and hand wrote a new title, she needed something innocuous, unrelated to her or Lillian. Finally, she wrote 'Repair Schedule' on the spine and slid the album back onto the shelf at the far end, along with what looked like other boat related books.

With nothing better to do, she decided to reacquaint herself with Jack, through the many other photo albums and books on the shelf, starting with the one marked 'Saffi'.

Chapter 20

Cap'n Skip sat in the Sunset Bar drinking his fourth coffee of the day, waiting for the non-existent customers to come along and charter his boat. As he sat quietly, he could see someone walking along the dock. After taking a closer look, he thought it was someone he knew from a long time ago, from a time in his past he wanted to forget; an era he thought he had escaped. Wishing to stay out of sight, he picked up his coffee and went inside the bar, no need to bring trouble to my doorstep if I can avoid it, he thought.

He sat in the farthest, darkest corner of the bar, behind an old-fashioned jukebox, and pulled his cap down over his eyes. He watched as the man stopped outside the bar. He peered up and down the dock and then looked at Cap'n 'Skip's boat which was moored outside the bar. Cap'n Skip subconsciously held his breath as the man asked his neighbours on the boat next to him if they knew where his was. Thankfully, he could see them shaking their heads. They knew better than to tell strangers where Cap'n Skip was, it was an agreement they had had for the past few years. He finished his coffee, threw a couple of dollars on the table and nodded knowingly to the barman as he casually walked behind the bar and out the back door.

He walked along the side of the building, and watched from behind the safety of the corner, as the man walked further along the dock, until he was out of sight. Time to pick up the hook and move for a few days, Cap'n Skip thought as he headed back to his boat. His neighbours told him all they knew; his inquisitor had left no name or message.

Perhaps a few days in the Spanish Virgin Islands is what I need, he thought and within thirty minutes Cap'n Skip had checked his boat, made sure Skippy the cat was on board, slipped his lines and was on his way. The sun would soon be setting, a perfect time to travel in the shadow of darkness.

~~~

Raoul continued looking along the dock, asking anyone and everyone if they knew or had seen Cap'n Skip. He knew nobody would give him any information, but he needed to feel like he was doing something to find him.

It had been many years since he had seen Cap'n Skip, for all he knew he could have ended up like Jack, at the bottom of a cliff. Raoul went into Road Town; he knew of a couple of bars where the unsavoury residents of the island hung out. One of them might be willing to give up some information about Cap'n Skip's whereabouts for a quick buck.

After buying a few beers and handing out a few dollars, he had the information he needed. Cap'n Skip was still on the island, chartering his boat out to day-trippers, not into anything illegal, staying out of trouble and keeping his 'record' clean, which Raoul thought was most unlike Skip. Maybe he's turned a new leaf after his time with Jack; perhaps Cap'n Skip doesn't even know about Jack.

Further enquiries led Raoul to believe that Linalli had not made it to the islands yet, and no one had seen anyone with Saffi or Andreas' description. It was time to report to Luis, no news was not good, but better to keep him in the 'know', Raoul was certain of that.

Chapter 21

For over an hour Andreas had been swimming, treading water, floating and calling on his VHF radio, and he had not seen one boat.

He continued to call on all the VHF stations, except channel 16, the emergency channel; he didn't want Tariq to know he was still alive; surprise was always the best element in any rescue operation. He checked his watch, he knew the tide would be turning soon, and that would be to his benefit. The current would take him back towards Puerto Rico, albeit very slowly, but he also knew the fishermen would soon be out to check their fishing pots. Hopefully, one of them would see him, or certainly hear him if he shouted loud enough. He floated on his back and watched the clouds glide across the sky and his mind wandered back to the late 1980s, back to his days with Jack, after Lillian had died. He remembered how Jack had told him of his plan.

After Father Tomas had sobered Jack up, Jack spoke to Andreas at length.

'I need something to give purpose to my life and take away the meaningless of Lillian's death. I need to find a reason for living'. The sadness still deep in his eyes as he spoke, 'I don't want to avenge her death, that would be pointless, but I want to take away the things that mean most to those who had killed her, their wealth, their money, their ability to continue to do business.'

'OK, I can understand that, what do you have in mind?' Andreas had asked.

'Have you heard about Operation Snow-cap? It's a new initiative set up by the DEA and the INM?'

'What's the INM?

'It's the States Bureau of International Narcotics Matters. It's been set up to stop the manufacture and transport of drugs into the US. Its remit will be far reaching.'

'How do you know about this; it's not exactly broadcast on CNN?' Andreas asked.

'Let's just say I've been monitoring a few things, and know a few people in the right places. Look, I'm not sure how I'm going to set this all up yet, and I know it will take time to gain the confidence of those in authority. But just think what it would mean to an organisation like the DEA to have 'a man on the ground'. To have someone on the inside, someone who could find out what the drug

gangs were up to, know what their movements are. We've enough old contacts we can call upon to help us out'.

As he spoke, Andreas could see that Jack was still thinking his plan through in his mind. He would use his pent up anger against those who had ruined his life, the thugs that had killed his wife without a second thought and left his only child far away from him and without a mother.

'How's it going to work, a bit like a DEA Falcon?' Andreas asked. He was still not sure where any of this would lead, but was very keen.

'A bit like that. We can use your knowledge from back then. It might be a bit out of date, but you know how they work, we could maybe get you back in there under false pretences, you know, fallen back into the old ways, in need of money, you know the sort of thing. Dangerous I realise, but no more so than anything you did before.'

'Yeah, but before I didn't know any better. I think we need to think this through before we rush into anything.' Andreas could already see his old boss in his mind and knew how suspicious he would be if he were to return now.

'Don't worry, I'm not going to rush into anything without planning this through thoroughly, but if you're not going to be with me let me know now before I tell you too much.'

The sound of an outboard motor brought Andreas out of his daydream, and back to his present predicament. He looked over to see the expected fishing boats checking their pots, he shouted and waved his arms frantically trying to catch their attention, he called on his radio and finally a fishing boat headed towards him, the fisherman standing on the front of his boat, waving back at him. He knew someone would find him, eventually; all he had to do now was find a way to get to Saffi and hope he wasn't too late.

Chapter 22

Saffi could hear raised voices, outside her cabin, Conrad and Tariq were arguing. She couldn't hear exactly what they were saying, but assumed they would be coming in to get some information from her soon. She began to panic. She tried to think of what Andreas would do, but that only made her feel worse not knowing what had happened to him. She had heard the gunshots after they had taken her below, and the sound of a body hitting the water, followed by more gunshots.

While locked in the cabin, she had sat among her father's things, imagining him there, in the cabin with her. What would he do in this situation? Then she heard someone unlocking the door; she flinched and curled back as far as she could on the bed. The door slammed open.

'Out NOW!' screamed Tariq. He grabbed Saffi by the arm and shoved her through the door and into the saloon. She could see her computer sitting on the table, open. 'You need to explain a few things.'

'I don't know anything, honestly. I don't know what Andreas was looking for.'

'Oh and you expect us to believe you do you? Well let's start with something simple shall we?' Conrad's eyes were glaring at her, searing through her own.

'It's just some stuff he asked me to help him with, nothing important.' She was panicking now.

'Again, I ask you to think why it is that I would believe you.' Tariq stopped and stared straight into her eyes. 'Exactly how long have you known Andreas, go on, tell me you've known him all your life, and you thought it would be a nice idea to pop over the Caribbean to have a little chat about some clues and a crossword, sort of a holiday romance, is that it. Give me break. What do you take me for, some sort of imbecile? Now shall we try again, with a bit more realism this time? Sit down and tell me who you were going to meet in the Virgins and why?'

Saffi began to sob, she really didn't know who these people were, or what they wanted, but she knew they were dangerous, and decided the best thing to do would be to co-operate. She sat down and looked at the clues again, remembering the last one she had looked at, and the words of the poem. She was glad now that she hadn't written any of it down, they wouldn't be able to find the answer to the last clue.

'I don't know his real name. Andreas called him Skipper or something like that.' She tried to be evasive, but to no avail.

'I think you mean Cap'n Skip, aka a very old friend of Jack's if I'm not mistaken.' Tariq replied, again not taking his eyes from her.

'I don't know. I don't know any of these people, or anything. It's just some stuff that Andreas has asked me to help with, to find some friends of Jack's.' She looked directly at Tariq, 'I think you killed the wrong person, if anyone knows anything about all this it was Andreas, so if you've killed him, then you only have yourselves to blame.' She was hoping they would tell her if Andreas was dead or alive.

'Oh you needn't worry about whether we killed the right person, Andreas has had it coming to him for a long time, and we shot enough bullets in the water to kill all the fish, as well as that shark Andreas. So I wonder if you'll be a little more helpful now, knowing that he won't be coming back to get you. Sit there and explain all you know to Ollie; he understands computers better than you think.'

Ollie sat next to Saffi, a look of guilt in his eyes, Conrad followed Tariq back up to the cockpit to check their position and set up a course directly to Tortola, the main island in the British Virgin Islands.

'I'm sorry Saffi, but the best thing you can do is be co-operative, and let me have all the information you have, otherwise the other two will get very nasty. You know I'm talking sense.' Ollie said moving closer to the computer.

'It was all a set up from the start with you, wasn't it? You asking me for a computer lesson. Why are you involved with these people, Ollie, you seem much more intelligent than those two?' She nodded her head up to the cockpit. 'Surely there must be something better in life for you to do than this.'

Ollie's demeanour changed, he became angry. 'The problem is, Saffi, you come from a very nice world, a safe one, one with jobs, and homes and security, and you've probably never had to worry about anything real in your whole life. There's always been food on the table and money in the bank, and with what your father has left you, if you ever find it, you'll never have to worry again.'

'What do you know about my father?' Saffi said quietly, she tried not to show any emotional response to what Ollie had just said. She still didn't know what Jack had left her, but clearly, these people wanted to find it before her. She now realised she was much happier before she knew about any inheritance, and would happily have let them have it if it had meant not losing Andreas. Then an even darker thought crossed her mind, if she had not come looking for Jack's inheritance, then she would never have met Andreas, none of this would have happened and he would still be alive. Tears began to roll down her cheek, why had she bothered chasing something or someone she knew nothing about.

'All you need to know is that your father took things that didn't belong to him, and my boss wants them back. Clearly, Jack has kindly left you some instructions on how to find it, so let's try one more time, show me the rest of the clues, where we have to go and who we need to meet. What you have to remember Saffi, is that we've been following you since the day you left the Bahamas. We already know where you've been and have already met up with those same friends of yours, most of them were very helpful and gave us the information we needed, some needed a little more persuasion.'

Saffi looked at Ollie with a start, 'you haven't hurt anyone, and none of them had anything to do with Jack's things, whatever it is you're after. They just told me about him, want sort of person he was, that's all. 'Her mind wandered back to all the people she'd met recently, some, but not all of them, could look after themselves, but others like Gus and Ma, she tried not to think about it. The more she carried on with this stupid hunt, the more people were getting hurt. She decided that she would tell Ollie everything; even if they killed her at least no one else would get hurt, that's what she hoped.

Chapter 23

Cap'n Skip left under cover of night for Culebra; he knew it would take him all night, but also knew it's where he could hide away for weeks at a time. He would anchor away from prying eyes while he let the 'heat' of why he was being sought out could die down. He knew he could trust the islanders not tell anyone he was there, that is if anyone were to ask.

Once beyond the protection of the smaller islands of the BVI, he headed southwest, into the open sea and away from any dangers in the shallower waters. He fed Skippy his cat, set the autopilot on the correct course, and his alarm clock to wake him every twenty minutes. Although he knew the waters well he wanted to ensure he would be awake when he reached the dangerous rocks surrounding Culebra, he would power nap for the next few hours while he would be in the open water.

It was a calm night and he watched the moonrise, and as it did, it hid the stars in the sky. He drifted off for his first nap, with Skippy in his lap. Twenty minutes later his alarm clock woke him with a start and it took him a few seconds to gather his bearings and remember why he was where he was. He quickly checked for any other boats in his immediate vicinity and then gave a more thorough check of the 360-degree view around. Leaving Skippy curled in the cockpit he went and checked his radar screen, there was nothing showing. He reset the alarm clock and dropped back into a more comfortable sleep, ready for when the alarm clock woke him again. At 2am he had covered 30 miles and could see the lights of Charlotte Amalie off to his right, he would continue to nap for another hour and then stay awake until he reached his favourite anchorage.

Cap'n Skip arrived in Culebra just as the sun was rising, he followed the red and green markers which guided him safely through the channel into Ensenada Honda, the bay on the edge of the sleepy town of Dewey. Fortunately, the sea remained calm and he managed to anchor safely and have coffee, before any of the other boaters had even risen. He would wait until 8am and then take his dinghy over to Mamacitas Bar, order a full breakfast and say hi to some old acquaintances.

~~~

When the fisherman saw Andreas in the water, he immediately increased his engine speed and headed towards him. As he drew closer, he slowed his engine and threw Andreas a life ring and a line. Andreas slipped the life ring over his head but struggled to keep hold of the line, he didn't realise how exhausted he'd become swimming and treading water all this time. He managed to tie the line around his chest and the fisherman helped him into his boat, where Andreas collapsed and breathed heavily while the fisherman got him a large bottle of water. Andreas tried to drink slowly, he knew how dehydrated he was, but gulped the water despite himself.

The Puerto Rican fisherman looked perplexed as Andreas tried to explain how he had fallen off a friends' boat, while on their way to the BVI. He said that his friends had not heard him go overboard, as they had the music playing very loudly.

'So your friends, they no turn back for you? They no seem like friends to me.' He said in broken English.

'Maybe not such good friends as I thought eh, but I'm glad you found me. Where are you from?' Andreas asked.

'You know the Spanish Virgin Islands? I'm from Culebra. I'll take you there, we'll be there soon. I can call authorities to contact your friends, yes.'

'No!' Andreas wanted to remain as anonymous as possible, but the fisherman looked stunned at his refusal. Andreas realised he needed to clarify the situation. 'Sorry, sorry! Culebra would be perfect and I have some friends there who can help me out, they can call my friends to let them know I'm OK,'

'OK, whatever you say, here, drink some more water and rest.'

Finally, Andreas fell asleep as the fisherman tidied his nets and lines, and tried to get back to Culebra as quickly as he could. The fisherman also knew not to ask questions of people who didn't want to give up too much information in this part of the world. Sometimes it's better to know nothing, than something, he thought wisely to himself wisely.

When they arrived at the town port, Andreas thanked the fisherman, took his address and promised to send him some money for his time, trouble, and diesel. Somehow, the fisherman knew that Andreas would stand by his word and he watched him walk away, along the canal towards the main town. Andreas had many friends on Culebra, and he knew one of them would offer him a bed for a few nights while he worked out his next steps, but first he would head straight to Mamacitas. He could use the hotel showers before having one of her infamous breakfasts.

As he walked into Mamacitas Andreas' mind was spinning, he was safe and relieved, but his main concern was Saffi. Where had they taken her, but more importantly had they hurt her? He knew he needed two things very quickly, a plan and a plane. Neither of which should not be too difficult to sort out. He was staring straight through to the bar as he walked between the tables of the dining area of Mamacitas, not seeing anyone, until someone called his name and brought him out of his trance and back into the real world.

'Hey, Andreas, is that really you, man? Damn, you look rough, like you need a shower and a good meal.' Cap'n Skip's unmistakeable English accent, tinged with too many years in the Caribbean, cut through Andreas' thoughts.

'Cap'n, man are you a perfect sight for sore eyes, and just the twist of fate I need right now, have you got your boat here?' Andreas asked.

'Good to see you too,' Cap'n Skip replied, sarcastically.

'Shit, sorry, I've not exactly had the greatest day, how are you man?' Andreas said, realising how sharp he must have sounded.

'No worries, what's up? You look like your world is upside down. Sit down, let me get you a breakfast ordered and you can tell me what's happened and how I can help.'

Cap'n Skip's heart sank when Andreas told him the news of Jack death; he had known Jack and Lillian for a long time. Andreas paused, while the realisation of what he was telling Cap'n sank in, before he continued. He couldn't believe what Andreas was telling him about the last few days racing around the islands, solving clues and catching up with Jack's friends. He was even more surprised when he found out that he was next on the list, and even more devastated to find out what had happened to Saffi.

'But why am I on the list, I don't have information from Jack, it's been years since I've seen him. More importantly, what are we going to do about finding Saffi?' Cap'n Skip asked.

'I think you mean what will I be doing to find Saffi.' Andreas said lowering his voice as their breakfasts arrived. They had moved to a secluded spot at the back of the restaurant, Andreas didn't want people seeing him just yet.

'No way man. There is no way I am leaving you to sort this out on your own, and from what you've been saying about Jack's friends you've already seen, there is no way they will let you do this alone either.' Cap'n Skip protested.

'Get real, will you. We haven't seen each other in I don't know how long, and you're ready to go on a wild goose rescue for someone you've never even met?'

'I may never have met her, but there are enough things Jack and Lillian did for me in the past, that means there is no way I'm not helping you now. Besides, you'll need a place to keep a low profile, and my boats anchored in the bay. The very least you can do is call Julio, he knows the right people, mainly in the wrong places, but they are probably the ones we need to find.' Cap'n Skip proffered.

Andreas knew he was right. There would be too many things to organise and not enough time to do everything if they were to reach Saffi as quickly as possible. 'Thanks Cap', I really appreciate it, and I know Jack would be glad to have you on board.'

'Talking of on board, I need to get back to feed Skippy, he'll be wondering where the hell I've got to. You ready. Breakfast is on me.' Cap'n said as he went off to pay the bill while Jack finished his coffee.

Andreas knew he'd made the right decision to keep Cap'n Skip alongside, he knew Jack from old and he knew how some of their adversaries' minds worked. He would call Julio from the boat.

Chapter 24

Saffi knew there would be no point in being obstructive to her captors. She knew if she co-operated they would take her to the next person on the clue list, Cap'n Skip. Knowing what Andreas had told her all about him, she knew he would help, if she could just get a message to him that they were holding her against her will.

She sighed as she sat at the computer, next to Ollie. 'I need to look at the clues to find out how to contact Captain Skip, or whatever his same is.' Saffi said.

'Before you do anything, you need to show me exactly how this plan of Jack's works, so that I know you're not up to anything you shouldn't be'. Ollie sat so close to Saffi that it her made her skin crawl, she knew she had to work out a plan quickly.

'OK, I'll explain everything I know.' She said reluctantly. 'There are two parts to each clue, the first part directs us to an island, and the second leads to something more specific on the island. Once we've worked out what that is, we put the answer into the programme and, if it's right, it shows us who we have to contact. It's quite simple really.' Saffi said feeling resigned at having given in to him. 'And we've not worked them all out yet.'

'Oh well you're bound to say that, but we were listening to you and Andreas, we know roughly where we have to go, so don't try to hide anything from us.'

I'm not trying to hide anything, but this is only the first half solution. Once we've worked out who we have to visit, that person then has to give me some other bit of information. That final piece of information gives me a grid reference to put the answer from the first part of the clue into the crossword.' It sounded complicated even to Saffi, and she understood what she was doing. 'After that, I don't know what will happen. We've only managed to put four of the clues into the crossword, and there are ten altogether. So I don't think it's going to be as easy as just asking me to work the computer for you, you're going to need me to actually talk to the people in the clues.'

'Oh we can be very persuasive, I'm sure we'll be able to find out whatever it is they need to tell you.' Ollie said pulling out a gun and placing it on the table in full view of Saffi, 'As I said before, we've already had a chat with some of your friends, and they told us all we needed to know.'

Ollie stood up and called through the companionway to Tariq, 'she's finally decided to co-operate, Cap'n Skip's first, head for

Tortola, and we know where he moors his boat'. Tariq nodded in agreement and Ollie sat next to Saffi again. 'So we know we have to go to the BVI to have a chat with old 'Cap'n Skip' and his fluffy old cat and find out what information he has for clue number five. We also know that you need to go to St Kitts, Guadeloupe and Dominica, so that makes clues six, seven and eight, so shall we see if you have managed to solve nine and ten, so at least we'll have a game plan?' He moved closer to her, pressing up against her as much as he could, he liked to watch her flinch whenever he approached her, it made him feel in control, a feeling that he was so far unaccustomed to.

Saffi felt the fear rising in her stomach, she knew she would have to tell him everything she knew, but wondered how long she would be able to hide the details of the last clue, and fortunately, she hadn't written anything about the clue or the poem. Reluctantly she opened the clues document.

'Just because we worked out which islands we need to go to, doesn't mean we worked out the second part of the clues.' She was stalling for time, she would go through the second part of each clue again and make Ollie do the hard work with her, she might be able to make this last until they reached the BVI. 'How far until we arrive?' she asked, hoping they were nearer than she thought.

'We have plenty of time for you to be as helpful as you've been so far, so shall we start with clue number six, St Eustatius, if I'm not mistaken.'

It took over an hour for Ollie to work out the second part of clues six, seven and eight before he had become frustrated with the whole idea, and hungry. He locked Saffi in her father's cabin once more, and suggested to the others that it was time to eat. Saffi could see from the porthole that the sun had already set and the sky was the same dark purple colour she had looked at back in the Bahamas when she first met Andreas. She thought back to the brief time they had spent together and she began to realise that she had slowly fallen in love with him, and now he was gone.

She began to feel that anyone she ever cared for was taken from her before she really got to know them. Firstly, her mother, then her father and now Andreas; she couldn't even contact Nana and realised that she hadn't been in touch with her for days. She wouldn't know of any of the trouble she was in, better that way she thought. Her mind wandered into dark thoughts that she knew she shouldn't. What would happen to Nana if she never made it back to England? Nana would blame herself for letting her go on such a ridiculous escapade. She would most definitely blame Jack for even thinking of getting me to go on this stupid trip. She leaned back on the bed and closed her eyes. She knew there was nothing she could do about Nana. She must concentrate on a plan to escape, but very quickly exhaustion caught up with her and she drifted off into a deep sleep.

She woke abruptly to Ollie shaking her shoulder. 'There's something here for you to eat.' He said as he pointed to the sandwich he brought. 'You'll be pleased to know that we're half an hour away from Tortola, so make sure you're awake when we arrive, you might have to go and find the Cap'n.' Ollie said as he walked out of the cabin, slamming the door and then locking it behind him.

Saffi stared at the sandwich laid before her, she wasn't hungry, and she thought of the wonderful meals she'd shared with Andreas. She looked out the porthole again to see the lights of the harbour in the near distance and wondered how she would get a message to Cap'n Skip. It had been hours since they'd thrown Andreas' body overboard. She checked the time, 8pm. She had to stop herself from crying at the thought of his body floating in the water, eventually washed up on a shore somewhere.

She looked around the cabin for anything that could help her, but all she could see were reminders of her family, stacked in photo albums she'd not yet had a chance to look at. She looked along the bookshelf and found a dictionary, perhaps I can make up an anagram of kidnapped or hostage, she thought, but soon realised that Cap'n Skip would have no idea what it meant. She knew he was the son of a vicar and scrabbled to think of scriptures she could remember that might help him realise the danger she was in, but it was all to no avail. She would just have to see what happened when she met him, and hope that he would understand what she was trying to say to him.

A few moments later, whilst eating the sandwich Ollie had brought for her, she heard scrabbling noises from up on deck, and she could hear the cockpit lockers being opened, and the engine slowing. She looked out of the window and could see they were reversing into a berth in a marina, which she thought was strange. Surely, they wouldn't want anyone to see them, but soon realised that it was quite normal for Jack's boat to be here.

Saffi strained to see what was happening through the porthole. She heard the familiar sound of the gangplank hitting the dock. She could hear someone else's voice up on deck, Ollie, Tariq and Connor greeting someone new, their voices were muffled but she could make out the names of Andreas and Cap'n Skip being said. She could hear people moving about above her, and then there was silence. They had left her alone on the boat, now would be her best opportunity for escape. She shook the door violently to see if it would move from its hinges, but it didn't budge. She banged and screamed as loud as she could, surely someone in the marina would hear her. However, unbeknown to Saffi, they were in a private marina, on a private dock, one controlled by Luis Leppe.

Finally, full of desperation she gave up. She knew she had no chance of escape whilst locked in the cabin. Even if she could escape, she didn't know where she was or what she would do even if she did get out. She realised that they had the perfect hostage in her, a useless female; all she was good at was feeling sorry for herself and crying. With nothing else to do, she decided to go through Jack's photo albums, she could at least find out more about Jack from them.

~~~

An hour or so later the sound of footsteps and voices on the deck above startled Saffi. She could hear Ollie, Tariq and Conrad laughing and jeering. She could hear in their voices that they had been drinking. She put the photograph album back on the shelf; she would pretend to be asleep if they came in the cabin. She could hear their footsteps come down the companionway, and heard a bottle bang on the table, the chinking of glasses and muffled voices filtered through to her cabin. Holding back the desire to move closer to the door, she lay very still and hoped they would fall asleep soon.

But they didn't. Instead, Tariq called Luis Leppe.

'El Jeffe, Tariq here.

'Have you located Cap'n Skip?' Leppe asked

'No, he's not here, nor is his boat.'

'Can I assume you have made sufficient enquiries, and not just spent the night in the bar?'

'We asked everywhere. We understand that Raoul has arrived here and is also looking for him.' Tariq said, but what he really wanted to ask Luis Leppe was whether he didn't trust them to complete the job.

'Yes I know. I sent him. Is he with you? Leppe wasn't about to get into a discussion with an underling, he needed to talk to someone he trusted.

Almost too scared to answer his boss, Tariq stuttered. 'We've not met up with him yet. I think he maybe at his hotel.' They knew exactly where Raoul was, but knew as soon as he appeared, he would take control of what they believed was their job.

'Well don't leave the island until you have met with him, he has my instructions, so make sure you carry them out.' Luis put the phone down, annoyed that Raoul had not made contact with these people, he was unsure of both their ability and their loyalty, coming only as a recommendation from Carina.

Tariq turned to the others, 'We have a choice, we can wait for Raoul to take control, or, we can take control of our own destination and fortune. We have all the information we need, plus the girl who is easy to manipulate. We could sort out this puerile business of the clues, find whatever it is Jeffe thinks Jack has left her, and be on our way to Brazil before anyone knows what's hit them.'

Tariq had no idea whether Conrad and Ollie had thought this far ahead, or whether they would want to take on the mighty Luis Leppe. Nevertheless, he knew this would be the only chance they would get at making any big money fast. The thought of spending the next few years working his way through the ranks of El Jeffe's organisation did not appeal to him.

'Are you sure we can pull it off?' asked Conrad.

'Risky if you ask me, the thought of what Jeffe would do to us once he'd found out, is not worth thinking about.' Ollie offered.

'That's why we need a plan, and we need to act fast. Raoul must know where we are, I can't believe he's not been here already.' Tariq said as he picked up the notes he had seen Ollie make regarding the clues. 'From here to Statia, one-day sail, grab this girl Abigail; get the information from her while we're on route to Guadeloupe. We drop her overboard along the way. We take a visit to the next guy on the list, what's his name?' Tariq looked at the notes. 'Pablo Francois, do we have any idea where he is on the Guadeloupe, or what he does?'

Ollie looked up from the computer, he had managed to work his way around the clues that Saffi and Andreas had completed, and the files that Jack had left them. 'I'm pretty sure he's one of the bridge operators on the River Salee. He should be easy to grab as that bridge only opens once a day, and that's before sunrise. He probably gets there fifteen minutes before the bridge is due to open.'

'But which bridge?' Conrad asked. 'That could be the sticking point.'

'What do you mean, which bridge? Tariq asked.

'There are two bridges, north and south. The north opens at five and six in the morning, and the south at five thirty. I don't imagine he operates both.' Conrad said sarcastically.

Ollie, seeing his chance to show his superiority over Conrad, interrupted. 'Well, there are two bridges and three of us. Two of us go to the north bridge, establish if he's our man, nothing violent until we know if its him, if it is we grab him. If not, we go to the south bridge and grab our man there.'

'I like you're thinking,' Tariq said. 'We'll need a car, I'm not taking this boat through that reef system, too dangerous and it will slow us down. We can organise a car while we're on our way to Statia. So we're agreed, we leave now, under the cover of darkness, and get as far on our way as we can. Ollie, you slip the stern lines, Conrad you take the lazy line and I'll get the helm.'

~~~

Saffi was still feigning sleep when she heard the engine start and movement up on deck, and then should felt the boat move off the quay. So much for grabbing the attention of Cap'n 'Skip, she thought. She was truly on her own now, no one to contact, not knowing where they were heading, or what was on the agenda. She began to sob.

Chapter 25

Back on Cap'n's boat, Cap'n fed Skippy the cat and Andreas set about calling Julio.

'No way, man!' Julio said, as Andreas filled him in with what had happened to him and Saffi.

It took Andrea fifteen minutes to explain how he'd been rescued, and completely coincidentally, met Cap'n' Skip. He then told him of their rescue plan, which of course involved Julio.

'I know she won't like it, but I think it will be best if you leave Jacqui at home.' Andreas said before Julio could make the suggestion.

'Absolutely man, no way do we need another woman getting grabbed by those bastards.' Agreed Julio. 'Leave Jacqui for me to sort out, she'll understand, in any case we'll need someone on the ground we can trust to organise things.

'In which case, make sure your internet and phone bills are paid up, we're gonna need decent communications on the ground. I think this might get rough, bring whatever equipment you'll need.' Andreas said.

'Can I assume that we won't be calling for the help of our friends in law enforcement?' Julio asked, already knowing what the answer would be.

'You have assumed correctly. Jack said in his letter that he thought there was someone 'on the inside', so we need to be careful who we trust. I'm only going to talk to people on Jack's list.'

They agreed that Julio would rent a plane first thing in the morning and he would meet Andreas and Cap'n Skip on Tortola, at Beef Island Airport. They knew they needed to act swiftly, but Cap'n wanted to get his boat, and more importantly, Skippy, back in safe dockage on Tortola. With everyone in agreement, Andreas and Cap'n set about the plan of action. They both knew that they were at a disadvantage, not knowing what Tariq would do, or where he would go next.

'Let's make the assumption that they will follow the trail of the clues and head for Statia.' Andreas suggested.

'If that's where the next clue sends you? Who were you going to meet?

'Abigail Jones, ever heard of her?' Andreas asked.

'Abi, the Guide, yeah, I know Abi. She was working on Tortola when I moved there. Helped me find my way around, get my gear together. You know the sort of thing. I always thought she and I would get it together, but every time we meet she gets dragged off to some other island, or a nature reserve or something.'

'Well she's next on the list, followed by one of the bridge operators on Guadeloupe, Pablo Francis. Another of Jack's acquaintances I've never met. Do you know him?' Andreas asked hopefully. All the contact information Jack had left him was still on Linalli. Tariq and his team would have all the information they needed, which left Andreas at another disadvantage.

'Nope, never heard of him, but I know that Abi knows most of anyone who's anyone on the islands, if she doesn't know him, she'll probably know someone who does.' Cap'n replied.

'We could save time if you called Abi, we wouldn't need to go to Statia then, and we could head directly to Guadeloupe. It might also be a good idea to warn her that Tariq we'll be coming to find her. Could be beneficial if she left the island for a while, that would slow Tariq down.' Andreas suggested.

'Better still we could get her to fly to Tortola and meet us there. Not only will she be out of danger, she'll be able to help us out better from there. Mind you, trying to convince Abi to do something she doesn't want to do may prove difficult.'

'A woman with her own mind?' Andreas said.

'Woman with her own mind, body and soul, and no-one's going to tell Abi what she can and can't do. In fact, she'd give Tariq a run for his money.' Cap'n replied. 'We need to approach this very carefully.'

'Make her think it's her idea to come to Tortola somehow?' Andreas suggested.

'No, I've got a better idea, one that appeals to her sense of duty. Where do we go after Guadeloupe?'

'Next stop is Pico, a boat boy on Dominica. After that I've no idea, Saffi and I were what you could say, interrupted.' Andreas grimaced at the thought of Saffi still be on board with those thugs. He could only hope that she co-operated and took them to the islands in turn, as Jack had set out. At least that way he would know where they would be in the next few days. He also realised now that this was another of Jack's ploys. By making them have to get more information from an actual person, it would mean that he and Saffi would never have the full story of where he had hidden her inheritance, not until the very end. Clever, he thought to himself, but he knew that Jack had always been cleverer than he ever let on.

'I know Pico. The only problem is you can never get him on the phone, no signal up that bloody river of theirs, God only knows how the crew of 'Pirates of the Caribbean' got on when they were filming there.' Cap'n said.

'Well, that's our plan is it? Coax Abi into coming to Tortola. See if we can get the information from her. Meet Julio, hopefully without Jacqui, try and establish who Pablo Francis is and somehow contact Pico to warn him to look out for Linalli.' Andreas said, not too sure whether he was proud of this plan or not, but it was the only plan they had.

'Right, where's my phone, I'll get onto Abi.' Cap'n said as he moved Skippy off his lap and into one of the cabins out of harm's way.

Chapter 26

Once out of sight of Tortola and on the correct heading for Statia, Conrad sent Ollie down to Saffi, to solve the final clues and establish the final part of this journey. Saffi heard the door being unlocked and wondered what was in store for her now.

'I hope you had a little nap while we were out, as it's time to put your thinking cap on again. You need to solve the final clue. As you can see, we're now at sea, a long way from land and no one is coming to find you, so you may as well co-operate. Not that anyone knows where you are, so it will just be easier if we get this over and done with.' Ollie grabbed her by the arm and pushed her through the cabin door to the saloon.

'OK, OK.' Saffi cried. 'There's no need to be so rough, it's not like I'm going anywhere. I fully understand the position I'm in. I'm not sure how much help I'm going to be. It was Andreas who solved the clues; I hadn't any idea about any of it.'

'Well let's just see what we can establish. You've only got two more to solve, so it shouldn't take too long.'

Saffi read out the ninth clue, she already knew the answer, but she made Ollie search out the information he needed. She wasn't going to make this easy for them. Ollie went up on deck to tell Conrad and Tariq that they would be heading to Martinique and the Trois-Islet golf course after they'd been to Guadeloupe.

'Some golf caddy called Salvador Hareau. Just one more clue to solve and then we're done, and then we can lose the girl.' Ollie said, pleased with his progress with Saffi.

'Not so fast.' Tariq interrupted. 'These people need to give us the final pieces of information. We need work out a way of how they're going to give us the information, without Saffi it may be more difficult than we think.'

'It won't be that difficult, when you're holding their best buddies' daughter as hostage, they're bound to give up the info we need. We keep the girl, she's leverage.' Tariq said.

'I agree, but I think we need to think this through before we go barging in. We don't know who these people are, how they knew Jack, or what friends they might have in high places.' Tariq said.

~~~

Back down in the saloon Saffi was desperately trying to think of a way to put Ollie off the scent of the last clue. As it were, she was still none the wiser where they were supposed to go. Although she'd found the poem, she hadn't found out what it meant. She heard

Ollie's footsteps on the companionway. She needed to send them off the trail tail, somehow.

'I've started working on the last clue.' She said as Ollie sat next to her. 'The first part reads," this *floating island has a place of memories, on which 'I'll nail' my own"*. I don't know about you, but a floating island sounds a bit odd. However, I've also been looking at the islands, going south, ones we're not going to. So far Jack has sent us down the islands, never back from where we've come.'

'Well, I'm glad to see you've decided to help. You know it will be better for you in the end. So, have you found anything of interest yet? Ollie asked.

'Well, nothing major, apart from Trinidad and Tobago. It might just be a tenuous link, but the Caribbean Guide refers to the oil industry, so I'm not sure if Jack is referring to an oilrig, you know a sort of floating island. I don't know if he ever worked on them. I know he was away at sea a lot, so that could be why the clue goes on about memories. Perhaps we need to look for names of oil rigs.' Saffi had no idea if this was going to work, it was after all a very thin link to floating islands, but Ollie took the bait.

'Yes, that could be it. You see, you are good at unravelling this, some of Andreas' magic must have rubbed off on you, shame he couldn't be here to congratulate you'.

The reference to Andreas cut right to her core, tears welled up in her eyes, but she fought them back. She would not let this thug get the better of her. She could hardly believe she was thinking this way; a month ago, she would have crumpled into a heap on the floor. She let the comment drop.

'The second part of the clue says *'A secret life, hidden beneath my blue eyes'*. I've an idea about this either, but my Nana. . .' she gulped at the thought of Nana not knowing what was going on, not knowing why she hadn't called, she knew she would be getting worried, but she continued,'... my Nana told me that Jack adored Frank Sinatra, and he's known as 'Blue eyes'. It could be a reference to one of his songs, maybe?' She said, clutching at straws.

'What sort of reference?' Ollie asked, not as convinced about this suggestion.

'That I don't know, I think I'll need to do a bit more research. It would probably be best if you left me alone to try to work it out.' She looked at him with imploring eyes. 'I'm quite happy for you to leave me here on my own, and you can help with the sailing.' Her mind was working overtime now. What she wanted was for Ollie to lock her back in the cabin so she could work on the real solution to the clue, but for that, she needed to be alone.

'Very clever, but I don't think so. There are too many things in here you could use as weapon. No, I think its best we lock you up, back in the cabin, where you can be of least danger to the others and me. I won't have to sit here and mind you like a little kid that way.' With that, Ollie grabbed her arm, Saffi managed to grab the guide and her laptop, and he threw her back in Jack's cabin and locked the door.

Her plan had worked. All she had to do now was to solve the real clue.

Chapter 27

The first part of the rescue plan had not gone well. When Cap'n phoned Abi, her colleagues told him that she was out on a hike, not due back for another four hours. He'd tried her mobile, which diverted to her answer phone, so he had left an urgent message for her to contact him. They had managed to contact Julio, who had convinced Jacqui not to come. He would meet them on Tortola the following day. The only thing left for Andreas and Cap'n to do was to get back to Tortola as quickly as possible. The trip would take about ten hours, and they would arrive just after sunset. Just as they lifted the anchor, Cap'n's mobile rang.

'Hi Skip, it's Abi here, I got your message, what's the emergency?'

'Abi, thanks for getting back to me so quickly, I was worried I wouldn't catch you in time. I've a real favour to ask.' Cap'n said, trying not to sound too panicky.

'Anything, shoot.' Abi replied. She knew she had a soft spot for Skip. Unfortunately, they were always in the wrong place at the wrong time to do anything about it.

'It's Skippy.'

'What, what about Skippy'. She said, not hiding the fear in her voice that anything bad had happened to her favourite cat. 'Please say he's OK.'

'Yes, yes, he's fine. It's me. I have to go into hospital for a small procedure, just overnight, nothing serious. But I can't get anyone to look after Skippy at such short notice, not anyone I trust that is.' He was hoping his ploy of acting like a helpless man in a medical situation, and her having to look after her favourite cat, might convince her to fly over today, or at the latest tomorrow morning. 'Obviously I'll pay for your flight and any loss of salary, it's just I'm in a real situation. The hospital has had a cancellation, and it will be months before another slot comes free.' He trailed off, trying to sound as pathetic as he could.

'Oh is that all, I thought someone had died and it was a real emergency.' She replied, teasing him. 'Of course I'll come over, anything for...,' she paused for dramatic effect, 'Skippy'.

'Oh Abi, you are an angel, a godsend, what would I do without you? Can you get the next flight out? Then I can get myself off to the appointment. I'll leave the house keys in the usual place, and you know where everything else is, and you know to help yourself to anything you want'.

'Not a problem, I'm just on my way down The Quill trail, but I'll call the office and get them to book me on the earliest flight. I'll be there tonight.'

He thought it odd that she hadn't mentioned Jack's death, perhaps she hadn't heard. In which case he would tell her when he met her at the airport. Cap'n was just about to end the call when Andreas was waving a piece of paper at him. He passed it to him while saying his farewell to Abi. 'That's great,' he paused as he read the note, 'one last thing, I don't suppose you have a number for Pico on Dominica?'

'Yeah, sure, back at the office, I'll drop you a text with it when I get back.'

Cap'n read further down the note and interrupted her again. 'And I don't suppose you know any of the bridge operators on Guadeloupe?'

'Well actually I do, we have all their numbers in the office, so we can check the bridge is operating, I'll send you them as well.' She stopped talking. Now she was confused. 'What on earth do you need the bridge operator numbers for in hospital?

He hadn't thought about this question, and struggled to think of an answer, until something suddenly came to mind. 'Oh, I met an English couple on a yacht who wanted to head that way, I told them about the river and the bridges, and told them I would try and get the numbers so they could check the bridges were operational, and the opening times. Perhaps, when you get back, you could keep an eye out for them. They said they might head your way. They're on a sailboat called Alhambra.' He hoped this sounded plausible. 'Thanks again, Abi, I'll see you tomorrow when I get home.'

'Oh, OK, I'll see you tomorrow.' She was going to ask a further question, but Cap'n had cut the call off.

Cap'n conveyed the information to Andreas, all they could do now was sail to Tortola and wait for Abi's text.

Chapter 28

SAFFI'S plan had worked. Locked in the cabin, she could try to work out the correct answer to the last clue. More importantly, she could work out where the other clues should fit in the crossword. She had nine of the ten answers, four she had already put into the crossword, and surely, it couldn't be that difficult to work out where the rest fitted, she thought. However, she needed to come up with a convincing argument about the final clue in order to put her kidnappers off the trail of the real answer.

She went to the shelf where she had hidden the photo album, retrieved the poem, and read it again to herself.

> *Her deep blue eyes, just like her mother*
> *The secrets beneath, she will uncover*
> *Our story finally told, our hidden truth*
> *Our love endured, beyond our Island of Youth*

The words of the poem were beautiful, and it was obvious to her that Jack had written it about her. What was not clear was what it meant, she had no idea what Jack was trying to convey. She looked for all of the five letter words in the poem and entered them into the clue page. STORY, nothing appeared. TRUTH, again nothing appeared, no name, no one to contact. She entered YOUTH and still no name appeared. She concluded there must be more to the poem than she could work out.

She opened up the Crossword page, where she had already entered the first four clues. She then looked for a pen, and in the back of the photo album, wrote the other five answers she had.

DRAKE
QUILL
SALEE
LAYOU
TROIS.

She looked at the crossword. There was only one word that began with S and ended with E. Therefore, 'SALEE' had to fit into Two Across. She entered the word, and then looked at the remaining words. DRAKE, QUILL, LAYOU and TROIS. She could see that the only word that would fit into Four Down could be

LAYOU, and now she could see that the only word that could fit into One Down would be DRAKE. She entered them into the crossword.

With two words left, QUILL and TROIS, she entered them into the crossword. First, she tried QUILL into Five Down, but then realised that this was wrong, as TROIS would not fit into Five Across. She reversed them, looked at the crossword and at the final missing clue.

'Y, something, something, T, something', she said quietly to herself. She repeated it, until it finally registered. YOUTH. The word YOUTH from the poem, *'Our love endured, beyond our Island of Youth'*.

However, she was still confused. YOUTH had not returned a person to contact when she had entered it to the answer sheet. With trepidation, she carefully typed the letters into the crossword. Y, O, U, T, H.

As she hit the enter button on the last 'H' various other letters in the crossword lit up in bright green.

'D, J, E, N, A, L, U, T, V, U'

Thanks Jack, she thought, another bloody anagram. She took a deep breath, and began the process of working out the anagram, forwards, backwards, and alphabetically.

D J E N A L U T V U
U V T U L A N E J D
A E D J L N T U U V

She was completely flummoxed. She couldn't make any words out of the letters. Certainly, not any island names that she could recognise. She could see LAND, END, LEND, TEND, NUT, DENT and so on, but nothing substantial. She decided to leave this for a while and look through Caribbean guide for inspiration in order to keep Ollie off the trail of this final clue.

She had convinced Ollie that this must be something to do with Frank Sinatra and one of his songs, so she wrote down all of the Frank Sinatra songs she could think, which unfortunately, was only two. MY WAY and COME FLY WITH ME. She opened the guide at the Trinidad and Tobago section, having convinced Ollie the first part of the clue was to do with oilrigs. She scoured the pages of information about Trinidad, but could only come up with one link, which was birds, at the Asa Wright Nature Sanctuary, *'home to 433 bird species.'* She could try to link this to 'Come Fly With Me'.

Unfortunately, none of the words had five letters and could therefore not fit into the crossword.

She continued reading about Trinidad and thought it sounded like a nice place to visit, if she ever got out of this mess. The realisation of her situation began to sink further into her darkest thoughts. Holding back the urge to cry, again, realising it would do her no good, she began reading the section on Tobago. Page after page she read about the wonderful sights and sounds of this '*Gem of the Caribbean*', until finally she began to read about Little Tobago, known also as Bird of Paradise Island. Another reference to birds she thought, and then, staring from the page was the ideal solution to falsifying this clue.

'*Several operators run glass-bottom boat tours, but the best is Frank's, based at Blue Waters Inn or Birdwatcher's Restaurant and Bar'.*

'**Frank's'** was in bold, staring out at her. She ran the idea through her mind repeatedly. 'Yes, it could work' she thought. FRANK has five letters, links to Frank Sinatra, Come Fly With Me, reference to birds and flying'. Obviously, when she put FRANK into the crossword, none of the letters would highlight as they had done when she put the correct solution into the crossword, but she would explain that she didn't know what Jack expected her to do with all this information, once she'd completed the clues. They would have to try to solve it themselves. She liked her plan, and decided to take all the other answers out of the crossword, so that Ollie could not see what she had solved. She would co-operate with them, but she wouldn't just hand them the solution.

She sat back, shut down the computer. She picked up the photo album again, and started to look through the photos of her parents, during travels and time together. What a waste of a young life, she thought. How awful must it have been too have lost someone you love so much. She began to understand the pain her father and Nana must have felt at the time.

Each page of the album showed another beautiful island, the crystal blue water, edged by white, sandy beaches, and fringed with palm trees. Beneath each photo was a date, the name of the place and a short description. As she turned another page, she couldn't believe what she saw. Her parents sitting on another white, sandy beach, surrounded by the ubiquitous palm trees, but this was not the surprising thing. It was what Jack had written below.

Lillian and Jack on our Isle of Youth - La Juventud, Cuba

She looked again; she couldn't believe what she was reading. Isle of Youth, or as in the poem, Island of Youth. More importantly the letters of LA JUVENTUD. It was what the bright green letters on the crossword had spelt out.

She picked up the Caribbean guide and turned to the section on Cuba; she looked at the map and searched for their 'Isle of Youth'. She found the island, just off the south coast of Cuba, in the Canarreos Archipelago. But the more she looked, the more she realised that the island was the same shape as her pendant. Or rather, the pendant was the same shape as La Juventud, The Island of Youth.

Chapter 29

Abigail did as she had promised and sent a text with Pico's mobile number to Cap'n, but she only had the work numbers of the bridge operators. This meant they could not contact the bridge operators until 04:30 in the morning, when they came on duty.

Andreas telephoned Pico, not wanting to be the bearer of bad news, Andreas was a little relieved to hear that Pico had already heard about Jack's death. He told Pico what he and Saffi had been doing, and how his name was on Jack's list of people to find. He continued.

'But now we're in serious trouble. Some of Leppe's boys have taken Saffi hostage on Linalli.'

'What the. . .' Andreas interrupted Pico before he swore.

'Yes, I know what you're thinking, but swearing won't help us. We don't know where they're going, or even if they are still on the boat. If Leppe's got involved personally, Saffi may well already be on a private jet, heading for Columbia.'

Pico took a deep breath, 'Sorry man, you're right. What do you want me to do?'

'I know it's short notice, but if you can get hold of as many fisherman and boat owners as you can, and get them to report back any sightings of Linalli. Anyone you can trust, who is out at sea. Just get them to look out for the boat. These people are dangerous. We don't want them to approach Linalli, just report back. We know they have to go to meet the people on the list, to get some additional information. So the chances are they'll be heading to Statia, Guadeloupe and then down your way, to Dominica.' Andreas said.

'OK. Do you want me to give out your name and number?'

'No. As I say, Jack believes there's someone who may have switched sides, and we don't want to draw attention to ourselves. His people don't know that I'm alive. Just tell your friends that you have some information for the girl on the boat. Say her grandmother is sick, and we need to get a message to her to phone home.'

'OK, I'll call you when I have any info. Will you be heading this way Andreas?'

'Yeah, we'll be flying down in the next day or so. I'll catch up with you then. Thanks again Pico.'

Andreas brought Cap'n up to speed with his conversation with Pico, but until they reached Tortola, there was nothing more they could do.

~~~

Cap'n docked the boat in Tortola just before sunset, and they were already on their way to the airport. For once, everything had gone their way, the wind Gods were in their favour and they made up good time. Abi's internal flight was due in at 8pm and Julio had already landed his plane and was waiting for them.

They saw Abi get off the plane from Statia and gave a sigh of relief that she was now safely out of Leppe's reach. However, her expression was one of confusion. Why wasn't Cap'n at the hospital? She thought. Was that Andreas she could see with him, and who was the other guy? She walked up to the three men.

'Can someone please explain what the hell is going on? Abi said, staring hard at Cap'n.

Andreas stepped in before Cap'n could speak. 'Before you get annoyed at Cap'n, this has all been done for your own safety, and I'll explain everything before we leave'.

'Before we leave? My own safety? Where are we going now?' She was getting very angry now. She didn't need anyone to look after her. They had better have a good reason to drag her away from work, she thought.

Cap'n looked her directly in the eyes. 'Let's get a drink from the bar and I'll explain. I do still need you to look after Skippy, if that's any consolation.'

Andreas got the drinks, and Julio got the bags and followed behind. He thought about how short Jacqui's temper could be, and he certainly didn't want to get on the wrong side of this woman.

They sat at a secluded table and Andreas explained the whole story again. Cap'n watched as Abi began to sob, as Andreas told her about Jack. Cap'n felt useless. Abi was inconsolable for at least fifteen minutes, and had continued to cry while Andreas told her of how she was on Jack's list.

Cap'n interrupted Andreas, and put his arm around Abi. 'So I know you're angry with us, and yes, we know you can probably look after yourself, but this is bigger than all of us put together. We needed to get you out of Statia, so they can't find out the part of the clue that you hold. We're hoping it will slow them down if you're not on the island.'

'But I don't have any idea what the information could be. I haven't seen Jack for over a year.' Abi said

'OK. Finding whatever it is that Jack left you is not important right now.' Andreas said. 'We can go to Statia another time and work out what it is. In the meantime, we need you to stay on board with Skippy, while we fly down to Guadeloupe and Dominica, find Linalli, and get Saffi off. That's if they're still on board.'

Abigail tried to convince them to take her with them, that she knew the islands' rainforests better than anyone did, but she knew it was pointless.

'If we need you further down the line, we'll call for you. For the moment, I just want to keep you and Skippy safe.' Cap'n said.

'And now it's time for us to go, we've already submitted a flight plan.' Andreas said.

The three men got up, Abi remained sitting, still overwhelmed by all she'd been told. Andreas and Julio bent and hugged her goodbye and walked away, leaving Cap'n behind. They could sense he wanted some time alone with Abi. He sat down next to her and looked directly into her eyes.

'Abi, I don't know how you feel, but this whole sorry saga has made me realise I need to be truthful to myself, and with those I care about.'

Abi stared back into Cap'n's eyes, her stomached twitched and her heart beat faster, hoping he would say what she wanted to hear.

'It's just, you and I, we're the same, I think. Free spirits, maybe a bit too carefree at times'. He said.

'Yes, I agree with that.'

'Well, I think I want to clip the wings of my free spirit, just a bit.'

She looked at him curiously, 'what do you mean?'

'I don't mean I want to stop being me. Oh, I'm not making myself very clear, am I?'

'No, not really. Why don't you just say what you want to say in plain English?'

'OK. Abi, when this is all over, I think we should turn our friendship into a proper relationship.' He stumbled, 'if that's what you would like.' He hadn't thought that she might not want to.

Cap'n needn't have worried. Abi grabbed him with both arms and kissed him, the most passionate kiss she'd ever given anyone.

'I though you would never ask.' she said.

They stood up and walked back to Andreas and Julio, arm in arm. Despite the circumstances, they could not stop grinning at each other.

Abi stood in the departure lounge and watched as the plane took off. She would have to pray that now, having found the love of her life, he would come back safely to her.

Chapter 30

Saffi hadn't realised how much time had passed, whilst locked in her cabin. Apart from aggressively shoving some food through the door and slamming it shut again, her captors had not bothered her. She had dozed frequently, between trying to work out the clues, and had slept quite heavily once she had solved the entire puzzle.

However, she was woken suddenly, by the boat rocking wildly. The waves were crashing over the bows and against the sides, more than she had felt previously. Each time the boat moved it was more violent than the last. She looked at her watch. It was four o'clock in the morning. She looked out of the porthole. It was pitch black. She could see tiny specks of lights in the distance, and assumed they were from an island, but she had no idea where they were. She could also see the waves smashing up the side of the boat and she could hear the wind howling and assumed that it was raining. Every now and then horizontal lightening streaked across the heavens, fusing each cloud with the next, a blinding whiteness creating a momentary negative to the blackness. She was beginning to get very scared. They were obviously in a storm, and hoped that Tariq and the others had as much sailing experience as they had said.

Not knowing if she was safer in the cabin or up with her captors, either way, she wanted to know what was happening and where the life jackets were. She began screaming and banging on the cabin door to get their attention.

~~~

Up on deck Tariq, Conrad and Ollie were facing their own nightmares. They were in a storm that had not been forecast, and it had encroached the Caribbean Sea, unannounced, and out of season. It had started slowly at first, lulling them into a false sense of security, but as the hours crept by, the storm clouds accumulated and hid the moon under a veil of black. In their haste, they had not fixed the autopilot problem that they had created to get onto the boat in the first place, and were having to hand-steer. Unaware that the wind and sea were taking them off course, as the sea continued to rise, building with each wave, they had to keep a vigilant watch, in continually diminishing conditions. Very quickly, the short and steep, following seas were above the top of the canopy. As soon as the sea lifted Linalli up on the first wave, pointing her directly up into the night sky, the sea was immediately throwing her back down into the ocean as the crest of the wave collapsed, just as the next wave picked her up and repeated the process.

Standing at the helm Tariq watched, as a continuous rolling mass of water tried to invade the cockpit. He shouted at everyone, 'Double check your safety lines are on securely', as the sea tried to eject them from the protection of the cockpit. The enormous seas engulfed his view. Every wave that crashed behind the boat became louder and larger than the last. None of the men knew the history of the boat and had no idea if she could withstand the deteriorating conditions.

'We need to let the storm take us, there's no point trying to fight it, where's our safest landfall, Ollie?' Tariq shouted over the noise of the wind.

'I'll go and check the charts and the plotter and see what our options are. There's land on our port side.' Ollie replied as he cautiously made his way down the companionway. As he did, he could hear Saffi screaming in the cabin. 'Oh God', he thought, in their panic, they'd all forgotten about Saffi. He quickly checked the charts and went back up to the cockpit and shouted to Tariq. 'We're about forty miles from Guadeloupe, with the storm running behind us, all the sails are reefed and a storm jib up, it will take about six of seven hours.'

'OK, if everyone's in agreement, we'll run before the storm. If we can make Deshaies, we can hole up there while the storm blows itself out. I don't believe that Jack would have a boat that can't stand up to a storm. And where the hell did this weather come from anyway? Did anyone check the forecast before we left?' Tariq asked.

'There was nothing on any of the weather sites, or the Navtex. It has to be an out of season storm. It may not get much worse, but I agree we should head for Deshaies.' Conrad agreed.

'We do have another problem.' interjected Ollie, 'We have another passenger we've all forgotten about. Saffi's in the cabin screaming. What do you want to do with her? I think we should let her out of the cabin in these conditions?'

'I don't want her up in the cockpit, but I agree she shouldn't be locked in the cabin. Get her out and explain the situation to her, and tell her to keep quiet. The last thing we need is a whining woman, as well as a whining storm.' Tariq said.

Ollie went below and unlocked Saffi's cabin. He found her sobbing on the bed, hugging her knees to her chest. She didn't know what else to do.

'Thank God you've heard me; I was so frightened. What the hell is going on? Are we in a hurricane?' she asked, visibly scared.

'No, it's just a big storm, it will be OK.' Ollie said, sitting on the bed, trying to reassure her. She may be their captive, but she needed reassuring. 'I'll leave the door unlocked, but you're to stay down below.' he said calmly.

'You're not going to leave me again, are you? I can't bear it. The storm's getting worse, I can tell.' Saffi said.

'I have to go back up on deck to help the others, you'll be safe, but you must stay down here, it's for your own safety. Don't open any lockers or cabinets, you don't know what's moved or become dislodged. I promise to keep an eye you. It will be all right, trust me.' Ollie said as he walked out of the cabin and back up into the cockpit.

'Trust you', Saffi thought, but she had no one else to trust, and for some reason she did trust him. Her mind wandered to stories she'd seen on the news of people who somehow become friends or trust their captors. She sat in the saloon, holding on for dear life, as the waves tossed the boat around in all directions.

Chapter 31

Andreas, Cap'n Skip and Julio got into the plane that Julio had chartered in the Dominican Republic. They each carried a bag of essentials, comprising mobile phones, chargers, radios, charts and contact numbers. They had sombrely waved goodbye to Abi.

'I didn't expect that reaction from Abi. How long have you been holding out to tell her how you feel?' Andreas asked Cap'n as Julio carried out his pre-flight checks.

'Only since the first day I met her. We just never found the right time or place to tell each other. We've always been on the wrong island at the wrong time.' Cap'n replied. 'It's just a shame it's taken something like this to put it all in perspective, and let each other know.'

'Well let's make sure we get you back in one piece, now that you've found the love of your life.' Andreas said, trying to lighten the mood, but all the while thinking about how frightened Saffi must be.

Julio raised his finger to his mouth, indicating that he was about to talk to Air Traffic Control. With the procedures out of the way, he headed down the taxiway, ready to receive his departure clearance. Within ten minutes, they were on their way to Guadeloupe, not knowing what to expect.

~~~

The journey was uneventful and they arrived in good time. Having checked-in and cleared customs they found the hire car they had reserved and were on their way to their hotel within half an hour.

'There aren't many hotels in Point-a-Pitre, so I picked one right at the entrance to the River Salee, so we can won't have far to go to get to the bridges in the morning, see if we can find Pablo before he goes on shift.' Julio said.

'That's good. As a favour for flying us here, you can have a lie-in in the morning Julio. Cap'n and I will set the alarm for 4am and we can each go to one of the bridges. The south bridge opens at 5 o'clock, the north at 5.30.' Andreas said, and confirmed with Cap'n that he would take the south and Cap'n the north bridge.

It was after mid-night before they checked into the hotel and went immediately to bed. The past few days had been exhausting, and they knew the next few would be more so.

~~~

Andreas woke suddenly at 4am, but it wasn't his alarm clock going off, it was the sound of thunder outside the hotel, and the night sky bleached white by the lightening as it flashed outside his window. Startled, he got up to see what was happening. There was nothing on the weather reports issued in the BVI. He looked out of the window, and with the realisation of the storm going on, his thoughts turned immediately to Saffi, and the fear for where she might be.

He switched on the TV and turned to the Weather Channel to see if the storm had reached the media yet? As he did there was a knock at the door, he opened it, knowing it would be Cap'n, but saw Julio standing there as well.

They all sat on the bed, watching the weather report, all knowing what the others were thinking, but no one saying a word, as news of Tropical Storm Olga was beginning to unfold on the screen in front of them.

". . . the formation of Subtropical Storm Olga, a low level trough began to develop along the eastern periphery of an upper level low, over the tropical Atlantic Ocean near 50 degrees West, Longitude. Waters in the region are still marginally warm enough to assist in subtropical development, near 28 degrees Celsius. Initially, the system was inhibited by strong south-westerly wind shear, which confined convection to the northern side of the system. . . the National Hurricane Centre has began communicating safety advisories about the system and its potential threats. The low-pressure system is beginning to show initial signs of low-level rotation on satellite imagery, as it continues to move west towards the Leeward Islands."

Andreas stood up and switched off the TV. He looked at the others. They all knew what the warnings meant. 'We may as well see if we can find Pablo, there's nothing we can do if Saffi is still on Linalli and out at sea. We have no idea where they are.' He said, trying to hide his worst fears.

Cap'n nodded his agreement. Julio looked at Andreas and Cap'n ad said, 'OK, you two head to the bridges, I'll get over to the Coast Guard to enquire if anyone is known to be out at sea.' Julio stopped and looked at Andreas again, ' and yes Andreas, I know, I won't mention the boat or Saffi's names, but I'll find out if anyone has called in a Mayday or a PAN PAN.'

'Sorry Julio, nerves! I think you ought to call Jacqui to give her the heads up and prepare for what might be heading her way'. Andreas said.

Cap'n looked at Julio, 'And while you're at it, can you call Abi to warn her too. My boat's safe enough in its moorings, but she may not want to be on board in a storm.' Cap'n's voice already sounding nervous for her.

'Will do. And when you both get back we'll go and tie the plane down more securely.' Julio said.

The three men looked at each other pensively. They knew there was nothing more they could do. They also knew they had to be quick about their tasks in order to get back to safety, in case Tropical Storm Olga became Hurricane Olga.

Chapter 32

Saffi sat in the saloon, alone and frightened. Every time a wave hit the hull, the boat jerked in every direction and she found it difficult to hold on and sit tight. The noise of the waves crashing against the hull and the wind through the rigging was deafening. Eventually, she could bear it no longer and stepped up through the companionway, peered into the cockpit, but did not actually encroach any further. She could see Tariq at the helm, spinning the wheel violently one way, then the other. All of them were soaked to the skin. Every bolt of lightning lit the sky a brilliant white, and just as quickly returned to the blackness the clouds created. The sun was not due to rise for another hour, but it would be impossible for it to break through the thickness of the storm clouds.

Saffi didn't speak, but stared at the enormity of the situation she was in, being held captive on her own boat, in a storm that wasn't forecast, heading for an island somewhere in the Caribbean, and she had no idea what to do about it.

Conrad saw her peering through the companionway. He bent down to her face, his face expressionless, 'You really don't want to be up here, and we don't want you up here. Let us deal with the weather, we do know what we're doing, I promise. If you really want to be useful, you can find us something to drink, and something simple to eat. Biscuits or crackers, anything we can just grab at.'

Saffi nodded. Somehow, their dire situation gave them some sort of camaraderie, not something she understood, but they all knew they were in this together, no matter what happened.

She went back down below, hanging on to anything in her reach, every time the boat lurched. She found some cans of drink, crisps and biscuits and passed them through to Conrad. Tariq and Ollie did not move from their positions. Tariq was steering, and Ollie was looking out, calling instructions. She dared not interrupt and went back below again, and sat in the corner of the sofa with her knees to her chest. Why was she here, what had possessed her to come? She could be at home with Nana, living a quiet, normal life, and then she thought about everything she had been through recently with Andreas and the thought of what she had seen and done recently, made her wonder if she did actually want to be at home with a normal life? Everything she had done with Andreas she had enjoyed. Maybe not the current situation, but the flying, the sailing, meeting new people, all those things had come so naturally to her and she had enjoyed every minute of it. Had Jack set this whole thing up, just to make her realise that there was more to life than a job as an accountant? After all, her mother had followed him to the ends of the earth, or so it seemed. Lillian had travelled with him at a time when no one really went off the beaten track. Had she inherited something from her parents that allowed her to enjoy this adventure? Was this Jack's plan all along?

~~~

She sat in the saloon, lost in her thoughts, until Ollie broke into them.

'Saffi, this is getting very dangerous now. We're going to try to get to a safe anchorage in Guadeloupe, a place called Deshaies, but it's going to get very rough over the next couple of hours. I promise nothing bad will happen to you if you do exactly what I say. You have your life jacket on, but you must stay down here. Under no circumstances must you go up on deck. We will deal with the storm and get you to safety.'

With renewed vigour, she laughed at him, 'and what will you do with me then, I wonder? I'm still your prisoner. Why should I listen to you, all you're after is my father's fortune, you don't care about me? You'll keep me alive for as long as it suits you. It would be much simpler for me if I just went upstairs and jumped overboard. Either way I'm dead. You're not going to keep me alive after you've got what you're looking for. So why should I let you get to it in the first place?'

She had no idea where her strength to retaliate had come from. Maybe she finally got the point that Jack was trying to teach her, no point being alive if you're not actually living!

She sat back, almost relaxed, considering the situation. Ollie had nothing to say to her. He realised that he would have to put her back in the cabin for fear that she would try to do something stupid. With rage filling his head, he grabbed her by the wrists and threw her back in the cabin, slammed the door and locked it. 'Try jumping overboard from there.' he shouted through the door.

Back on deck, he explained to the others what had gone on, and that he had locked her back in the cabin. 'I believe the ghost of Jack has just risen in his daughter, like the proverbial phoenix, I think we will have to watch her like a hawk now.' He said. The others nodded their agreement, but knew their first concern was to concentrate on fighting the storm and getting to a safe haven.

Chapter 33

Before leaving for work, Pablo Francois had double-checked that every shutter, every door, and anything that could come loose, was secure. He, like everyone else in the islands, had woken to the sound of Tropical Storm Olga. He had quickly checked the weather stations and the National Hurricane Centre to see if they had predicted a track for Olga. Although he doubted anyone would come through the bridges, it was still his responsibility to ensure that everything was secure in such times. He looked in on his sleeping children, and kissed his wife goodbye, as he did every morning, whatever the weather.

His route to work didn't take that long, and the winds were not too strong in-land as he left home. When he reached his bridge station, there was someone already there, waiting for him. Andreas stepped forward, away from the shelter of the cabin, and held his hand out in greeting, hoping not to startle Pablo. After all, Andreas knew about Pablo, but Pablo had no idea who Andreas was.

'Hi.' Andreas said tentatively. 'I'm sorry to disturb you before you've even started work, and in such horrible conditions, but my name is Andreas Romani. I'm a good friend of Jack Simpson. Are you Pablo Francois?' Andreas stopped, hoping that the mention of Jack would help the situation, not knowing whether Pablo had received the news of Jack's death.

Pablo shook Andreas' hand, thinking it had been at least a year, or more, since he'd seen Jack. 'Yes, I'm Pablo Francois, how can I help you?' Pablo asked, always wary of anyone purporting to be a good friend of Jacks.

'Do you mind if we go in the cabin, this might take some time?' Andreas said, shielding his face from the wind and rain, which was getting heavier by the minute.

Something about Andreas rang true in Pablo's mind, he recalled Jack talking about him. 'I need to make some routine checks on the bridges before I do anything else, if you don't mind waiting?' Pablo said as he unlocked the cabin door. They went inside; Pablo pointed to a chair and indicated for Andreas to sit.

'I don't imagine anyone's going to be going through the bridges in these conditions, but you never know. I couldn't believe it when I woke up to this storm. You'd think the NHC would've spotted this one and given us a bit more warning.' Pablo said as he poured himself a coffee from his flask and offered Andreas the same.

'Thanks, but I've had my fill of caffeine this morning already, and I won't keep you long.' Andreas replied.

'OK, but I have to call the other operator to make sure no-one's coming through, we only give boats a ten-minute window to show themselves, after that they have to wait till the following morning.' Pablo said, not waiting for an acknowledgement from Andreas, but got on the phone to the other bridge operator.

Andreas took the opportunity to send a text to Cap'n, informing him that he had located Pablo and that he should go back and help Julio secure the plane at the airport.

A few moments later, Pablo put down the phone and turned to face Andreas. 'Seems like everyone has their sensible hats on and are staying tucked up in their cabins, riding out the storm securely somewhere. Now, how can I help you Andreas, you said you're a friend of Jack's. How is he?'

Andreas broke the news gently to Pablo, who was visibly very upset on hearing the news. He, like everyone, held Jack in high regard and had a special relationship with him.

'I can't believe it. I know it's been over a year since I've seen him, but that's quite normal for Jack. The wife and children will be devastated when I tell them.' Pablo poured yet another cup of coffee, offering one to Andreas, who accepted this time. 'However, you still haven't said how I can help you. I don't imagine you came all this way just to tell me this news in person. Is there something else?'

Andreas started at the beginning, from when Saffi arrived, and finished fifteen minutes later asking if Jack had left him anything personal, or odd. He also asked him if he had received any reports of boats out at sea, having told him of Saffi's kidnapping.

'I'll get straight on to the coast guard, I can't believe it, and she must be petrified.' Pablo said, picking up the radio receiver.

'OK, but don't mention the boat name or Saffi, we don't know who Luis has on the inside.' Andreas said.

After he called the Coastguard, Pablo explained that there had been no reports of any boats in the last four hours. He then went on to tell Andreas a few stories of how he had helped Jack hide out in the mangroves over the years. Andreas now knew that Pablo could be trusted, and obviously why Jack had him on his list. He would also be another pair of eyes, which would only aid their search.

'What about anything that Jack may have left with you, a trinket or gift. Anything that would help us solve the puzzle?' Andreas asked.

Pablo thought hard. 'I can't think of any gift or strange object, but maybe. . .' he stood up and went to his workbag, opened a side pocket and took out a torch. He handed it to Andreas. 'Last time Jack was here, he left this on the Nav Station, over there.' Pablo pointed to the operations unit overlooking the River Salee. 'By the time I'd found it, he'd already left and was going down island. I left him text messages about it, and he just said he would pick it up next time he came through the bridge. Could that be what you're looking for?'

Andreas looked at the torch. It was nothing fancy, a typical, waterproof pocket torch. The sort any sailor would have lying around their boat. Then he looked at it more closely. Set into the wrist strap was a stone. A crystal stone, the sort of thing a girl would have in a necklace, not something a man would have on a torch. Next to the stone was a round, metal tag with 'XJ-5A' engraved into it.

'That's it.' Andreas exclaimed, 'Five across and a stone for the pendant. This is what we're looking for. Can I keep this?' Andreas asked, without thinking.

'Well, I suppose so, if it's going to help, it seems to make sense to you, and not to me.' Pablo said, not really knowing what else to say.

Before leaving, Andreas asked Pablo to lay low for a while, take a few days off. They still had no idea where Linalli, Tariq, and crew were, and whether they would come looking for Pablo. Andreas and Pablo promised to call each other if either of them heard any news.

In the meantime, Andreas went back to the hotel, not really knowing if he had achieved anything or not, only time would tell.

Chapter 34

Tariq checked his watch. 'Time to change shift guys, it's the only way we'll stay alert in these conditions. Ollie you take the helm, Conrad you keep a 360-degree watch and I'll check our position and get a weather update, if there's one.'

'If it's possible, get the kettle on, we could do with something hot inside, I'm sure I've seen some of those thermal mugs with lids.' Ollie said as he took over the helm.

Although the storm was getting worse, the boat was riding the waves well and they all knew they needed to keep their strength up in these conditions, even if was just a mug of coffee grabbed at frequent intervals.

Five minutes later Tariq appeared in the companionway with two mugs of coffee. 'There's no real update from the National Hurricane Centre, Olga's still running on its predicted course, up the islands and on to the Virgins, but I think it's going to get worse before it gets better. I'm not sure what it will be like when we get to Guadeloupe.' He said.

'Well at least we're not still in the Virgins. I reckon it'll be nearing hurricane strength by the time it gets there.' Ollie said as he battled to and fro, hand steering the boat.

'My only real concern is that I can't make out much on the radar. We're far enough out that there aren't any rocks or shoals but I've no idea who else is out here. You know what some of these yachties are like, we're only just out of hurricane season, and they'll already be moving their boats up and down the islands.' Tariq said.

'What's wrong with the radar?' Conrad asked. 'It was working OK before.'

'Yes, I know, but with the size of these waves, it would be useless to use. Even with the 'gain' at its least sensitive, it's still showing nearly every wave around. I can't work out if I'm looking at waves or other boats, and what with the rain, our visibility is almost zero.' Tariq said. 'Hopefully things will be a little easier to see when the sun comes up.'

'What do you mean when the sun comes up, it's been up for half an hour, but it's not had any effect on the amount of day light we've got? I don't think I've ever seen clouds so thick and black.' Ollie said.

'Do you think its worth heaving-too?' Conrad asked. 'It might be a better option to see if the storm will die down and it will make it safer to get into Guadeloupe.'

'I'm not sure it will be worth the effort. The NHC have said its moving west and north, so we are going to be getting the fall out of this storm for a while, I still think we should get to Guadeloupe as quickly as we can. Hopefully by then, it will be OK for us to get off the boat and move Saffi elsewhere on to the land, while we decide what to do next. No-one knows we're out here, Luis can't get hold of us while we're out at sea, and even if he knows we're caught in the storm, he doesn't know where we're going, and this will put further distance between us.' Tariq said, and Ollie agreed.

'We've reduced the mainsail, and put up a storm-sail, and we can put out a sea anchor, if the following seas become too dangerous, that will slow us down and stop the boat broaching. Saffi is safe down below, and I still think this is the best course of action in these conditions.' Ollie and Conrad knew this decision wasn't open for negotiation.

'Can I suggest that in order to stay alert, and conserve energy, there should only ever be two on deck, and the other one of us can take a thirty-minute rest every hour.' Conrad said, and the others agreed.

~~~

Locked in her cabin, Saffi knew there was nothing she could do; she would wait and see what happened when they reached the shore. In her predicament, this would still be her best plan of action. All she knew was where she had to get to, once she had somehow managed to get free from Tariq, Conrad and Ollie. Even so, the more the storm continued, the more frightened she became. If she ever managed to get home and watch reports on the BBC of hurricanes and other disasters, she would know firsthand how everyone in the islands was feeling - alone and out of control in such awful conditions.

~~~

After another hour, the men changed shifts, two up on deck, and the other below. They had not had a chance to eat or drink anything, and had not bothered to check on Saffi. The storm had raged on, increasing wind strength and wave size, and each of them were grateful that Jack's boat was able to cope with the ferociousness of the storm. As the sun rose higher, the sky became a little lighter, and their ability to keep a daylight watch made life a little easier. They knew they were nearing Guadeloupe and with that came other problems.

'Have you checked the chart to see how far out the sea bed begins to shelve up?' Tariq ask Conrad who was on navigation duties.

'I guess within the next hour we should start to see the waves increase in size, but they shouldn't get too steep as it shallows quite gently around Guadeloupe. I'm more concerned that we'll be able to make Deshaies with the direction of the wind. We may end up being pushed too far east and if that happens we'll be in real trouble.' Conrad said.

'Let's not think about that now, we'll wait to see what the next hour brings us. When we change watch we'll see how far east we've been pushed and make a decision then.' Tariq said.

However, they didn't have to wait that long before the wind and sea increased to such ferocity that they knew they would be in trouble.

~~~

Suddenly, there was almighty crash of thunder and lightning lit up the sky, like an exploding bomb, and a huge wave hit Linalli on her beam with such force it threw Ollie from his bunk. Above the noise of the storm, Saffi's scream was so loud everybody heard it. Ollie ran to her cabin and unlocked it. When he opened the door, he could see the cause of Saffi's screaming as she ran toward him and clung to him for dear life. She was soaked threw and water was pouring in through the cabin porthole which had cracked with the strength of the last wave that hit the boat.

'Ollie, please don't lock me in there, I'll drown. The water just crashed through the window like it was paper. Please, please don't make me stay in there.' Saffi's earlier bravado had left her, and she had returned the helpless hostage she knew she was. She clung to him and sobbed, she had never been so frightened in all her life.

'It's OK Saffi, you can stay out here, but get out of the way so I can do something with the porthole and stop the water coming in. Make yourself useful and let Tariq know what's happened. Tell him we need to pump the bilges.' Ollie said as he rushed into the cabin to help stop the ever-increasing amount of water from entering through the porthole.

Saffi did as Ollie asked and told Tariq what had happened.

'OK', Tariq replied. He knew neither he nor Conrad could leave the helm. He shouted toward the companionway to Saffi. 'To your left, the Nav station, that's where all the charts are kept, you'll find a switch on the electrical panel marked 'bilge pump'. Can you see it from where you're standing?'

Saffi looked over at the panel with at least thirty buttons on it, fortunately for her, Jack was meticulous at labelling everything on board, and Andreas had briefly explained the panel to her. 'Yes, I can see the switch.' she replied.

'Good, now go and turn the switch on for at least a minute, and then every two minutes turn it on for another minute until Ollie has sorted the porthole out. Can you do that?' Tariq asked. He could see how frightened she was and realised this would keep her occupied until the leak was under control.

Saffi sat at the Nav Station, periodically turning the bilge pump on as instructed, and hanging on for dear life every time the boat swung violently from side to side. After five minutes, Ollie came out of the cabin and shouted up the companionway to Tariq and Conrad.

'We need to find something strong enough to place over the window and tape it up. It won't fix the problem but it will stem the flow of water until we can find a better solution. The window is cracked and there's a hole in it, so it needs something sturdy. I will see what I can find down here. I'll keep Saffi on bilge pump duties.' He looked over to Saffi for acknowledgement that she was OK. He just saw fear reflecting back from her eyes. However, she also had an idea, something that Andreas had shown her when she was first on the boat, something at the time she didn't think was important.

'What about an old life jacket. In the other cabin there are some old-fashioned life jackets, you know the sort that are made of polystyrene or something. Andreas had told her she could throw them out, as they had replaced them with modern ones. Can't you cut a bit out in the shape of the window and tape that into it.' She said, not knowing if this was a good or bad suggestion.

Ollie could have hugged her, if he wasn't so aware of the seriousness of the situation. 'Where are they, in the forward cabin?' he asked.

'In the cupboard, they're just thrown in there, I don't think they've been touched for years.' and at the sound of her own voice she now knew more about Linalli than she realised, and that was all because of Andreas. She knew she had to put his memory to back of her mind and deal with the situation in hand.

Ollie opened the cupboard to find two life jackets. He grabbed one of them and with his knife started to tear off the outer orange plastic covering. He looked at Saffi, 'Perfect.' He said and ran to the far cabin. 'Saffi give the bilge pump one long last pump and then come in here and hold the blankets and pillows up to the opening, it will stem the flow while I cut this to size.'

Again, doing as Ollie told her, she held the bilge pump on for another minute and then ran to the cabin. Inside she could see seawater still gushing in through the porthole as the waves hit the sides of the boat, and Ollie was standing in about an inch of water. Taking in the situation she grabbed the pillows and blankets, pushed them up against the porthole, and held them as tightly as she could while Ollie cut the old life jacket to size. Water continued to come through, but not as fast as before. She was kneeling on the bed, which was soaked through by now and it was difficult for her to get any purchase against anything at all. She used all her strength to keep the bedding in the porthole, and her arms and legs where shaking, she had no more energy left.

'When I say, I want you to take out the blankets while I push the polystyrene in place, I'll hold it there while you go and get anything you can find that will fit into the gaps around the edge, tea-towels, pillow cases, anything. Then stuff them in as tightly as you can. Understand?' Ollie said looking at her directly. Saffi nodded in confirmation as the adrenaline took over from any fear she had before.

'OK, on the count of three. One, two, three.'

Everything went like clockwork as Ollie jammed the polystyrene into the porthole. His expert use of a knife had ensured that he had cut an almost perfect wedge. Only two or three gaps remained around the edges. Saffi ran back with a bag of old cloths she had found in the same cupboard as the old life jackets. Together they ripped the cloth into smaller pieces and began jamming them into the gaps. Then, using the gaffer tap he found earlier, Ollie taped the whole porthole up.

'It will hold for now, but not for long, we'll need to keep coming in here and checking the port hole, can you do that for me?' Ollie said. He knew he had to keep Saffi occupied below decks, and it would keep her mind off the storm.

'I'll keep pumping the bilges and checking the water level in the cabin. If anything changes I'll let you know'. Saffi said. She understood the magnitude of the situation.

~~~

Ollie went to the cockpit and updated Tariq and Conrad; he looked around at the sky and took in the enormity of the storm they were in.

'What are our chances of getting to Guadeloupe safely?' He shouted above the noise of the wind and the sea.

'We'll get there, but I'm not sure we'll make Deshaies, the storm's pushing us in the wrong direction and I think we're going to end up in the 'Cul de Sac' Tariq shouted back.

'We'll never survive in there, there are too many reefs. It will be suicide. There must be another option.' Ollie said. Looking toward the island of Guadeloupe as it began to show itself upon the horizon.

They all knew they had no other options, but this would be the worst place for the storm to push them. The storm was driving them so hard and fast that they all prayed that it would have passed by the time they were forced into Guadeloupe's reef system that protects the inner shores of her north coast.

~~~

Tariq, Conrad and Ollie tried to prepare the boat, as well as Saffi, for what was going to be their worst nightmare. They were at the mercy of Tropical Storm Olga, and nothing they had tried, could stop the wind and sea pushing them into the Grand Cul-de-Sac Marin, a large bay on Guadeloupe's north coast, that runs between her two landmasses. The river would have been a perfect 'hurricane hole' but, they were too late to even try to enter the channel. Tied up among the mangroves a boat can sit out a hurricane in relative safety. However, not for the four souls on board Linalli caught out in the storm.

'Can't we contact the coastguard?' Saffi said, realising immediately what a stupid thing she said.

'Even if we weren't holding you against your will, and on the run from God knows who else, do you really think that the coastguard would even attempt to come out in these conditions. Tariq replied with such venom in his voice that Saffi knew not to say another word.

Conrad was at the helm and Tariq was desperately looking for somewhere they could try to head for, somewhere with a bit of protection.

'Ilet a Fajou is right on the edge of the reef system and the entrance to the marked channel is on its eastern side. We're about six miles away, if we keep the island to the south of us until we pass it, we might be able to get some protection from the island. At this speed we'll be there in less than an hour'. Ollie suggested.

'It's an idea, and I really can't see anywhere else, without getting caught in the reef system.' Tariq agreed. 'I want everyone's safety lines attached when you're in the cockpit. Keep Saffi down below and get her to keep an eye on the bilges. You did a good job fixing that hole. We'll see how long it lasts. Hopefully we can get into some calmer water.'

Tariq and Ollie returned to the cockpit to relieve Conrad. Saffi nodded to him as he came down the companionway, but he said nothing. He was exhausted, and his eyes showed the fear everybody was feeling. He sat down, shut his eyes, laid his head back, and within minutes he was asleep.

~~~

While Conrad was asleep, Saffi noticed something that looked like a 'walkie-talkie' on the navigation table. With Tariq and Ollie in the cockpit and Conrad asleep, she moved over to the table. Although she didn't know what it was, she assumed it was some kind of radio. Trying to hide what she was doing, she sat down and started the bilge pump again, she managed to pick up the radio and slide it into her waistband, underneath her top. Then, as instructed, she went back to the cabin to check on the water level and the porthole.

She closed the cabin door behind her, sat down on the bed and looked at the radio she had concealed under her top. There was an on/off button on the top. She turned slowly and it clicked on. It made a 'beep' noise and the screen glowed orange and displayed a number '16'. She knew now that it was a hand-held VHF radio. When she and Andreas had first gone sailing, he had shown her how to use the main radio, and explained that Channel 16 was the emergency channel. She turned the volume control up a little and squeezed the transmit button on the side. She had no idea what she was going to say, but she went ahead anyway.

'Hello, hello, MAYDAY, MAYDAY.' She knew she had to say that. 'Can anyone hear me? My name is Saffi and I'm being held prisoner on the boat Linalli.' She waited, but heard nothing.

She moved to the furthest part of the cabin, with her back to the door, turned the volume up and tried again.

'MAYDAY, MAYDAY, my name is Saffi, can anyone hear me?' This time she heard a crackle from the radio. She tried again. MAYDAY, MAYDAY, this is the boat Linalli, we're caught out in the storm and we're near Guadeloupe, can anyone hear me?'

'Vessel calling MAYDAY, repeat your vessel name and state your position'. The reply came, louder this time.

Before responding, Saffi went back to the door and checked that Conrad was still asleep, she could hear Tariq and Ollie shouting at each other above the noise of the storm. She closed the door and went back to her position at the end of the cabin.

'My name is Saffi, I'm being held captive on the boat Linalli, we're near Guadeloupe, but I don't know where, they mentioned a 'Cul-de-Sac'. She said as loudly and as clearly as the situation allowed.

'Are you a sailing vessel or a motor boat and what is the nature of your MAYDAY? Over.'

Saffi looked at the radio stunned, what do they mean what is the nature of my MAYDAY. She pressed the transmit button again. 'I'm in a sailing boat, in the middle of a hurricane and am being held captive by three thugs. What else do you want to know, please come and get me?' She replied desperately.

'OK Saffi, I want you to change to another channel. Channel zero nine. Please confirm you have understood. Channel zero nine. Over.'

'Yes I understand, channel zero nine.' Saffi replied and using the down arrow on the radio clicked down until it displayed zero nine. She heard the man's voice calling her again.

'Saffi this is the coastguard; can you hear me? Over.'

'Yes, I can hear you. Please help me. I don't know what to do.'

'Saffi, my name is Leo, can you tell me where on the boat you are and if you can see out of a window? Over.'

'I'm in a cabin, at the front of the boat, there is only one window I can see out of, but it's taped up because a wave smashed through it, there was water coming in and we had to cover it up.' Saffi said, knowing she was babbling.

'OK Saffi, good, that's fine, is there another window hidden behind any books or anything that you might be able to look outside. Can see any land? Over.'

Saffi looked around the cabin and soon realised that Jack had made a shelf along the other side of the cabin and placed all his books and manuals along it. She moved across and started pulling the books off the shelf. Behind them was a porthole. She looked outside and peered through the rain and sea spray. In the distance, she could see land. She picked up the radio and transmitted again.

'Yes, yes I can see land through the other port hole.'

'Good Saffi, now what side of the cabin is the port hole on, and how far away do you think the land is? Over.'

'The port hole is on the left of the cabin and I really can't tell how far the land is, about ten miles, maybe.' She replied.

'That's good Saffi. Now are you facing the front or the back of the boat? Over.' Leo knew he had to make his questions simple enough for Saffi to understand, in order to get the important information from her. This question would at least give him some idea of where they were in relation to Guadeloupe and what direction they were heading.

'I'm facing the front of the boat and the port hole is on the left hand side of the cabin.' She began to realise why he was asking such questions and had looked out the porthole again. 'The land is sort of at an angle in front and ahead of me, in the sort of eleven o'clock position on a clock.' She said, she'd remembered Andreas using this term when they were in the plane.

'That's very good Saffi. Now I want you to keep calm, I need to pass this information onto my colleagues so that we can decide on the best course of action. Leave the radio tuned to channel nine and I will get back to you as soon as I can. Do you understand? Over.'

'Yes, I understand, I'll keep the radio on channel nine and wait to hear from you. Over' She said tentatively, but what did he mean, 'check with his colleagues, surely they'll send a rescue boat for her, what else would they be thinking of doing?

But Leo didn't talk to his colleagues about the best course of action, he immediately got on the telephone to Luis Leppe and gave him an update of the conversation he had just had.

Chapter 35

Andreas sat in the hotel room, listening to the sound of the wind, and watching the torrential rain pour down the windows. He was monitoring channel 16, which had been silent all day. He never believed for one minute that Tariq or the others would transmit a message. They knew that would alert Luis Leppe to their whereabouts. Then he heard Saffi's voice, and her attempt to make someone listen to her MAYDAY. His biggest fear was that Leo, the coastguard she was conversing with, was one of Leppe's men. Not knowing who he could trust, Andreas had to find out if the coastguard actually would plan a real rescue operation. He flipped his phone open and dialled the one person in the coastguard he knew he could trust.

'This is Matt Fennis of the US Coastguard, please state the nature of your emergency and let me see if I can be of assistance.' The pre-recorded message on Matt's phone said. Andreas sighed.

'Matt, pick up the phone, its Andreas here, and it's important. Really important.' He waited patiently as he knew Matt would now be sauntering from the kitchen, back to the staff room, with his mid-morning coffee and doughnuts. He knew that coastguards training taught them not to rush into anything, and Matt never rushed if it meant spilling his coffee.

'Yo', Andreas, what gives, what's the panic? You know it's really bad timing to call me at coffee break.' Matt replied, not knowing how important Andreas call was.

'Matt, we have a situation on our hands, one I didn't tell you about sooner. Perhaps I should have done, it concerns someone close to us, well me especially.' Andreas spoke slowly. He wanted Matt to understand what he was trying to convey without mentioning Saffi's name. He knew he could trust Matt, but as always, never trusted who might be listening in on all their calls.

'Right, this situation, does it involve the storm that's currently heading my way, and could there be a sea worthy vessel in danger?' Matt knew to keep the reply ambiguous.

Andreas thought hard about how to reply and then he remembered what he had given Saffi when they visited. 'Yes, in a way. Do you remember that saltshaker you gave away recently, and how sad you would be, if I told you that someone has stolen it from me? Would that make you very angry?' Andreas hoped that Matt would understand what he was saying.

'When you say it was stolen, do you mean it was forcibly removed from your care?' Matt knew exactly what Andreas was getting at and understood not to mention names or places on the phone.

'Yeah, you could say that. They took the saltshaker and threw me away, if you get my drift, and I have been trying to find it ever since. Well today I heard a rumour that it might be lost at sea and in the hands of those who don't really care much for salt.' Andreas was hoping that he wasn't being too obscure, but he had no other options. He knew that one of Leppe's employees would be listening in, and he would already know that Saffi had put out a MAYDAY call, stating her rough position. The only bit of luck on his side was that no matter how much Leppe paid, no pilot would be able to go out in this storm. His only hope would be Matt.

'So where did you hear this rumour.' Matt asked, wondering how Andreas would get this message across. He'd been in a briefing all morning, getting everyone up to speed on the storm and its potential track, and had not been listening to the radio. Andreas had called just as he'd come out from the Ops Room, and no one had mentioned anything about anyone calling in a MAYDAY or anything. He knew as well as Andreas, that Leppe had people on the inside, even on 'his inside' and they may not have passed that message along yet.

'It was an advert I heard on the radio, something about the May Day celebrations this year, in Guadeloupe. The message was very clear that they need help, and quite urgently.' Andreas had to hope that his cryptic message made any sense at all, because he sure as hell didn't have any other ideas what to say.

'How many people do you think are involved? Matt asked, clearly understanding everything Andreas had said.

'Well I understand that they already have three additional members, who seem to want to keep the whole thing to themselves.' Andreas replied.

'How many do you have that can help, and where are you?'

I have three helpers already signed up, all in close proximity. How many can you get?' Andreas said, knowing the conversation was getting surreal, but he was glad that he and Jack had often had similar conversations when working undercover, and realised that probably everyone Jack had known, would communicate in a similar way when required.

'It's gonna be difficult with this storm to get anywhere fast, but leave it with me and I'll make some enquiries as to who would want to be interested in such an event. I'm sure they won't be too hard to find. Can I call you on this number?' Matt asked.

'This is the only number I have at the moment, I don't think we have a lot of choice in the matter, but we'll talk about the May Day Celebrations when we know more. I'll be in touch. And Matt,'

'Yes.' he replied.

'Thank you for your help in this. It is most appreciated by those that matter.'

'I know my friend; I'll be in touch.'

~~~

By the time Andreas had finished on the phone, Julio and Cap'n had returned to the hotel room.

'We've secured the plane, but it sure as hell is windy out there. I'm concerned about the lightning strikes. There's not much around the airport to deflect any lightening that might be headed that way.' Julio said. 'Did you get anything useful from the bridge guy?'

'Yes, he was very helpful, gave me a torch that Jack had obviously left for us to find, it's given me another crossword reference. He's a nice guy, said he knew Jack really well. He's gonna listen out for anything that might be useful.' Andreas said moving back to the window to see if the storm had abated any, it hadn't.'I don't suppose you two had the VHF on while you were out?'

'It was on, but we were at the plane most of the time, why, have you heard something?' Cap'n asked.

Andreas repeated what he'd heard on the radio, and then of the coded conversation he had with Matt. 'So now we need ideas of what to do. We've no idea if Leppe knows where the boat is, or whether he's in any position to attempt to take control of her. There's no way we can go out in this weather, I'm not sure what else we can do.'

At that moment Andrea's VHF radio squawked into life. He'd left it on Channel 9, hoping that Leo would get back to Saffi. They huddled around the radio and listened intently.

Chapter 36

Saffi jumped as the radio 'spoke' to her.

'Saffi, this is Leo, can you hear me?' He spoke clearly and confidently.

Leo Dubois didn't like to do what he was about to, but his brother owed too much money to Leppe. Leo had been trying to clear his brother's debts, built up over the years from his drug abuse. Leppe had always said that if he 'helped out when it was needed', he would clear his brother's debt, and that he and his family could move on. He only hoped that his involvement in what he was about to do would be enough.

'Hello, Leo, this is Saffi.' She spoke quietly, having once again checked that no one could hear her in the cabin. She had continued to go back and forth from the navigation table, pumping the bilges and checking the water levels in the cabin. 'Can you hear me OK?'

'Yes Saffi I can hear you. Has anything changed in the situation, are you still in the same position? Can you still see the island on the same side of the boat?' Leo asked. He kept checking over his shoulder to see that no one could hear what he was saying.

'That's correct, we don't seem to be moving very fast, the land is still quite a long way off. Are you sending someone to help me?' She asked, the expectation in her voice hiding any other feelings.

'Yes Saffi. I've checked with my superiors and they are sending a rescue boat to you within the next thirty minutes. It will take that time to launch the boat in these conditions. I want to you to continue to do what you're doing and not tell anyone on board about this conversation. You must not let them know that anyone is coming for you, they might make things worse for you if you do that. Do you understand?' He said, again checking over his shoulder. He knew there would be no rescue party coming from the Coastguard, but he had no idea if Leppe would be sending some sort of 'Greetings Party' for this woman and her captors.

'Oh thank god for that, thank you, thank you Leo. Do I need to do anything to let them know where we are, I can try and find some flares or something?' Saffi replied, not actually knowing where the flares were on the boat, or how to use them, even if she managed to find them.

'No, no, just sit tight and they will come to you. Leave the radio on channel nine and if there is anything else I need you to do, I will call you. Is that all clear?' Leo said, not waiting for an answer, instead it switched the radio back to monitor Channel 16.

Saffi had no idea that she was responding to no one when she replied. However, she was also unaware that Andreas, Cap'n, Julio, Matt and the bridge operators, had been listening in, and had all assumed the same thing. They knew the Coastguard weren't going to be making any rescue, but they had no idea if Luis Leppe was.

~~~

Raoul answered his mobile when he saw Luis Leppe's number appear on the screen.

'I have received word that the scumbag Tariq has taken off with the girl, and that they are caught in this irritating storm. It appears that they are stuck off the coast of Guadeloupe. No doubt they will try to make landfall and get the girl off the boat. How did you let this happen?' it was a rhetorical question. 'I need solutions, and I need them now. What do you suggest we do Raoul?'

Raoul always thought it humorous that the so-called 'master' of the drug world always asked for his opinion first and then took the suggestion as his own.

Calmly Raoul replied. 'In reality El Jeffe, there is not a lot that can be done at this moment. I am still in Tortola and the storm is heading my way, only a fool would attempt to go out in this weather. It would be like serving your own death sentence if anyone were to go out in a plane or a boat.' Raoul answered, knowing that this would save him from having to send any of his underlings out into such conditions. He did not have the same casual approach to death as his boss did. Good men are always hard to find, no point losing them to the elements, when there are enough other enemies they could be fighting.

'These were my thoughts exactly. We must not waste good men. How long do you think it will be before you can get to Guadeloupe? Surely this storm cannot last forever.' Leppe knew he was saying the right thing, but his patience was wearing thin. Not only had Tariq stolen the only chance he had of getting his money back, Tariq was also at least three steps ahead of him. He would not tolerate this situation for long.

'The NHC are predicting that it will be past the Virgins within twenty-four hours, I can have a plane down in Guadeloupe eight hours after that.' He knew it would only take him four, but he also knew that whatever he said Leppe would knock two hours off, thereby giving him an additional two hours to get things ready.

'Make sure you're there six hours after the storm has passed, and report to me as soon as you are off the ground. Is that clear?' Luis said, frustrated that he could not make things go faster. He was desperate to get hold of Jack Simpson's daughter and deal with her accordingly.

Raoul smiled as he heard his boss utter the last sentence, he had worked for him long enough to know how predictable he was. He would be there in four hours, two hours ahead of whoever else Leppe sent to spy on him. Double crossing was the nature of this game, and now no one knew who was on whose side.

~~~

As predicted, Luis immediately phoned another employee and told him to be in Guadeloupe as soon as humanly possible. There would be a bonus for him if he made it before Raoul.

Chapter 37

After listening to the VHF radio, Andreas turned to the others.

'I don't know about you guys, but Leo doesn't sound like he's being completely truthful to Saffi'.

'What do you want to do?' asked Cap'n.

'I don't know. Anyone got any suggestions?'

'What's happening with Matt? Is it worth calling him to get an update?' Julio asked.

'No, I don't want to draw attention to us being on their trail, we'll wait for Matt to call us, but I can't sit here and do nothing.' Andreas was now letting the panic set it and the others knew it.

'What about Pablo, the guy at the bridge. You said he was a friend of Jack. He must know some people who can help, being the bridge operator. Let's give him a call and see if he can give us some ideas.' Cap'n suggested.

'Good idea', Julio added, 'and what about the pilots at the airport. I'm sure there would be someone willing to help. It has to be better than sitting around here waiting for something to happen that's out of our control.'

'You're right,' Andreas said, realising he had to take control of the situation and pull himself out of this self-pity. 'OK, Julio you get back to the airport and see what you can find out, Cap'n you call Pablo and see if he'll help.'

'What are you going to do?' Julio asked, not knowing what else there was to do.

'Me, I'm heading down to the marina at Pont-a-Pitre, there are some guys I know, and I'll see if I can get hold of a decent rib. If I was in Tariq's position in this storm, I'd be heading for Ilet a Fajou to try to get some protection from behind the island, and if that's what they do, I want us to be there waiting for them.' Andreas replied, now ready for action. 'Keep your radios dual tuned to 16 and 09, and if you have any updates click three silent blips on channel 16, then move to channel 84 and hope that no-one follows us there. Keep the conversation low key and as cryptic as you can. If we have nothing in two hours, meet back here.

~~~

It only took a couple of minutes talking to Pablo for Cap'n to realise that Pablo had access to many things and people.

'I'll contact any fisherman I know, they can start to scour the area without looking suspicious, when they get back out to sea.' Pablo suggested.

'That's great, but no-one is to risk their lives in this storm, no-one goes out till it's safe to do so'. Cap'n replied. 'Andreas and Julio are meeting me back at the hotel in two hours. You can join us and give us any news you have then. We're trying to maintain radio silence as much as we can.'

'I understand, I'll pass the message onto the fishermen and see you in two hours.'

~~~

Julio had similar fortune with the pilots at the airport. They all knew Jack from years gone by, and agreed to take off when it was safe, and start searching for the boat and Saffi. They would report any sightings back to Julio at the hotel via text message, rather than trust anyone in the control tower, or anyone else listening in on the radio.

~~~

Andreas was also getting help from an old associate, Marcus, who offered to take him out in his rib when it was safe to do so.

'I have an 80hp outboard that will get us out to Ilet a Fajou in a matter of minutes. The rib's low enough that we can go under the bridges and get through the river without having to wait for the bridges to open.' Marcus explained. 'We can go through the river now and wait at the north entrance. There are enough safe places in the mangroves where we won't be seen, while we wait for the weather to calm down before heading over to the island.'

Andreas was happy with this plan and sent a brief text to let the others know what he was doing. He would contact them if he had any news, and followed Marcus to his Rib.

'Put this on, before we get going, and attach the safety strap. I don't want to have to rescue you first.' Marcus handed Andreas a life jacket and safety strap. 'We still have to take it carefully while the wind is so strong.' Marcus shouted to Andreas. 'I know this rib looks sturdy, but some of these winds could still flip us over until we're in the mangroves proper.'

It had been a long time since Andreas had been through the River Salee, and as the bridges only opened before daybreak, he had never been through during daylight hours. He hadn't realised how winding the river was through the mangroves, so many places for a small boat to hide away, or to ride out a hurricane he thought, as Marcus carefully navigated through to the south entrance.

'What are the maximum conditions you can go out in this Rib?' Andreas asked, trying to make some sort of conversation while they were making their way through the river.

'The manual says she's a Class C, Inshore Rib, so, up to a Force 6, but we've been out in stronger, when we've needed to. It really depends on how big the sea is, and how many I have on board. With just the two of us, it's a tricky one to answer as the payload is down, but we'll see what the sea state is like when we get there. Hopefully the reef and islands will break up some of the bigger waves.' Marcus replied, only looking back to Andreas briefly, every few seconds. His full concentration was on steering the boat through the river and working against the winds.

Andreas nodded in silence, as he hung onto the boat. Although they were in the river proper now, the storm was still raging and picking the sea up inside the mangroves. Because Marcus was driving the rib slowly, it bounced off every wave it hit, and the ride was very uncomfortable. However, they reached the north bridge quite quickly and tied up to one of the huge buoys provided by the authorities.

'We'll sit here, in the mangroves, until the storm dies down enough for us to go out into the reef system and take a better look. There's nothing more we can do until then.' Marcus said.

Andreas was frustrated, but knew that Marcus was right.

Chapter 38

Saffi continued to work the bilge pump in the cabin; she had hidden the handheld radio in a locker. Conrad tried to sleep until it was his time to go back on deck. The storm had remained at the same intensity, but the wind direction had changed, as Tariq knew it would. They were now clearly heading for the 'Grand Cul-de-Sac du Marin', but no one on board knew where they would end up.

The last thirty minutes had felt like hours, Linalli was tossed around as though she was made of paper, but she was strong enough not to break up, and dealt with the big, confused seas much better than her occupants. Slowly the entrance to the enormous bay opened up, and it would now take all of Tariq's strength to try to steer the boat behind the island in the middle of the bay, and into what he hoped would be calmer waters.

'Conrad', Tariq shouted over the howling wind, 'come up here on deck and help me out, while Ollie watches the chart plotter for the depths. This whole area is full of coral reefs and shoals and as we have very little steering, it will be our only hope. Ollie, I want to keep at least five meters underneath us, do you understand. The minute the depth starts to decrease I want you to shout headings to me, in order to avoid the shallows.' Tariq knew he had to stay in command, he shouted his instructions and watched as Ollie and Conrad got into their respective positions.

'Saffi, you continue to do what you're doing, keep an eye on the bilges and the water level in that cabin, and don't bother with any more drinks, we need all our concentration to get behind this island.' Tariq didn't wait for any acknowledgement from Saffi. 'Fifteen minutes each at the helm in these conditions is enough for anyone.' Tariq said as he took control of the helm from Conrad.

But Saffi had other ideas.

~~~

The more she thought about it, the more Saffi realised that she would have more chance to escape, as they got closer to land. Rightly or wrongly, she thought that if she let the bilges fill up, this would hinder their ability to sail the boat, as it slowly sank. She had no idea if this would work, or how dangerous it would be. Nor did she know what effect it would have on the boat, as far as she was concerned, she knew the coastguards were coming, and that's all that mattered.

She continued to go to the bilge pump, but only switched it on for half the time she had previously, then she went back to the cabin, and rather than trying to stop the flow of water trickling through the porthole, she removed the entire polystyrene plug and let as much water in as she dared, without getting wet. She then put the plug back in and sealed it up, but not nearly as tightly. Each time a wave crashed over the boat, more water came through the porthole. She checked that the hatch above her was unlocked and that it was big enough for her to get out. When the time came, and the boat started to sink, she would climb out through the hatch, to the safety of the coastguard – or so she thought.

However, within minutes, she could hear all three men screaming at each other up on deck, she ran to see what was happening. Conrad was hanging over the side of the boat, held on only by his safety line. Tariq was desperately trying to control the boat, as Ollie was trying to get Conrad back inside the cockpit.

'Saffi, come up here and strap yourself on, help me get him back on board.' Ollie screamed.

Without a second thought, she ran to help him pull Conrad back onto the boat. It didn't occur to her to let them struggle, or even let him fall over board, what would it matter to her. In fact, it would have made life a lot easier, only having to deal with two captors. However, her compassionate instincts took over, someone needed her help, and she could do nothing to stop herself from running into the cockpit, and with all her strength she helped Ollie pull Conrad back into the safety of the boat. He was alive, but unconscious. This caused Tariq a dilemma.

~~~

Conrad lay on the cockpit floor, unconscious, and in a potentially dangerous position. He would be in everyone's way, and unable to keep himself secure.

'Saffi, you get down below and Ollie, try dragging Conrad by his feet and pass them down to Saffi, then try to get him under the arms and slide him down below. Saffi put some blankets on the floor to soften his landing.' Conrad shouted to them both.

Saffi did as instructed, but found Conrad's concern for another human being's safety completely out of character. She knew he would be in the way, but why worry about his landing. In any case, she took the pillows from the cabins, placed them on the floor and waited at the bottom of the companionway. She saw Ollie struggling to drag the dead weight of Conrad to the top of the stairs, he positioned Conrad's legs over the stairs, Saffi grabbed them, but his weight was too much.

'Wait a minute, I have an idea.' She said and turned so her back was facing the stairs. She sat on the middle stair, her feet just touching the floor and placed Conrad's legs either side of her shoulders. 'Can you lift him now?' She shouted up to Ollie. She heard Ollie grunt under the strain of the dead weight, but soon felt the weight on her shoulders. She managed to stand, whilst holding onto the stair rails with one hand.

'Move forward slowly, Saffi.' Ollie shouted. 'When you've got his weight supported, can you turn around and face me?' He asked.

Standing with the weight of Conrad on her shoulders, she held on as much as she could before she turned around to face Ollie.

'Good, now you can see what I'm doing, I can hold his shoulders, you can move backwards and I can then ease down the stairs. Now, on the count of three. One, two, three.' Ollie shouted.

Saffi stepped backwards, very carefully, holding on with one hand to steady herself. Ollie lifted Conrad's head and they brought him down and laid him on the floor.

'Excellent, now I can drag him into the main cabin'. Ollie said, whilst picking Conrad up under his shoulders. 'Get the door open Saffi'.

Saffi's heart sank. He would see what she had been doing and now she would have no chance of escaping through the hatch when the Coastguard finally arrived. She had to think quickly.

'Wouldn't it be better if you just laid him in the other cabin, I've to keep the bilges pumped and keep and eye on the hatch in the cabin, he'll be in the way if you put him in there?' Her voice desperate.

'No, this will be safest place for him, now open the door.'

Saffi did as Ollie said and he dragged Conrad backwards through the boat, toward the open cabin. Just as he stepped over the bulkhead and through the door, the boat lurched suddenly and they both heard the noise of the crash as the boat hit the reef. Saffi screamed. Ollie fell and door slammed shut. Within seconds, the boat was listing and she could hear Ollie trying to get to door open and shouting at her.

'Get upstairs and find out what's happened, tell Tariq I can't get the door open and there's water coming in fast.'

Saffi stood in bewilderment, paralysed by fear, and trying to stand upright as she realised they had come to a halt, the wind and sea screaming and crashing all around her.

'Saffi, do you hear me, what's happening?' Ollie shouted, whilst banging on the door.

His voice brought her out of her panic-induced trance and she ran up to the cockpit, and could not believe what she saw when she came through the companionway.

Chapter 39

Although it seemed like longer, only two hours had passed since Andreas and the others had set out to find help from people on the island. However, it was clear to see that the storm was abating, albeit slowly. From the rib, Andreas looked through his binoculars to check if he could see anything in the bay.

'I don't believe it.' Andreas said, handing the binoculars to Marcus. 'Over on the far side of the island, a boat's crashed on the reef and I think it's Linalli.'

Marcus refocused the binoculars and scanned the horizon, and found what Andreas was looking at. 'What do you want to do? It should be OK to take the rib over there now?'

Although he wanted to get to Saffi as soon as possible, he thought better of the idea.

'Not yet. Let's get the others here, with some back up. We don't know what we're going to be getting into over there.' Andreas said.

'We can monitor the boat from here, if it looks like it's getting more unstable, we can do something then.' Marcus agreed.

'OK, you keep watching the boat and I'll text Cap'n and Julio'.

~~~

As Andreas received acknowledgement from Julio, that they were on their way, Marcus could see something happening on the boat.

'Look in the cockpit, it looks like a woman, but I can't see anyone else. What do you think?' Marcus passed the binoculars back to Andreas, and without waiting for an answer, started the engine.

'That's Saffi, I'm sure of it. The boat looks like its listing further, and she's struggling to hang on, no wait, she's gone back down below.' Andreas said, and nodded to Marcus to go.

Although the wind and rain had eased considerably, they still couldn't go at full speed; the sea was still too big, especially over the reef. Then without warning, Saffi's voice was on the VHF radio.

'MAY DAY MAY DAY MAY DAY, can anyone hear me? Then silence.

Andreas grabbed the radio, he didn't care who heard now. 'Saffi?' He shouted down the radio. 'Saffi, it's me; I'm on my way, just hold on tight. Who else is on the boat?' He asked cautiously, but didn't really care what she replied, he was going to rescue her, right now.

'Oh my god, is that you Andreas? I thought you were dead.' Saffi replied. 'Where are you, I can't see you?'

'OK Saffi, we're on our way, just hold tight. I say again, is there anyone else on board?' He needed her to answer, it was crucial he knew who was on the boat.

'Conrad is unconscious, he nearly fell overboard, so we put him in the forward cabin, that's when we crashed and Olli is now in there with him. When I came back up on deck and I couldn't find Tariq. We've hit the reef and water is coming in. I've got a life jacket on. What do you want me to do?'

'OK Saffi, I want you to stay calm and get yourself to the highest point of the boat, away from where the water is coming in. Is that possible?'

'Yes, I think I can get over to the other side.' She replied.

'That's good Saffi, now hold on tightly. The waves are still going to be coming over the side, and could easily wash you overboard. Have you got anywhere you can put the radio, in a pocket or something?'

'I'm using the main radio, down at the 'Nav Station', I've hidden the handheld in the cabin where Ollie is trapped, I was using it to call the Coast Guard, they should be here soon.' She replied.

'OK, not to worry. Leave the radio on as loud as possible. If I need you to do anything I will just call on the radio, you might just be able to hear over the noise of the waves. We'll be with you soon. Don't worry Saffi. I'm coming to get you.' Andreas said.

Without saying anything, Marcus had already increased his speed and they were heading towards Linalli. Within seconds of speaking to Saffi, Andreas' phone 'beeped' informing he had text messages. He read them quickly.

'Cap'n and Julio are just coming through the second bridge, on your other boat and have got some help with them. I'm not sure about the Coast Guard coming, if Saffi got a message to them, they should be here by now. I knew my gut feel was right, and Leppe has someone on the inside.'

~~~

Moments later, they were alongside Linalli, and Andreas could see Saffi clinging to the shroud and guardrail on the portside. The boat had stopped listing, but how much internal damage she had sustained would be anyone's guess. Marcus brought the rib as close as he could, and Andreas tied a line onto the mid-ships cleat.

'Saffi, are you OK?' Andreas shouted to her.

She was just about to answer when, from out of no-where Tariq scrambled across from the starboard side of the boat, and grabbed Saffi around her neck. She screamed, but managed to hold on with one hand to the shroud, as Tariq pulled her backwards. At the same time, everyone heard the thwack thwack noise of helicopter blades directly above. Saffi looked up and thought it was the Coast Guard, and nearly let her grip go as they sent a rope ladder down, but before she could, Andreas appeared on the deck in front of her, with a knife in his hand.

'Let her go Tariq, before she goes overboard.' Andreas shouted at him.

'Oh I don't think so, this prize is mine, and the information she holds is worth more to me than even Leppe realises, this little lady knows too many people and too much information to let her go back to you.' Tariq replied as he increased his grip around Saffi's throat.

'And you think you're going to get away from here, the others are coming, the real Coast Guard are on their way, and it's over Tariq.'

'What do you mean the real Coast Guard?' Saffi croaked as she tried to ease Tariq's grip. 'Aren't they the Coast Guard?' and she indicated with her eyes up to the sky and helicopter above. She could see someone leaning out of the helicopter, shouting at Tariq.

'Oh no, my dear, the Coast Guard you called, just happen to be under our control, that helicopter has to take you and me far away, somewhere where it will be just the two of us.' Tariq replied, breathing heavily down her neck, indicating that he had more on his mind that just the information she held.

Saffi shivered at the thought. 'Andreas, do something.' Her voice full of all the fear that Andreas was feeling throughout his body, but out of the corner of his eye he spotted a hand just coming over the toe rail, then another, followed by two more. In the commotion, no one had seen Cap'n and Julio come quietly alongside Linalli, on the starboard side, out of everyone's view. With stealth-like actions, they had climbed on board, Andreas knew he had to keep Tariq talking, and away from the rope ladder dropped from the helicopter.

'It's no good Tariq, she doesn't know anything more than I do, I've solved all the clues, I've found the answers and been and got what belongs to Saffi.' Andreas said. He could see Saffi was about to speak, he interrupted her. 'It's OK Saffi, what's yours is safe, with people who care for you, and won't let anyone else touch it.' He looked at her, hoping that she could read his eyes.

'There is no way you could have solved the clues, found the money and hidden it again. Do you think I was born. . .'?

Before Tariq could finish his sentence, Julio and Cap'n had crept up behind him and in one swift motion, Julio grabbed his legs and

Cap'n grabbed him around the neck. Cap'n and Tariq fell backwards and crashed onto the deck of the boat, and Cap'n held him in a headlock grip, while Julio grabbed Saffi, and rushed her back to Andreas.

'Get her off the boat. We'll deal with that piece of scum.' Julio shouted as he ran back to help is friend, who was now in a stand-up fight with Tariq.

Saffi clung to Andreas and wouldn't let go, she didn't need to say anything, as he helped her down to Marcus. By the time he had got her into the Rib and he'd climbed back on the boat, he could see that Tariq had managed to knock Cap'n unconscious and Tariq was now hanging off the rope ladder, climbing up furiously towards the helicopter, with Julio only two rungs below. Andreas watched as Tariq kicked and swung the ladder around, trying to knock Julio off, as the helicopter tried to stay steady in the still strong winds of the dying storm.

Andreas looked up. He could just touch Julio's leg, and called up to him. 'Let him go Julio, don't get yourself killed, you've already saved the one person we came for. You know it's the right thing to do. Jump and I'll break your fall.'

With that, Julio took in the whole scene and knew that Andreas was right, he'd also seen his friend, Cap'n lying on the deck. They needed to get him back to safety. He jumped from the ladder, and Andreas caught him. As the helicopter sped away, they could faintly here Tariq calling, 'It's not over. I'm coming to get her, and all of you.' By that time, Andreas had helped Julio get Cap'n into their Rib, he could see Marcus and Saffi were already safely in the mangroves.

'What about Ollie and Conrad'. Julio asked.

'We'll come back when the weather's calmer and see what's what. I'm not wasting any more time out in these conditions. We have no idea what damage Linalli has taken, it's too dangerous to risk.' But everyone knew Andreas just wanted to get Saffi back to safety.

Just as they reach the river entrance, another rib appeared out of the mangroves. It was the Coast Guard and Andreas called them on the VHF, 'We're coming back, wait at the entrance, and we'll debrief you there.'

'That's a roger, we'll tie up on the buoy.' Matt Fennis replied to Andreas' relief.

~~~

Tariq clung to the rope ladder, as the helicopter pilot dealt expertly dealt with the gusts of winds still present. He watched as Andreas lead Saffi to safety and out of his reach and he knew his chance of getting his hands on Saffi's inheritance were now slim. He would have to think fast, before Luis Leppe caught up with him.

He wasn't worried about Ollie and Conrad, with them out of the way, it would leave even more money for him, but he would need to get back on board Linalli to get the final clues. He knew Saffi would have been working on the clues before the storm struck, but he didn't know how far she had got solving them.

He carefully climbed the rope ladder, clinging on for dear life as the ladder swung wildly in the wind. He didn't look down, nor did he look up, not until he reached the top, when someone leant over, grabbed him by his arms, and hauled him into the helicopter. He lay face down on the floor of the helicopter, taking large gulps of air, relieved at finally being safe. Slowly, he got on all fours and looked up and at the face staring down at him, and immediately hung his head back down having stared straight into the eyes of Luis Leppe.

Leppe nodded to one of his men and instantly the henchman grabbed Tariq from behind, in one swift movement got a firm grip around Tariq's neck, and twisted him so that he was now half sitting, half standing. Tariq kicked his legs violently, but to no avail, and he knew it. He knew he would need to surrender. He was outnumbered, but not out-smarted, or so he thought.

'So you thought you could double cross me?' Leppe sneered. 'You should have known better than that.'

'No, no, you've got it all wrong, it was the others, and they said all along that they weren't going to give you the information. I tried to reason with them, but they wouldn't listen.' Tariq was desperate. He knew he needed to think of something quickly before Leppe threw him out of the helicopter.

'How long have you worked for me Tariq?' the question was rhetorical and required no answer. 'Have I not treated you well over the years, is there anything you have ever wanted for, or needed?' Leppe's voice was almost a whisper now. 'And you repay me like this. I'm very disappointed.'

'It wasn't like that; you've got it wrong.' Tariq struggled to speak his throat was being squeezed tighter.

'Don't answer me back.' Leppe screamed. 'Do you think I am an idiot?'

'No, no, I'm sorry El Jeffe, forgive me, but I swear it was the others. Let me prove it to you.'

'How? Why should I waste any more time and money on someone who has lied to me, and tried to cheat me out of what is mine? Give me one reason why I shouldn't throw you out right now?' Leppe nodded once more to the henchman, who manoeuvred Tariq to the edge of the open door, he deftly held him just close enough for Tariq to feel the strength of the wind on his face, the raging ocean one thousand feet below.

'Because I have all the answers to the clues.' Tariq lied.

Leppe didn't acknowledge him. He just nodded at the henchman who brought Tariq back inside the safety of the helicopter. Tariq panted, knowing now that he had to find out the answers to the remaining clues.

Chapter 40

Saffi knew she was safe but she was shivering all the same.

'There's a blanket under the seat.' Marcus said, and indicated to Saffi. Get it round yourself and hold on, it'll be a bit rough until we get back into the mangroves and the safety of the river.'

'What river is this?' Saffi asked as she wrapped the blanket around her. She didn't know who this man was, but she knew he was taking her to safety, and to Andreas. She knew introductions would happen sooner or later.

'The River Salee.' Marcus replied. 'Why do you ask?', but still concentrating on driving the Rib.

'Two across.' She said to herself, and a smile lit up her face.

'Two across?' Marcus questioned.

'Pablo Francis, the bridge guy.' Saffi couldn't believe she could remember the clues and answers; let alone the name of the person she was supposed to meet.

'Yeah, that's right, he's one of the bridge managers, and he's been helping Andreas and the rest of us trying to find you. Do you know him?' Marcus was confused. This wasn't quite the conversation he was expecting to have with someone he just rescued from an out of season Tropical Storm. But then, everything about today had been confusing. He looked at Saffi, who by now had slid down in the rib, closed her eyes and was asleep.

Marcus drove carefully; he did not want to wake her. He knew to go back to the marina, where he knew Andreas would meet them.

~~~

When they arrived at the marina, he secured the rib on the dock, and shook Saffi's shoulder gently. She murmured and opened her eyes slowly.

'Where are we, and where's Andreas?'

Realising she had no idea who he was, Marcus replied. 'It's OK, I'm a friend of Andreas', he's on his way, and he's just a few moments behind us.'

In a matter of minutes, Saffi could hear Andreas calling out to her. The very sound of his voice sent her whole body into a meltdown of emotions. Marcus helped her out of the boat, just in time for Andreas to whisk her up into his arms.

'Oh Saffi, are you OK, did they hurt you, or touch you?' he whispered in her ear.

'No, they were a bit rough, but I'm fine, now that you've got me. Please don't ever leave me.' she said, as she began to sob uncontrollably.

'I'm never letting you out of my sight again.' Andreas said, as he held her as close as he could. He led her back to the car where Julio and Cap'n were already waiting for them and drove back to the hotel.

~~~

Matt Fennis looked at his team, 'OK boys, you heard what Andreas said, one-man unconscious, one man trapped, and no idea of conditions down below, damage or weapons. We take this nice and slow, we watch each other's backs and no one takes any risks. Do you hear me?'

The four-man team had worked with each other for many years, and knew how each other thought, how they moved and how they acted in any given situation. They had risked their lives enough times to know when to say 'enough is enough!'

They brought the Coastguard rib around to the starboard side of Linalli to assess any damage. Matt could see a makeshift bung rammed into the broken port light, it seems to be holding tight. He banged on the hull and shouted. 'This is the US Coast Guard; can anyone hear me.' He waited for a few seconds and banged again. 'I say again, this is the US Coast Guard, can anyone hear me. This vessel is now under the jurisdiction of the US Government. If you do not make yourselves known to us, we will assume that you are hostile and will take this vessel by force.' Again, he waited.

Matt Fennis repeated these last words one final time. 'OK boys, lets gain entry, and I say again, watch each other's backs, just because they haven't answered, doesn't mean they're not waiting for us.

Matt and his first officer, Greg, boarded Linalli and walked along the deck to the cockpit. It was difficult as Linalli was resting on the reef at a thirty-degree angle, but these were quite common conditions, in their line of work. Using well-trained hand-signals Matt indicated that he would go first and for Greg to cover him. Before they began down the companionway, Matt made eye contact with Dan and Josh, who had been under instructions to check through the deck hatches to see if they could see anything. Dan replying with hand-signals indicated that one man was down, the other not seen. Matt entered the companionway with caution. One-step at a time, fully aware that the boat could move at any moment. At the bottom of the steps, he indicated to Greg to come down, looking all around, but he could not see anyone. Not taking anything for granted, he slowly turned to enter the rear starboard cabin, and was caught off guard by Conrad screaming and tearing out of the cabin door. He rugby-tackled Matt to the ground, knocking the wind out of him, but it was to no avail, as Greg and the others were on top of him in seconds. The three of them had him handcuffed in moments, while Matt went through to the forward cabin where he found Olli just coming around.

'I advise you both to keep your mouths' shut until you've got yourselves a lawyer, cos anything you say, WILL be used against you.' Matt said has he and the others manhandled them into the rib.

Before Matt radioed the station to ensure the correct authorities were on the dock to meet and arrest Conrad and Ollie, he sent Andreas a text. 'Scum apprehended. Do you want to see them before the authorities get their hands on them?'

Andreas' reply said it all. 'Thanks, but no thanks, I have everything I need right here. Catch you later.'

Chapter 41

Saffi woke up and couldn't remember where she was. Sunlight filled the room as the curtains lightly billowed in the gentle breeze from outside. She had woken half a dozen times in the night, each time not knowing where she was, but as soon as she saw Andreas lying next to her she remembered she was safe, and instantly dropped back into a deep sleep. However, this time, when she woke Andreas was not lying next to her and she began to panic; she needn't have worried. He'd left a note on the table, along with croissants, fresh orange juice and a note.

> "I hope you slept well, and are a little bit more rested than last night. You looked so peaceful lying there, wrapped in your duvet, that I daren't wake you. I was just glad to get the chance to watch you. I can't believe how lucky I am to have you back.
> I won't be long. We've gone back to Linalli to see what the damage is, or at least what we can salvage. I've left my phone on, if there's anything you want brought back, just call me, otherwise we'll be back just after lunchtime.
> I've left you some breakfast, but if you need anything else, just call for room service.
> I can't wait to have you in my arms again.
> Yours forever
> A"

She heard his words in her head and could not believe that he was alive. She knew for certain now, that she was in love with him.

She placed the letter on the table, poured a glass of orange juice, and tore the croissant apart; it wouldn't have mattered what it was, she knew that it would taste wonderful. She thought about what she wanted from Linalli, and realised that what she wanted most of all, was Linalli, safely returned to a marina. Not just because there were her father's memories on the boat, but, she realised that Linalli "was" her father, and suddenly she wanted to be as much a part of what was his life than she could have imagined. She thought of all the people he had arranged for her to meet, of all the stories of their time spent with Jack, and the importance of what he had been doing. He had done all of that, and had tried to protect her at the same time. Her emotions got the better of her, tears ran down her face, and then she thought of Nana. What was she going to tell

Nana, she hadn't spoken to her since she'd left the Bahamas? The more she thought about it, the more she realised she should not call her until she was more stable in her own mind. She also realised that although she was now safe, she had yet to tell Andreas that she had solved the clues and the crossword and that they needed to go to Cuba. Now she knew what Andreas needed to bring back from Linalli.

Chapter 42

Andreas' heart ached as he walked away from the hotel room. He never wanted to let Saffi go, ever again. However, he knew they needed to get back on board Linalli, to see what damage the impact had caused. He locked the door as he left, and had arranged for Pablo to sit outside, on guard. He knew no one could get to her in this hotel, but it made him feel better, and Pablo had insisted he wanted to help Jack's daughter in whatever way he could.

When he came out of the lift, he found Cap'n and Julio waiting in reception as instructed.

'She OK?' they asked in unison.

'Sleeping.' Andreas replied. 'Have you called Abi and Jacqui?'

'Yep, they're arriving this afternoon, flights are back on schedule, and I think they get here within an hour of each other. Reception knows their coming and will send a car when they know the flights are on time.' Cap'n spoke for Julio as well.

'Shall we do this then?' Andreas said with renewed vigour in his voice. 'Matt will meet us at the marina, he's letting us use the rib and one of his officers is coming with us, so we do everything by the book. We take no risks, but I'm going to try my damnedest to save Linalli, it's what Jack would have wanted.'

They nodded their agreement as they walked out of reception and into a Jeep Andreas had arranged. At the marina, Matt Fennis was waiting, as agreed, and the rib already to go. Everyone knew everyone, so no one bothered with formal introductions.

The journey this time through the River Salee was beautifully calm, noises of the tropics sounding in the mangroves, the sun high in the bright blue sky. Once through the river they followed the marked path, through the coral reef, the water was blue, but not clear. Nobody would have believed there had been a storm the day before, not until the island came into view and they saw Linalli listing over. No one said a word; they kept their thoughts of what they might find on board to themselves.

Matt secured the rib to Linalli's stern and Andreas climbed on board first, the others gave him a moment to himself, they knew he would indicate when he was happy for them to get on. Matt had tried to insist that he get on board first, to check the safety of the vessel, but he gave up arguing with Andreas, and knew he would want to do the same if he was in Andreas' place.

Andreas looked around the cockpit, it looked surprisingly clean and then he walked toward the companionway and bent his head down into the saloon. Linalli was listing at about 20 degrees, the seawater about knee deep at the deepest part. Unbeknown to anyone, Saffi had inadvertently left the automatic bilge running, which had helped for a while until the power ran out, when the seawater had reached the battery bank. The original leak in the forward cabin port light was above sea level, so no more water had come in, but there was water getting in somewhere else, fortunately very slowly.

Andreas went back up to the cockpit. 'OK guys, come aboard. From first glance it doesn't look too bad, but we have a leak somewhere in the hull.' He helped the others as they climbed aboard and let them go below.

'I'm going around the starboard side, see what damage can be seen from the outside.' Matt told Andreas. 'I've got snorkel gear on board should we need to go beneath her.' He said, as he slipped the line and manoeuvred the rib around the stern of Linalli to the starboard side.

When Andreas went below, Julio and Cap'n were already putting together a manual bailing system of buckets. 'Let's get what water we can out, see if we can spot anything.' Julio said. 'Batteries are shot.' Cap'n interjected.

However, Andreas didn't hear them. He opened the door to the main cabin where he knew they had locked Saffi away during her ordeal. He visualised her sitting on the bed, scared, blaming him for getting her into this mess. How could he ever repay her? Would she ever forgive him, or get over this? He sat down awkwardly on the bed, books and photo albums strewn all over the place. He could see where she had jammed the pillows and life jacket into the broken porthole and could only image what she must have been going through. Then his phone rang, the number withheld, he didn't say anything when he opened the phone.

'Andreas? It's me, Saffi.' her voice quiet, not knowing if she had the right number.

Andreas breathed a sigh of relief. 'Hi! How are you feeling, are you OK?' They hadn't had a chance to speak since the night before, Saffi had collapsed in the car, and he had carried her to his room, and put her straight to bed. He had no idea how she felt about him.

'I'm fine, if not a little, well, exhausted. Where are you?' she asked.

'On Linalli.' He said nothing more.

'How is she, will she be OK?' Saffi almost didn't want him to answer, fearing the worst.

'I don't know yet, we've only just got on board, I'm in the main cabin, it's a bit of a mess, there are sodden books everywhere. I don't really know where to start.'

There was silence.

'Saffi, are you there, are you OK?'

Somehow, with all her might, she searched her memory for things she needed him to bring back. 'I'm fine. I'm just trying to remember what I did with some things. In the cabin, do you remember the photo album we looked at, the one with the poem?' She asked.

'Yes, the one called blue eyes or something.'

'Yes, that's the one, but I had to rename it to hide it from them, I called it Repair Schedule, I think, and I put it back with all the other boat manuals, you need to bring that back with you and the computer, if it's still OK, that is. I didn't tell you, I've solved all the clues and the final bit of the puzzle.' she paused, 'we need to go to Cuba.'

~~~

Matt secured the rib to the mid-ships cleat and started inspecting the hull. Fortunately, the wind was blowing from the opposite side, causing the waves to lap against the port side of the boat, giving him a protected area of flat sea in which to work. There were a few superficial scratches, but he could see no major impacts above the water line, but as she was listing at 20 degrees, he had no idea what might have happened below the water line. He knew he would have to dive on the hull to get a full inspection, but should be able get a reasonable idea from snorkelling around the hull. He leaned into the locker, got out his fins, mask and snorkel, and got into the water. Unfortunately, the storm had kicked up the seabed and the visibility wasn't as good as it could have been. He began by swimming just along the water line, his head just beneath the sea. Again, he could see superficial scratches and cracks, but nothing major, but he knew there must be something or there would not have been the amount of water there was inside of the boat. He swam down, about a meter, and back along the hull. At first glance, nothing looked out of place or untoward. He knew however, that they would have to get the boat off the reef somehow. He swam down to the keel to see if it was stuck in the reef. It was, but not too badly. He would need to discuss the situation with the others.

Back on deck, Julio was furiously bailing water while Cap'n was using the hand bilge pump. They knew they needed to get as much water out before they could see any damage there may be. Then they could decide whether they would be able to get her back to shore. Julio and Andreas heard Matt call from the cockpit.

'Guys, how's it going with the hand bilge?' Matt asked, looking down into the saloon.

'We're getting there. It's not as bad as I thought it would be?' Julio said coming up into the cockpit and threw another bucket of water over the side. Andreas joined them up on deck.

'What's the prognosis Matt?' Andreas asked, expecting the worst.

'I swam down and there doesn't appear to be a breach in the hull. I've checked the path the boat took to get onto the reef and the entry route is a straight line. She must have started taking on water, which then made her topple and list. We won't know how much water she's taking on until we've cleared out down below.' Matt replied, matter of fact, but that was his job, he could not afford to be emotional about this boat.

Andreas called down to Julio, 'how long till she's empty?'

'About done now, we should be able to see how much water she's taking on.'

The others came down below and all four of them stood, like expectant fathers, waiting to see how much water came back into the boat. Julio had already lifted the flooring so that they could see into the bilges as much as they could. Andreas was expecting the worst, but hoping for the best. Initially nothing happened, but then very slowly a trickle of water started seeping into the bilges. Andreas sighed in relief, as he realised that the flow did not get any stronger.

'OK, what are our options?' Andreas asked the others.

Matt was first to step in. 'If we assume that this is the full strength of the flow of water, but I imagine it will increase when the boat is moving, then we should be able to manually pump it out as we go. But first we need to decide how to get her off the reef and then see if the engine starts, which I doubt it will.'

'Will that cause a problem or is your rib big enough to tow her back, and where are we going to take her. We can't go through the bridge, it doesn't open during the day, and believe me, I've tried to get special permission to open them in daylight, and that's a no go.' Andreas replied.

'Yeah the rib will cope fine, and I think we'll just be able to get into Port Louis. It's only five miles North West of here.' Matt said. 'With regard to lifting her off the reef, our best option is to un-weight her, the keel doesn't look jammed. We'll need to fill as many containers we can find with sea water, and then we attach them to the boom, which we let out over the side, obviously keeping a line attached to bring the boom back in, so that it doesn't go over on the other way with all the weight. It's a tricky manoeuvre but there are enough of us to handle it. Once she's level, we'll try the engine. After that, we will need to get her off the reef. We can use the rib to push the bow around, and hopefully she will slide out of the clutches of the reef.' Matt said.

'Just like that.' Julio replied. He and everyone on board knew enough about boats to know that nothing ever goes according to plan.

'Yep, but before we do anything, let me contact Port Lois and let them know we're on our way, and I'll call my guys to meet us there with dive gear, so we can see what the real damage is.

'Can one of them go by the hotel and collect Saffi, I'll text her to let her know their coming. She wouldn't want to miss this.' Andreas asked.

~~~

After what seemed ages, trying to find and fill containers, and then attach them to the boom, Matt was finally happy.

'Does everyone know what they're doing? We need this operation to go as smoothly as possible.' Matt said. His face was serious, his mind concentrating, and his heart thumping. Everyone nodded. 'OK, on the count of three, Julio will swing the boom around slowly. Andreas, is the line secure?'

'Yes skipper.' Everyone had assumed that Matt was in charge, and correct protocol took over without question. They all knew this was going to be a delicate operation.

'Cap'n, how's the water level?

'Staying low, with a slight to steady flow, but the manual bilge is keeping up, skipper.' He could not leave his post of pumping the hand bilge.

Matt stood at the helm of the rib, the engine in idle, his hand poised over the throttle.

'Julio, are you ready on that boom line?'

'Yes skipper'. Julio replied immediately.

'OK everyone, this is it. One, two, three.'

Julio controlled the boom mainsheet, letting it out carefully and slowly.

'Easy does it, just an inch at a time, we need to be able pull the boom back the moment she's righted herself.' Matt instructed.

Inch by inch the boom moved out, over the guardrails and towards the side of the boat. Everyone was holding their breath, waiting for any indication of movement on the hull. Then, without any effort, but with the weight of the containers, Linalli began to right herself.

'Slowly does it, that's it, a few more inches, and when I say, Andreas, bring the boom back into the centre?'

A few moments passed, that felt like an age, and then everyone could feel Linalli begin to float.

'Now, Andreas, slowly but firmly.' Matt said as he put the rib into idle forward and gently pushed the bow of Linalli off the reef. 'OK, once the boom mainsheet is secured, try the engine. Make sure you've centred the helm.

No one breathed as Andreas turned the key, but he knew it would be to no avail. He had seen the amount of seawater in the engine compartment, but he tried anyway. Nothing.

'OK, leave it.' Matt shouted, 'you'll only make it worse if you keep trying. How are the bilges holding up, is there any more flow of water?' He shouted from the rib. Andreas called down to Cap'n and repeated the question.

'They're OK, no real change.' He replied. 'I've got it under control.'

'They're holding up.' Andreas told Matt. 'What's next?'

'Right, Julio, you start emptying the containers, no need to weigh her down unnecessarily, Andreas come and take this tow line, we'll need a bridle tied on at the bow. Then get Julio to come on board the rib with me, he'll need to keep an eye on the tow line, and we'll take this very, very slowly. It's about five miles to Port Louis, so it's going to take a while. Andreas I want you on the helm, to counteract the movement of the rib, and Cap'n just stays below bilging, but he must let you know the minute anything changes with the water level.'

Andreas acknowledged his understanding and walked the towline to the bow, Julio began emptying the containers and everyone sighed. The whole operation had taken less than thirty minutes and so far, had gone very smoothly. Julio emptied the last container and then jumped onto the rib, and when Matt was happy with everything, he opened the throttle, very slowly, and began steering the two boats in the direction given of his GPS waypoint.

~~~

Saffi had read Andreas' text and wasn't sure she had understood him. How could they be towing Linalli to a harbour, but she got herself ready and told Pablo what was happening.

'That makes sense.' he said when she told him they were taking the boat to Port Louis.

'Really, I don't think I understand at all, but the Coast Guard will be coming to get us in an hour.' she replied.

'Well, they can't bring Linalli back here, they'd have to go through the river, it's too long to go around the outside of the islands, and the bridges only open at 4am. At least this way they can get the boat to a marina where they can see what the real damage is. I expect Matt has arranged for divers to meet them there, it will be a slow and difficult job to bring her back.' Pablo replied, not talking directly to Saffi, but more thinking the operation over in his mind.

Saffi didn't reply. She didn't have the faintest idea of how you would get a boat off a reef. Especially one that was leaking, and then get it back to a harbour five miles away, but decided that it would all probably be explained to her when they arrived. She and Pablo waited in reception for the car to arrive.

~~~

The journey had gone without hitch, Cap'n had kept pumping the bilges out and kept the water at bay, but very little had come through, Andreas had steered Linalli in line with Matt's rib and Julio had kept a vigilant eye on the towline. As they approached the entrance to the harbour, Matt called on channel 16 and within minutes another rib appeared with Matt's team and they gently guided Linalli inside the safety of the harbour, and tied her alongside the harbour wall.

'We can only put her on the very edge of the harbour wall, it's too shallow to bring her all the way in, but it should be enough to get down and take a look.' shouted Greg to Matt.

'OK, that's fine. I think Andreas will want to go down with you, do you have spare dive gear with you?' Matt replied.

Greg nodded in the affirmative and radioed to Josh to bring out extra dive gear in the other rib.

'Thanks,' Andreas said, 'I definitely want to see what's happening on the hull, and thanks for everything you've done today. Without you and they guys I'd be up The Indian River without a guide.' Andreas continued.

'Pleasure was all mine, you know I wouldn't have let you, or Jack, down.'

Andreas waited patiently for the other rib to arrive with the dive gear. As the boat arrived, he could see that Saffi was also on board and her face gave away all her emotions. She could hardly contain herself when the rib pulled up alongside Linalli. Andreas leant over and helped her on board, and she immediately wrapped her arms around him and let all her emotions fall from within her. She sobbed as he held her close.

'It's OK, it's all over now, you're safe, and surrounded by many friends. Nobody is going to hurt you now.' He said. They sat down in the cockpit while Josh put the dive gear on board and waited until Andreas was ready.

'I'm going to dive down on the hull to see what damage the reef has caused. I want you to stay here with Julio, it shouldn't take more than 15 minutes and then you can tell me about Cuba!' He held her face in his hands and gently kissed her, tasting the salt of her tears as he did so. He then indicated to Julio to sit with her while he put the dive gear on.

Andreas and Matt slid into the water and began the inspection from the stern to the bow. Matt took photographs with an underwater camera. When they had finished they both surfaced and looked up to a row of expectant faces. Andreas removed his regulator from his mouth, 'There's nothing obvious on the hull, but the fact that there's a crack along the keel line will probably be the cause. We've taken photos, but I think she'll need lifting, so we'll have to get her back to Pont a Pitre Marina,'

As he and Matt got back on board Linalli and removed their dive gear, Andreas looked at Matt. 'I don't really want to take her the long way around, but I'll need help if we're to take her through the bridge at night.'

'That won't be a problem. We'll use two ribs and take it nice and slow. If everyone's up for it, we can move her tonight.' Matt said, knowing that everyone would agree.

Chapter 45

That night, before moving Linalli back to Pont a Pitre Marina, Andreas drew up a rota, which allowed everyone time to get some much needed rest and food, while one person would stay on board to pump the bilges as necessary. They would need to be ready for a 4am start to take her through the river and the bridges.

During the day, both Abi and Jacqui had arrived and Cap'n and Julio had brought them up to date on what had happened respectively. Meanwhile Andreas and Saffi started her laptop to see if it was in working order, and more importantly, to discuss going to Cuba.

'So while they had you locked in the cabin, you worked out that the final destination is Cuba?' Andreas asked, as Saffi the laptop sprung into life.

'Well, it was a process of elimination. Once I'd worked out all the answers, I just had to work out where they fitted in the crossword. To be fair, with the words I had left, there was only one solution.' She said. 'When I entered the last letter of the last word, a whole bunch of letters lit up bright green.'

She opened the crossword and showed it to Andreas. He, like Saffi, saw the letters 'D, J, E, N, A, L, U, T, V, U' illuminate. 'And from this you worked out we need to go to Cuba.'

'Well, with a little bit of working out using the anagram technique, and the fact that, if you look through the photo album I told you about,' she opened the album at the required page, 'you'll find a photograph of Jack and mum.'

She handed the album to Andreas. He could see quite clearly what Saffi had seen, written underneath the photograph, 'Lillian and Jack on our Isle of Youth - La Juventud, Cuba'.

'Well I'll be buggered, that old devil is sending us to El Pueblito. I never thought I'd go back there.' Andreas said, as he continued to look at the photo of his old friend, and thought to himself, I wonder if you realised your dream my old friend.

'How do you know he wants us to go there, wherever there is? He hasn't left anymore clues.' Saffi asked.

'It was our one and only 'bolt-hole'. No one knew we ever went there, it really was 'our secret hide-out'. . . but apart from that, it has the best diving in the world, amazing fishing, and a beach so white, and sea so blue, you can't believe your eyes. Thank you Jack.' Andreas sat back, closed his eyes and smiled, and remembered the good times they had spent at El Pueblito, La Juventud. This was clearly a good place.

'So, what do we do next?' Saffi asked.

'Once we've lifted Linalli out of the water, and we're happy that any repairs can be done, we can fly ourselves over there. We'll have to stop and refuel in the DR, we can drop Julio and Jacqui back if they want, and then fly right onto the airfield at Cayo Largo. Saffi, you are going to love it there. Once you're there, you'll forget any of this ever happened. It's somewhere you can finally relax for a while.' Andreas said, his smile so wide, his face so happy, Saffi couldn't help but smile with him, and finally relax.

~~~

After they had informed everyone of their final destination, it didn't matter how much Saffi and Andreas protested, they knew all along that everyone would insist on coming along with them.

'Tariq is still around, and Luis Leppe is like a dog with a bone, you know he won't let this lie. You don't know what they found out from Saffi.' Julio protested. 'I know she says she didn't say anything, but they had access to her computer, the clues and anything she'd worked out. If Saffi worked it out, so could Tariq. It's not safe for you two to go alone.'

'I'm with Julio on this one Andreas, and besides when was the last time any of us were there, let alone there together?' Cap'n said.

'OK, OK, I get the picture, but if you're so convinced that they're maybe trouble, then we drop Abi and Jacqui off when we stop to refuel in the DR. I know they won't be happy, but those are my terms.' Andreas said. 'And yes, I know what you're thinking, we should leave Saffi with them, but this is where Jack wants her to go, she needs to see this through to the end.

~~~

Andreas was right, Abi and Jacqui spent the whole flight to the DR complaining bitterly. Saffi agreed with them, if she was going, then surely sure they should be able to come along. However, Andreas was adamant and they left the two women at Puerto Plata Airport. Although they continued to complain, the women knew it was the right thing to do.

The flight to Cuba's Cayo Largo Airport would take a few hours. Julio and Cap'n flew the Cessna he'd rented the week before, Saffi and Andreas sat in the back going over the clues and information they had. They still didn't know why Jack was sending them to La Juventud, The Island of Youth.

'If you look at the picture of La Juventud, compare it to the pendant Jack left me.' Saffi handed Andreas the pendant. 'Can you see all the markings on the back, the little letters?' she asked as she pointed the letters out to him.

'Yes, what do they mean?'

'Do you remember when we were with Gus and Ma?'

'Yes.' He answered, still confused.

'Ma had a pendant, almost exactly like this one, but hers had a gold stone that came out, and underneath it was inscribed, X Jack 1A. It was Jack's way of telling us where to put the answers in the crossword. You remember the salt pillar.'

Andreas interrupted, 'Yes, it had the green stone inside, which gave us the crossword grid position. Yes, I remember all those things.'

'Well, there's a whole bunch of people I didn't get to meet, what were they meant to give me, would it be the final bit of information that we need? Does it all revolve around this pendant and we've lost sight of that fact.' Saffi said, taking the pendant back and looking at it one more time. 'The back still has all the inscriptions, and I don't have the stones that fit in there. I'm just wondering if it's some kind of map.'

'Without going and meeting those final people, I don't think we'll ever know, I think we're just going to have to go on good old 'gut feel', and I've a feeling I know exactly where we need to go.' Andreas said.

Saffi was about to protest when Julio signalled to them to put their headphones on. 'We're thirty minutes out and have been given permission to land, seat belts tight?' he asked. They nodded and Saffi looked out the window at and the amazing view below. Having been at sea for the last week, seeing the sea from the air gave her deeper appreciation of what she had been through, over the last few days. Not just the fear her captors had invoked, the dread that Andreas was dead, and the terror of the storm, but now she realised that this adventure would be ending very soon, and she didn't know how she felt about that. Would she ever see Andreas again, and how would she live without him, back in her normal life in the UK? She closed her eyes and tried not to think about that ever happening.

~~~

Saffi was jolted back to the present, as the plane landed at Cayo Largo International Airport. She looked at the runway and smiled. How this could conceivably be regarded as an 'international airport', was beyond her. Inside the airport, while Julio cleared them through Customs, Saffi could see the lists of daily flights on the departure boards, it appeared that Cayo Largo was busier than she realised.

'Some of the hotels here are fantastic.' Andreas said, reading her mind. 'Everything from huts on the beach to four-star luxury, but we're not going to touristy bit.' He said as he hailed a cab outside the terminal building. 'El Pueblito, por favor'. He said to the cab driver, as he loaded their bags.

'Ah, 'the village'.' Cap'n sighed as he said the words.

'Ooh 'the village'.' Julio repeated. 'I can hardly wait.'

'So you've all been here, you know where we're going?' Saffi asked.

'Yop!' They replied in unison

'You'll see soon enough.' Andreas said, and none of them said another word.

~~~

After a short ride, the cab stopped at a 'reception' building, and on the other side of the road, was a marina. Saffi could see large fishing boats on the docks, as well as sailing boats. She got out of the cab and looked around her. The place was like nothing she'd seen before. Next to the Reception building was a row of wooden cabins, and on the other side of the Reception, was a bowling alley. Beyond that, she saw a sign directing you to a disco and the 'Pirates Bar'. Now she could why the Andreas and his friends liked this place. Fishing, sailing, bowling, log cabins and a bar, all within walking distance of a runway. What more would any of these three men want in life? She smiled. She was beginning to understand Jack a little more now, she thought.

Andreas interrupted her thoughts. 'Ready?'

'Ready for what?' Saffi asked.

'Ready to unravel the last clue?' he said.

~~~

The four of them walked into Reception and a young woman, smartly dressed in the hotel uniform greeted them with a warm smile. 'Good afternoon, how may I help you?' Her English was perfect, but tinged with a hint of a Spanish accent. 'Do you have a reservation?'

Andreas spoke for all of them. 'I'm sorry, we don't, but do you have any rooms available? A twin and a double?'

'I'll just check.' The receptionist said. 'You're in luck, we have rooms available. If I could take a copy of your passports and ask one of you to fill in the registration forms.'

Andreas got the passports out of his flight bag and passed the form to Saffi to complete.

'Typical.' She said, 'get the woman to do the paperwork.' as she sat down at a small table to complete the form, but as she was filling out their details, something on the form looked familiar, the hotel logo. Then she looked around her, the logo was on the reception desk, and the clock on the wall was in the same shape as the logo. It was the shape of the island, La Juventud, but more importantly, it was the same shape as her pendant. It was as though the logo was an image of her pendant. Thinking it was just a coincidence, she continued to complete the form. However, at the bottom of the form, underneath where she needed to sign her name, in the smallest of letters she read 'Island of Youth: Proprietor - Saffrina Simpson'.

As she read the words, the pen fell from her hand, and at that moment, the receptionist returned with their passports and looked as white as a ghost.

'Miss Simpson, I'm so sorry, I did not know you were coming, we were not informed, please accept my apologies. Let me get Stephano to take your bags.'

'Stephano!' Andreas said, repeating the receptionist's words. 'Then you must be Maria?'

Everyone stopped and looked at Maria, who could not control herself now and ran towards Andreas. 'Is it really you, Maria? Really?' He said, and wrapped his arms around her, lifted her up and swung her round.

'Stephano, Stephano, come quickly, you will never know who has arrived.' Maria called into the office.

Julio and Cap'n sat down and Saffi just stared. Could this be THE Maria and Stephano, the orphan children she was named after? How could that possibly be, and how is my name on the bottom of the paperwork, she thought. It was all too much for her to take in, and no one noticed that she'd fainted with shock.

When Saffi came around, everyone was sitting around her, including Maria and Stephano. Andreas helped her up and gave her a glass of water. 'It's OK Saffi. I think you passed out, with the heat, probably.' He said.

'No, I think I passed out because of the shock. Have you seen what's on the bottom of this registration form?' she said as she handed him the paperwork?' Saffi said.

'Never mind about that, I want to introduce you to Maria and Stephano, you know, the children I told you about.' Andreas said.

'I think it was that and what's written on the bottom of the paperwork, is what made me faint.' Saffi said, pointing to the bottom of the form.

Andreas looked more closely at the registration form, and at the name at the bottom, and then he looked at Saffi. Does this mean what I think it means?' He said.

'How should I know, I've never been here before, how can my name be on the paperwork?' Saffi said.

Julio took the document from Andreas, looked at it and then passed it to Cap'n.'He did it; he bloody did it!' Cap'n said.

'Did what, who did bloody what? Can someone please tell me what's going on?' Saffi asked.

Maria came and sat next to Saffi. Can I call you Saffi?' she asked politely. Saffi nodded. 'I feel like I already know you so well. Your father always showed us photographs he had of you, growing up, he missed you so much.'

'Are you saying Jack used to come here?' Saffi asked, looking at everyone.

Maria looked confused. 'She doesn't know?'

'Know what?' Saffi was getting quite annoyed now. 'What don't I know?'

'Your father, Jack, he built this place, the marina, the cabins, the bars, everything.' Stephano said.

Saffi, for once, was silent.

'And you own it now Saffi, he did it all for you. He put it all in your name so no one could get at it.' Andreas said quietly. 'It was always for you; this is his legacy to you. This is your inheritance.'

Chapter 47

It had taken a while for everything to sink in, everyone confirming to her that 'it was true, she owned everything in El Pueblito'. Spending the rest of the day with Maria and Stephano, hearing the stories of how, with the help of Father Melia, they left Columbia. How Jack and Andreas had made arrangements for them to come to La Juventud, and how Jack had worked hard to make his dream a reality, a reality for Saffi.

The following morning, Maria gave Saffi a guided tour of what she now owned, while the guys relaxed in the Pirate Bar with Stephano, telling him of the last few weeks and what Saffi and Andreas had been through. Saffi had insisted that they arrange flights for Jacqui and Abi to come to the island, which they had done, they would be arriving later that day.

That evening, after a wonderful meal together, celebrating the end of Saffi's ordeal, they all headed off to their respective wooden cabins. Saffi took a long shower and finally relaxed in the arms of Andreas, under crisp, jasmine scented, bed linen. They made love as though they had never been apart. Saffi finally felt safe in the arms of the man she loved.

~~~

In the middle of the night, Andreas was woken by a noise outside on the veranda. He slid out of bed, trying not to disturb Saffi, he slipped behind the curtains to see what the noise was, just as there was an almighty smash as the window shattered and a large stone hit Andreas right on the forehead. He fell backwards, unconscious. Saffi jumped up and ran to Andreas. Without Saffi seeing anything else, Tariq came silently from behind the curtain, grabbed her from behind, and placed the handkerchief, soaked in chloroform, over her mouth. She collapsed and he dragged her out of the room into a waiting jeep. Tariq reversed down a dirt track and to a waiting speedboat. He lifted Saffi over his shoulders and dumped her limp body into the boat.

What Tariq didn't know was that the whole scene was being played out on the CCTV, and the Security Guards had already come running to Andrea's assistance. They woke the others and told them what had happened. Within a few minutes, Andreas had come around, and he and the others had taken a speedboat from the marina, and were in full pursuit.

Out in the bay Andreas could see a large motor boat at anchor and he knew exactly who was on board, he was glad now that he had told everyone to come armed. Perhaps finally they could be rid of El Jeffe.

~~~

When Tariq reached the motor yacht, two more of Luis Leppe's men grabbed Saffi's arms and dragged her on board the boat. They knocked on El Jeffe's cabin door and threw her onto his bed after he had given permission to enter. After they left he locked the door. The Captain had already started the engines and was raising the anchor by the time Andreas reached the motor yacht. The marina security guard held the speedboat alongside as Andreas, Cap'n and Julio climbed on board as quietly as possible. Andreas dealt swiftly with the first of the guards on the motor yacht, taking him from behind and breaking his neck in one quick movement, then threw him overboard. Julio and Cap'n dealt with any other guards they came across with the same precise movements. Meanwhile, Andreas moved silently around the boat, to try and find where they had put Saffi. However, the noise of bodies being thrown into the sea had alerted Tariq to their presence, and he was now in pursuit of the intruders; he knew it was Andreas.

Tariq knew this boat intimately, and could move around it like no one else, without being seen. He peered slowly around the wall and saw Andreas moving along the outer deck, looking in the cabins. Tariq aimed his gun and fired, missing Andreas' head by millimetres. Andreas opened a cabin door and stood behind it for protection, and began firing back at Tariq. The gunfight continued until they were both out of bullets, Andreas knew this would end in hand-to-hand combat and he swiftly removed his knife from its scabbard.

Meanwhile Luis Leppe sat in his stateroom, listening to the battle outside, but he didn't move, that's what he employed the guards for, to do his battles for him. They would soon dispose of Andreas and his 'little friends' he thought. He would wait patiently for Tariq to finish with the annoyance that Andreas had become and wait for Saffi to stir; he would then enjoy interrogating Jack's daughter. 'One-day Jack, I will find her, and I will take away from you all that you hold precious.' He had taunted Jack with these words so many times, and now he would carry out his promise. His only sadness was that Jack was not alive to know that he, Luis Leppe, had finally beaten him.

~~~

Having eliminated the guards, Julio and Cap'n carried out the remainder of the agreed plan. Cap'n would go to the engine room and disable the boat's engines and Julio would take control of the bridge, both disposing of any of Leppe's men in the process. Both had seen Andreas up on deck as they moved to their respected parts of the boat, but neither had seen Tariq approach him. On hearing the gunshots, they knew that they had to stick to the plan if they were going to rescue Saffi and deal with Leppe once and for all. They knew she would never be safe and rid of the threat of Leppe while he was alive.

Cap'n had no difficulty in taking the engineer by surprise and disposing of him, all he needed to do now was find the fuel shut off valves and turn them off, which would immobilise the boat.

Julio moved silently towards the bridge, he could see the Captain at the helm controls, concentrating on getting the boat to maximum speed; the captain had his instructions, and knew not to disobey them. Just as Julio was close enough to strike, the engines came to a shuddering halt; Julio knew that Cap'n had succeeded in his role.

'What the. . .' the captain shouted, as he grabbed the radio to shout at his engineer, and ask him what the hell was going on.

It was the perfect opportunity for Julio; he grabbed the captain from behind and wrestled him to the floor. Although the captain was a big man, he was not strong, nor was he young, and he fell with ease. Julio did not intend to kill every one of Leppe's employees, just disable them so that the authorities could deal with them accordingly. This man probably had no idea of the true extent of Leppe's empire. He took his gun and with its butt hit him with enough precision to render him unconscious for a long while. Julio dragged him out of the way and tied him up. Back at the helm Julio radioed Cap'n on their walkie-talkies to give him power to the engines, not a lot, just enough to stop them drifting. As he said this, he looked out of the window; he could see another boat heading their way. He radioed Cap'n again,

'We've got company; you might want to get up here.'

'Coast guard?' Cap'n replied.

'Nope. No lights, completely stealth, maximum speed. Through the 'bino's' I see two on board, minimum. I suggest you take up an appropriate position.' Julio replied. 'I'll stay here and keep you informed.'

'Wilko.' Cap'n replied quickly, as he switched the fuel shut off valves back on, and returned power to Julio.

~~~

'You won't get away with this.' Andreas said as he positioned himself ready to take a lung at Tariq. 'Everyone knows about you, we've had Conrad and Ollie in custody for long enough now to know exactly what you had planned. It will be interesting to see if Leppe knew about your take over plans.'

'Him. El Jeffe. He's out of date now, an old man in this business. It needs new, young blood; he has no idea about modern technology, where the real money can be made nowadays. The way he runs things, he would have been out of businesses in a year or two, without my help. No, best I take control now, make sure the business is run properly, in a modern world.' Tariq replied as he lunged at Andreas, knocking him to floor.

The knife battle between the two militarily trained men was as expected, they both endured knife injuries to their extremities. The fight made all the more difficult while the boat wallowed in the lumpy sea, while Julio tried to get the boat moving again.

But it was not to be Andreas' pleasure of inflicting the fatal knife wound into Tariq. If only Tariq had looked around him and seen where he had been shouting out his intentions against his boss, he would have seen that they were standing directly outside the cabin they had dumped Saffi's limp body, outside Leppe's cabin.

~~~

At the bow of the motor boat, a small powerboat arrived, its occupants unaware they had been seen en-route. The taller of the two men threw a fisherman's anchor over the bow of the motor boat, and he then helped his companion climb the line. Once on board, the first man helped the second on board. The two of them, dressed completely in black, only the whites of their eyes visible, moved with precision along the walkway of the boat to where they knew their prey would be. They took up their positions, unseen by anyone on board, and waited silently.

~~~

Luis Leppe's blood boiled. He had taken Tariq and his companions in long ago, when they were street boys and needed 'direction'. He had treated them like his own children and this was how they were going to repay him, with treason. Leppe did not need to take revenge on people like Tariq; he just disposed of them, quickly. He moved to his dresser and pulled open the top draw. Inside was an array of weapons. He would not shoot Tariq that would not give him any pleasure; he would need to take his life with his own hands. He took his knife, and moved to the window, twisted the blinds just enough that he could see what was going on outside his cabin. Saffi remained unconscious on the bed, impervious to all that was happening around her.

Leppe waited until Andreas and Tariq where directly outside his door, he chose his moment well. Andreas lunged at Tariq with all his might, and as he did, Leppe opened the cabin door; Tariq and Andreas fell to the floor, stunned. Leppe grabbed Tariq around his neck, and dug his knife tip into Tariq's artery.

'Betray me, would you.' Leppe whispered angrily into Tariq's ear.

'Never, El Jeffe, it was the others, they planned everything. I always protested to them, you gave us everything. Without you we would be...' Tariq pleaded, but Leppe didn't give him the chance to finish the sentence, he finished it for him.

'Nothing. That's right, you would and are nothing.' Leppe's voice was controlled and cold, and with one swift movement, he slit Tariq's throat, and dropped his lifeless body to the floor.

Leppe turned to Andreas, who had seen Saffi on the bed and was now desperately trying to wake her up. She stirred, but was still drowsy from the chloroform. Leppe did not attack Andreas as he had expected. Instead, he walked slowly over to his dresser. Leppe knew he had Andreas 'on the back foot' and was in control of the situation. Andreas would do nothing to endanger Saffi. Leppe slid the draw open and, wiping the blade of the knife, returned it to its rightful place, and then withdrew a gun and attached the silencer. He didn't need it, but he disliked the noise a gun made without one.

'You won't use that; you still need me.' Andreas said, his voice calm, he'd been in trickier spots than this in the past, and he continued to bring Saffi round.

'Again, Andreas, you are wrong. It is not you that I need, but Saffi.' Leppe said as he withdrew the chair and sat down, the gun pointing directly between Andreas' eyes.

'Saffi knows nothing.' Andreas said, thinking of a plan, and hoping that at any moment Cap'n or Julio would come through the door to assist him. 'I moved everything Jack owned before she solved Jack's ridiculous riddles. You don't think I would have let her know where anything was, do you?'

'Oh my dear Andreas, do you think me that foolish. I know all about the Island of Youth. I watched Jack build it up over the years. Don't you realise that I have friends in many places that can tell me everything I need to know. The fact that Saffi owns all of it is all I needed to know. And now I have Saffi. All I need her to do is sign it over to me and I will have won. I will have finally beaten that pathetic creature Jack Simpson'.

Anger took over Andreas in a way he had never felt before. He hurled himself at Luis Leppe with such strength and surprise that it stunned Leppe and they both fell to the floor, Leppe's gun going off in the process. Saffi screamed, having finally gained consciousness, but not knowing where she was or what was going on. Both Andreas and Leppe turned towards her and Leppe got the better of Andreas, throwing him off, punching him in the face as he did. Andreas flew back to the floor as Leppe ran to the bed and grabbed Saffi around the neck, his gun pointing at her temple.

'Go on then, kill me, you were going to all along.' Saffi said, somehow taking in her surroundings and all that had happened. She had worked out exactly who Luis Leppe was and she would be defiant to the end, as her father would have wanted. Tears ran down her cheek as she finally realised that she thought of Jack as her father now, and then the silence was broken.

'Saffi be quiet.' a voice said from behind the door.

Leppe and Andreas both turned to the door expecting to see Julio or Cap'n, but the door remained closed. Although Saffi could not see who the man was, but it was a voice she recognised, a voice from her past. But while they were all concentrating on the man behind the door, there was a smash of glass from the other side of the cabin as another man swung through the window, feet first, and landing behind Leppe, pointing his gun directly at the rear of his head.

'It's over Leppe, no-where else to run.' the second man said, as he removed his balaclava.

'Raoul!' Leppe's voice roared with surprise. 'Another betrayal.'

As he said it, the cabin door opened and the first man stood there, his gun aimed directly at Leppe's forehead, with his other hand, he also removed his balaclava and said, 'You're not the only one to have friends in all places and, he's right Leppe, it really is over now.'

But he didn't wait for Leppe to answer, he squeezed the trigger of his gun as the bullet hit him straight between the eyes, they all watched as Leppe fell to the floor. Out the corner of his eye, Andreas saw Saffi falling, but he managed to catch her before she fell to the floor. He wrapped her in his arms and led her to the bed; he sat her down where she began to sob. She knew her ordeal was finally over as she looked over at the man in the doorway, and up into her father's eyes.

Epilogue

Sitting in the Pirates Bar at the 'Island of Youth', it didn't take long for Jack to explain to everyone the plan he had set in place five year's previously. It took longer to apologise to everyone for lying to them and making them think he was dead. It took longer for Andreas to apologies to Saffi for having known all along.

Jack and Andreas knew that eventually Leppe would try to take Saffi. It would be his only holdover Jack. They knew they had to get her out to them in such a way that she would suspect nothing, but in a way that both Jack and Andreas would always have control of the situation. Saffi had protested that they had used her as bait all along, and this angered her more than anything did.

'He would have sent someone to get you anyway.' Andreas had explained.

'The moment you were old enough, and had enough hate for me, he would have found you.' Jack said. 'It was the only way I could protect you. All those years ago I had to start to extract myself from your life, make you hate me.'

'But the letters, Switzerland, the pendant, it's so, so elaborate, why couldn't you just have gone to the police or someone?' Saffi argued.

She still had not understood her father and Andreas' involvement with the authorities, the DEA, the Caribbean Governments and police departments, and probably never would. It was too unbelievable for anyone to believe, and Andreas and Jack had always agreed that no one should ever really know what they did.

'It was the only way Saffi, the only way to bring Leppe out in the open. We had to make him follow you, so that we could finally be rid of him, and for you to be safe. It was a risk I had to take, to protect you for the rest of your life.' Jack said, not caring about the tears that were falling down his face. 'But I wasn't expecting Tariq to be able to get to you.'

'I'm sorry Jack, I was careless.' Andreas said, knowing that he had let his oldest friend down, when Tariq took control of Linalli.

'No, you weren't to know that Leppe had control of Carina for all those years. His organisation was far reaching.' Jack said. 'You did everything as we planned, and more. We could only have control of so many elements, there was always going to be a risk using the boat.'

Saffi interrupted. 'Will there be any more of Leppe's organisation coming after us.' She looked worried now.

'No, the ringleader is gone. They will disperse and find new a new boss, or maybe just go back to normal life with the money they've earned. Only Leppe had an interest in me, we go back a long way.' Jack said, but his eyes said it all, and Saffi realised in that moment, what Jack was saying.

~~~

Luis Leppe was the man who had shot her mother, and was the man who eventually killed her. It was always going to be Jack against Luis Leppe, until Jack could find a way to take revenge for killing Lillian.

In the process, he and Andreas had worked against the drug barons, and with the Drug Agencies, they had helped enormously, but in the end, it had all been about revenge, or was it love?

~~~

In that moment, Saffi understood. Looking around her at the now familiar faces of Julio and Jacqui, Cap'n and Abi, Maria and Stephano, and of course Andreas, and all the people Jack had instigated that she met, she realised that this wasn't about money or inheritance, it was all about the love and friendship of all these people.

All these people had helped Jack get over the loss of his one true love, Lillian. These people were Jack's family now, they had helped him survive the most painful part of his life and without them, and he may not have made it through.

She realised now, that she could no longer despise him for having left her as a child, now that she understood it was to protect her. She could only love him, the way all these people loved him. The way they had shown her, in their stories they had shared with her of their time spent with Jack and some of them with Lillian. The fact that any one of them would have been prepared to give their life to save Jack, and now she realised, they would do the same for her. These people were now her family and she would embrace them that way, the way they had embraced her.

'I have one question.' She said, looking at Jack. 'Did Nana know about any of this?'

Jack didn't answer, but his face said it all, Nana had been involved right from the start. Jack had told Nana everything many years before, and they had agreed that this would be the only way to keep Saffi safe. Nana of course was not happy with what had happened, but despite everything, she had always trusted and loved Jack, and she would do whatever it took to keep Saffi from harm.

Then he spoke, 'She only had one request, 'You bring her back safe to me when this is all over.' he said, smiling at Saffi, but Jack had done better than that.

'Nana and Benedict are arriving here, on the afternoon flight, to make sure I kept my side of our bargain.' Jack said.

The end

Printed in Great Britain
by Amazon